I0534422

i

Shots, Plots & Diva Down

Louise Furley

Louise Furley
Copyright 2022
All Rights Reserved

Shots, Plots & Diva Down

ISBN: 979-8-9859963-6-4 (Paperback)
ISBN: 979-8-9859963-5-7 (eBook)

AUTHOR'S NOTE: This book is a work of fiction. Names, characters, places and incidents are products of the author's imagination or are used fictitiously. Any resemblance to actual events or locales or persons, living or dead, is entirely coincidental.

The scanning, uploading and distribution of this book via the Internet or any other means without the permission of the publisher is illegal and punishable by law. Please purchase only authorized electronic editions, and do not participate in or encourage electronic piracy of copyrighted materials. Your support of the author's rights is appreciated.

WARNING: this book contains dark themes, addiction, child endangerment and domestic violence.

Cover art by: *Pixel Mischief Design*
Photo: *Courtesy of Shutterstock*

Shots, Plots
&
Diva
Down

Chapter One

The room buzzed in excited chaos.

A colorful blur of the most beautiful young ladies in town dressed in glitzy gowns fluttered about, laughing and gossiping, getting their makeup done and their glorious manes styled like movie stars.

Waves of crimson tresses swinging down her back, Lareina Wittgenstein sashayed into the salon, her body sheathed in a leopard print dress as tight as a second skin. Heads turn at the sly beauty with the undulating hips. She looked sultry, wild, and pure trouble.

Just inside the threshold the perfect hourglass figure hesitated, her left palm pressed against the doorframe, the other hand set on the curve of her waist posed like a sensuous S.

She loves to make an entrance but this time she has a mission. Inside, most noticed her dramatic entrance, the deliberate pause for attention. Several girls glared before quickly looking away lest the young woman latch her fearsome gaze upon them.

Glancing around the crowded room, Lareina spotted her target. Heavily outlined Cleopatra eyes narrowed to mean slits, the sumptuous lips contorted in a grimace disfiguring her beauty into a Franken-witch.

Clenching her manicured fingers into furious fists, she stalked in six-inch heels like a leopard about to rip apart its prey, straight to an unaware girl sitting in one of the many salon chairs.

Without warning, Lareina grabbed the back of the chair and shoved it hard, sharply propelling the girl around, then she slammed her hands on the chair arms stopping the chair abruptly to face her.

The girl's neck whipped back and forth like a willow branch, flinging her hair in her face.

"Hey!" the girl squawked, swiping at her long brunet hair with both hands to see.

Peering through the mess of hair, she sputtered angrily, "Who the-" seeing the fuming redhead glaring at her, the surprised girl's jaw dropped, brown eyes shifted guiltily like a dog that had just eaten the pie on the counter.

She licked her suddenly dry lips, gulped the lump in her throat and croaked, "Oh, uh, Lareina, hi- hey how are- what, uh-"

Blam!

Lareina slapped the stuttering girl across the face.

Smothered gasps ricocheted around the room.

Shocked by the unexpected attack, her mouth gaping like a fish out of water, the girl cringed back expecting further onslaught. A scarlet handprint brightening on her cheek, she blinked dumbstruck through the tangle of brown hair that twitched with every blink.

Letting the cowering girl stew to wonder what's coming next, Lareina checked her freshly painted nails for damage. Satisfied the nails were still flawless, a smug smile creased the smooth olive complexion.

Calmly fluffing her thick waves with her fingers, Lareina's face returned to its natural Latina loveliness.

No one moved or spoke, you could hear a pin drop in the salon as everyone held their collective breaths.

Seated along the back of the shop, girls sitting under driers strained without moving to hear what was going on.

Lareina's smile straight-lined as she leaned over and planted her hands on the chair arms.

Recoiling, the girl held up quivering splayed fingers to protect her face from further abuse. She pulled her knees up and mushed back against her chair trying to meld into the black leather.

The rest of the shop's occupants froze in curious astonishment watching the two young women like rubberneckers passing an accident. Getting involved in Lareina Wittgenstein's business was never a winning move.

Lareina grasped the girl's wrists pulling them apart. She positioned her face, high cheekbones sharpened, within inches of the stunned girl's face and stuck a finger to her frightened nose.

A flap of false lashes, winged eye liner like an eagle's swoop and a sneer of red lips Lareina snarled, tapping the girl's nose, "You," she tapped with each word. "Finella Finestone," tap- tap- tap "stay away from Adonai Alamanni. Adonni is mine. You got that?"

A hard last tap, then, "Got it?"

Finella's eyes blinked with every tap. Before the stupefied girl could respond, Lareina grabbed both of Finella's arms, yanked her out of the chair then shoved her.

Arms flailing like windmills, Finella tottered off balance backwards in her sky-high heels. Salon cape billowing, she fell like a sack of potatoes flat on her butt. The cape dropped over her head, her skirt bunched up around her thighs and her legs landed ungainly spread.

Dismissing the girl with a haughty sniff, Lareina turned and swiveled the vacated chair back around to face the mirror.

Not bothering to fix the tight leopard dress that had ridden up her rather thick thighs, she settled her curvaceous figure in the salon chair with her Louboutin heels on the foot bar like nothing happened.

She looked up at the makeup artist standing like a dumbfounded statue with a blush brush in her hand.

"I'm ready." Lareina smiled at her own reflection.

3

Resisting the urge to run, Regina shrugged, set the blush down, picked up a white paper napkin and pinned it around Lareina's neck. Then she layered a cape to cover Lareina's clothes.

After clearing her throat, as if the assault hadn't just happened in front of practically the whole world, she asked politely, "How are you today, Miss Lareina?"

They both ignored the hapless girl on the floor who climbed to her feet, palm print glowing red against her even redder face and scurried out the door still wearing the salon cape.

Lareina didn't respond to Regina's greeting. Discussing pleasantries with the help was beneath her.

Used to her rudeness, Regina lifted Lareina's hair out from under the cape clasped around her neck. "You have the most beautiful hair, long, thick, a lovely delicious kind of burgundy color. Did you inherit it from one of your parents?"

Lareina didn't once look directly at the thirty-something hairdresser with the short choppy blonde hair dressed in a peasant blouse and capris. She treated her like she treats all the help, they are there to serve her.

Never taking her eyes off her image in the mirror, Lareina said, "My father is German and my mother was born in Venezuela, but actually I give it some help from a bottle, duh!" She laughed snidely, having a cosmetic's certification, Regina should be able to tell when a hair color is real or fake. Honestly, the woman was useless!

Regina's brow arched. "Really? Your little sister, Talana, has hair sort of the same color as yours, but more of a rich auburn, more natural looking, and she has such pretty green eyes, yours are more, um, just brown. Hey, how come she doesn't have your accent?"

Lareina frowned, then brightened. "Of course I can understand your interest in me. I mean, really, who wouldn't be?" Her head turned side to side to get a full view of herself in the mirror.

4

Then the childhood memories flooded, she frowned again. Shoving the memories aside in her brain, she preened. After all, she did love attention, any kind.

She said, "Well, my older brother Talco and I were raised in Venezuela until late middle school when we moved to America, here to California." Her face darkened. "Try to get it straight, Talana is my half-sister."

"Oh?" Regina opened a tube of primer and squeezed a drop onto one finger.

"Oh yes. Mama," Lareina's lips twisted bitterly at the re-emerging memory, her brows pulled so low they almost came together in a hard V. Slinking down slightly in the chair, her shoulders rose up to her ears.

Staring blankly at the floor, she said, "When I was four and Talco was around seven, she and Daddy separated for a few years and my mother got herself a new boyfriend, which is why Daddy came back around. Except by then Mama realized she was pregnant.

"When she had the baby, I don't know what happened with the other man but Mama and Daddy left Venezuela and dumped Talco and me at our aunt's house for years while they went through their terrible thirties.

"But they kept Talana with them and raised her like she was both of theirs and not the fruit of mama's betrayal. In fact, they treated the bastard baby better than they treated their *real* children." The angry bitterness distorted her beautiful face again.

Regina dotted the primer in sections on Lareina's face then using her fingertips she spread around a light layer.

Lareina allowed the painful memories to roam around in her head for a moment then straightened her back and squared her shoulders. Like hitting a light switch, the animosity cleared from her expression allowing the patrician loveliness to return.

Calmly she continued with her story, "I guess as a way of holding her over Daddy's head, Talana has our mother's last name, Castilla. My brother uses it too, it's our middle names, but he uses it as his last name.

"He and Daddy were always at odds and I guess that was a passive aggressive way of digging at him. Talco couldn't be bought with expensive gifts like I was."

She squinted at the mirror. "I'll have you know my eyes aren't just plain old *brown*. I prefer to think of them as cinnamon and sugar, *sparkly* brown. Besides, many a boy has told me he could fall happily into my dark pools and drown!"

Pulling off the lid of a tube of concealer, Regina squelched her response, *you bet those boys wanted to kill themselves listening to you jabber on and on and on about yourself*, but she did not need to be on Lareina's bad side so she bit her acid tongue.

Pushing aside the words, *and you could be arrested for that battery you just committed*, she said instead, "Well, you both got your good looks and fab figures certainly from your mother. You girls have such voluptuous shapes like- like Sophia Vergara."

Lareina nodded in agreement, her eyes staying on her reflection.

Regina babbled on, "Even as young as Talana is, at 14 she's already blossoming into a posh young lady with a bodacious body. Plus, she has that little extra something special that just draws people to her. She's so striking and nice, like a sweet Spanish rose."

Looking up as two more young ladies entered the boisterous room she missed Lareina's venomous scowl.

"Oh, there's those gorgeous girls," Regina crowed. "Pepi Nok and Cheyne Somerset. They make me think of glazed marble bookends, you know like perfect statuettes only different colors, dark and light. Ya know?"

Not seeing Lareina's growing anger, Regina kept on, "Except Pepi isn't exactly deep dark, more of a syrupy honey color." She stopped talking with one hand holding Lareina's chin, the other clutching the concealer tube and stared at the pair.

Lareina jerked her head to get Regina's attention back on her.

Regina smiled automatically at Lareina's reflection. "So, since you're 18 now you're in the Miss Gable Belle Pageant this year?"

She held Lareina's chin to tilt her head up while she dotted then smeared concealer over a few barely visible uneven tones on Lareina's skin.

That done, Regina closed the tube, dropped it on the makeup tray and studied the assortment of foundations to choose the perfect one for Lareina's particular shade of olive complexion.

Lareina tipped her head sideways to get a look at her profile in the mirror. "Oh yes, I am too old to be in the Miss Peony Princess with those juvenile 16 year olds, Pepi and Cheyne."

Her lower lip stuck out ruefully. "Don't you think they have such stupid names? Shane is a guy's name she can't even spell it right, and what the heck kind of name is Pepi? What's Pepi s'pposed to be? They're just stupid." She sniffed.

"They are way out of my league anyway, they wouldn't stand a chance against me," Lareina declared. "They're even out of my sister Talana's league; she won the Miss Ruby Glow last year."

Regina sighed. "Wow, there's so many pageants I don't know how anyone keeps track of them."

"Different seasons out here in northern California mean different pageants, even in this dead-end town. That's why there's a few of us from each of the pageants on the parade floats next week for the May Day Parade," Lareina explained.

Regina dotted then patted the foundation on Lareina's face with her fingers. Her brows rose. "Oh?" She smoothed the foundation with a tiny square sponge. "You don't like our picturesque town?"

Using her pinky, Regina pushed a bristle of blonde hair off her own temple and dipped the sponge lightly into a cup of water then smoothed some more of the foundation evenly down Lareina's neck.

Lareina rolled her eyes and her lip curled. "Ugh. Are you kidding? Talk about a one-horse town. Cut off from the rest of the world by the forests on one side and the river on the other, I can't wait to get out of here."

Still smoothing the lotion, Regina gushed, "My husband was born here, we met out east at a party while I was visiting relatives.

He couldn't wait to come back home here. Such a darling little town."

Lareina opened her mouth to comment but Regina rattled right on,

"The main city is so easy to get around, designed like a European square with surrounding streets in ragged lines, and pretty, rustic villages scattered along the scenic countryside. I take my nieces to the park, they can't get enough of the statues and fountains.

"My husband loves boating and fishing on the Merestic River, and the kids love skating on the frozen lake and skiing down the mountains in winter. Ahh, and the forests," she sighed.

"They are breathtaking. Horseback riding the trails through the fresh jade woods in the spring, the charming neighborhoods colorful and smoky smelling from burning leaves in the fall.

"The stately old Victorian houses up near Lighthouse Way are gorgeous. Why, even in the winter the city is powdered frosty white, the steeples sloped with glistening snow. And so quiet like you're in a cotton cocoon-"

"Will you shut up for crying out loud?" Lareina pulled her head away from Regina's hands.

"Who cares about your boring little life! You're one of the reasons I want to get the heck out of this godforsaken tedious humdrum. Scenic- who cares- I want parties and dances, and rage concerts and- fun, excitement."

Regina's frown did not put Lareina's tirade off a bit. "Not this boring town with its boring people with nothing to do and people like you with no aspirations for more. Big fat bore. Charming? More like zero sophistication."

Across the room girls squealed in delight when Cheyne Somerset and Pepi Nok arrived.

Cheyne greeted everyone she knew with hugs and kisses.

Leaving her friend to the mushy stuff, Pepi hailed their fellow beauty queens with breezy hellos.

Cheyne and Pepi waited until twins, Collie and Holly Eden vacated a couple of salon chairs.

Careful not to muss their fresh hair and makeup, the twins hugged Cheyne and grinned at Pepi aware that Pepi was friendly but not a hugger.

Collie burst out excitedly, "Isn't this just the best! We were chosen to be on the parade float too, we are so honored, we can't wait!"

At the same time her sister Holly exclaimed, "Yeah, we get to be in the parade, on the floats, we are so excited, can't wait! See you at the photo-op!" The two carrot-topped, freckled faced girls giggled and bubbled out the door.

Pepi and Cheyne smiled at each other.

"They're this excited now," Pepi said, untying the band on her long braid. Even as beautiful if not more than the other beauty queens, Pepi was more of a tomboy than most of the others.

She seldom wore jewelry or makeup, and today was no different, besides she was still in her soccer uniform. Splitting the thick curly hair apart she pushed it back off her shoulders where unbound it spun itself back into fat ringlets.

She laughed and declared, "Today is only the photo session for promotion of the event, they are going to explode when they actually get *on* the float!" The two girls laughed good-naturedly together.

Cheyne said, "I can understand how they feel, Pep, I'm pretty excited too, and honored. But I think really our names were drawn out of a hat to keep things even."

She modestly shook her head, highlights flickered in the wave of blonde hair, crystal blue eyes shone like twin spotlights. Gold bangles on her wrist clinked and tinkled with her every gesture.

A girl swung a covering over Cheyne to start her hair and makeup. She said, "Oh no, Cheyne, my cousin Cindy said everyone was chosen because of their looks. Even Collie and Holly Eden. I think the sponsors thought with their bright orangey

9

hair and millions of freckles they would add flavor and color to the float."

"That may be true, Celeste, but the twins are pretty in their own unusual way," Cheyne responded. As she was swung around in her chair she spotted Lareina Wittgenstein. She threw her a big toothy smile and friendly wave.

Lareina stuck her nose in the air as if she didn't see Cheyne's gesture and resumed studying herself in the mirror. Cheyne's face fell.

In the chair next to her, Pepi consoled her friend, however there was a firm edge to her words. "Don't feel bad, Chey, we have tried all year to be friendly with that girl. Forget about that mean queen. Who cares, right?" She crossed one toned leg over the other.

Her grandmother swore she was running before learning to walk. Pepi played everything from soccer to tennis to baseball since she was very young. Her legs were athletic yet curvaceously long for her petite stature.

"I guess…" Cheyne's weak smile was a little dispirited. "It's just that-"

Celeste, Cheyne's chubby cosmetologist pushed her glasses on top of her short curly hair and said, "Oh that Lareina Wittgenstein is so vain and stuck up, unless you're a good looking guy or can do something for her everyone else is just invisible to her. You should have been here earlier when the flame-haired twins came in. They were in tears the poor dears.

"They had run into Lareina at the application desk and she was just vile, they said. Turned her nose up at them like they smelled and made comments like 'carrots should be eaten by rabbits, not be felt sorry for and put in parades.'

Another stylist spoke up. "And that wasn't the rudest, she told Collie her name was perfect because she resembled the dog with the long nose so much, and Holly looked like a clown with her bright orange hair. Can you believe it? Wait 'till I tell you what she just did to poor Finella Finestone!"

"Oh yeah, that was so mean!" While talking, Celeste snapped the cape closed around Cheyne's neck and swung her chair around to face the mirror.

Pepi and Cheyne shook their heads listening to the troubling tales knowing the nasty behavior was Lareina's trademark.

Another cosmetologist, Simone, shook a cape open and draped Pepi with it.

Celeste stood behind Cheyne for a second, drawing her fingers through the soft blondeness, studying her reflection to determine her skin tone.

Satisfied she knew what she wanted to do with Cheyne, she turned to her counter. On top of the left side of the counter lay a blow dryer, its wires tangled in the wires of two curling irons, several cans of hair spray and mousse, a glass jar containing blue liquid with a half dozen combs submerged in it.

The front of her blouse was tucked in over her muffin top, the back hung out slightly in the back but not enough to cover her ample derriere, Celeste pulled the top drawer open further to select from an array of pots of shadow and blush, foundation and eyebrow pencils, liner and so on.

The cosmetologist tapped short, sausage plump fingers against her lips while deciding where to start. She wiped a hand on her jeans and picked up a roseate tinted foundation.

She said, "You're a bit on the pale side except for those rosy cheeks, Cheyne, so I'm going to beef up your color a little. Really, Lareina should take a page out of your books, hon, she should be more like you two. You're drop dead gorgeous just like her, but you're sweet and kind to other people. You know you both would make stunning models, are you going to-"

"Thank you Celeste, that was nice," Pepi interjected from her chair. "But we're both too short to be models, and we have other plans. Yeah, there's a lot of money to be made modeling, but it sounds so monotonous, and," she shuddered, "you have to endure strangers touching and groping you all the time when you're half naked. No thanks, not for me."

The cape covered part of her body. Half a leg, an elbow and the tips of her sneakers were exposed. She fumbled under the cape pushing it so that every inch of her was concealed like a turtle pulled in its shell. Out of sight, untouchable.

Cheyne said, "We only do the pageants to raise funds for our school class. I like the dressing up and makeup and fussing, but it's like pulling teeth to get Pepi into the glam mode. Right, Pep?"

She leaned sideways, poking her friend with a finger.

Pepi pretended to scowl at her teasing friend. "Uh huh." She stuck her tongue out at Cheyne which made them both giggle.

Simone had tied a black apron over her long lanky body in blue jeans and tank top. The apron bulged and drooped in the front from scissors, combs and pins stuffed in the pockets. She bulged in the backend too, but that was God-given.

She set a bottle of amber hued foundation on the counter. Then changed her mind and pushed the bottle towards the back of the counter. "

You really don't need much makeup, Miss Pepi, your skin already glows, your lips are a natural pastel pink that I couldn't produce chemically if I spent a week mixing sticks and glosses. And those spectacular eyes, mmm," crossing her arms, she shook her head. "Nothing could make them prettier, I can only showcase them."

Embarrassed, Pepi squirmed. "Yeah, okay, so can we move on?"

Simone smiled at Pepi's humbleness and pulled her fluff of hair out from under the neck of the cape. "So, hon, how do you want your luscious ringlets done? You're lucky your African American hair is so soft and manageable, I have to constantly use relaxers and perms on mine, what a pain."

The cocoa skinned woman pulled Pepi's hair back and swung it up in a high ponytail. "What about this? The light sparkles on all the different shiny shades of brunet."

Pepi's pulled in her tiny pillow poofs of lips as she contemplated the soft spirals bouncing from Simone's hand. Her unusual eyes, such a light grey they looked like silver tinsel, turned up at Simone.

"No, I think today I'd like it down, in maybe a braid. It's likely to be windy on the moving float, it'd be a hassle trying to tame those curls and keep them out of my face."

Simone nodded. "Good idea. But I think a fishtail over one shoulder would be a more current style, edgy, sophisticated yet almost casual. I can string a ribbon through the braid and brush shimmer on your lids and lips, you'll look like a starlet. That Lareina is going to be green with jealousy when she sees you two bombshells!"

Pepi glanced at her friend Cheyne in the chair next to her who shared her grin. "I can't wait to see what Saturday brings."

Chapter Two

The day of the parade finally arrived!

In light jacket weather under a dome of pure blue sky, people lined Main Street waving streamers, laughing and eating from food stands dotted up and down the avenue.

The littlest kids perched on fathers' shoulders to see it all, yelling and waving tiny flags on sticks.

Escaped balloons sailed up and away to the sounds of instruments tuning; bleeps and honks and strums filtered through the rising crescendo of street noise.

The sound hushed when Aura High School's band came marching down the street with trumpets bellowing, drums pounding, cymbals clanging, the crowd roared their approval.

The first band strutted along the street, proud as shiny new pennies.

When the band disappeared around the corner, baton twirlers in flashy gold and red dresses danced and sashayed right behind them, pirouetting and expertly catching batons they tossed high in the air.

People craned their necks to see what was coming next.

Pepi and Cheyne gathered up their long skirts to climb on board their designated float.

Her brown hair slivered lightly with grey, Mrs. Britton, holding a clipboard and pen, directed in a high loud voice to the girls where they were to stand.

Periodically, the sharp boned but podgy around the midsection woman lifted her glasses on a multi-colored beaded chain around her middle-aged neck to peer at the clipboard, then she'd drop them where they'd jiggle and jump on her floral printed bosom with her every gesture.

Other girls already on the float were finding their places, smoothing dresses, primping and doing last minute hair combing.

It was a perfect day for the parade. A shade cool, yet pleasant weather with clear skies and the sun was already warming up the day.

The brisk wind would lighten as the day grew. Some of the girls wore sweaters they would remove when the floats started their journey through the streets teeming with noisy merrymakers.

Cheyne went to her spot to the right front of the float.

There was a railing covered in flowers for the girls to hang onto and lean against as they waved to the public.

Feeling so sophisticated in her white gloves, Cheyne smoothed her saffron colored gown over the ruffled petticoats that made her look like a Chantilly bell and looked across the float to Pepi who was also settling into her place on the left front side. Cheyne waved cheerfully at her.

Pepi grinned and waved both hands back up and down like she was Minnie Mouse in her gloves, but really she looked like the perfect southern belle in her indigo and silver chenille dress.

The hairdresser had threaded a matching ribbon through the fishtail that spread like a loosely braided tawny stream across and down the front of her chest.

Pepi waved at the other girls scattered around the fancy float like beautiful bouquets.

On the other side of the float, a girl in pink taffeta a few feet from Cheyne leaned towards her. "Boy did we luck out, no squalling little kids or Queen Lareina on our float!"

Cheyne smiled but didn't say anything. Her hair had been pulled up and pinned with the tresses in one loose curl flowing down over one shoulder. The wind lifted and tossed the wound locks.

"I heard Lareina was a no show," another girl said from her perch on the float. Brandi was actually a male that dreamed his whole life of being in a pageant. He loved the peach dress with ruffles at the bodice and hem his mother had purchased for him for the event. He was a true beauty who had won his position honestly.

"Here we go girls! Hold on! Listen to me!" Mrs. Britton called out shrilly as she heard the engine turn on. A gust of wind blew her floral dress so hard it embarrassingly outlined her angular body with middle-aged spread.

While talking, she tried to push the flapping skirt down, attempting to maintain her dignity, which was blowing away with the wind.

Breathless, pushing the salt and pepper hair out of her eyes, she continued her instructions in a high-pitched, Sunday school teacher voice.

"Now remember, hold onto the railing. Do not lean over it, don't throw anything over it. You will not use your cell phones, and not possess any food or drinks. You just give that little pageant wave we all practiced. Always behave like ladies, and of course the most important- smile!"

She started to say more, but the float suddenly jerked forward then backward, then swayed a little.

"Oh!" Mrs. Britton exclaimed, staggering.

The girls squealed and grabbed the railing, but then the float got its sea legs and moved smoothly forward, slow and sure.

Mrs. Britton hurried to her covered seat in the middle of the float.

They were the third float in the parade with many more behind them. As they passed the crowds, the teens waved and smiled, the people waved back and cheered.

Chapter Three

After what seemed like hours, the floats circled back to the street they had started from.

Instead of giggles and girlish chatter, moans and groans permeated the area as each float came to a shaking halt and the engines shut down.

The girl in now disheveled pink taffeta standing beside Cheyne brushed a hand across her face, sighed heavily then slumped.

Crossing over to her friend, Pepi stretched her back and twisted her neck to get the kinks out. "Wow, Chey," she said, "that was a lot harder than I thought it would be. My back is in agony from standing so long. Feels like burning knives stabbing down my spine."

Cheyne nodded tiredly. "Yeah, my mouth is major stiff from smiling so much and so hard!"

The girl next to her said, "And our poor hands, waving, waving, waving, I'm surprised my arm didn't snap right off and fall to the ground and get trampled by the drum majorettes!"

The three girls laughed together.

Pepi glanced around their float.

Earlier, all of the pageant girls were gleaming and polished and perfectly coifed. Now, hair straggled, makeup ran, dresses were wrinkled and smudged.

Mrs. Britton was the first one off the float scurrying off to find the nearest restroom.

Pepi smiled at Cheyne. "But it was so much fun, it was worth it!"

Cheyne nodded, smiling blearily she agreed. "Oh, it was really great, I'm so glad we got to do this, but I'm thinking about a cold soda and a hamburger, I'm starving."

"Yeah," Pepi approved. "Me too. Let's go change quickly. Do you want to come, Marie?" She asked the pink taffeta girl that now looked like a wrung out dishrag.

"No way," Marie yawned. "I'm going home to bed. I'm too tired to even eat."

Pulling at parts of her rumpled poufy dress, Pepi said, "You might like to dress up in this fancy ball gown crap, Chey, but I can't wait to get this costume off."

The three girls climbed off the float with the other participants.

People who had volunteered decorating and running the floats helped them down, then began gathering up fallen garlands and plucking ribbons off the float.

The subdued girls joined the throng of tired, hungry pageant princesses flowing down the street to waiting rides, some lived within walking distance.

Parents had arrived to pick up the littlest girls and walked with the crowd to their cars. Half went in one direction, half in the other.

Cheyne and Pepi passed one float after another. Once glorious and lovely, they were now dusty and bedraggled. Loose streamers floated in the wind, spent flowers littered the street.

Suddenly, piercing screams peeled from up the street.

"Oh my god! Oh my god! Help! Help!" A woman's frantic shrieks brutally fragmented the sleepy aftermath of a happy day of music and beauty.

After stunned hesitation, everyone surged up the street towards the screams.

At the end of the street, people were circling a float like gulls around a shrimp boat.

Cries of horror rent the air as Pepi and Cheyne joined the multitude.

"What is it?" Pepi asked.

Cheyne on tiptoe craning her neck said, "I don't know I can't see."

Then people started falling back from the float, gagging, screaming, crying.

The two girls watched in dismay as people covered their mouths, shoved out of the crowd and ran away shouting down the street.

As folks left, others took their place and reacted the same way. Several ran to the grass a few feet away and vomited.

Parents grabbed up the young children, covered their eyes and ran.

Breathless, someone running past, cried in distress, "It's the last float, it didn't go out because a few of the girls didn't show up so they cut out the last float. You can't believe what's-"

Cheyne and Pepi rustled forward, bumped by people who were running away and nudged between others that were too shocked to leave.

"Oh- my- gosh…" Pepi's words drew out in disbelief at the horrific sight in front of them.

The girls stood, hands clamped over their mouths, eyes white and wide.

In the center of the float, the splendorous Lareina Wittgenstein lay mangled, sprawled on her back in a congealing pool of blood.

Auburn pigtails splayed like two giant eyelashes above her head, her makeup gunky and blotched, heavy liner smeared crookedly around open lifeless eyes. Red circles of blush bright against her bloodless skin gave her a clown face.

Her mutilated body appeared broken in half, like someone had snapped her over their knee then tossed her out the window to slam brutally onto the float.

Blood had gushed from sharp metal fixtures on the float that had stabbed holes through her body when she had landed, saturating her outfit into a horrid sticky mess.

Flies buzzed in growing numbers. Dressed in a ball gown like a lovely, fairytale Disney Princess Ariel, she was horridly incongruous with the grotesque bloody scene.

Viewers fell back as if they could become victims too by just being near the violent fatality, until just Pepi and Cheyne were the only ones standing there.

It seemed everyone ran off in hysteria, but no one called the police, so the teens each pulled out their cell phones.

Cheyne dialed 911, and struggling to keep her shaking voice coherent, relayed the scene.

Then both girls took pictures with their phones. They photographed the float and the body from all angles. Pepi even went up a few steps on the building the float was in front of and took sort of an aerial picture.

Pepi shivered then said to Cheyne, "How ghastly. I guess other people would think we're sick ghouls for taking pictures."

Cheyne agreed, taking stock of the dead body and everything on the float. The only thing that looked out of place was Lareina.

Cheyne's attention went from scrutinizing the float back to Lareina. Pondering the images, she said, "There's something peculiar about the way she looks."

"Yeah, Chey, she's dead," Pepi replied drily.

"Not that part, but Lareina herself. I can't put my finger on it. But yeah, we needed to take the pictures. From journalist class we know how quickly a crime scene can be corrupted and it's more important right now to conserve the scene at least by photo than to worry about what people think of us."

She turned her head at the sirens coming down the street and stated redundantly, "The police are here."

It was over an hour before the police allowed Cheyne and Pepi to leave.

The officers confiscated Pepi's cell claiming they'd return it as soon as they had copied the pictures.

Blushing and stammering, Cheyne was bad at lying, she denied having her phone. She didn't like to lie but they had Pepi's photos and things happen by accident sometimes, pictures get deleted, phones get lost, all sorts of things can happen.

Not that she didn't trust the police, but Cheyne held onto her phone just in case to preserve the photos.

Now that the adrenalin rush from when they had first seen the body was depleted, with the already long day in the parade culminating in the tragedy of Lareina's atrocious demise, the girls were truly exhausted.

One of the officers drove the girls to Pepi's house.

They dragged their weary bodies out of the car, stumbled up the middle of the yard on the cement path, then hobbled up the porch steps to the tan two-story with white trim and shutters.

A child's bike lay against the wrap-around porch. Rockers, wicker chairs, and a scattering of mismatched tables welcomed people to sit a spell.

In the big back yard, a bountiful vegetable garden basked. Her way of relaxing, Pepi's grandmother, Elma Mae loved to piddle in the garden, planting, weeding, harvesting, canning, one with nature and God, and enjoying the healthy gifts year round.

The young ones learned the labor and love of miniature farming. In the summer, Elma Mae would be sitting in a wicker rocker snapping peas from the garden into a basket and listening to her grandchildren talk about their lives and dreams for the future.

Tulips in all colors were breaking ground lining the front of the house. The rose colored azaleas under the bay window were still asleep, wrapped tightly in green gloves.

Trees just coming out of winter spread their bony white arms waiting for the leaves to burst and fill the yard with every shade of green.

The pungent smell of newly cut grass from Pepi's older brother Thomas' earlier mowing, made Cheyne sneeze as she plodded behind Pepi into the house.

"Here you go girls, this will chase away the willies." Elma Mae set two steaming cups of chamomile tea dolloped with sweet honey in front of the teens.

The aroma of chocolate melting and pastry from the pie Elma Mae had baking in the oven, and the warm cheery kitchen was comforting.

At 67, Elma Mae, an older version of her pert granddaughter but with little round glasses, was still working and did a lot of yoga. Although her hair was graying, she liked to stay fit and wear tailored suits. Unfortunately, she still battled the bulge, she liked her food too much.

She was always trying to drop ten pounds, but they refused to budge. Her tongue clicked behind small poofs of pillow lips that were a slightly larger version of Pepi's.

Cheyne's grandmother, Marylou was there too. She bustled around the kitchen and the girls, patting first one of their heads then the other like a nervous Nellie.

Cheyne leaned over her hot tea, her eyes closed. The vapor warmed her face with soft whorls before dissipating leaving a fine dewy film on her skin.

Relaxing a bit, she sat back, opened her eyes and looked around. "It's way too quiet in here, where are the children?"

Pepi's brown brows rose, she had hardly noticed the quiet, she was so used to a constant buzz of noise and commotion of young children running and yelling, playing and crying in the house. She asked her Gram, "Where are they?"

Pouring herself a cup of tea, Elma Mae set it on the table then joined the girls. She added some honey and cream, stirring until the tea was a savory heath bar color.

Taking a careful tiny sip, she set it down quickly, it was still too hot to drink. "Well, the minute I heard the news about the," she searched for a benign word, "...parade, I had their Auntie

Lettie come and take them to her house until, well until things settle down or get resolved or, whatever…"

She tried the tea again. It was perfect, like Goldilocks, not too hot, not too cool. "Lettie is on the other side of town, but she will drive them to school. Thomas of course is up in his room listening to music, as always."

Marylou added, "You girls were on your way out too."

Elma Mae nodded, set her cup down. "Yes, we spoke with your family, Cheyne, about sending you girls somewhere away, with a relative, but a detective called and said since you got involved with taking pictures and such, you had to stay available for any further questioning or deposing."

"Your mother, Cheyne, my daughter," Marylou sighed. "She wouldn't allow you to leave with anyone anyway. Said she wanted you in her sights."

Cheyne rolled her eyes. "No kidding," she muttered. "I'm always amazed when she lets me stay overnight here, she's so, controlling."

Elma Mae's best friend, Cheyne's grandmother, Marylou got up and returned with a plate of freshly baked pecan chunk cookies and two glasses of milk, she set them on the table.

"These will help calm the quivering in your tummies." Shaking her head, she 'clucked-clucked' and sat down at the table.

The setting sun streamed through the bay window glinting off the snowflake chandelier and crystal glasses on the table like a fairytale tea party making the aberrant day seem a little less eerie.

The ladies sat at the round kitchen table in the middle of the room rather than the long table with the cushioned bench in front of the bay front window.

Cheyne took a couple of sips of the nurturing herbal tea.

Ignoring the mild-apple smelling tea, Pepi reached for the icy glass of milk with one hand and a cookie with the other.

"Such an ordeal for you young girls. Something you never should have had to deal with in your lives much less at such a young age. Bless my soul," Marylou patted her heart.

"What a horrendous sight for you to behold on what had been an honor and a lovely day."

Marylou was growing old gracefully by dyeing her hair, maintaining the bright, corn silk blonde of her granddaughter's, and although her full curves were plumping, it didn't slow down her shopping.

She fit the image of an aging Hollywood actress from an era long past, like an elderly Marilyn Monroe. Unlike her granddaughter Cheyne, who loved gymnastics, Marylou decried any type of exercise.

She always said 'if God intended us to exercise she wouldn't have invented cars and elevators.'

Taking a bite out of a pecan cookie, Elma Mae said through a mouthful, "Wasn't a great day for Lareina either."

Marylou wrinkled her nose at her friend and snatched a cookie. "Uh huh." She bit off half the cookie, crumbs fell scattering the table and her lap. Licking a finger she dabbed at the escaped crumbs and guiltlessly licked them off her finger.

Pepi and Cheyne nodded mournfully.

Cheyne said, "We thought the police would never let us go. I left a message for Lareina's little sister, Talana, to call if she needed anything. The poor thing, she's going to be so-" her mouth dropped, her eyes shifted back and forth. "Uh, I want to say brokenhearted but…"

Pepi choked, crumbs flew out of her mouth. She coughed then quickly gulped some milk. Wiping a tear, she said, "I don't think brokenhearted would be the right word. Shocked maybe, but brokenhearted, I don't think so."

"Yeah, but she still must be hurting," Cheyne replied. She set her elbows on the table, resting her chin in her hands. She stared gloomily at her tea.

Elma Mae added some more honey to her tea, stirred it a second then took a couple of sips. She licked her lips, then said, "I hate to speak ill of the dead," she made the sign of the cross quickly over her heart.

"But I can't say I ever heard a good word about that girl, and especially her behavior towards that darling little Talana. Talana only ever looked up to her big half-sister, but Lareina wouldn't give her the time of day, shunned her and was downright mean to her." She saw Cheyne eying the honey pot and handed it to her.

Marylou smoothed her long skirt over her crossed legs and nodded emphatically. "So pretty on the outside, and so- uh, so the opposite on the inside. Makes me think of an exquisitely painted Easter egg that had spoiled within."

She shook her head regretfully. "Well," brushing crumbs off the table into her palm she dusted them onto her empty plate. "Like you said, El, mustn't speak ill of the poor dear, she was so young, and to die so dreadfully. We'll add her and her family to next week's Bible Study prayer list, remind me, El." She winced.

She hadn't seen the pictures, didn't want to thank you very much. The description from Pepi and Cheyne had been so awfully bone chilling and grisly, it popped goose bumps like chicken skin clear up and down her arms!

Still in her soiled gown, Cheyne sat back and crossed her arms over her chest as if to shield herself from, whatever evil was lurking in their safe little Lilliputian-esque town.

Both teens' gowns entirely covered their chairs and draped on the floor.

Across the table, Pepi was untwining the braided fishtail. When it was all loose, she combed her fingers through the locks then shook them back off her face.

The light grey eyes somber, she frowned as the sickening picture of Lareina on the float drifted through her head.

"She must have just gotten ready for the parade. Her makeup and gown didn't look quite- I don't know, like she'd dressed in a hurry. Maybe she was getting ready and she heard someone at the door. I remember her complaining that she would be home alone as the others in her family all had to be somewhere else, and she was mad because she would have to call for a taxi."

"Oh yes, that was yesterday." Cheyne nodded. "She said she'd have to carry the dress and have to cram it into a taxi with no one to help her. We offered to pick her up, but she said no thanks. I think she didn't want to be seen with us- what does she call us- teenyboppers."

She picked up a cookie, her pretty face a map of puzzlement. "I thought the same thing, that the makeup and dress were weird, messy, crooked, kind of childlike, and the pigtails, those were the oddest. That prima donna probably hasn't worn pigtails since she was in diapers."

"Maybe she was just in a hurry," Elma Mae offered.

"Or she was having fun, or trying something different," Marylou said.

They all looked askance at each other because that did not describe the not-lighthearted Lareina.

The four sat quietly, each picturing poor doomed Lareina all alone, her dress over her arm, trying to keep it from wrinkling during the ride to the parade. Rushing about getting ready since she was always late, maybe putting her makeup on in the taxi.

"The question is," Elma Mae said, getting up to get the pie out of the oven. "Why would anyone kill Lareina Wittgenstein?"

Chapter Four

The crowd at the funeral was huge.

Half of the high school was there. A few to pay their last respects, most to see what a dead person looked like. Especially one their own age, and one of the most beautiful diva, stuck up, and wickedly mean girls in town.

The mass of attendees wandered about unsure of what they were supposed to do. Like a compressing fog, the people nervously wandering here and there, mostly more curious than bereaved.

The good news was they got to dress up. No jeans, flips or t-shirts today. The yard was peppered with wedge stilettoes tripping over the grass, cleavage for days, and so many hair extensions Rapunzel and her entire village could have been covered!

Winter winding down with spring on the horizon, mornings were still cool with brief sprinkle showers, soon though the downy clouds huffed away and it warmed up by mid-day.

Green nubs on trees budded like tiny opening hands. Birds suddenly in love chased each other from wire to wire, and wildflowers were springing up everywhere. None of which the deceased would have enjoyed, cared about or noticed even if she wasn't deceased.

The enormous funeral home contained numerous offices. Large grooming area for the deceased, three chapels and three other rooms for varying religions. Along with several viewing rooms, heaven forbid the dead had to wait.

The wide driveway arched right up the glossy pavers of the celestial sphered building to the entrance.

Under the gables, the palest of blue lights shone down on two alabaster Grecian columns. Cloisonné urns on both sides of the gigantic double doors sported a dazzling array of spring flowers.

Cheyne arrived with her parents and two younger brothers. Older sister Suchie Rose was out of the country.

As they entered the building, Cheyne paused to gaze up at the vaulted atrium, painted sky blue with cotton clouds and floating cherubs like a cosmic ceiling.

Instead of giving her a peaceful heavenly feeling, it gave her the willies.

She hurried to catch up with her family as they passed through the vestibule. Their shoes clacked across the tiled lobby under a high ark-shaped ceiling with dozens of other people speaking so nervously loud, the sound echoed off the gold and ivory papered walls.

They followed the crowd until they funneled through a broad doorway into a receiving room.

Outside, the afternoon had turned brilliant. Natural sunlight trickled through the narrow floor to ceiling windows highlighting the gold lamps on the walls and specks of gold in the wallpaper. The carpet and heavy wine drapes helped muffle the sounds.

There were already a few dozen people crammed in the room, but the noise level had dropped dramatically. Piped in dulcet music, a gentle backdrop to the whispers and subdued tones. The lamps on the walls shed muted golden light adding to the somber ambience.

Cheyne's keen blue gaze searched the chamber until a flurried motion across the room caught her eye.

It was Pepi. She was standing with her grandmother Elma Mae. Her siblings, older brother Thomas, younger brothers twins

Bud and Kevin, and two younger sisters, Starly and Tina, were not there, but two aunts and several cousins swarmed Pepi and her grandmother.

Cheyne saw Pepi whisper something to her grandmother.

Elma Mae looked over at Cheyne and smiled and nodded. Her normal walk energetic yet always held back with a vague wariness, it took Pepi a moment to get over to Cheyne, the room was so stuffed with nosey posies.

Moving away from Cheyne's family, the girls jokingly air-kissed both cheeks, a jab at the housewife reality shows on TV where the upscale women always greet each other even if they just saw one another 30 minutes ago.

They both quickly put their hands over their grinning mouths to stifle their amusement, it was after all a funeral, and one of someone they had known pretty well.

"Isn't this spooky?" Pepi whispered to Cheyne.

Cheyne nodded, biting her tongue.

Pepi whispered again, "I like that black mini-dress, the ruffle around your legs looks sort of like a mermaid skirt but short."

Cheyne grinned. Her voice hushed, she said behind her hand, "I got it a while back but had no reason to wear it until now. Is your satin, blue slip dress new? I don't think I've ever seen it before. Nice pop with the matching bow."

A little sheepish, Pepi smoothed the skirt of her dress. "Yeah, Gram got it for me for Easter Sunday. I hate to admit that I don't own a LBD, can you believe it? I hate dismal colors, but I brought my black jacket to cover the blue. Gram insisted I wear a dress, I can't wait until I can shed this thing and these heels."

She glowered at the high heels that were sure to cause her blisters. "It's still windy, I hope the bow stays in my hair, I sprayed the curls heavily but you never know."

"You worry too much about your hair, Pep," Cheyne admired. "It's beautiful, with soft full curls, it's so pretty the way they scroll down your back in five fat ringlets."

She lifted one ringlet letting it curl around her hand, then she laid it back gently. She could feel Pepi stiffen from her touch.

"Well," Cheyne sighed, ignoring her mother trying to get her attention. "Someone told us that Lareina, I mean her uh, what do you call it– seeing- viewing-" she bit her lip. Pepi just shrugged.

"Whatever it's called," Cheyne went on, "is uh, in another room. They said there's a whole setup of pictures of Lareina, of her growing up and stuff, and a guestbook to sign besides the one on the webpage. Anyway, I guess we need to pay our respects. You want to go over with us?"

Pepi gulped, nodded.

Seeing the girls whispering, Cheyne's mother frowned at them and motioned for them to come to her.

The girls pasted on solemn expressions, closed their lips and moved unenthusiastically to join Cheyne's family.

In her best June Cleaver voice, Laura Somerset said in a whispered scold, "Girls, this is not the time or place for gossip. Please control yourselves. You may visit later." She patted her blonde hair nervously holding onto Cheyne's brother, Danny's hand

Her husband John, held tightly to Cheyne's other brother, Mikey. Laura linked her arm through John's and the girls tagged along behind as they moved like snails through the crowded room.

The group slowly made their way over to where Lareina's family was sitting on wine colored velvet chairs lined in front of the farthest wall receiving the guests.

The lower part of the walls were paneled in wood, the upper was papered in a regal gold and ivory pattern.

Managing again to separate a few feet from her family, Cheyne leaned over to whisper in her friend's ear, "Oh gosh, look at poor Talana, she looks so desperately heartbroken. But even though drowning in tears, those exotic green eyes are still striking."

Pepi nodded in agreement. "Yes, I'm afraid she's the only one who really cared for Lareina. Except of course for Lareina's brother, Talco. He looks pretty broken up too."

The girls grimly watched the grieving brother and sister, tears streamed down Talana's face.

Tall, rigid as a soldier, his tanned, olive skin paled in grief, Talco looked like he was struggling to hold back his emotions. Also auburn-haired like his sisters, his face was stiff, his eyes identical green to Talana's were stoic with unshed tears.

Pepi whispered again, "Doesn't Talco have the same last name as Talana, and not Wittgenstein like Lareina?"

Cheyne nodded and whispered back, "Yes, although his father was also Lareina's, Miss Mallon, our Sunday school teacher, you know what a relentless gossip she is, said Talco had a falling out with him a long time ago, and his middle name was his mother's maiden name, Castilla, so he just dropped the Wittgenstein. Isn't he handsome in his uniform?"

Pepi said dreamily studying the young man, "Oh yeah. I love those dress blues. The reason why I want to go into the military is to wear a uniform." She laughed quietly at Cheyne's goofy look at her.

"No really, I'm kidding. Of course you know the reason I want to go into the military is to live my passion for my country, and to fly. Except I want the Air Force and Talco's Marines. He does look dashing. I heard he just did two tours across the sea, got back six or so months ago."

Smiling, Cheyne said, "Oh yeah, he's hot. I don't know why Lareina didn't go with the Castilla name too, her name would have been prettier, Lareina Castilla.

"Besides, although they spoiled her rotten, she was always so disparaging of both parents, she held on to her grudge that they left her when she was a kid. She really needed to forgive and let go. You saw how it ate at her from inside. I think that's why she was so spiteful and angry all the time, so ugly on the inside but gorgeous on the outside. Eventually that anger would have warped and gouged her beautiful face, destroying the outside too."

Pepi murmured almost inaudibly but her own open wounds came through clear, "I can understand her anger. Can identify with her somewhat, with the fear of being kept away. Even though not alone."

Cheyne leaned her head gently against Pepi's, feeling her stiffen from the physical contact, but she didn't pull away. "I know, Pep, but it's okay, you're okay now-"

Laura Somerset shot her daughter a withering look and mouthed the words, "*Be quiet.*"

Keeping her face deadpan, Pepi jabbed Cheyne with her elbow.

Cheyne softly stepped on Pepi's foot.

They both struggled not to burst out laughing. What was it about extremely serious events or situations that made a person want to inappropriately giggle?

It took a few minutes before they reached Lareina's family.

Her mother sat like an empress on her chair, dabbing an embroidered handkerchief at her eyes. Her husband stood like a sentry at her side, his face pinched anguish.

Talana had been standing as several aunts and uncles and a few cousins sat sniveling, taking up all of the chairs. But her young knees kept buckling so her brother had gotten her a chair too.

Father and son chose to stand rather than sit, although not next to each other.

After they paid their respects, Cheyne and Pepi moved with groups of people into a chapel for the actual funeral.

They weren't able to sit with their families, it was so crowded they barely got seats together.

Regardless, Cheyne could feel her mother's eyes burning her like a laser across the room. So she sat with perfect posture and bit her tongue to keep it quiet. She tuned out the priest's droning as she daydreamed about her own future.

The somber ceremony finally ended.

The teens slipped away, mixing into the crowd that poured out the back doors and was now moving in an ebb and flow through white wrought iron gates to the cemetery acres behind the grand funeral home.

It was blue and heavenly going in the building, but greyly austere coming out the back.

The winter green lawn all around the building was neatly clipped, hedges professionally manicured.

Sadly, the rows of brooding tombstones sprouting ghoulishly in the cemetery beyond were depressing and macabre. It looked like an avalanche had roared through leaving behind a mishmash of square or arched rocks.

"Ahh," Pepi breathed in deeply, deliciously, then exhaled long and loud. "Finally, fresh air and room." She stretched her arms out, did a tiny pirouette.

"I felt so scrunched and smothered in that building, and too many different kinds of overpowering perfumes and stinky cologne. Ick." Her snub nose wrinkled, she wiped at it with the back of her hand. "It was like being in a department store."

There were tarred paths leading through the cemetery, but with so many people the girls found themselves making their way on the grass through slightly crooked rows of headstones.

Some new and erect, others, even on the grounds of a well maintained cemetery were crumbling, decaying, the elements slowly erasing the etched names.

The girls nervously glanced at ground plaques with cups of faded plastic flowers, stepping gingerly, hoping to avoid stepping on- someone- and hurried to where people gathered around Lareina's burial site.

There were too many people for chairs to be supplied except for the immediate grieving family members, so the crowd swayed and mingled, shifted and wriggled, waiting for the mournful event to end.

High above, perched in a tree, a lone bird chirped, musical to some, grating to others.

Pepi looked up at the bird. "You think he's calling for a friend, or saying goodbye to Lareina?"

"Maybe he just likes to sing." Cheyne tilted her head back and closed her eyes letting the warmth and light of the sun embrace her face, listening to the happy bird tweeting above.

The morose feelings melted away, she opened her eyes and gazed around. Suddenly she grinned and waved.

Pepi looked to see whom she was waving at, but could only see a sea of people. "Who're you waving at?" she asked.

"It's Miss Milan our very favorite teacher. I think she's with her sister. She's talking to a woman that looks just like her but a little older," Cheyne replied still smiling.

"Huh, you say favorite because you love English and journalism. I agree, she's really nice, a plain Jane but nice. If that's her sister with her, her sister is ten times prettier than Miss Milan. But *my* real favorite teacher is my ROTC instructor, Captain Raleigh." Pepi sighed. "If only I was like 10 years older..."

Cheyne laughed. "Sure, his wife and kids would just love that. Come on, let's stay back here, I really don't want to see the casket go in, it would be too...too..."

"Morbid?" a deep voice said from behind the girls. They turned around.

"Hey Karey, what's up?" Her voice unusually shy and demure, Pepi greeted the tall young man who joined them. Her cheeks turned pinkish when he took her hand and held it longer than necessary.

Square jaw, broad shoulders, clean cut with short neat hair and mischievous dark eyes, much darker than his coffee colored skin. Karey Kissoon, a senior, was two years ahead of Pepi and Cheyne.

"This is so awful, poor Lareina," he lamented, his deep voice a bare whisper. "No one would wish this terrible thing to happen to their worst enemy. She was...challenging...but she still deserved a full life." He smiled sadly down at Pepi who was staring at her feet.

The lightness of the spruce spiced air was drenched by a ton of potent perfumes.

Cheyne's lips pursed, she nodded. "Maybe if she'd had more time she could have realized what a- a- difficult person she was and changed herself. But, it's too late now." She picked at a sleeve, pushed her hair off her shoulders and wondered where the noisy bird had gone.

Louise Furley

Pepi nodded in agreement, looking everywhere but at the handsome young man in front of her. She didn't trust herself to speak.

Karey looked around the cemetery with a studied air of nonchalance, then turned to Pepi. His voice low and husky, and just a shade shaky said, "So uh, Pepi Nok, that dress is a knock-out. I mean, um, you're a knock-out in that dress. Sapphire blue is my favorite color."

"Thanks, Karey," Pepi said in a tiny polite voice.

The three stood uncomfortably, their glances bouncing off each other, the ground, the crowd, the sky.

Karey fiddled at his tie with two fingers, rocked his shoulders then said, "So, um, what are you girls doing after this, uh, this is over?"

Twisting her purse chain around her hands, her legs swaying slightly, Pepi grew warm. Wrestling with her jacket, she was surprised when it airlessly slid off.

Karey folded it neatly and laid it over her arm.

"Uh, thanks." She held her purse in both hands. Answering him, she said, "We're supposed to go to the open house for refreshments, and then we're going back to Cheyne's house to watch her little brothers while her parents go-"

"Oh," Cheyne cut in. "I forgot to tell you. Mom changed her mind, she wants the whole family to go to Auntie Martha's together for dinner. So you're free." She kept her expression serious although the look on Pepi's surprised face almost made her laugh out loud.

Pepi's surprise quickly turned to suspicion, but Cheyne just innocently looked back at her.

"That's great, I uh mean, oh. So, anyway," Karey cleared his throat, brushed a nervous hand through his short neat hair. He crossed his arms over the stiffness of his buttoned down shirt, then set his hands on his hips.

"So that means you'll need some dinner. How about, uh, my family is going to Pizza Point tonight would you like to join us? Do you need to ask your folks if it's okay?"

36

Pepi's lips separated, aware she'd been ambushed. Her eyes darted to Cheyne who looked way too uninterested in the conversation, then hopped to Karey who was trying to cover his obvious nervous eagerness with blasé coolness. He managed an uneven smile waiting for her answer.

Pepi's mouth hung for a second. She looked up at his friendly, fine-looking face, impossibly lucent ebony eyes willing her to agree. She nodded, replying shyly, "Um, I, uh, sure, I guess. I'll check with my grandma but it should be okay."

Karey broke out into a huge grin. He had perfect teeth except for one slightly crooked one that made him look amiably approachable. "Well, then. That's great."

His words rushed as if he was afraid she'd change her mind, "I'll see you at the reception and we can go after. So don't eat too much!"

He lightly touched her arm, turned to Cheyne, flashed her a happy smile. "Nice to see you, Cheyne," then back to Pepi. "I'll see you in a few, okay?"

Pepi nodded wordlessly, just blinked perplexed grey eyes at him.

Karey long-legged it easily through the crowd, stopping here and there to greet people he knew. He is a very popular basketball player in the high school. The girls watched him, he was so tall, he was easy to see.

Pepi swung her heated face, catching her grinning friend. "I knew it! I knew you lied about going to your aunt's for dinner! What-"

"Oh don't be silly, Pep, it was written all over the guy's face. He's crazy about you and I wasn't going to let you run him off. He's perfect for you, two gorgeous sporty people," Cheyne said. "And, you didn't flinch when he touched you."

Pepi scowled at her friend. "I do not fli-" she broke off at Cheyne's knowing look. "Anyway, he did it so smoothly, gently," she said in dazed wonderment. "I barely felt his touch."

Her fingertips lightly set on the spot where Karey had touched her arm. She watched as Karey disappeared around the side of the building to the parking lot.

"He's obviously smitten, normally he's one of those cool, calm, collected kind of guys, really friendly and outgoing, but not in a nerdy kind of way, and again, he kept touching you, it was so cute."

Cheyne rattled on before Pepi could get a word in, "We see him every year at that big youth group jamboree at Christ School, so you have the same strong faith. He has tons of friends, practically every girl in school swoons over him. They'd kill for a date with that hot jock. And here he is blushing and stammering while talking to you- oh yeah girl, he's got it bad." Nodding emphatically, she crossed her arms and tapped her toe, the curlicue skirt flouncing with the movement.

A wall abruptly shut down over Pepi's face. Her lips tensed, lids lowered, her body rigid she half turned to walk away, but not before Cheyne caught the misery she tried to hide.

Her voice gruff and low, and heavily desolate, Pepi said, "Let it go, Chey." Her tone hardened. "I don't need a man in my life. I don't need anyone."

Cheyne winced at the raw pain in her voice.

Pepi had quickly erased the torment in her face, but couldn't disguise it in her voice. She looked about to flee.

Cheyne caught Pepi's arm to hold her from leaving. She held tight at first as Pepi pulled away.

Her lips close to her friend's ear, she whispered, "Pep, I know better than anyone your wretched lousy excuse for a childhood." Cheyne still held Pepi's arm, but relaxed her grip, holding onto her friend like she was a frightened kitten.

"But girl, you gotta let go of the darkness or it'll break you apart, it'll keep your heart and your gut raw. It wasn't your fault what happened to you. You deserved better. You deserve better."

Pepi still half turned away, her lids squeezed shut, she clutched her purse and jacket tight to her chest.

Seeing her agitated friend wasn't going to bolt, Cheyne let go of her.

Flicking her blonde hair off her shoulder, she set her hands on her hips and stated firmly, "I am not letting you run him off. He's too good of a guy, he'll make a great boyfriend. He's good looking, plays sports, is smart, he can be your rock. And," she grinned craftily, "you guys will make adorable babies!"

Pepi tried to scowl, but didn't quite manage, tried an excuse instead. "Come on, Chey, you know I have so much on my plate right now, with schoolwork and ROTC and soccer and-"

"Yeah, yeah, you're a busy chick. Every girl can make time for romance. You'll thank me later when you're bouncing those babies on your knees."

Pepi just about choked. "Geez girl, I'm 16, give me some time already. Besides, you know I have plans for the Air Force. I am going to fly and I'm not letting anything or anyone get in my way." She crossed her arms firmly over her chest, tiny lips like mini pink marshmallows pressed in a firm line.

Cheyne smiled slyly. "Uh huh. Isn't Karey also in the ROTC?"

Rolling her grey eyes, "Okay girl, knock it off, you are so annoying when you have a point to press," Pepi smiled slightly.

The bruising darkness lifted for now, Pepi grabbed her friend's arm and tugged her. "Come on, let's go before you have me married and pregnant!"

Chapter Five

Prim English/Journalism teacher at Aura High School, Megan Milan set her briefcase on her tiny kitchen table in her tiny house and popped it open.

Humming, she pulled out several notebooks, a USB drive, pens and a laptop.

The setting sun strew waning rays of sunlight through the open curtains leaving barely enough light to see.

She hated to close the flowery curtains and shut out the evening's inflorescent stars and moonlight even though she'd been warned again and again by friends and neighbors the dangers of a single woman in her mid-twenties living alone leaving the windows wide open for every Tom, Dick and rapist to peep in.

Megan dearly loved to sit in the semidarkness and gaze dreamily out at the roughhewn orb high up in the night's sky.

Feeling the moon's silver coolness caress her face, she would fantasize about her Prince Charming coming someday. As dashing and muscular and courageous as his gleaming white stallion, to whisk her away to Never-Never Land where they would have a dozen kids and live happily ever after.

She opened the laptop and hit the power button then went to a counter and switched the radio on. It was set to the easy listening channel of late 1990's love songs.

She turned it down low as a pleasant background, but not a distraction. Singing along to a song she liked, she ambled over to a cupboard where she took out a candle, carried it to the table and lit the wick.

"Ahhh," Megan deeply breathed in the fragrance, dropping the spent match on the tablecloth. Lush floral scents of roses and lavender filled the small room.

Roses adorned the wallpaper and her dress like colorful rosary beads.

An exceedingly hopeful romantic, Megan had decorated pretty much everything in the miniature house from sofas to pillows, curtains to bedspreads with one type of flower or another as if the immersion of romance from inanimate objects could envelope Megan, and draw real romance to her like a magnet, finally blessing her with the love of her life and children she had always yearned for.

Megan typed for hours, long after the stretched shadows disappeared and the dying candle sputtered spasms of orange and yellows with its last breaths.

Clouds passed over the moon's metallic sheen, shading its beacon now even higher in the firmament.

Hunched over the computer in the meager twilight, she finally sat back, stretched her arms and neck, wiggled her fingers, rubbed her tired eyes.

Yawning, she picked up the teacup but it was empty. She shook the primrose-covered teapot she'd made two hours ago but it was empty too.

"Fine," she muttered. "I can take a hint, it's time to stop." Leaning over the computer, she gazed with drained unfocused eyes, pushing the page-up key until she got back to the beginning of her novel.

So far, she had three chapters completed. An elbow on the table, she set her chin in her hand and pondered the title; 'She Screamed.'

Yawning again more deeply this time, she pushed in the USB drive to save the material, then shut the computer down and closed the lid.

Sighing sleepily, she sat back in her chair. Memories of the brief tour she did overseas in the Peace Corps drifted through her tired mind. Pictures played like a movie.

She had been teaching at a ramshackle school she was assigned to in a deplorably poor village far away from a city, deep in the harsh jungle of Hasguaga, an indigent town in rural Africa.

So remote there was no electric, no phones, no running water, and the makeshift school had only ten students. Two of the ten were sisters. Mereea was five and Shralin was three.

Megan smiled remembering the day Shralin finally spoke for the first time since they'd been brought there half a year ago. She had simply said 'thank you' when Megan pushed a cup of warm tea into her baby hands.

She couldn't help it, Megan had to hug the little girl who had never seen Megan because her eyes were bandaged. The child warily hugged her back.

Eventually, her sister Mereea who seldom spoke and never smiled, told in brief spouts here and there what had happened to them. The serviceman who had brought the children to the school added what he had garnered from some of the whispered rumors in the closest village.

The girls' mother, pretty Yalania, was a pitifully young teen who had been sold in marriage to a young, high-ranking military man by her family.

Although youthful himself with darkly bronzed good looks of an eagle, her husband was an unspeakably sadistic man. He beat Yalania ruthlessly, daily.

It didn't take long before the sheen faded from her raven hair. Cigarette burns on her arms and legs, cuts and bruises all over her body had turned the young mother into a quaking, vacant-eyed, scrawny zombie. She couldn't even nurture her daughters, Mereea and Shralin, identical mini-me's with their black hair and black dots of eyes.

One day, hearing horrifying screams, Yalania was drawn to the shrieks coming from the living room.

Inside, she was struck by the shocking sight of her husband assaulting baby Shralin and a bloody screaming Mereea pounding him on his back with her tiny fists pleading for him stop.

Yalania's vacant look was replaced by a burning rage.

Snapping to life, she rushed over, grabbed a liquor bottle and tried to bash her husband in the head with it. Regretfully, she was no match for the powerful militia trained man.

He snatched the bottle from her, smashed it on the table breaking it, then without a word he viciously slashed it across little Shralin's face- cutting her eyes- With zero emotion, he hurled the bottle across the room and turned to Yalania.

The young mother cringed back in terror. She held up paper-thin frail hands trying to ward him off. But it was like holding a bull back with a feather.

Ignoring her skinny flailing arms, he wrapped his muscled hands around her neck and squeezed. Immediately her eyes bulged, her teenaged face swelled beet red.

The room was blood-soaked bedlam.

Shralin knelt shrieking, her tiny hands covering her bleeding eyes.

Mereea torn between going to her sister's aid or to her mother's just stood so freaked, her mouth popped open and closed with no sound coming out.

Her mother made choking sounds as she clawed at her husband's hands. He shouted, cursing insanely at them all like they were at a circus.

Laughing like a manic hyena at the poor helpless females- he squeezed harder, crushing, squeezing every last drop of oxygen out of Yalania's throat until she stopped moving and grew limp.

Then he let her go. She dropped to floor like a Raggedy Ann doll.

43

Shralin couldn't see what happened, she kept screaming.

Mereea stood frozen, stunned, eyes like shocked lightning.

The husband looked down with no compassion at the young teen mother lying throttled on the floor.

Her eyes were already turning opaque staring blindly into the beyond, the color in her skin fading.

Then the fiendish brute looked at Mereea and pointed, "This is all your fault. You screamed." His lunatic laughter only grew louder at her stricken face.

The insane man started towards the terrified girl then suddenly veered to the door.

A tarnished, brass glass lantern sat on a table near the threshold. Smirking, he picked it up. Turning the knob, his snarling face glowed yellow when the flame flared and grew. He turned to the two little girls.

Shralin was kneeling, tiny shoulders heaving in piercing sobs sounding like a lamb being ripped apart by a wolf. Blood poured out between her fingers pressed over her eyes.

Mereea knelt beside her and wrapped her arms around her little sister while keeping her terrified eyes glued to their depraved father.

With one last look at his two sobbing daughters kneeling huddled together on the floor, he laughed, the merciless inhumane laughter of the very devil himself. He opened the door, said, "Goodbye my darlings, I'll see you in hell!"

Then he threw the lantern to floor where it shattered and immediately went ablaze. In seconds the carpet caught fire and rushed at the children.

Their father slammed and locked the door behind him.

No one knows how they got out. Mereea never said. Her story always ended at her mother's hair and skin crackling as the flames consumed her and moved towards the girls.

Everyone assumed they probably escaped through a window.

A serviceman was training in the woods when he came across the pathetic bedraggled girls barely clinging to life. Under a tree with their arms wrapped around each other, they lay starving, bloody and burnt, spent, waiting to die.

Wild dogs were zoning in, snarling and snapping, creeping closer and closer. The serviceman shot at them until they ran off then he picked the children up and brought them to the school.

Neither girl had uttered a word in the first three months then Mereea spoke a little, telling their story in jibs and jabs.

They ate voraciously, their only comfort, food. Mostly they sat silently like broken dolls.

The teachers and Peace Corps' rotation of doctors and nurses could only clean them up, feed them, teach them, and give them the best medical care they could while keeping them hidden at the school.

One day one of the teachers had gone into the nearest town 30 miles away to get supplies.

The town was tiny, a rural village, with just one store that contained only bare basics. But there was electricity and phones, running water; some people had vehicles.

While there, she'd heard a tale of two little girls that allegedly had murdered their mother, and their father had been obligated to kill the girls for the sake of his family's pride.

Although speculation was that the truth was seriously distorted, the children after all were hardly more than toddlers. The father was known for being a savage vicious man even when not provoked.

When the teacher had returned, after a brief meeting, everyone decided it would be best to keep the children hidden, let their dangerous father think he'd succeeded in killing his daughters.

The teachers felt they were too young to be considered credible witnesses, therefore, they decided it would be fruitless to go to the authorities, and to do so would only put them out there, and the father would undoubtedly go after them to silence them.

Megan had tried to bring them back to America with her, but she was unable to do it legally without exposing them to the law. Which might incarcerate the children in a juvenile detention, or a

45

deplorable orphanage, or worse, their abhorrent father could find them. There was just no way for her to smuggle them out.

Eventually, just before her tour expired, the doctors were able to stash the sisters on their private plane and flew them to Switzerland.

Megan had tried periodically to find the girls and see how they were doing, but she hadn't been able to locate any word about them. It was as if they just vanished, like they'd never existed. Which for them was probably for the best.

Sitting in her floral kitchen, Megan let the tears fall to her hands clasped tightly in her lap.

She had decided she could write the children's story and maybe down the road it would bring light onto their travails, as well as others trapped and abused in that far away poor village, Hasguaga.

"But enough for tonight, girlfriend," Megan ordered herself, wiping her eyes. She left her work on the table, stashed the USB drive in what she hoped was a safe place from fire or flood or some other catastrophe, and headed off to get ready for bed.

She needed her beauty sleep to look her best for that dopey wedding her sister was making her go to tomorrow.

Chapter Six

Megan attempted to smother her yawn.

The wedding was a huge bore.

She watched her older sister Margo dancing her legs off, laughing and flirting.

Megan was not ugly, just plain. She was called cute when she was younger, but she had grown into a nondescript wallflower, slim, medium height with brown hair in an easy to maintain chin length bob, and puppyish round brown eyes.

Her sister was the pretty, vivacious one, she always got asked to dance or date while Megan was treated like she was everybody's friend.

It was amazing how two women with basically the same coloring and features could look so different just depending on what shade, size and where those features were placed.

Both ladies happened to be single at the moment so Margo had practically twisted Megan's arm to have her accompany her to the wedding.

"There are always single men at weddings, Megs," Margo had said, trying to convince her sister to go. "Brothers and brothers-in-law, and cousins and nephews- gee it's like going to one tree and having a choice of a bunch of different types of fruit to pick!"

"Oh yeah, sure, that's what I want, a fruity guy," Megan remarked sourly.

However, Margo cajoled and begged and finally Megan gave in.

Now, Megan looked down at the bedazzling dress Margo had loaned her. Back at the house Margo had said, "None of those schoolmarm outfits you wear, not today. You're too young to be buttoned up to the neck and skirt past your knees."

"But Margo, I am a teacher and I can't afford to be dressed like a slut, what if I run into a student or their parents? I have to maintain a proper image."

"Yeah, yeah, yeah, whatever."

Megan had gotten tired of Margo yapping at her so she gave in, and here she was at the most boring of all weddings, dressed in the skimpiest dress she'd ever worn in her life. Spangled gold with spaghetti straps, décolleté neckline so low she had to wear a jacket in the church, but so hot now at the reception she had to take the jacket off.

Not used to showing so much skin, she could hardly cross her legs the skirt was so tight and short she was afraid every time she moved she'd expose herself!

She also regretted letting Margo talk her into wearing Margo's stilettoes. She wasn't used to such high shoes and Margo's feet were a quarter of a size smaller than hers, her feet were killing her- it was actually a blessing she wasn't asked to dance.

Besides that, there was only one decent guy in the bunch and he was with Margo, the charismatic one in the family.

The only thing Megan liked about her outfit was the glittery gold barrette that held back one side of her hair. Margo told her it gave her a sexy look with the side swept up.

Megan felt her sister was trying to pump her up so she'd have more confidence and relax a little more, and flirt. She laughed wryly to herself. It didn't look like she was ever going to even have to the opportunity to flirt with anyone.

Even if she could flirt, or knew how to flirt, it wasn't something she had ever considered something she could do. She knew she'd feel gawky and foolish if she tried.

For a moment, she imagined herself twirling a lock of hair and batting her eyelashes at some guy, and- she was right, even in her own mind she looked goofy. She shook the illusion away. *What a silly dolt you are,* she told herself.

Sighing, Megan hid another yawn behind her hand. She gulped the last of her ginger ale and looked around the room wondering how soon she could drag Margo away-

Oh No, she couldn't believe it, there were several students that had graduated a couple of years ago standing in a clutch near the band. *Great, just what she needed, there would be pictures of her in seconds all over social media, jeopardizing her job.*

She hustled to her feet, keeping her head low and sideways, using her short brown bob and gold clutch to cover half her face she bee-lined for the door.

Keeping her head down, she hurried down the hall tugging the tight skirt back down clumsily with one hand and praying she didn't break her neck in the heels that threw her ankles in all directions.

Halfway down the hall, she gratefully turned into the first door she came to.

She shoved the door open.

A little out of breath, she looked up and blanched.

Worse than the ballroom, she had burst into the hotel's bar.

Everyone looked up as she made her awkward entrance stumbling when her heel caught the change in carpets.

Too embarrassed to turn around and leave, she regained her balance and walked as coolly as possible to the bar working hard not to toddle in the hateful heels.

Setting her the gold clutch on the bar, not sure of how much of her underwear she showed, and unused to chairs without arms or backs, she gripped the bar with her fingers, bemoaning the manicure she'd gotten talked into, and climbed up on a barstool.

Even at average height, her feet dangled and she had to stretch to reach the bottom rail without losing a shoe to secure herself.

Feeling she was going to topple over or slide off any second, scared to let go of the bar, she latched onto the edge to steady herself like holding onto the saddle of a rocky horse.

The bartender, long, lean with a small beer belly and stringy blond hair moseyed over. He leaned in and said in a low voice, "Honey, we don't let professional girls in here you know."

Confused, Megan said, "I'm a teacher, that's professional, why wouldn't I be allowed in here?"

The bartender laughed. "Oh, it's okay if you're a teacher. I meant *working* girls, ya know what I mean?" He winked. Rolling his white sleeves further up his forearms, he braced his palms on the counter.

Even more confused, Megan sputtered, "I find that I don't understand what you mean?"

The bartender set a cocktail napkin in front of Megan. "It's the dress, doll, you look like...uh... flashy, like a, forgive my French, you look like a streetwalker."

Seeing her genuine confusion, he believed her. "Never mind, Miss. So what's your pleasure?"

Finally understanding what he was saying, Megan's brown eyes widened, red blew up her face. "Well, I can assure you-"

The bartender shook his head, smiled kindly. "I get it, you're a teacher, don't worry, you're okay. What'll you have?"

Embarrassed to the teeth, Megan started to say she didn't want anything thanks for asking, but she didn't want to make things worse, and she'd look like a child she thought if she ordered a soda like she wanted.

"I'll, uh, have uh, a glass of white wine please," she said very primly. She tried to cross her legs and almost fell off the stool.

The bartender sucked in his amusement and left to get her a glass of house white before he embarrassed her further by laughing at her obvious greenness.

"Well, *that* was sure smooth," Megan muttered, regaining her balance. She decided she'd drink her wine as fast as possible and get the heck out of there before she *really* did something humiliating.

Keeping her head down, she peered around the room. Typical of any hotel bar, it was medium-sized, lowly lit, square tables that would seat up to four people, half had patrons at them, were sprinkled the room.

The bar was a straight line, the carpet red, walls beige covered with photographs of the hotel as it changed over the years.

Megan sat hunched at one end of the bar, a handful of guests were seated in the middle and the bartender was down at the far opposite flirting with an attractive young woman.

The bartender quickly went to washing glasses as soon as a young man joined the woman.

Gulping the first Chablis the bartender brought her went down like vinegar, but by time she finished it she felt so much better that she ordered another. And then another.

Three men sat in a huddle a few seats away from her. They had looked up when she had first blundered in, but paid her no attention after that.

The alcohol oozed through her body, warming and tingling her. Her arms were suddenly all shivery and rubbery and her feet were numb. She giggled. "Oo!"

The wine was making her feel more risqué than she'd ever felt before because she didn't really drink. Christmas 3 years ago she'd had a half a glass of champagne. According to Margo, she'd had to be helped to bed.

Megan doesn't remember anything other than bubbles tickling her nose and making her sneeze, it all went blank after that.

Her eyes fluttered lightly closed. A blissful smile graced her thin lips, relaxing some of her normal primness and inducing a

51

rare suppleness. Her shoulders swayed right, left, in her mind she was moving sensually to the slow, sexy, throaty blues music playing from speakers on the walls.

Her pleasantly woozy head rocked side to side. She felt happy and really truly tranquil for the first time in a long time. And attractive. *Yeah, I am attractive* Megan announced silently to herself firmly.

Continuing to sip, the sips grew longer and less time passed between them, she paid for the drinks and tipped as she went.

After several glasses of wine, she became emboldened from the liquor. She pushed her heavy lids open and glanced discreetly several times, at least she thought she was being discreet, over at the men a few feet away.

After all, she was dressed in a spectacularly sexy dress and hot shoes, why waste it? Maybe this was her night to get herself a boyfriend!

She tried to make eye contact with the cute blond guy in the middle, but his gaze was blank, he looked through her like she was a window.

Maybe another drink will help her become bold enough that for once in her prudish lifetime she would be the initiator; for once *she* would do the asking! Just one more glass of liquid courage and she could do it, she knows she can!

So intent on her plans of getting a date and drinking and staying atop her stool, she didn't notice the young men who had been in the ballroom that she left to get away from had wandered in and were now joining the three men she had been contemplating asking for a date.

Oh dear, Megan frowned.

Worry and annoyance wormed through the liquor-induced cotton wool in her head. She needed to hide fast, she didn't want those ex-students to recognize her- why didn't they just get drinks at the bar at the reception for heaven's sake!

Before she could swivel on her stool and make a get-away, the young men had already picked up some cocktails from the bartender and moved off and back out of the bar.

Keeping her head turned away from the entrance, Megan drew a deep grateful breath.

Waiting to make sure they didn't return right away, she pulled a compact out of her purse and checked her makeup. When Margo was applying it earlier Megan had protested it was way too heavy, she looked like Mila Kunis playing Elizabeth Taylor for crying out loud- but now, looking through blurry inebriated eyes she decided she looked quite beautiful, like Mila Kunis playing herself!

Her confidence soared. She reapplied her lipstick, unaware with her blurry vision and loose hands she had lined some of the outside of her lips. She straightened the glittery barrette and patted the bottom of her bob.

Smiling at her fuzzy reflection, she snapped the compact closed and slipped it back in the purse. Tucking the clutch under her arm she clumsily slid off the stool to her unbalanced feet.

Now or never, while she has the alcohol infused nerve in her she's going to make her move! Smoothing and pulling down the tight short glam dress, she straightened her shoulders and brazenly stepped over to the men.

Hardly wobbling at all on the high heels, she boldly plunged into the middle of the group.

Slithering between one of the other men to stand in front of the blond, with a watery smile and blurry eyes, Megan shouted, "Hi, I'm Megan!" Not realizing how loud she spoke, she pushed back the gold barrette that slipped again in her fine hair and now hung crookedly by only a few hairs.

A fan of vintage films, she smiled like she pictured the old timey sex kittens did.

The men all looked at her with mild surprise, and barely suppressed animosity. If Megan had not been so intoxicated she would have seen the danger in their eyes.

"What's *your* name?" She slurred inelegantly to the blond.

Chapter Seven

"Wow Cheyne, that was a phenomenal dismount!" The Phys Ed teacher exclaimed.

The other girls clapped.

The teacher laughed, "I gotta say though, it looked a little bizarre and extreme, are you going to be able to repeat it or was it a fluke?"

Built like SpongeBob Squarepants with a bowl haircut and masculine mannerisms, it was rumored Ms. Blankenfoor played in the lady pool and was in a relationship with the Latin teacher, Ms. Palmer.

The upbeat Phys Ed teacher was very supportive of her students and seldom reprimanded them, always cheered them on, encouraging and praising even the slowest and heaviest. She was very popular with most of the student body.

Cheyne stood for a second on the mat catching her breath. Blushing a little, she pulled the band around her ponytail tighter then flicked the blonde tail back behind her head. Wiping the chalk off her hands on her leotard, smiling, she pattered in her bare feet over to the teacher.

"You called it, Ms. Blankenfoor. It wasn't actually the move I'd planned. I had kicked and swung scissoring too hard around the top bar and found myself twisting while going around one too many times and had to improvise. But I think I can duplicate it."

"I hope so. With the semi's coming up a few months after spring break we'll need all the extra extraordinary routines we can get!"

Cheyne opened her mouth but Blankenfoor cut her off with a square hand held up and a grin. "Remember, I'm a Phys Ed teacher, not an English teacher."

The teacher turned to the rest of the room and announced with a clap of her square hands, "Okay girls, that's it for today. Everybody out, and I mean everybody. Overtraining causes injuries. See you all on Wednesday."

The girls put away any movable equipment, grabbed their towels and water bottles and headed for the lockers.

Thirty minutes later after a fast shower and her hair back up in a clean but wet ponytail, Cheyne grabbed her gym bag and headed for the door.

"Hey-"

Cheyne almost bumped into Pepi as she was exiting the locker room.

"Hey, sorry sistergirl." Cheyne apologized. "You got here right on time. We have just enough time to stop by Starblinque Boutique on the way home. I've just *got* to have those fuchsia earrings. I hope they're finally on sale, they will go perfectly with my prom dress I'm planning to buy for the Summer's End Dance!"

A corner of Pepi's mouth turned up. "Girl, you need to get a date first. In the meantime you need to move past your allowance and start looking for a job. I saw some help wanted signs in the Fresh Food Sandwich Shoppe. They need people to work in the ice cream section. You want to go there tomorrow after class and apply? You don't have practice do you?"

Cheyne shook her head. "No, there's no practice until Wednesday, then we're done for spring break. I'll ask my mom. She's against me getting a job right now with all the stuff I have going on, schoolwork, gymnastics, journalism team, school paper and the chores I have to do at home. But I think if the hours are not that much she might agree."

"Okay, sounds good," Pepi said with a wide grin. "Let's go to Starblinque's. I called Grams already and told her what time I'll be home."

Hefting backpacks over their shoulders, they left the school and walked down the street where they could catch the city bus.

Hours later, giggling wildly like teenage girls, which they were, Cheyne and Pepi left the boutique, each carrying a small bag in their hands and backpacks heavy on their backs.

Hitting the sidewalk, they strolled side by side, Pepi with her energetic but guarded walk, and Cheyne, her hips with their feminine sway still managed to be a half a beat ahead of her wary friend.

Pepi moved like she was always expecting- something, and not something particularly good.

"Whew!" Pepi puffed out a breath of air. "I'm beat. We should just catch the bus." They flopped down on the bus bench and stuffed their purchases in their back packs.

"Mom's going to be peeved, the sun is already setting and it's going to be another 20 minutes before we get home. I'd better call her." She pulled out her cell but as she started to dial sirens wailing down the street caught her attention.

As the earsplitting yowls and horns blasting grew closer, the girls covered their ears. In seconds one police car after another streaked past with sirens blaring and blue lights strobing.

When the sound finally died enough to hear, Pepi said, "Gosh, I counted like 15 police cars and 4 fire trucks!"

Cheyne nodded. "Yeah, I can't believe how far behind the ambulances were. I'd hate it if it were me waiting for them! It looks like there must have been a huge accident somewhere. I hope it's not on our way home. I'm gonna say a quick prayer for them."

"Me too." Pepi said just as the bus pulled up.

Chapter Eight

While a giddy Megan Milan dressed for her date, her sister Margo hen-pecked around her.

Pushing shoulder length rich chestnut hair behind her ears, she wrung her hands following Megan from closet to drawer to closet. "Really, Megs. That is so not like you to get picked up like a- like a- well like a tramp! Why I-"

Standing in front of a vanity with a mirror in a curved frame, Megan ignored her sister's rants and lined her lips with her new Ravishing Red lipstick then smacked them.

Running a finger, the nail in matching red over her teeth to make sure they were clear of lipstick, she stood back to look at her reflection. Squinting at her image, she asked Margo, "The lipstick and nail polish were an early morning impulse buy. What do you think?"

Margo's expression told her exactly what she thought.

"Come on, Marg, after my success in snagging a date with that good looking Devin, I decided I needed to class up my action, wear makeup more often. You know I've never worn red before, I always thought it was too flamboyant, too daring for my pallid complexion. But I think it really adds some, oh, va-voom to my looks, don't you think so?"

Margo's frown not approving, she sniffed, "Next you'll be buying red shoes."

Megan smiled sideways at her sister. "You know, the thought did cross my mind." She laughed at her sister's expression. "Don't worry, that's not going to happen any time soon!"

"Listen Megs-"

Megan cut her off, "Really, I just can't believe the blond hunk at the bar agreed to go out with me." Not that she remembers their entire conversation, just bits and pieces. Thank goodness she'd written down what he'd said on a note and put it in her purse.

She could hardly believe her luck when she woke the other morning. Of course she had a nasty, blinding headache and upset stomach, but once she retrieved the note when she returned the purse to Margo, part of the night came back to her.

She was thrilled beyond belief. She had a date! And he was hot! And- she had done the asking- her knees almost buckled when she thought about that.

But maybe that was the price of the hangover, not having to remember what she said and how she said it. She was just going to be glad of the outcome and not worry about how intoxicated she had been.

Now finally, she didn't avoid mirrors, hating to look at her plain reflection with her brown bob, puppy round eyes, pale skin and skinny lips. Who knew how fantastic makeup could make her look?

Never one to mess with her hair after she combed it one time in the morning, she now teased, smoothed and poked at it, trying to keep her hands busy to halt them shaking from nerves.

The last thing she was going to do was admit to her sister that she couldn't believe her audacity in approaching a total stranger, albeit a cute one, and asking him out. Forget that she was to go meet him at a bar in a part of the city that she had never been to before.

To be honest, she had seldom been anywhere near that, well, seedy section of town. She smiled confidently at her sister.

"I'm starting a new stage in my life, the new Megan Milan. Ever since writing my exposé story I've been stirred with, oh I don't know, I guess a tiny rivulet of courage is streaming through my veins. I just feel like I've been meek and mild and letting life do and guide me, well, now I want to *do* life. I may even grow my hair out to my shoulders. Guys like long hair."

"Sure Megs, I'm all for you coming out of your shell, a little at a time, safely. But really, going out with a man you know nothing about-"

"I know, I know, Margo. I am not a child. I am meeting him in a public place."

"Yeah, where?" Margo asked.

Megan blushed, her eyes downcast. "Uh, well we're meeting at the Dhreu House for cocktails and then-"

"The Dhreu House!" Margo gaped at her in disgust. She pushed her chestnut hair behind her ears. The full curls danced around her shoulders.

Her hands dropping to perch in irritation on her hips, she ranted, "That miserable dump? Are you kidding? Really, sis, I don't think-" she followed her sister as Megan roamed around the room picking up a sweater and purse.

Her keys in her hand, Megan scowled absently, trying to focus, she didn't want to forget anything. "Oh calm down," she said patiently to her sister, "it's just for drinks to get to know each other a little bit without a crowd around. Then I'm sure he'll take me somewhere nice for dinner."

She worked to keep the uncertainty out of her voice, but her sister knew her too well.

"Listen, Megs, maybe I should go with you, you don't have to-"

Megan wiped the second thoughts off her face and ushered up a confident smile. Squaring her slender shoulders and speaking in her most haughty teacher voice, she said, "Don't be ridiculous I am perfectly capable of taking care of myself. Besides, you just got through reminding me as soon as I leave you're heading out of town for that expedition. I'll be fine."

She grinned at her sister. "Oh, Margo, you have no idea, he is *so* dreamy, *so* good looking, blonde hair combed neatly but looks like it has a mind of its own, and the palest blue eyes I've ever seen. And," Megan clasped her hands, twisting them and rolled her shoulders up to her ears. "Oh Margo, he's got this accent. I can't tell from where, but, oh it's romantic, deep, low, hard to hear, makes you move in closer to listen. He-"

"I got it Megs, he's hot. But he's still a stranger. I can cancel the-"

Megan shook her head. She stopped and took her sister's hands, her smile soft and warm in her genuine love for her only sister. "I will be just fine. Now don't you worry. I'll call you tomorrow with all the delicious deets. Okay?"

Margo looked sternly at her little sister. She had always mothered her even though they were close in age. She had to admit Megan was beaming, she looked the happiest Margo could remember seeing her in a long time.

With a heavy sigh she shook her head, "But Megs, still... a total stranger-"

Megan dropped her sister's hands. "I'll call you tomorrow, I promise. Do not worry about me. Have a safe trip."

One last look in the mirror to check that the rose chiffon blouse with the scalloped collar was tucked neatly in the pencil skirt, carrying her purse and sweater over her arm and a quick kiss to her sister's cheek, she hurried out the door in pumps with one inch heels before she changed her mind.

The drive to the bar took 45 minutes.

Sitting in the car in a parking lot, Megan turned off the engine and sat for a second, working up her nerve.

Thinking about what she was about to do, she realized she had never gone to a bar before alone. Actually, she couldn't even remember a time went she went to just a bar with no restaurant attached.

"Gee, I am sheltered." She sighed. The fact that the area was less, well, a lot less reputable than the main city of Corbiestep, Megan had not previously had any reason to go near this area.

Finally gathering up the nerve to get out of her car, she trotted self-consciously down the trash strewn alley and out along the walkway scarred and pitted from long hard years of use.

Megan had to watch her low heels didn't catch a rut and make her fall. A few empty cars were parked along the curb at meters. This section of town flanked way outside of the main city square.

She passed a tattoo parlor, smoke shop and used book store. The city air had a sooty, cigarette smell mixed with rotting garbage.

Feeling like someone was watching her, she furtively peeked over one shoulder then the other.

A couple of unkempt men, carrying what looked like bottles of booze in paper bags sat on the stoop of a closed shop across the street. Taking quick swigs from the bags, they darted cagey glances at her.

Down the end of the street was a construction site closed down for the night. Orange cones and striped barricades blocked off the area.

The realization she was in a bad section of town with the light fading fast, spurred her feet to move more quickly. She was sure that her date would walk her gentlemanly back to her car later.

Letting out a hearty breath of relief, finally, she reached the bar. Suddenly painfully shy, *thank goodness*, she murmured to herself, the door was propped open so her entrance shouldn't be that noticeable.

She pretended not to notice the H and e on Dhreu House were broken off the front of the fairly decrepit building, and the b, r, and n of the blinking neon Beer and Wine sign in the window were burnt out, but the neon sign still buzzed.

Skirting the peeling paint of the open doors, Megan clutched her purse, sweater and a bag tight to her chest and stepped gingerly over the worn and torn Welcome mat inside that was supposedly to wipe one's dirty feet on, but apparently was not used very much because scores of muddy footprints crossed the faded and scraped wood planked floor.

Most of the footprints ended at a pair of construction workers sitting hunched over the bar nursing foamy mugs.

Without moving her head, Megan searched the room. Her shoulders sagged.

Devin, the cute blond she had made the date with was nowhere to be seen.

The dingy, dimly lit place was small with only a square U shaped bar that ran the length of the wall to the left, five booths along the opposite wall that were all empty, and seven tables scattered through the middle of the room.

The occupants in the tavern consisted of the two construction workers hunched at the bar, the lone bartender drying glasses and a barmaid sitting over at one of the tables texting or playing a game on her phone.

Oh yeah, playing a game, Megan decided when she heard the familiar screams and beeps from Angry Birds.

The only other occupants were a couple that judging by the way they were noodling at one of the booths in the shadows at the very back, were probably on a clandestine date, and lastly there was a man sitting at a table smoking a cigar and reading a newspaper. So much for no smoking inside laws.

Well, she couldn't stand in the doorway gawking, so she reluctantly pulled out a chair at a table nearest the door.

The entire bar was made out of wood. Wood floor, wood tables, wood panels, actually panels painted a faux wood; the bar was the nicest thing in the structure. Varnished a deep mahogany, the lights hanging from the ceiling cast copper aureole halos on the glossy counter.

However, the rest of the room reeked disreputably shabby. The table tops of the booths along the wall were once white with silver and gold speckles but now were yellowing, and the tears in the red vinyl seats were covered with silver tape.

Megan looked up once and resolved not to do it again. Above her head, thick dusty webs clung from beam to beam. Feeling like

Little Miss Muffet on her tuffet, she shuddered, picturing a spider dangling over her head ready to drop-

Taking a wet wipe out of her purse, she opened the package and wiped the chair and a spot in front of her on the table.

The table was gouged and scarred by burnt cigarettes. People had carved their initials and obscenities into the wood top. She also wiped the chair next to her where she sat her purse and a shopping bag, then laid her sweater carefully across that back of her chair.

She had stopped on the way and picked up some shoes she'd had repaired at the shoe shop. She didn't want to leave a shopping bag on the seat in the car and invite robbers, and her trunk was so packed with school supplies and projects she just went ahead and brought it in with her.

Looking at the bag on the chair, she felt kind of silly now for bringing it in. Her fidgety hand pushed the ashtray that had been emptied but not wiped clean across the table out of nose range and waited, for a long time for the gum-popping, young barmaid to come to her.

Eventually, in a uniform of worn, holey jeans that dragged on the floor, and a tacky, tight black t-shirt, the sulky, with more hair hanging in her face then around it, the barmaid, leaned a skinny hip against the table while she took Megan's order.

Megan sipped her ginger ale as slowly as she could, but lag as she may, the big hand on the clock kept moving until it passed the little hand 60 times.

Two other men had come in, glanced at her, had a couple of drinks, used the restroom twice then left, more came in to replace them all planting themselves at the bar.

The occasional bursts of raucous laughter and arguments, and heavy metal music made Megan dreadfully antsy. She waited a little while longer, but finally had to admit she'd been stood up.

She paid her bill, collected her purse and sweater and with half disappointment and half relief, left the bar.

Evening had fallen in the short time she was inside, with most of the street lights knocked out by rocks or bullets, it was hard to see.

Picking her way carefully down the beat up street, the sound of her heels tap- tapping down the sidewalk rang abnormally loud in her ears in the quiet barren night.

Although it seemed she had the street to herself, it made her jittery that anyone could hear her coming a mile away.

She regretted now that she had been too cheap to pay the meter out front and had parked in the free parking in the back. Because now she had to walk down a very dark alley to an even darker, poorly lit parking lot.

By the time she reached the parking lot, she stopped suddenly. "Darn it," she said snapping her fingers. "I forgot my shoes."

Megan turned around, the long dark, homicidal alley and the parking lot were so eerie with no one around, so quiet and surrounded by a scraggily wall of fir trees casting restless shadows.

The trees looked like faceless, tall, triangles of men staring down at her. She decided she could come back tomorrow in the daylight.

Hurrying across the lot to her car, Megan was careful not to trip and fall.

Chapter Nine

After stopping for some fast food, exhausted and disheartened, Megan pulled into her driveway and shut off the engine.

Sitting motionless for a few minutes, she just stared at her home. She had a sweet little house.

White gingerbread trim with matching shutters, the pastel yellow of the one story house would pale when brilliant daffodils bloomed across the front in April.

The yard was framed with a low hedge separating her from her neighbors on both sides. The Jeffersons on one side and the Fitzgeralds on the other were both gone this week visiting relatives.

The lights that usually blazed so homey in their windows were extinguished tonight, making the neighborhood spooky and lonely.

Their three houses were separated from the others in the neighborhood by several empty lots and partially hidden by a bristly host of trees on every swale to the end of the street.

Megan sighed. Her house was pretty and feminine and tiny, she had a job she dearly loved, a small group of intimate friends, and was very close to her family. But, she wanted more.

She wanted a bustling big house filled with boisterous children and a loving husband.

She sighed again and gathered up her sweater and purse, pushed open the door. *It'll come*, she thought, *I just have to be patient.* She didn't have the energy to walk around through the kitchen so she went in through the front door.

Not bothering to flick on the lights, wearily she dropped her purse and sweater on a table next to the door; too despondent to care when she heard them fall to the floor.

Padding across the tile with her eyes almost closed, she headed towards the hall that led to two teeny bedrooms. She'd watch TV for a change, in bed.

She didn't turn on any lights because she knew her house like the back of her hand even in the pitch-black night. But after taking only three steps the hairs on the back of her neck prickled. She hesitated.

There wasn't any sound except her breathing, but something didn't feel right.

Turning back to the table by the door to switch on a lamp, she tripped over something squishy like a pillow. She bit her lip when she stepped on something that crunched like broken glass. Catching her balance, she reached for the lamp- but her hands only hit air!

Trying to stem the sense of panic rising in her stomach, she slapped at the wall until she caught the light switch and flipped it on.

"Oh my gosh!" she cried out loud.

Standing in the entrance to the living room, Megan couldn't believe her eyes!

The room had been practically turned upside down.

Her tall secretary desk was lying on the floor with all the contents spilled across the rug. The cushions on the couch were thrown on the floor, some even had slashes in them and the stuffing pulled out. The guts of the couch had been ripped out, her few paintings and a clock had been torn off the wall, the TV and stand and the side tables strew broken in front of her feet.

Her mouth agape, she looked around. Stupidly she ran down the hall to see if the bedrooms were ravaged too!

Her heart hammering, she flew into her bedroom-

It was the same. Drawers dumped, mattress pulled hanging half off the bed and slashed too, clothes hauled out of the closet and thrown in a pile in the middle of the room!

Megan dashed from room to room and back down the hall, no room had been left untouched. Even the kitchen was destroyed.

Every drawer had been pulled out and cupboards opened, fridge and pantry emptied, all the contents thrown in ruined piles over the entire room.

How she didn't trip over anything was a miracle. Hurrying over to the wall phone, she snatched it off and with shaking hands dialed 911. It never occurred to her to leave the house.

She was standing in the kitchen on trembling legs when the police came, her arms wrapped tightly around her body.

The first policeman to arrive on the scene chastised her for being inside and brought her outside to wait for them to clear the house.

She should have, he admonished her, run outside to a neighbor then call 911.

Megan knew she had acted imprudently, but really, the thoughts had clamored and bounced around inside her head, she hadn't even been able to think, couldn't catch her breath.

The 911 dispatch had to ask her several times for her address. The operator had told her to leave the premises in case the burglars were still inside, but the words hadn't penetrated the chaos in her static brain.

After the place was searched and cleared, a detective joined the scene. He brought her back inside to her kitchen. He up-righted the table and two chairs that didn't have broken legs and helped her sit at the table.

"Miss, uh," he dipped his eyes at his notes. "Miss Milan. I know this is a terribly frightening experience, but I do have to ask you more questions. Can you handle that?"

Louise Furley

Her head spinning, Megan sat staring blankly, body quivering, chest heaving with frantic pants, her bones had turned to mush.

Giving her a few moments to collect herself, the detective kindly made her a pot of tea.

The microwave currently lacked a door, so he searched the debris and miraculously found an unbroken teacup, then rather quickly located a metal teakettle only slightly dented.

The water boiled, teabags dunked in, he waited about three minutes before pouring her a steaming cup. He took her hands and wrapped them around the teacup then sat opposite her at the table.

Her eyes drifted down to the tea then up to the detective. It was hard for her to focus with the quaking and the steam, the detective appeared across the table in a wobbly mist.

He reached over and patted her hand. He hadn't removed his coat but he had opened it.

"I know this is a shock, Miss, um," eyes dropped quickly to his notes again, "Milan. I'm Detective Douglas James." He waited for her breathing to calm and her eyes to stop twitching.

She absently blew on the tea then sipped. The strong brew did have a calming effect, as did the detective's calm deep voice. She smiled wanly. "Thank you Mr., um, Detective uh, I'm sorry what did you say your-"

"James."

"Yes, Detective James. You are very kind." She pressed a shaky hand to her dizzy head, the tea and strong presence of the detective were helping her head stop spinning.

"You must have done this a thousand times yet you still act with compassion and patience. I appreciate it, truly." She peered over the rim of the cup.

She was surprised to see a quite good looking man sitting across from her. The clichéd overly used term 'ruggedly handsome' was coined for this man.

Douglas James was tall, rangy, with door spanning shoulders, square chin and totally smoldering dark eyes. The coat and loosened tie, quiet black shoes, and neatly combed hair in need of a trim, were a sort of uniform that made her think of the cop shows she watched.

He leaned back comfortably, crossed one leg over the other then set a hand on his knee. He did not get himself a cup of tea.

"Yes, well, I know this reprehensible intrusion makes you feel- violated. It is a traumatic experience to come home and find your place tossed."

Her head bobbed in short spurts. "Destroyed is more like it. But yes, it's unbelievably traumatic. My house has been raped." She smiled weakly, quipping badly, "Without even getting dinner first."

Detective James appreciated humor, though as gallows as it was and an old joke. In nerve-racking moments such as this, it let him know she was okay, well, at least as okay as she could be under the circumstances.

He smiled back. She was definitely a docile wallflower, yet she had moments of plucky wryness. A corner of his mouth pulled in forcing a dimple.

Megan's eyes were irresistibly drawn to the dimple.

"That's it, keep a stiff upper lip," he said with a slight grin. "So then," he pulled a small notebook and pen out of his pocket. "I know they already asked you these questions, but maybe you've thought of something since the first responders took your statement."

"I understand," Megan said demurely, her eyes still on that dimple. Pulling her gaze away, she looked up at his smoldering eyes, *oh dear*- butterflies kicked in her stomach.

With the harrowing day and this handsome policeman, she wondered if he would catch her if she should happen to faint... *Maybe, maybe he could be her prince to rescue her from-*

She crossed her ankles and tucked them modestly behind a chair leg and cupped her tea with both hands.

Momentarily, the nastiness of being stood up and her house being burglarized slipped to the back seat. She wriggled her lips trying to maneuver them into what she hoped was a beguiling smile, whatever that meant. It's not like she played the coquette every day!

At least she was still in her chiffon blouse and skirt and not in the sloppy sweatpants she usually hung around the house in. She glanced around for her shoes, she'd lost them somewhere-

"So," Detective James' smile was courteously kind. "Have you any idea who did this? Anyone you know might want something of yours, is mad at you, any suspicious characters in the neighborhood recently? Any bad break ups? Any valuables missing?"

He leaned one forearm on the table, pen hovering over the notebook, the smoking hot eyes waited patiently.

Megan's bottom lip pulled in. Absently chewing off the Ravishing Red lipstick, her eyebrows drew down, she shook her head, the bob swished against her chin.

"No," she answered, picking at her nails. "I've thought about it while they were searching the house and questioning me, but I draw a blank. I have really nothing of value like expensive jewelry or a lot of money. Not many schoolteachers are millionaires. My TVs and computer are still here."

Her stomach twisted remembering her computer and televisions smashed on the floor, it hurt. It was inconceivable that anyone disliked her that much to inflict such damage, and pain, and fear.

"I don't know why anyone would want to hurt me," her voice tapered off tiny and sickened.

James folded his hands. "Oh no," he saw the pained look strike her plain face and quickly reassured her, "I'm sure it was just a random burglary. Especially with the neighborhood half empty what with the vacant lots and few lights it would look like easy pickings."

He flipped through the notebook hoping but not believing what he said. One of the first responders had said to him just before he brought her in, 'How could anyone have such immense loathing against this simple little schoolteacher with those puppy dog eyes to destroy her home?'

No, with this much destruction, it was personal, someone really hated her or they were looking for something. But what could the teacher possibly have that was that valuable or important?

He kept reading to keep his daunting thoughts off his face.

"So," his eyes on his notes, he said, "the first responders relayed that you said nothing was missing. You didn't really have the opportunity to do a diligent search." Wryly he glanced around, one brow arched. "How can you tell nothing is missing?"

Suddenly the hysterical energy from the frightening evening drained out of Megan leaving her limp as a kite with no wind. Her shoulders slumped, eyes drooped.

She pushed back the brown bob with both hands then clutched her hair, pushing it to cover her eyes. She sat still for a few moments, he waited.

Then, she sat back, smoothed her hair away from her face. Mascara was now smeared around her eyes.

The strain showing, she struggled to compose herself. Keeping her voice calm, mature, she took a breath and told him, "Under the circumstances I did a fairly cursory look around. It's kind of creepy you know, looking at my things a stranger touched. But, no, I can't say that anything is missing. Obviously it's hard to tell with everything-"

She drew an arc with her arm gesturing to the floor covered with yanked off cupboards and their contents hurled to the floor. "In broken piles, but I'm pretty sure nothing of value is missing."

Even the refrigerator had been emptied, jars smashed and the back of the fridge ripped open, like someone really thought something could be hidden back there. She shook her head, it was mind boggling, just insane.

Detective James' expression didn't waver. A burglary with nothing taken and she didn't surprise them, they had been long gone by time she'd arrived home. And that it had been a rare time that there were no neighbors home to call the police was pretty odd.

However, he'll investigate although it'll be pretty difficult to find the perpetrators. Usually the police get contacted by pawn shops or people tell on each other to solve these kinds of cases. It doesn't appear there's going to be any witnesses coming forth. He closed the notebook and stood up.

He asked as he pocketed his pen and pad, "I assume you have no security cameras or an alarm system?"

Her lips pulled in, staring at the table she shook her head.

The CSI were moving about checking the doors and windows for a sign of a break in.

Detective James had come in through the front door which was undamaged, he only got a fleeting glimpse at the kitchen door however, with his experienced eyes he thought he saw pry marks around the door knob.

Her palms on the table, Megan tiredly pushed to her feet.

"You should call a locksmith as soon as possible to fix the door if it was used to gain entrance. We can have one of the officers nail a board across if for now if you'd like. Just let the officer who first spoke with you if you want him to do that for you."

James motioned with his head at the officer who stood near the kitchen door. "All right, well, that's enough for now, Miss Milan. Of course you should not stay here alone. I'm not saying they'll be back but you know..." He walked towards the door.

The other officers had gone. A CSA was hanging around to speak to Megan about what happens next, and give her victim impact info.

Obviously he was not offering her his couch. "I'm packing a bag and going to my sister's," Megan said wearily. "She's out of town on a seminar or my eardrums would be blistered right now from her screaming."

Megan glanced sadly around her little rose garden kitchen. The comfort was gone, now everything about the house gave her the willies. She didn't know if she'd ever be back.

She walked the detective to the door and was disappointed for the second time that night that the good looking officer was now all business and didn't say something like maybe he'd check on her in a few days, or ask for her number, or- *oh you're such a silly romantic goose,* she reproved herself for her outlandish thoughts about the detective.

Here she was, stood up, house burglarized, a disgusting mess that'll take weeks to clean up, and she's having some kind of idiot fantasy about a cop she just met!

Sometimes she acted like a ridiculous teenager, boy crazy, her mother would have said. The trauma from the burglary must have addled her brain.

Shaking her head, she resignedly waited for the CSA to complete the paperwork.

Chapter Ten

On Monday, Cheyne sat at the kitchen table eating dinner with her family. She took a slice of meatloaf, a big dollop of mashed potatoes and a spoonful of corn.

Sipping ice tea with fresh mint in it she listened to her two younger brothers prattle on about their day. At 8 and 6 the things that interested them the most right now were riding their bicycles and playing with their cars and trucks.

Her own thoughts wandering, Cheyne loved to watch the old daytime shows like Leave it to Beaver, Good Times, the Dick Van Dyke show, What's Happening, Bewitched, nice normal family shows.

To Cheyne, her parents resembled young versions of Doris Day and Rock Hudson. She glanced at her mother and father and mused, maybe more like Bewitched's Darrin and blonde Samantha with the twitchy nose.

Her mind drifted dreamily listening with one ear until her father spoke. *Having Samantha's witchy powers would be so cool-*

"Hey, did you guys hear about the bomb explosion on Claridge Street?"

"John, please, that's not talk for the dinner table or for children," Laura Somerset admonished her husband. She put a small pat of butter on both boys' potatoes.

Cheyne's head popped up. "Bomb? Is that what all the police were for?"

Laura shook her head vehemently at her husband and passed the basket of rolls to her youngest, Danny. He took two. She frowned at him but didn't say anything. She took the pepper shaker from Mikey who was twisting the top off.

John looked happily around the table as he shoveled in a huge forkful of ketchup-smothered meatloaf. Pushing the meatloaf with his tongue to one side of his mouth, he said, "Oh come on, dear, it's the real world," he chewed, kept talking, "we shouldn't shelter them. They need to know what's going on out there."

While swallowing, he stabbed another piece of meat and shoveled it in. "We can't have them in rose colored glasses for Pete's sake."

"I don't want rosy glasses, that's for girls!" Mikey announced.

"Who's Pete?" Danny asked. He picked up a roll and tried to shove the entire thing in his mouth at once. Half went in, he pushed at the rest to get it all in.

Laura said, "You see, John, they are too young for-" she pushed Danny's hands away and pulled at the roll with her fingers until she got the whole mushy dough out and dropped it on the plate.

Wiping her hands on a paper napkin, she shook her head when she saw him eying the last bun in the basket.

"Nonsense." Her neatly trimmed, late thirtyish, pleasant looking husband cut her off. He was still dressed in his work clothes of starched, long-sleeved white shirt and black slacks.

"It's life. They see it on TV anyway, they need to know it's for real and real people get hurt. We've let Suchie Rose go to the other side of the world for the love of-"

Slathering a tablespoon of butter on her mashed potatoes, Cheyne watched as the butter quickly melted on the steamy potatoes. Sprinkling salt and pepper she swirled the potatoes with her fork mixing in the seasonings and creamy butter, took a taste. Perfect.

She took another mouthful then interrupted her father. No one wanted to hear another tirade about her 21-year-old sister off with her sorority sisters to do a few semesters in Istanbul.

"So what happened, Daddy? Pepi and I saw the police and fire trucks while we were waiting for the bus. It looked really serious. We were in the mall in a shop in a dressing room gabbing so I guess that's why we didn't hear the blast."

Setting her fork down, she buttered a soft warm roll and took a bite out of it. She rolled her eyes up sideways at him waiting for him to continue.

A naturally easygoing man, he was clean-cut, medium weight with short dark hair. The boys looked like their dad while Cheyne and Suchie-Rose got her blonde locks from her mother.

"Well, since you asked," knife in one hand fork in the other, John leaned forward like he was telling a scary story at a campfire.

"Friday, just after dark, a sleazeball bar downtown blew up. Like- it was deliberate. It was from a bomb. There was an enormous explosion. Wood and debris shot up sky high. They said they found bar stools and glass blocks away. It was nuts, fireworks had nothing on it! The place was demolished, practically leveled."

"Wow, was anyone hurt?" Cheyne exclaimed, shocked and spellbound by the small town's unheard of abominable incident.

Her mother gave up trying to stop her husband from talking, she got up and poured the boys each a glass of milk and sat back down.

John replied, "Oh yeah, no one could have survived the blast. The news said a bartender, barmaid, a couple of patrons, around three or four, they weren't specific as they still need to contact next of kin, were killed. It was awful, indescribably gory, the news said body parts-"

"That's it. You boys come with me. Cheyne-" Laura stood up and gestured to the boys to follow her. She just shook her head at her daughter who was obviously intrigued with the tragic horror of last week's bizarre event.

Mother and sons left the room. The boys had been involved in their own conversation about army men and hadn't been listening anyway to their father.

"Wow, that's so freaky, Dad, after last week with Lareina Wittgenstein dying mysteriously and all." Cheyne shook her head, gobbling the last of her bun.

"But," John continued, enjoying telling his story. "The authorities say they have a person of interest in custody already. Surveillance cameras at a drug store across the street taped everyone coming and going.

"They zeroed in on a woman who entered the bar with a bag, but when she came out an hour later she didn't have the bag. Apparently, according to the paper the police actually recognized her from a later call."

"Why would anyone do such a thing? Gee, that's crazy, Dad," Cheyne said, still eating but slowly. This deadly activity was way out there for their normally peaceful, friendly little town. First a beauty pageant contender murdered and now a bomb!

John sat back, took a few sips of his coffee. He nodded. "Oh yeah, really abnormal for this uneventful burg. That sort of terrorist type stuff never happens here. It's really kind of scary." He didn't sound scared though, more agog with speculative interest.

"Terrorist?" Cheyne dropped her bun.

"Yup." John leaned back, clasped his hands behind his neck cradling his head. "They say the lady came back from overseas a while ago. It's so mysterious and fascinating, you know? They think she's in one of those terrorist pod things. You might know her. She's a teacher in your school."

Afraid of what she was going to hear, Cheyne asked warily, "Did they say who?"

"Yup," John nodded. "A Miss Megan Milan. Do you know her?"

Chapter Eleven

As soon as class was over, Cheyne dashed down the corridor until she found Pepi charging just as fast towards her from her science class.

"Let's go," Cheyne said breathily to Pepi.

Both in jeans and light sweaters they hopped on their bicycles chained out front of the school, tossed their backpacks in the baskets, yanked on helmets and tore out of the schoolyard and down the street.

They pedaled furiously, wordlessly, conserving their energy until they reached Pepi's house.

Dropping their bikes on the grass, they rushed inside scaring the wits out of Pepi's grandmother.

"Lordy, girls, where you coming from in such a hurry?" Elma Mae set a basket of clean laundry on the sofa and plopped down next to it. She pulled out a shirt and started folding it.

"Nothing, Gram, we're just going to my room," Pepi answered.

The girls hurried up the stairs.

Pepi's room was the size of a walk-in closet. Nonetheless, she felt lucky, the other siblings had to share rooms. As the oldest girl Pepi had her own private sanctuary.

It looked just like a teenage girl's room with posters of mostly music celebrities on the walls, but also a few military pictures of jets and planes mixed in. Her favorite, a Stealth, was over her bed so it was the last thing she saw before falling asleep.

A desk and chair that had seen better days sat under the window so she could look out while studying. Pepi had painted the knobs and border violet on the white wood dresser and bookcase.

Elma Mae had made the ruffled curtains, white with violet trim.

Kicking off their shoes, the girls flopped down on the matching duvet.

"Can you believe it?" Cheyne asked her friend. She chewed on a pink nail, her stomach roiling from the disturbing news.

Pepi's curled ponytail flailed back and forth as she shook her head. "No way, it's too freaky. Ever since you called last night I've been riveted to the news and googling everything, but there's very little information right now."

"Well," lying on her back Cheyne crossed her legs, leaned back on her elbows and scowled. "I don't believe it. Miss Milan is too nice, I've known her for years and I've worked on projects with her, even at her house. She's really the best.

"One day she had the TV on in the background and there was a commercial for feed the kids, you know, starving big-eyed children with swollen bellies."

"Yeah, I can't watch that stuff, it breaks my heart," Pepi said. "Our chem class got together last year and did a fundraiser, we're already working on our next one."

Cheyne's face fell, the blue eyes sad. "It kills me too, those poor little darlings." She sat up and crossed her legs tailor style.

Gesturing animatedly with her hands, she said, "Anyway, Miss Milan happened to see the starving children and her eyes just welled up, she had to excuse herself to the bathroom.

"She told me one time that every time she sees a starving child or one in harm's way it reminds her of some little girls she took care of while in the Peace Corps. She has a picture of the sisters on her bookcase. One of the little girls had bandages over her eyes. I just don't believe Miss Milan would do anything to hurt anybody. She has an American flag in her classroom for Pete's sake."

"But the news says they kind of caught her red-handed," Pepi commented. She sat up facing her friend, her legs crossed.

Nodding, Cheyne's expression turned serious. She pressed her lips together flattening their bow shape. Wrapping her arms around her knees she hugged them to her chest. She shook her head determinedly.

"No. I refuse to believe it. There's more here than catches the fly. Maybe she's being framed."

Pepi mirrored her. Pulling her knees to her chest, she set her chin on a knee. They were both quiet for a moment, mulling over the senseless situation.

Cheyne's sigh was frustrated. "I wish we could do something, help her somehow."

"But what if it is a frame, what can we do? We're not the police," Pepi offered, then fell quiet again. Then, she perked, a small grin pushed the rounded, high cheek bones higher.

She held a hand out gesturing while she spoke, "Hey, though, remember when the money was missing out of the drawer when we sold candy in the lunchroom and you and I sleuthed and found out Valerie Duggan was the thief? She wanted tickets to the concert and decided to get them the easy way."

"Yeah, Cheyne agreed with a grin. "We learned she had her heart set on going to the concert and knew she had no money. She had previously asked us for free candy, telling us that her parents had cut off her allowance when they caught her smoking."

"Uh huh," Pepi chuckled. "On a hunch, we went to the concert and scoped the place out. Lo and behold, Miss V. Duggan herself sauntered right in and plopped her butt right down in one of the most expensive seats in the house."

The two teens thought a minute, recalling the circumstances of how they had brainstormed some steps and analyzed the situation.

Valerie broke right away when confronted with the evidence.

Pepi spoke again, "And remember when Burt Banton's puppy was stolen? We tracked it down by questioning all the neighbors and building a timeline of who saw what, who, when and where, discovering from the grocery store bagger that Joey Simpson had bought dog food when he didn't own a dog. And we brought the puppy back to Burt."

She pulled simple stud earrings she rarely wore out of her tiny ears like all of her petite features, and reached over to set them on the end table beside the bed.

Cheyne nodded. Then she slowly looked up at her friend, at the same time Pepi smiled.

Her grin growing, Cheyne pounded one fist into her hand emphatically and declared, "We're going to get to the bottom of this. We're going to prove Miss Milan is innocent!"

She held up her hand- Pepi slapped it in an enthusiastic high-five.

Then Pepi said soberly, "But like I said before, Chey, we're not the police. What can we possibly do?" She pulled over her stuffed bear that she has slept with since she had been brought back home. Holding it on her lap, she laid the side of her head on it while watching Cheyne's brain work.

Cheyne thought hard for a moment. Her brow furrowed, lips pursed.

Then, snapping her fingers, she said resolutely, "First off, we have to figure out a tactic to get into the police station and talk to her. And I think I have an idea."

Chapter Twelve

Cheyne had a cousin who was a corrections officer. The next day she called him earlier in the morning, right after breakfast.

Ready for a little playacting, she took a deep breath while waiting for him to answer his phone. He picked up after three rings.

After he said, "hello?" She responded in her friendliest voice.

"Hi Jamie, how's Sandy and the little ones?"

She let Jamie rattle on for a few minutes describing his children's recent hijinks. When he trailed off she said, "So, um, listen, Jamie, you know that journalism class I'm in?"

"Sure, Grandma had shown us all the award you got for the article you did on those disgraceful puppy mills in town. She was really proud of you going undercover and busting them and all."

"Yeah, well, someone had to look out for those babies. Anyway, I've been tasked with doing a feature on that woman, you know, the one they think set off that bomb downtown that killed those people?" She tried to keep her voice even keeled, she didn't want to sound needy or like she was doing something wrong.

"Uhh..." Jamie sounded uncomfortable seeing where she was headed. "She's, uh, she's a terrorist, Chey. She's kept isolated, no one is permitted near her until the Feds come and get her. Even the detectives aren't allowed to question her any more. I don't think it would be safe-"

Cheyne cut in cheerfully, "Oh, I'll be perfectly safe, Jamie. You know, the lady is my journalism and English teacher, I know her very well and she's quite harmless. Pepi and I will come around lunchtime when there's the fewest people there and I'm sure it'll be no trouble at all for you to kind of slip us in unnoticed. We'll be only a few minutes, I swear Jamie, I promise."

"But- but- I can't-"

Cheyne whizzed right over his objections, "Alrighty then, cuz, thank you so much! Pepi and I will see you later, around 12:30. Thanks again!" She clicked off quickly before he could respond.

The girls attended their morning classes then hopped on their bikes at lunch break and rode across town to the jail.

A relatively small jail in a small city was combined with the Town Hall in the heart of Corbiestep's center square.

Nothing tremendously exciting ever occurred in the city so the authorities were a bit backwoods with procedures on housing an infamous prisoner.

Besides, she was being charged as a terrorist- *"But after all,* the mostly male governing body said, *she was just a woman, and a small, thin, meek one at that. Why waste money and manpower bringing in any extra uniforms to keep her secured?"*

Pepi had read that Miss Milan was being held there until government agents came to take her.

The girls carefully chained their bikes and helmets to a bike rack on the side of the jail.

They each carried notebooks and press passes hanging on neck straps they had been given from the school.

Louise Furley

Cheyne had been sent on several assignments to interview people for the school newspaper and the teacher, Miss Milan actually, had given the young reporters official looking ID's.

Both girls decided to wear black slacks and buttoned down white blouses to appear professional with their hair tied back in severe buns.

They stood at the steps to the red brick jail, three stories yet it still on the diminutive side. Administrative personnel, records, etc. were located on the first floor, prisoners on the second, and a cafeteria and offices including the corrections officers that monitored prisoners on the third.

The accommodations and staff were appropriate for a town the size of Corbiestep. Satellite police stations were scattered throughout the city.

The courthouse was several blocks away, and in the event the small jail grew overcrowded, prisoners were transported to a bigger jail in their sister city, Whaleport.

The girls tucked in their blouses and made sure their ID's faced out.

Pepi frowned at Cheyne. "Really Chey, I'm not sure about that hat, it's a bit over the top don't you think?"

Cheyne smiled and patted her fedora styled hat. It was a popular style with celebrities trying to look edgy, but to Cheyne it made her feel she looked detective-ish.

"Seriously Chey, the hat maybe, but you need to lose the shades and the trench coat, where'd you get that coat anyway?" Pepi rolled her light grey eyes, disapproving the absurd outfit.

"My dad's closet." Cheyne pulled off the glasses and tucked them in her purse, untied the coat's belt and unbuttoned it so it didn't look so private eye-like, then just decided to chuck it and the hat into her bike basket.

"Fine. I don't want to overdo it, but I need to feel the part, you know? I have to do something to harden up this cherubic face I was given so I'm taken seriously. Come on let's go in, are you nervous?"

84

Pepi said, "I wasn't until we got here. Now my heart is beating like a rock star's drum. Let's go in before I change my mind!"

Up the steps they went, then scooted through the front door.

Once inside they came to a halt. Never having been in the jail before, they stood awkwardly checking the place out, not sure where to go.

The lobby was empty of people. A window to the left was for requesting records, it had a 'closed for lunch' note up.

Plaques honoring officers lined the wall, and next to the window a glass cabinet contained awards for community projects and trophies.

The Employee of the Year announcement hung on the other side of the records window, and placards decrying crime as well as crimestoppers' information and a few wanted pictures covered the rest of the walls.

Across the room, an officer sat at an information booth, his face behind a newspaper. A security station behind him led to two closed glass doors.

The station consisted of a metal detection booth and a small conveyor belt next to it with an x-ray machine for purses, briefcases, etc. to pass through. The girls took a few tenuous steps towards the desk.

"Uh oh," Cheyne uttered under her breath when they were about halfway to the information desk. "That's not Jamie on the front desk."

The girls slowed. "Who is it? Where's Jamie?" Pepi asked tensely, holding her notebook to her chest.

"I don't know that officer at the desk. We might need to go to Plan B," Cheyne whispered.

Pepi whispered back, "What's Plan B?"

Cheyne shrugged. "I'll let you know as soon as I think of it. In the meantime, smile, smile big and friendly and nonthreatening."

Pepi harrumphed then muttered, "I am never threatening."

The girls approached the front desk acting like they went there every day and were expected.

The newspaper now spread out on the desk, the officer continued to read. White hair, bushy mustache, overweight, over 50, coffee stains and other unidentifiable things on his uniform of white shirt and green slacks, he did not look up. He flipped a page over in the paper.

"Well hello there, sir," Cheyne enthused, "you must be new. I've never seen you before. How do you do?" She graciously held out her hand to shake.

Hunched over the paper, keeping his head down, using one finger, he pulled reading glasses that didn't appear to be his as they were pink with cat's eye rims like older ladies wear, slightly down his nose and peered over them with watery blue eyes up at first Cheyne and then Pepi, and then he dropped his gaze to Cheyne's outstretched hand, then back up to her face.

Cheyne exhibited her most glorious smile, all bright and white and trustworthy.

The officer leaned back, took the glasses off, set them on top of the newspaper, and crossed his arms over his chest resting them on his big belly. "What can I do for you young ladies?" Definitely condescending but he probably thought he sounded nice.

"Well," Cheyne set her forearms on the desk and leaned in conspiratorially. "My name is Cheyne Somerset. My cousin is an officer here. You must know him, Jamie Phillips?"

The officer didn't blink.

Cheyne kept the smile plastered on. "So, uh, he said it would be okay for my colleague, Pepi Nok," she nodded to Pepi who smiled large too, "and me to interview the prisoner, Miss Megan Milan. We work for the paper," she and Pepi both lifted and flashed their ID's then dropped them before the officer could read them. "Of course we will be as quick as we can."

Pepi spoke up, "Can we please have the correct spelling of your name for the article?" With notebook open and pen poised, she looked at the nameplate on his uniform.

The bushy white brows arched. "Well, uh," he sat up straight, pillow sized breadbasket pushed against the desk.

"That's Officer Denton Dempsey, D e m p s y. Do you know when the article will be coming out, my wife would sure get a kick out of me being kind of a celebrity, you know, written up in the newspaper and all." He beamed, pleased with himself.

Cheyne gave him another full wattage smile and said, "It should be in Thursday's paper. Make sure you look for it!"

She started walking quickly towards the hall, Pepi a step behind. "Is she this way?" Cheyne asked over her shoulder.

Officer Dempsey pulled his tonnage off the chair and shuffled after them.

"Wait, Miss, we need to secure your purses and you can't take any electronic equipment like cell phones inside the jail. Here, I'll put them in this locker for you."

The girls kept their notebooks and pens, but handed over their purses. Dempsey put them in a locker then very importantly handed they key to Pepi like he was giving her a key to the city.

"There we go ladies, all straight. Please, come with me quickly, I need to get back to my post ASAP, there's usually a dozen people here, but today a bunch of people are either out sick, out to lunch or whatever, the rest are upstairs so I'm pretty much it for an hour or so."

He led them around the metal detector and buzzed the locked glass doors, they automatically swung open.

The girls followed his jangling keys and jiggling body down the hall then up the elevator, he was not a stairs kind of guy.

Chapter Thirteen

The girls held their breaths, they couldn't believe it worked!

Officer Dempsey didn't realize Cheyne had meant the Aura School weekly paper, the Newsnotes, not the city paper. Students called it the Snoozesnotes because there was not that much interesting news going on weekly in the school.

Dempsey brought the girls to a tiny claustrophobic interview room and let them inside. With only a single fluorescent light panel overhead it was dim and depressing.

"I'll be right back, the prisoner is sequestered nearby. Don't leave this room." He took off.

Pepi and Cheyne cautiously entered the cramped room.

Four plastic chairs looking like they were purchased from Walmart surrounded a plastic table about the size of a card table. There was nothing else in the room, not even a trashcan.

"Whew!" Cheyne exhaled loudly, dropping her notebook on the table. "I knew we were taking a chance with Cousin Jamie, but realistically I never thought anyone would let us do this!"

Pepi sagged onto one of the chairs and set her pen on her notebook. "Seriously, letting two teenagers into the county jail to interview a terrorist that just blew up a bar and killed several people and the Feds are coming to sweep her away, just goes to show how a person's vanity allows them to overlook – SERIOUS-stuff."

She picked up the pen and twiddled it between her fingers. Chewing the end, she swung her head to Cheyne. "Now that I said it out loud, really, Chey, what are we doing? How safe is this? We don't know, what if she really is a-"

Officer Dempsey ushered Megan Milan into the room. "I'll give you 15 minutes, girls, you have to be out before the crew comes back." He looked less sure than he had a few minutes ago.

He closed the door, they heard the key turn in the lock.

Megan hovered timorously just inside the doorway, so thin now she looked like a frail child. Dressed in an orange jumpsuit with CORBIESTEP COUNTY JAIL printed in black block letters across the front and back, she stood with her handcuffed wrists hanging awkwardly in front of her.

The plain face was wan and uncertain and deeply frightened. All traces of the Ravishing Red lips and nails were gone, the bob fuzzy. Eyes bloodshot and puffy from crying hung huge in the pale face, her cheeks had hallowed, colorless lips dry and cracked.

Obviously surprised to see the girls, she didn't have the energy to ask what they were doing there, just stared at them bewildered. At this point, she already felt like she'd fallen down the rabbit hole and this was all a miserable horrifying dream. If only she could wake up-

Cheyne stepped fast over to Megan and threw her arms around her beloved teacher. "Miss Milan, we've been so worried!"

Megan dropped her head on Cheyne's shoulder broke down and sobbed big shoulder quaking cries.

Pepi came over and joined them, patting Miss Milan lightly, uneasily on the back. It took a few minutes for them to calm down. Megan wiped her tears with her sleeve, the handcuffs clinked with every move.

"Come on, let's sit down," Pepi said, pulling out chairs.

"I don't understand, what on earth are you young girls doing here?" Megan asked, still wiping her eyes with her orange sleeve. Her shoulders rounded and her head bowed as she sat down dejectedly at the table. She'd grown so thin her shoulder blades stuck out.

Cheyne gently touched her teacher's shoulder then sat down. She clasped her hands together, set them on the table on top of her notebook. Her eyebrows drew down in straight lines.

"Miss Milan," her caring voice turned grave. "We know there's something wrong here. *I* know you would never ever hurt anyone. I know how proud you are of your country. I know how your heart broke over leaving those two brutalized orphans overseas. Someone who cares that much over strangers can't possibly be capable of hurting anyone."

Megan burst into tears again, shaking her head, the lank bob swished across her pinched cheeks. She raised her head, the puppy round eyes swimming with tears overflowed, cascading down her hallowed cheeks. Her chest heaved with gut wrenching sobs, she covered her face with her hands.

Not sure what to do, the girls sat motionless waiting for her to get control of herself.

After a few moments, the tears lessened. Shallow breaths and hiccups shook her rail thin body as Megan struggled to restrain her distraught emotions.

Plucking pieces of hair stuck to her wet face, Megan hiccupped, sniffed, said, "You're right, Cheyne." One sleeve soaked, she wiped her eyes and nose on the other one.

"I would not, could not do the things they are accusing me of. Not in a million years. I don't know anything about bombs or the like, I don't even like guns. I'm so scared." Wailing, sobs racked her wasting frame, her head dropped, tears splatted like tap shoes on the table.

Cheyne leaned forward and patted Megan's hand. "That's why we're here, Miss Milan. We are going to prove you innocent."

Her head lifted, Megan blinked, sniffed. "You're going to what?"

"Yes," Cheyne said determinedly. "But listen, we don't have much time. First, why on earth do the police think you did this?"

Megan gulped and sniffed, wiped her nose and eyes again, she had to raise both hands to do this due to the handcuffs.

She hiccupped and sat back in her chair shaking her head mystified. "This entire episode has run through my head like a nonstop video the second they came to my sister's house and hauled me off to jail. But, I just can't make heads or tails out of anything." The confused brown eyes big and round in the strained face.

After a heaving inhale, Megan went on, "It's the craziest thing." Sniff. "The police said they have a tape of me going into this bar with a package and coming out without it. I mean... I did, go there I mean, with uh...uh a package, but it was just a pair of shoes, old shoes.

"My house was burglarized that same night and apparently one of the policemen who made the report recognized me from the tape. I had moved into my sister's apartment, she had freaked out and raced home from a seminar when she heard about the burglary."

Her eyes drifted back and forth as she remembered. "The police barged in with warrants, bull-dozed right over Margo frightening her to death. They wouldn't say why they were there or what they were looking for, and then Margo said that later that day they did the same thing at my house.

"She had to give them the key or they said they were going to break my door down!" She shook her head in horror and disbelief.

"They confiscated my notes and computer and everything. Even though the computer had been smashed they said they still retrieved stuff. They said I had googled bombs and terrorists and overseas, and that I had, in the past, been over there. Well, yes, of course it's no secret I was in the Peace Corps.

Cheyne and Pepi nodded at her, they'd heard some of her stories of her time in the Corps.

"You know about the school I taught at, and the injured sisters I tried to help. I'm writing a book about that time, about the girls. I researched stuff. But I *never* researched bombs or about terrorists, I can't imagine where they got that from.

"They won't believe me. It's hopeless, I'm going to go to prison for the rest of my life." Tears gushed, anguished lines deepened in her face, she was beyond scared.

Cheyne's heart bled to see her lively teacher, even prim and proper she was normally so vibrantly excited about life and especially her students, now in such staggering despair.

Megan Milan knew each and every one of her students, current and past, all of their idiosyncrasies and worked with each of them to bring out the best in every unique child.

As plain as Megan was, when she was teaching, those puppy eyes shined, her thin lips curved up so high it looked like even her ears were smiling. Some of the kids had named her 'the elf'.

But now the once animated eyes were flat, dull except for the fear twittering in them, hopelessness underlined with purpled shadows. The once joyful lips curved down now, her face deflated like an airless balloon, once again demure and timid.

"Oh my, gosh," Megan suddenly jolted forward gripping the edge of table with her fingers, the handcuffs jangled against the plastic. "I just realized, terrorists can get executed! I might be-"

Cheyne stroked her hand gently and said, "Miss Milan, back up the bus- beep-beep. Let's not go past one day at a time. You have us on your side. You don't realize how powerful we can be, and tenacious."

Pepi slanted a look at her friend.

With stern resolve, Cheyne repeated, "Yes, tenacious, like trying to get a crown away from a runner up in a pageant. We won't give up."

"Isn't that supposed to be trying to get a bone from a dog?" Pepi asked.

"Whatever," Cheyne said. She reached across the table and held her teacher's hands. "I swear to you we will never give up. We will get to the bottom of this even though we may be just young women,"

"*Very,* young women," Megan added.

"Yes, very young," Cheyne admitted. "But that will be our strength. People will underestimate us. We got in here didn't we?" One yellow brow rose slyly.

Every part of Megan's body was rigid as if to protect herself from further denunciations.

At Cheyne's determined look, a tiny weak smile softened the terrified schoolteacher's rigidly held mouth. Megan looked from one girl to the other and back again. The pair sat there serious as a heart attack staring back at her straight in the eye. *Could it be possible?*

"We know your family hired an attorney, we will stay in the shadows, let him or her do their work. Our concern is that the police may not look any further for suspects because they have you. But the truth will out, you'll see, we'll bring it. I promise." Cheyne crossed her heart with a finger.

Pepi opened her notebook. "What we need first, Miss Milan, is your accounting of absolutely everything you did and who you saw and where you went the past, oh, say we'll start with the last several weeks, or even month."

For a moment, Megan just looked back and forth at the two earnest teens in front of her. Then, she let out a deep breath and relayed with as much detail as she could remember about her whereabouts, who she spoke to, etc. for the past weeks including the burglary.

She was hesitant to talk about her behavior at the bar at the wedding, and then the aborted date, but Cheyne pressed her to recall every detail no matter how embarrassing or insignificant.

"Miss Milan," Cheyne said gently. "We only want to help you, we're not going to judge you. At this point we have no idea what could be important, even a tiny irrelevant detail could be a clue to everything. You must tell us all. It won't change our opinion of you."

Megan's head bowed in shame.

Cheyne bent her neck to peer up at Megan, she caught her eye and smiled warmly.

Megan wiped at new tears. Her hands in her lap, her shoulders were rigid up to her ears, she released them with a heavy croaky sigh. In halting embarrassed words, she told them about the wedding and the stood up date, even the stupid shoes in the bag, resisting the urge to press her hands over her mortified flaming cheeks.

Pepi scribbled furious notes. She stopped, tapping the pen angrily on the notepaper she said, "Are you kidding? How rude, stand you up like that, men!"

Cheyne laughed at her, even Megan managed a small tremulous smile.

"Yeah, listen to you with all your non-dating experience. Anyway," Cheyne smiled gently at her teacher, "this wedding, the events around it and after, the men, something sounds funky. Have you told us everything you can remember?"

Huffing out a held breath, Megan crossed her arms, leaning them on the plastic table and hunched over. Her forehead wrinkled as she tried to recall everything and everywhere and every person she had come across for the past few weeks.

Megan shook her head, unfolded her arms and sat back with a beleaguered lament. "Really, I can't think of anything else. This is ridiculous, they must have me mixed up with someone else. I mean, sure, that was me in the tape. I was at that bar, and the bar blew up that night," she croaked.

"But I didn't even hear about it until I saw it on the 6 o'clock news the next morning. I mean, I thought it was such an amazing coincidence that I had been in that bar that night for the very first time, and," she shivered and made the sign of the cross over her heart. "I thought for the grace of God it could have happened when I was in-" She shook her head side-to-side in disbelief.

Her voice grew high and squeaky. "But setting the bomb? Me? I- I, it wasn't me..." Losing it again, her shoulders started to shake, she dropped her face in her hands and wept.

Both girls got up and came to stand beside her, hugging her, even Pepi this time.

Megan wailed, "What if I'm being framed? I'll never be able to prove it- and why frame me of all people?" Her ragged weeping grew louder until she was crying deep, body jerking sobs.

Pepi separated from the others went back and sat down on her chair. She jotted some thoughts down in her notebook.

Reading over what she wrote, she said loudly to distract the suffering teacher, "I think maybe the date was a ruse to get into your house so they could sabotage your computer and search for, for..." She looked up.

The other two, wet faced, waited.

"But search for what?" Cheyne asked.

Setting her pen down, Pepi scratched her arm, staring down at her notes waiting for something to jump out at her. Without looking up, she said, "I don't know. There's not enough states yet to put this map together."

Cheyne smirked. "You mean like puzzle pieces for a puzzle?"

Pepi looked at her, crossed her arms. "So, you think you're the only one with the acronyms?"

"Metaphors." Cheyne laughed.

"Whatever. Show off." Pepi dropped her hands to her hips.

"Girls," Megan's teacher's voice albeit feeble rose from the dead. Smiling wanly, she embraced the Cheyne again. A hint of roses shone slightly in her ashen face. "You girls make me feel better, just being you."

The door opened, Dempsey slid inside pulling the door half closed behind him. He was alarmed. "You gotta go, people are starting to come back, you can't get caught in here!" He motioned vigorously at the girls to get out.

Cheyne patted Megan on the shoulder and leaned over giving her a gentle kiss on the cheek. "Don't worry, Miss Milan, we'll figure it out. You saw something or someone I'm sure, you just don't know yet what it was. If anything else comes to mind get word to us. We'll check back with you in a couple of days, or sooner if we discover anything."

Dempsey ushered them quickly, not gently out the door.

Megan called out after them, "Go with God- be careful!"

When they got outside the room, Dempsey said in a low anxious out of breath voice, hefty jowls joggling, "Listen, forget about putting me in your article, in fact, maybe you should just let it drop. I shouldn't have let you in there and it'll be my job if anyone finds out. Go down the stairs, don't let anyone see you coming from up here. I'll meet you out front. *Hurry*."

He rushed his jumbling girth back in the room to get Miss Milan to return her to her cell, they could hear his pile of keys jangling hastily down the hall.

Downstairs, the girls collected their purses from the locker and gave Dempsey the key back. Pepi said cheerfully, "Oh don't worry, Officer Dullupy- we'll keep your name clear out of it!"

Dempsey called out, "It's Demp- forget it." He watched them scurry down the tiled hall and out the front door.

"Whew," he dragged his arm across his brow. "That was close, what the heck was I thinking letting a couple of kids sit alone with a terroristic murderer?"

Chapter Fourteen

In Pepi's kitchen, Cheyne sat on the cushioned bench at the table, her back at the big bay window that curved out over showering fuchsia azaleas.

Facing out the window on a chair opposite her friend, Pepi laid the side of her head on her arm on the table and closed her eyes.

Cheyne crossed her arms, set them on the table, then rested her chin on an arm staring off into space. Their notebooks and dozens of loose sheets of paper cluttered the table along with empty glasses of soda and plates of sandwich crumbs.

"What is going on here?" Pepi's grandmother came into the big bright kitchen taking in the girls sprawled at the table.

"Homework that tough? It's Saturday, girls, take a break. I thought all the end term tests were done. Spring break is next week." She pattered to the fridge took out a bunch of fresh collards and a package of rice and set them on the counter.

The kitchen gleamed in mostly white with tangerine accents on towels, curtains and chair covers. Over the sink a cluster of herbs thrived on a shelf in front of the window soaking in the warm sun.

The kitchen was the most popular place for Pepi's family to hang out. She had stood on a stool after she had been returned home from that devastating time watching Elma Mae and helping cook and can fresh vegetables from their garden over the years. Now at 16, Pepi had all the unwritten recipes documented in her memory.

Pepi rolled back in her chair, stretched and yawned like a filly. She slapped her hands down on her notebook. "Oh Grams, you know Miss Milan, you know, we told you about her and her situation? Well, Chey and I went to-" her eyes darted to Cheyne who imperceptibly moved her head back and forth.

"Uh, we decided we were going to investigate, I mean, study her case and write an article..."

Without looking at the girls, Elma Mae shook her head muttering. 'Chickin Lickin Good' read the front of her apron she'd put over her blouse and slacks. She filled the sink with water to soak the collards.

"Uh huh, an article, you say." Muttering some more, she pushed the collards around, drained the sink then filled it again and swished them some more.

She turned and faced Pepi, wiped her hands on the apron, set one palm on her hip. "Child, I've known you most of your life and you too," she nodded at Cheyne. "I know exactly what you're up to. I have people you know, I hear things, your cousin Jamie for instance,"

Surprised, the girls jerked their heads to stare guiltily at each other then back to Elma Mae. Pepi said, "Uh, we..."

Elma Mae stepped over to the stove and turned up a burner. A big stew pot was already on it, the aroma of smoked ham hock and sautéed onions saturated the room, Cheyne's growling stomach was hard to ignore.

Stirring the pot with a wooden spoon, Elma Mae cut her granddaughter off. "Don't even think about lying to me, Persephone Emberlee Nok. Grams knows everything, you should know that by now." She went back to the sink and drained the collards then proceeded to strip the leaves from the tough stems.

The girls dropped their heads and sat silently.

When Elma Mae had the collards cooking, she came over and sat herself on the edge of the cushioned bench next to Cheyne.

"Now then," she looked at Pepi then Cheyne who sat like castigated schoolchildren. "Pepi, I know I've coddled you since I brought you here from that horrendous wicked-" she bit her tongue and wiped under her glasses with a finger.

"Anyway, I won't pretend to order you to stop what you're doing, it was a dangerous foolish thing you did going to that jail. Lord, you could have gotten hurt- anyway," brownberry eyes gazed pointedly over at Cheyne.

"And don't you think little girl, that you're in the clear. At the moment, your Daddy and Grandma Marylou know what's going on, they haven't yet apprised your mama of your activities. However," she looked from one sheepish girl to the other.

"We know dadgum well that no matter what we say or do, you're going to do what you think is best anyway, just be more secretive about it. We didn't raise you to be pig-headed and sneaky, don't know where you get it from."

The girls snuck peeks at each other without raising their heads.

Elma Mae sat back and motioned broadly at the paperwork scattered all over the table. "Now, tell me what's happened so far. What are you doing, what is all this mess?"

Pepi sighed and gave her grandmother a brief overview of all that had happened so far.

"Well then, why the sorrowful looks?" Elma Mae asked.

The teens stared at the mess of papers and notes like they were in Chinese. "Grams," Cheyne said, "we just don't know what to do. Where to start, how to-"

"Oh for pity's sake." Elma Mae pushed her heft off the bench and went to her stewing greens. She stirred and added some seasoning then covered the pot. She turned back to the girls, her glasses steamed up.

"You watch enough cop/CSI shows, what do they do?" She pulled off her glasses, wiped them on her apron and slipped them back on.

Both girls shrugged their shoulders.

"Ohh," Elma Mae rolled her eyes, sighing loudly like the girls were the dullest pencils in the pack. "You girls are both as smart and honest as salmon swimming upstream. Cheyne," she nodded at the blonde, "you are creative smart."

She smiled at her granddaughter and said, "Pepi, you're the logical one. You," she nodded at Cheyne again, "you are 99.9% honest but you can stretch things."

She turned quickly to Pepi as Cheyne opened her mouth. "Pepi, you are 200% honest but you need to learn some flexibility."

She smiled smugly at the pair, then shook her head again at their obtuseness. "Anyway, back to the CSI/police. They set up a murder room. They pin up all the data and pictures and make a timeline of people and events, list witnesses, victims, any people involved at all, their backgrounds, prior criminal history.

"They list where Miss Milan has been and whom she's seen. Then you start interviewing people- who saw what, when, where, check alibis, cross reference everything and everybody. Look for connections. Do I need to spell it out for you?" she spouted in exasperation.

The girls grinned at each other and quickly gathered up their papers. "Oh no, Grams," Pepi said, "we got it, we're good to go. We're going upstairs to my room-"

"Stop," Elma Mae ordered.

The girls froze, confused. "But you said-" Pepi protested.

"No," Elma Mae said, "it's too small in there and I don't want you gawking at murder stuff when you're trying to sleep or study. You can use my office at the back of the house. Just move my stuff in a neat pile out of the way. Go on now, what are you waiting for?"

The girls eagerly filled their arms with their information and made for the hall.

Elma Mae called out as they left the kitchen, "Stop."

The girls poked their puzzled heads back in the door.

Elma Mae was putting on another pot for the rice. "You will keep me and Cheyne's father and grandmother, *and the police*, abreast of everything, all the time. Where you're going, who you're talking to. No more going to the jail. Period. I mean it. Got it?"

The girls nodded so hard their heads bobbed like the bobble cat in the rear car window.

"Go," Elma Mae said, grabbing some butter and salt for her rice water. She smiled hearing their mutual "Yes Mams" and footsteps running down the hall.

Days later, Pepi and Cheyne stood in the middle of the study. A desk in the corner was piled with notes, papers, laptop, newspapers, school registers, etc. The round table in the center of the room had contained reams of pictures, graphs, lists, newspaper articles, a few papers still littered the table but most had been taped up on the wall.

Three chairs surrounding the table took up the center of the room. A navy blue leather divan with two end tables and lamps was against one wall, the desk cornered in another, they had shoved the only comfy cushioned chair under the window framed by dark blue curtains so it was out of their path.

The rest of the room was beige carpet, white walls, a floor lamp, bookcase, and a stack of books piled on the floor next to the door. They had moved some of Elma Mae's paperwork into a box and put it in the closet, they didn't want to get things mixed up.

Gazing intensely at the papered wall they didn't hear movement behind them.

"Well now, would you look at that." Cheyne's grandmother Marylou said in admiration. She and Elma Mae wandered into the room. They stood for a moment taking in all the pictures and other papers taped to the wall.

The girls turned at Marylou's voice, but rather than being pleased with their achievement, they looked unhappily stymied.

Elma Mae said, "Wow, that's a lot of work you two have accomplished, I am impressed! Where'd you get all that stuff?"

Pepi shrugged. "We wrote out a plan, did like a circular map with Miss Milan as the center with ideas going out from the center like spokes in a wheel, then we cut it in half and each went in pursuit of the most information we could obtain."

Cheyne said, "We had some help, Lareina Wittgenstein's little sister, Talana, asked if she could help, we had her look up people in the yearbook that Miss Milan had told us were disgruntled with her due to bad grades or whatever, even other teachers with sour grapes from some reason or other"

"We also had her checking on old school newspaper articles and current ones, looking for any reason why someone would want to have her arrested, framed," Pepi added.

Her eyes moving over the information they'd catalogued, Cheyne said, "Talana also reviewed the tape that the news had put online to see if she could discern something the police had missed, or give us an idea in which to proceed."

"So then what's the problem?" Marylou asked, watching Elma Mae stroll over to the divan.

A crisply dressed businesswoman, Elma Mae sat down graciously on the edge of the divan then smoothly slid back. Straightening her white blouse, she crossed one blue slacked leg over the other and laid an arm along the back of the divan. She pushed her glasses up her nose and regarded the girls with engaged interest.

Marylou, the image of a fading glamorous Hollywood movie star, made herself comfortable in the chair under the window pulling the hem of her lacy white dress over her knees, crossed her ankles neatly and leaned a forearm on the nearby desk.

"And stop doing that to your faces, you'll get wrinkles," Marylou ordered the frowning girls. She curiously reviewed all the work on the wall and nodded, impressed.

Both girls tried to smooth out the disconcerting feelings that had manifested in their brows and mouths, but they still looked perplexed.

Cheyne moved to stand directly in front of the murder wall. She tucked the tips of her fingers in the back pockets of her faded jeans, swaying back and forth in her well-worn cowboy boots. The long blonde hair tied in a ponytail swished across the back of the pink short sleeved sweater as she looked up at the wall.

Her lips pulled in as she cocked her head. "We're missing something."

The four women studied the papered wall.

Elma Mae was a much older, close copy of her short, pert-nosed, athletic granddaughter, except Elma Mae wore glasses over berry brown eyes and her hair was braided tight to her head, she also had a little extra meat on her still sporty but fine boned body even with the daily yoga.

Like most African Americans, her elder skin had barely wrinkled.

Pepi must have had a different ancestor somewhere along the line because she had softer, wavy hair and silvery eyes. Pepi liked to experiment with her hair. It was usually in several long, fat clove-colored ringlets, but recently she put in a sprinkling of blonde highlights. She liked the way the buttery lights bounced off her dark honey skin.

Cheyne also looked just like a mini-me of her grandmother.

Marylou described her own shape these days as a touch over ripe and full bodied like her favorite Cabernet. Her natural blonde hair had gone half grey, she died it regularly now to keep its golden sheen.

A hair band held the wispy hair back tumbling just to her shoulders. The sky blue eyes were just as mischievous as her granddaughter's, and Cheyne's slender figure was blooming into the same beautiful curves Marylou had in her youth. Marylou still had a great figure, there was just more of it now.

They continued their conspectus of the wall.

Marylou pushed her chair back to face the girls rather than the window. "How come there's nothing there about Lareina Wittgenstein?"

Pushing a thick ringlet off her shoulder, Pepi crossed her arms over the front of the pale violet T-shirt. Her distressed jeans were tight on her lithesome legs, her feet cozy in brown moccasins she always wore around the house. "What does Lareina have to do with this?"

From the divan, Elma Mae said, "Child, we haven't had a murder in this little burg in ages, what are the chances of one of a young woman and then a bombed saloon framing another woman in a short span of time? It's all too curious, too bizarre."

"I agree," Marylou said. "I believe if you find out who killed Lareina you'll discover who and why Miss Milan was set up as well. It could be because Lareina was killed first, that Miss Milan may have known or seen or heard something, and had been framed for a crime to discredit her maybe?"

"Yes, that makes sense," Elma Mae agreed with her friend.

Cheyne and Pepi turned to face each other.

Pepi said, "I guess we haven't really thought of Lareina since the funeral except to be friendly to Talana. Besides, they haven't come out conclusively in the news whether she was murdered, committed suicide or it was a freakish accident."

"She might have just been looking out the window at the floats while getting dressed to see how late she was, leaned over, then tumbled out- and down," Cheyne suggested.

Marylou chortled sarcastically from her corner. "Children, really, the way the newspaper described her broken, twisted body," she rubbed her arms, "take my word for it, it was murder."

The room was silent as each pictured the poor dead beauty queen lying in a pool of her own blood with metal pieces stabbing through her like she'd been thumbtacked to the boat. Actually, the tacks were pointing up and she had been impaled on them.

Cheyne nodded, turning her palms up. "I remember those windows, they were small and high, it would really be hard to accidentally fall out, so it has to be either be suicide or murder. I can't imagine the vain Lareina killing herself. I guess the two weird incidents could be tied together."

She turned to peruse the murder wall. The only murder wall in town that had a flowered border with sequined hearts in the corners, stars instead of dots on the timeline, notes written in glitter on the wall and a sad face sticker on Miss Milan's photo.

Elma Mae pushed heavy against the divan scooting to the edge and placed her hands on her knees.

The room was silent while the four women thought about how to pursue information about Lareina, and how she could possibly be connected to the framing of Miss Milan.

Chapter Fifteen

'TERRORIST SUICIDE IN COUNTY JAIL WHILE AWAITING FEDERAL TRANSFER!' the newspaper proclaimed two days later.

Cheyne practically broke her neck in a short sundress and cowboy boots riding her bike as fast as she could to Pepi's.

Just as she got there, Pepi came flying out her front door.

Cheyne threw her bicycle to the ground and the girls ran to each other, hugging and crying.

Muffled against Pepi's shoulder, Cheyne cried, "Miss Milan, Miss Milan, I can't believe it!"

After a minute they stood apart, both faces tear streaked. Pepi hadn't even tied her sneakers before running out of the house, the shoelaces straggled on the grass like white worms.

They moved to sit on the steps of the wrap-around porch. Dashing at her tears with her hands Cheyne said wretchedly, "I don't understand, she seemed so strong and optimistic when we left her."

"Maybe she didn't want us to know or thought we'd tell and they'd watch her, I don't know." Pepi said.

Cheyne crossed her arms and hugged her knees.

Rain just before dawn had cooled the air. A mist draped the trees like a filigree shroud dimming the light of the early morning.

As they sat, pinpricks of sun pierced the haze, blades of green grass dappled with raindrops sparkled through the gloom. Silky air and flourishing wildflowers mingled with the aroma of wet earth.

Two yellow butterflies wafted from tree to tree oblivious to the end of Megan Milan's life. A breeze drifted down the tree-lined road shuffling the bushes and stirring Cheyne's dress.

"Miss Milan and I talked a lot about our lives and stuff when we worked late on the paper." Cheyne smiled solemnly at the memory. "Even though she said she felt silly, she used to tell me her dreams of a prince coming for her on a white stallion."

Her face fell, tears threatened. Setting her palms on her knees, shoulders slumped, she muttered, "So now her prince will never come. So sad."

Wiping at her eyes with her knuckles, she leaned over, set her elbows on her knees and set her chin on her hand wistfully watching more butterflies dance around the overcast yard like fireflies glinting through the murk made by the incisions of sunlight. She tried to wrap her brain around the devastating news.

Plucking at the fringe on the hem of her worn jeans, her chin propped on her knee, Pepi's head bobbed up and down as she spoke, "I don't know, really, who knows if maybe Jesus comes for us riding on a white stallion in a brilliant stream of effervescent white light."

She cocked her head sideways, her cheek on her knee watching Cheyne struggle with tears and a broken heart. "Maybe?"

Cheyne sat up sending her friend a lopsided grin and raised brow. "Effervescent? Pep, your vocab is totally growing, I am 100 impressed, girl."

A short laugh, Pepi said, "It's from hanging around with you so much, you're rubbing off on me. Next I'll be blonde- look out!"

"No doubt. You should try it, blondes have more fun they say. Join our club." Cheyne picked up a lock of her hair, drew it under nose like a mustache and wiggled her eyebrows.

Pepi waggled a ringlet at her friend. "I'm already starting, Chey, look at my highlights."

Cheyne squinted and leaned closer to look at her hair. "Harrumph. Barely see 'em. Let me get at it, I'll have you looking like Beyoncé."

Pepi laughed shaking her head. "No thanks girl, I ain't no hip hop star, I'll keep things subtle, just like me."

Cheyne shook her head back and forth in pretend disapproval. "Too bad, I'd like to sail along on your rock star shirt tail. BTW, you were doing so well and now you revert to ain't? I'm so ashamed." She shook her head again hiding an impish smile.

Pepi leaned back on her arms, crossed her legs. "Ha, with you as my teacher I can only get better."

Unfolding gracefully and gliding to her feet in one lissome fluid move just like the gymnast she was, Cheyne stood up brushing off her sundress and rubbing her arms, it was chilly.

"Well, sitting here's doing us no good. We need to do something."

Pepi stood up too, nodding. "Let's go talk to the detective in charge."

Cheyne agreed, her smile grim. She waited, kicking at remnant puffs of bulky haze that clung to the grass while Pepi ran in the house to get a jacket and tell her grandmother where she was going.

Closing the door behind her, Pepi tossed a sweater to Cheyne.

"Thanks," Cheyne said. They climbed on their bikes and took off towards town.

Once they arrived at the Public Safety Building, five levels of plain brick and hundreds of windows, surprisingly the girls didn't have to wait long for Detective Douglas James to come out to the lobby where they sat on benches waiting.

"Ms. Nok? Ms. Somerset? Please come with me."

They stood up in the waiting room painted pale green with benches and chairs to wait on, stained carpet and scuffed walls and followed the man a few inches over average height through the door and into a wide open office space crammed with modules and people. Noisy people.

The busy staff rushed around, phones rang incessantly, doors opened and closed, elevators dinged, and surly people dragged in and out in handcuffs.

Veering off down a hall they passed numerous offices before turning into the last one on the right.

Detective James closed his door to the racket. "Come on in and sit down." He gestured to two chairs in front of his desk.

He went around and sat in his padded chair on wheels. As soon as they were seated he politely asked, "So, what's going on, what brings you girls here?"

He appeared fairly young for a detective, still, years of arduous experiences etched his face. His phone rang, but he ignored it. The blinking red light indicated he already had messages.

Taking turns, the girls told him the story from the beginning.

He sat patiently, his long legs crossed, ankle over knee, one hand on his thigh the other lay on the desk. White shirt, the long sleeves rolled up and the tie in a loose knot around his neck, a suit jacket slung over the back of his chair.

When they got done relaying all they knew, he uncrossed his legs, folded his hands together. Large hands looked like they'd done hard work in their lifetime, calloused, strong, not the hands of a paper pushing city boy sitting inert at a desk all day.

Pressing his palms on his desk, he leaned forward. "So, let me get this straight. You think Lareina Wittgenstein was murdered, although the coroner's report hasn't yet been made public, you know some people believe it was suicide."

He held up a hand as Cheyne opened her mouth. "And you say you believe Miss Milan was framed regarding the bombing of the building and has also now been murdered? You believe the two alleged murders are somehow connected, and you want to help? Did I get that all right?"

Cheyne nodded with a tight smile. "Yes, it sounds crazy cray-cray but we believe it's true." Pepi nodded emphatically with her.

Detective James worked hard to keep from sounding patronizing. Leaning back, he smiled benevolently, the dimple Megan Milan had found so entrancing deepened.

"Girls, I appreciate what you're saying, and it's really courageous of you to want to help, however," he paused as they waited expectantly. "This is police work. I can't approve of you young girls getting involved in *any* way."

Their crestfallen faces would have lanced the heart of even the toughest cop on the squad.

Regardless of his rejection of them, the resolute girls crossed their arms and sat in determined silence, lips pressed firm they stared unwaveringly at the detective.

He waited stoically.

They all sat silently glaring at each other. The girls' unflinching chins in the air.

Drumming his fingers on the desk, he tried to out wait them, but eventually realized he was going to lose the battle. Giving up he expelled a laborious breath.

Pinching between his eyes, he rubbed his forehead, pushed back a lock of hair. He'd been so busy the last few weeks he hadn't had time for a haircut. The back of his brown hair was growing over his collar.

Using his most forbidding expression that normally cowed the most hardened of criminals, he glared at one girl then the other.

They didn't blink.

Sighing again, clearing the aggression from his expression, but maintaining a stern no joking seriousness, he leaned forward. His voice low, he said, "I shouldn't tell you…"

The girls also leaned forward, eyes wide that he was about to spill something important.

Clearing his throat, he went on, "All right. You are on the right path. Both women were murdered. We're still not sure about

Megan Milan's involvement with terrorists or the bomb, we haven't been able to tie her to any known groups here, but she's been overseas in poor countries she-"

Cheyne cut in angrily, "Really Detective, we know Miss Milan told you about the story she was writing and researching and that she had been across the world in the Peace Corps."

"She also denied researching terrorists or bombs," Pepi said. "She believed whoever is framing her, hacked into her computer while she was waiting that night at the pub and put that stuff there. She made a burglary report that night."

"Yeah, why would she draw attention to herself like that, calling the police?" Cheyne asked. "Terrorists commit their dastardly acts then disappear before they can be captured. We believe she'd been set up to be at the pub. I'm sure your experts can prove the entry dates on the computer were done while she was not at home while her computer was there."

Pepi chimed in, "We believe her frame and murder may have had something to do with the book she was writing. Or, she saw or knew something about Lareina's murder."

Her energy high already from hitting the soccer field yesterday afternoon and a pre-dawn run this morning, Pepi's body vibrated like a tuning fork. She wriggled to the edge of the seat and tucked her hands under her thighs to keep from slamming them on the table in frustration.

Detective James laced his fingers and tapped his thumbs together. "Sure, it's a little fantastical," he said, "but you could be right. I guess we can look into those possibilities. However, who's to say that Miss Milan herself didn't enter that research information that very same night from a different computer making it appear it was from her home computer? Not even an expert analyst can prove who entered the data."

Rolling her eyes, Cheyne said, "Please, computer wiz's can certainly ascertain where info is downloaded to. They can determine whether Miss Milan used a different source to download stuff. Besides, I bet that the surveillance video from the bank cameras across the street will prove that Miss Milan was at the pub the entire time the info was downloaded."

"And other than a laptop locked in a safe in the office, and the staffs' own cell phones, there weren't any other devices found at the pub that could have done the deed," Pepi added. "The whole pub wasn't destroyed and the CSI's did a thorough search through the rubble for anything electronic that could have been part of the bomb."

At James' arched brows, she shrugged and told him, "We read the news reports as well as we have a source-"

"Pepi!" Cheyne snapped sharply to cut her off. She didn't want her cousin at the PD to get in trouble for letting them review some of the event reports.

Pepi looked chagrined. "Sorry."

James didn't bother asking, he figured the girls wouldn't give up their source. "But what has any of that to do with Ms. Wittgenstein's death? As you say you believe they might be entwined?"

Pepi unzipped her leather jacket, it was warm in the stuffy office. The detective had a nice big window he could have opened for some fresh air.

Out the window she could see a circular drive at the front of the building. In the center of the drive in a round patch of grass was a statue of a policeman standing proudly holding a badge up in one hand and the American flag in the other.

Parking was on the sides and back of the building. A lawnmower hummed louder then quieter as it passed by the window.

Pepi glanced around.

Messy desk, files piled everywhere, bookshelves crammed with statute books and more files. There was no filing cabinet, just an in and out box on his desk along with the compulsory pen/paperclip/other odds and ends holder, stapler, tape.

There were no personal photographs anywhere, but three paintings of different water scenes graced the wall albeit slightly crooked. One, a picture of a man standing in a river in waders trout fishing, the other two were of sailboats.

At least the paintings prettied up the typical governmental blah painted walls, the industrial strength carpeting was on its own. Pepi bet her allowance he was a dog kind of man.

"Yes," Cheyne said, "they most assuredly are associated. It's too coincidental and we-" she gestured at Pepi, "don't believe in coincidences."

"For sure," Pepi chuffed.

Cheyne propped both hands on the edge of the desk. "We intend to do our own investigation, we- I am a reporter and I have the right. You could help by giving us a little information to save us some time."

Blonde tendrils escaped from the ponytail and delicately framing her heart shaped face, her brilliant smile would have won over the oldest hobbit in Bangladesh, Detective James was no match.

He looked from Cheyne to Pepi's more serious, earnest face, sat and thought for a moment. He'd heard from the female officer at the front desk that they were beauty queens and he surely had no doubt about it.

The girls waited patiently. He tapped his fingers on his desk a couple of times.

"Okay, okay, fine. I have a feeling trying to force you bullheaded girls to not get involved will only make you try harder and be sneakier. I can't have loose cannons running amok. You'll be in a little bit less danger if I'm aware of your every move."

"Excellent!" Cheyne relaxed back in her chair, she heard Pepi let out the breath she was holding. Her forearms on the chair arms, Cheyne bent forward just a bit. "What can you tell us that you know so far?"

One corner of the detective's mouth pulled in denting the dimple, dusky brown eyes reflected health and vitality. He dragged his hand through his dark brown hair trying to flatten the recalcitrant waves. He smiled.

"I knew you girls were going to be tough the second I answered your call." He sighed with half admiration for their pluck, and half with resignation that he was letting children be involved in a murder investigation. The only way, he decided, to keep them safe was to keep tight tabs on them.

Knuckling his strong jaw, he folded his arms on the desk. Looking from one to the other, he rubbed the beginnings of a sandpaper five o'clock shadow, sighed again then said, "All right. The coroner did confirm both women were murdered."

Cheyne could feel her eyes filling. To guess was one thing, to have it confirmed stung her heart. She could see Pepi wipe at one of her eyes. They both sat back and straight up.

"We established that Miss Wittgenstein went uh, out from a window on the 5th floor of the Boderland Hotel that you girls, um, contestants got ready in for the parade."

Blinking back their tears, the teens sat still and silent with big eyes trained on James.

"The investigators saw evidence of her being in that dressing room. Her purse and street clothes were strewn over the area. It didn't appear that she was hit or-" he hesitated, "or assaulted in a, uh, sexual way." His gaze dropped to the desk.

It was very uncomfortable for him to mention this kind of information to teenaged girls.

He looked at them. The girls waited, their expressions were intense, but not embarrassed.

Feeling the heat rolling up his neck, he continued. "Her, uh, Miss Wittgenstein's neck had been broken before the fall." He glanced at the open file in front of him.

"It appears the incident occurred as the floats were leaving. The victim was killed and then thrown out the window. She landed in the last float that didn't go out."

He hesitated, the warm brown eyes flickered from one to the other, but the girls didn't interrupt or allow their poker-faces to reveal what they were thinking, or how they felt about this incomprehensible act.

Clearing his throat, he went on. "Apparently, besides the victim, a few other girls didn't show, so that float was going to stay parked. That's why no one noticed her until later. The um, culprit probably killed her then waited for the floats to go. Undoubtedly when he saw the last float was empty and not going out, he figured it would be a while before the body was noticed and give him," he took a breath, "or her, time to get away unseen."

Pepi and Cheyne sat as still as polished statues. They both blinked hard to keep the tears at bay at hearing the grisly circumstances of their fellow contestant's vile death.

"The killer made sure the other floats were already down the street and out of sight before dumping, um, dropping the body out the window." He peered at the girls again for their reaction.

Not wanting him to leave anything out or stop talking, they were careful to cover up their feelings. They just stared at him, waiting for him to continue.

Exhaling the tension in his chest, he flipped a couple of pages in the file, reading a few lines. His arms on the desk, he steepled his fingertips and looked back at the girls.

"So, uh, there were bruises, uh, fingerprints, handprints around her neck. The blood in the float was from her body getting impale- uh, pierced from metal objects when she landed."

He waited. He could see the girls now struggling to maintain their stoicism. He wasn't even sure he should be telling young girls this gruesome information, but he had already started.

"So, um, then Miss Megan Milan," he opened a file on his desk, flipped a few pages over in it. He looked up from one girl to the other.

"Someone had tried to make it look like she had committed suicide. She had told the guard she wasn't feeling well so he took her to the infirmary. Later, she was found...uh...well they thought she must have somehow stolen some drugs from the infirmary and overdosed.

"But it wasn't medication that killed her, they're pretty sure it was poison. They're doing tox screens now, we won't know for a few days at the earliest what it might have been." He took a breath and confided, "The coroner said it looks like arsenic."

Losing her struggle to remain stoic, Cheyne squeezed her eyes shut, blinking back tears. She held a trembling hand up and coughed behind it.

Opening her eyes, she looked straight up hard at the ceiling to keep her control, hold the tears back, then lowered them to level a steadier gaze on the detective.

"Who could have poisoned her?" she asked James. "Wasn't she in isolation in a secured cell far back at the end on the second floor?"

Pepi shot her a look.

Detective James' eyes narrowed. "I don't even want to know how you get your information, actually, I do. I should know to prevent this happening again, we'll discuss that later. Anyway," licking a finger, he used the tip to rifle through the open file.

"It's apparently a slow acting poison. There are a myriad of ways it could have been done. Anyone coming in contact with her food or drink at any point could have furtively doused it. Trying to find out who did it, how, and prove it is probably going to be nigh impossible."

Pepi started to say something, he cut her off, "I'm not saying there won't be an investigation. I am saying the copious amounts of people and time that her food could have been tampered with is astronomical."

Letting everything sink in, he continued, "But, that doesn't necessary confirm it was murder. It still could have been suicide. You know, a young woman facing the rest of her life in jail- or worse, frightened, ashamed, her career destroyed, family broken, dispirited. It's a horrific agonizing way to die but she could-"

"You are wrong. You did not know her." Cheyne was angry. Bending at the waist closer to the desk, she set a furious hand on it, her neck like a metal rod aimed at the policeman, the eyes spat blue fire.

"She may have been timid to you all, but to her students," she took a deep breath, expelled it, then squeezed her hand into a fist like she wanted to pound it on his desk.

"To us she was a rock, our mentor. When there was resistance from the faculty or whatever, she boldly stuck to her beliefs. Why, she braved uncivilized ferocious jungles to bring education to indigent children that might never get a chance to learn. No," she shook her head, blonde hair swishing.

The cherubic face unyielding, toughened, she brought her steely gaze up to the detective's. "She would not kill herself. She would have kept faith and hope to the bitter end."

Pepi glared at him, her eyes narrowed, letting her ire show. "Yeah, you don't know her, she had guts. We told you about the orphaned sisters..."

Detective James nodded, feeling taxed. "I know, it was in her statement. We have her computer, and there was a story on there about two little girls who killed or were killed by their mother or something, but a lot of it had been deleted.

"You could tell because big chunks of story were missing, names missing, and some obscure stuff added. We know some of the stuff wasn't written by her because the spelling and grammar were atrocious. As an English teacher, Miss Milan wouldn't have made those egregious mistakes." He didn't see the girls nodding in agreement.

"We're trying to recover the deleted info, however it appears someone spent some time writing a ton of nonsense to fill in and cover over the deleted info, so it may be lost forever."

He stood up. One hand tucked in his pocket the other loosely pointed at the girls. "So, this is the agreement. You keep me apprised of everything you do and everyone you talk to," he held up a hand to stop their objections.

"I'm 100% on that otherwise I'll see you are totally and fully grounded including after school activities until this is over one way or the other. I will be in touch with your parents today of course." James wasn't stupid, he knew the girls could find a way out of their homes and get themselves in deep trouble. The best thing was to let them think he was letting them sleuth.

He figured in a day or so they'd grow bored with the tedious aspects of detective work, questioning endless people, reading every written report, reviewing video tapes, on and on and on. Eventually, hopefully really soon, they'd give up and carry on with their normal activities and forget about the murders and mayhem.

The girls rose as well. Cheyne said, "What about your side? We tell you our progress and we expect you to keep us in the loop-100%- or no deal. We're clever and discreet, we can unearth so much information and you wouldn't even have a clue what we've done."

Pepi said, "So-"

Detective Douglas James pressed his knuckles on the table, his arms rigid he leaned over the file. He looked at the file then out the window, finally settled on the teens staring unshakable at him.

"Okay, okay, seeing how determined and shrewd you are now, I can't wait until you girls are grown and are hassling some other poor governmental slob."

He smiled, they grinned, shook hands, sealing the deal.

Chapter Sixteen

Tangy BBQ and molasses baked beans tantalized the neighborhood.

Living only a few blocks away going from the middle-class to the upper class neighborhood, Cheyne walked to the party carrying a plate of sugar cookies as a hostess gift.

School was finally out for spring break. Chalessa Chung's backyard was teeming with people. Her wealthy family loved to start off spring break with a prelude to summer with a BBQ/clambake.

The grill was the size of a mini cooper and every part of it was being used. Ribs, chicken, burgers, dogs, potatoes and corn on the cob roasted under the closed dome, smoke poured out the sides.

On the right side of the grill, four burners held kettles boiling up clams and other delights. Some guests came laden with potato salad, coleslaw, cake, etc. all was placed on two long tablecloth covered tables with paper plates, napkins and cutlery.

There was enough food to feed Texas. Another table held various soft drinks, iced tea, punch and lemonade, clusters of small tables and chairs shaded by red umbrellas rounded the pool area.

As American as the food was, to the side of the immense yard under a parasol of bamboo palms and sculpted boxwoods was a red pagoda. The majestic yet miniature structure radiated an air of peaceful harmony.

The corners of the gold roof turned up over a blubbery smiling Buddha sitting behind a fountain surrounded by lady ferns and feathers of lavender.

Dressed in a pink short-sleeved blouse, white jeans and white sandals, her hair swung loose past Cheyne's shoulders, the front tucked back behind her ears to display dangling sparkly pink earrings.

She knew it was too matchy-matchy and all this pink would nauseate Pepi, but she glossed her lips pink and painted her nails the same pink.

Cheyne found the hostess to make her greetings.

Chalessa was in Cheyne's grade, her family threw the most lavish parties. For her Sweet Sixteen they had hired a celebrity band and the florist had layered a pink and red rose petal blanket over the entire back yard including the pool.

Her black hair long and straight, Chalessa had been dressed in a traditional satin tang dress, red and gold like the pagoda, with capped sleeves and a lotus flower design.

They'd built a temporary bridge over the pool so she could be brought in by horse drawn carriage and could hold court in the center of the dreamily lit pool with all her peasants making homage to her.

Unfortunately, things didn't work out quite the way they'd planned. The horses wanted nothing to do with the bridge, they balked. One tried to back up dancing frenetically while the other railed back on his hind legs and dug the air with his front hooves.

Horses whinnied, people screamed, the handler ran in and rescued Chalessa. After taking the horses away they substituted bringing in a big gilded chair for her to sit on, shaken but still supreme.

It rocked uneasily on the rounded bridge but Chalessa pretended she wasn't worried that any second she'd be dumped into the pool. Blown up swans circled her skating gracefully atop the shimmering blue water.

Today, a much more casual Chalessa in jean shorts and a cropped top, when not seated on her throne danced barefoot to music streaming from speakers attached to the house and in some trees, the pool was filled with bikinis and jocks.

A huddle of young people off to the corner caught Cheyne's attention. Amongst the huddle she recognized some of Lareina's friends, surprisingly she did have some.

Cheyne got a plate, piled it with ribs and potato salad, tucked an unopened soda can under her arm and moseyed nonchalantly over to the huddle. Ever so slowly, a nibble here, a 'let's see who's in the pool' look there, she mingled herself into the group.

Unfortunately, they were the smoking group and they were also the ones that ultimately spike every punch bowl at every party. They hadn't yet, at the moment they were only spiking their own under-aged drinks.

Cheyne scooped a forkful of potato salad, hovered it in front of her mouth, she said to the girl next to her, "Hey Frieda, what's goin' on."

Mousy frizzy hair too damaged to maintain a platinum blonde luster anymore swished like quills without any feathers as Frieda Mills giggled.

Tossing her cigarette butt on the ground, not bothering to step on it, she said, "Not much." She glanced around sharply then took a quick drink of the soda can she held.

Cheyne's nose wrinkled. "Whew, what's that, tequila?" The sickening astringently sweet smell from the soda can was obviously liquor the teens thought they could disguise in the cans.

Frieda giggled again. "Yeah, those adults are so dumb, they are so clueless to what we're doing, ha!"

Showing off, she took a huge swig- big mistake- her tongue blew out, her eyes sprung like a sprinkler, she fell into a coughing fit- tried to catch a breath, wheezed like an old geezer then started choking.

Cheyne slapped her on the back. Frieda's face burned red, her mouth gaping as she gasped for air, the caked on makeup smeared from the sudden tears and rolling sweat. Hacking away, it took a few moments for her to recompose.

The others in the group shot her dirty looks, they didn't want attention drawn to them. They drifted away leaving Cheyne and Frieda standing alone.

"You okay?" Cheyne asked the teen patting her on the back.

Frieda coughed and wiped at her eyes with a napkin. "Yeah, yeah, I'm good," cough cough.

"You know," Cheyne said in a conspirator's whisper, "I was gonna slip in some vodka, ya know, get a little toasted..." She nibbled at a rib.

Coughing and wheezing lessening, the stark white pallor of Frieda's skin flushed, then the alcohol fire made it suddenly glow like Rudolph's nose. Her glassy eyes wiggled, she greedily looked at Cheyne, but Cheyne's expression remained impassive.

Frieda squeaked through a burning throat, "Yeah, so, did you?"

Swallowing, Cheyne replied, "Nah." She wiped her mouth with a napkin. "Gosh, these ribs are gooey." Sucking the bone dry, she tossed her plate into a trashcan nearby and cleaned her hands with a wet wipe.

Popping the tab on the soda, she guzzled the root beer. Soda dribbled down her chin then she remembered the straw she'd stuffed in her jean's pocket, pulled it out and stuck it in the can.

Frieda's sparse brows arched. "Why not?" She was feeling cocky now that the booze coursed hot through her veins and she could breathe normally again.

"Parties are dull without a little, you know, liquescent fun," Frieda said as if she had years of experience drinking alcohol. "We can't smoke weed because the 'dults would be able to smell it." She rolled her eyes, now taking smaller nips of her drink.

Chewing on the end of her straw, Cheyne shrugged. "Whatever. I just read the other day in Glitz and Chickz Magazine that weed shrivels your brain, and alcohol dries out the skin and causes premature wrinkles, and boys can smell it on your breath when you're kissing, and per a poll they took, boys do not like their girls smelling of booze. They say it's like kissing a snarky sewer. And," she sipped, "it not only dries out your skin and nails, it also strips the shine from your," her eyes slid up at Frieda's frizzled mane, "hair."

Frieda's hand went to her hair in dismay. "Really? Wow, like I never heard that before..." She stared at the back of her hand, turned it over and studied her peeling nails. "No wonder..."

"Yeah, sure, anyway," Cheyne tucked a hand in her jean's pocket, looked around the decorated yard and deck. "Nice spread and all."

"Mmm," Frieda mumbled. She'd pulled out a compact and was staring at her face and hair in the mirror.

"So," Cheyne said, "how about that Lareina, wasn't that just awful?"

Her nose in her mirror, Frieda said, "Yeah, awful."

Clearing her throat, Cheyne said, "I uh, I hadn't seen Lareina since the Saturday before the parade, what about you?"

Frieda was one of Lareina's BFF's, but secretly she was a little relieved her friend was gone. Lareina was mean and scathing and demanding equally to everyone, friend, foe, acquaintance, stranger, family.

Plus, Frieda thought she might have a chance with Lareina's boyfriend, Adonai Alamanni, now that the belittling queen was out of the way.

Still checking herself out in her mirror, Frieda replied, "Let's see, last time I saw her was like, it was the night before the parade. We'd had a big fight. The next day my ma made me go stay with my father in San Diego for a week. Visitation crap, ya know?"

Cheyne mentally crossed Frieda off the suspect list. "Oh yeah, boy do I know. So, what'd you fight about?" Not that it was any of Cheyne's business but Frieda was so wrapped up in her study of herself she was only half listening.

"Um," Frieda thought a second. "Oh yeah, it was about Adonai."

"Her boyfriend?" Cheyne asked.

Frieda nodded, her nose back in the mirror, she picked at her flaky skin. "Yeah. I thought since she was seeing that other older guy on the sly that maybe I could step in with that dreamhunk Adonni. Little did I know at the time that Finella Finestone was also trying to move in on Adonni."

Cheyne's ears perked. "Other guy? You said Lareina was seeing some other guy?"

"Hmmm." Frieda took one last look at herself then closed the compact tossing it in her purse that hung over one shoulder. A hand on a pin thin hip, legs like sticks encased in grey capris, she stood with one leg stuck straight out with the foot turned out sideways, and scowled.

"Yeah, she wants her cake and eat it too." She flipped her hair back, fuzzy pieces caught on her shirt collar. "I mean, I caught a fast glimpse of him once when he dropped her off at my house. I dug the black SUV, looked expensive."

Half loaded now, her fleeting attention drifted to newcomers entering the party.

"So," Cheyne touched her arm lightly bringing her attention back. "What did he look like? The guy in the car,"

"Huh?" Frieda focused her blurring attention vague as it was back on Cheyne. "I don't know, hard to see him as he was inside with you know, blacked out windows, heavy tinted.

"But, really, from what I could tell when she was all huddled up next to him, I mean she was practically on his lap the slu- uh, anyway, he looked like he was at least like 10 years older and 10 pounds heavier and shorter than Adonni. I mean, Adonni is a babe."

Her eyes glazed, mouth curved up as she pictured the regally handsome Italian young man. "I mean there's just no comparison. If she doesn't know any better then she should just give Adonni to me and go carry on with her supervisor dude."

She sniffed, turning her long pointy nose in the air, pulled her compact back out and clicked it open.

"Supervisor?" Cheyne asked, trying not to sound too interested.

"Uh huh," Frieda's face was back at the mirror. She turned her head side to side, ran her fingers through her feathery hair. "Some honcho over at a warehouse or something. Squinting at the mirror, she asked, "Do you really think alcohol dries out your skin and nails?"

"Yeah. Makes you look way old before your time. Besides maybe getting cancer, you can lose your teeth too from too much drinking. So, do you know his name? The supervisor?"

One shoulder shrugged. "What was it, it was really weird," she pondered. Her face brightened like a gritty day's clouds lifting. "Oh yeah, I remember. It was something like Kibbet reminded me of like Kermit the frog but not. Ya know what I mean?"

She smiled at Cheyne, grey-green eyes matching her grey-green sleeveless blouse looked Cheyne up and down. "I love pink," she sighed, "but it doesn't really go well with my complexion."

Cheyne said nothing about the sallow girl's complexion. She asked, "Do you know anything about him, like is he from around here, did he go to school here?"

"Nah. All I know is that Lareina had gone to this warehouse or to some shop in front that was connected to it, for something, and stumbled across this supervisor guy. Ugh," she rolled her eyes.

In a deprecating voice, she mimicked her deceased best friend, *"Oh, he is so mysterious, searing midnight eyes and rakish black hair and moustache, imperial nose like a hawk."* Frieda snorted.

"According to Lareina, she said his foreign looks were exciting, and she found him, '*oh,*' she'd said, '*he seemed so freakin' dangerous.*' She said that made her hot."

Cheyne's eyes widened. "Really? You mean she found the danger sexy? Why did she think he was dangerous?"

Frieda crossed her arms in front of her flat chest. Her eyes dropped to her chest, the corners of her mouth pulled down. The padded bra had not really filled her out much more. She shrugged narrow shoulders.

"I mean really, who knows? Lareina could be so flaky. I think she liked that she couldn't boss him around, and, oh I don't remember why she said she found him dangerous. Who cares, I just wanted Adonni. That's my nickname for him, Adonai is too hard to pronounce properly."

Cheyne thought for a moment. The music grew louder which caused the guests to talk louder. Shouts of laughter, a shriek here and there rose out of the party crescendo.

A dozen or so guests danced on the patio under colorful paper lanterns suspended from trees. People splashed in the pool. Food was starting to get dropped here and there and the breeze gently toted empty paper plates and napkins around the area.

Tucking loose blowing strands of hair back behind her ears, Cheyne suggested, "Maybe her little sister Talana knows."

Her pointed nose puckered. Frieda said scornfully, "Duh, not. Lareina wouldn't give that child the time of day much less discuss her love life with her."

She turned a full 360 scoping the place to see who new had arrived. Well over tipsy now, she squinted trying to make sense of the blurs.

"The only other person as close to her as me, maybe closer is Gwin Jardine. They grew up together in diapers, but I don't see her here. You know her, teased blonde, wears the skintight skirts. I think she had her boobs done because they sit up high you know," Frieda demonstrated on her own skimpy chest.

"She hasn't been around much, her family goes to Shawash Island for spring break and the summer. I think she left before the parade. Anyway," she yawned, bored with the conversation.

Actually looking at Cheyne for the first time, Frieda muttered, "Listen, I got to get going, I haven't eaten yet, you know. So, like I'll see ya around, girl."

The girls smiled vaguely at each other and Frieda awkwardly shuffled off. It was difficult to walk in pointy-toed stilettos on the grass and then the grouted tile. The grey Capri pants flapped against her skinny stick legs with her staggering steps.

Cheyne wandered a bit, ate some steamed clams, nibbled on an ear of corn, chit-chatted here and there but she didn't gather any more information about Lareina's goings on so she grabbed a brownie and headed home.

Chapter Seventeen

Instead of dropping it or propping it against something, for once Pepi used the kickstand.

She stashed the bike on the side of the house hidden behind a bushy sycamore tree. A sapling, thank goodness the stinky, sticky winter buds were gone.

Yellow police tape was tacked across the front door forbidding people to enter. Up the steps, she tried the door but she knew it would be locked.

She roamed around the yard picking up rocks and flower pots on the porch looking under them and running her hand over the top railings attaching the porch to the house. She even checked under the welcome mat in front of the door hoping to find the hidden key Miss Milan had mentioned.

But the teacher had been so muddled she couldn't remember exactly where she'd put it. Pepi had an idea.

Standing on tiptoe, she craned her neck to look where one of the top railings attached to the house and then down to the ground directly below. "Aha!"

A silver key almost buried in the dirt under an English ivy vine was just barely visible. Someone had accidentally knocked it off or the wind had blown it.

Gleefully, she knelt on the porch landing then rolled on her stomach careful not to scratch her bare legs in the jean's shorts on the cement. Stretching her arm she reached for the key, it was inches out of reach.

Heaven knows she did not want to have to climb into the garden getting pricked by twiggy bushes or bitten by a spider to get the key. She squirmed over a tad further.

Groaning, she stretched and reached, extended her fingers to their limit, wiggled some more inches closer, her hips started sliding off the porch, she swung her arm- grunted then-

"Yes!" She snatched the key up and scrambled to her feet.

She glanced over both shoulders to make sure she wasn't being watched. Fortunately for her the way the house was positioned the front door wasn't clearly visible to the neighborhood.

Plus, the adjoining two neighbors were still away and a jungle of budding trees, high winter grass and dense shrubbery shielded the other houses up the street that were also separated by overgrown empty lots.

Brushing off the front of her white polo shirt, she held her breath and shoved the key in the doorknob. It stuck a little but thankfully it turned. She grabbed the yellow tape, it looked like it had already been torn once and reattached.

Quickly, she pushed aside the tape and slipped inside, closing the door behind her.

"Oh- my- gosh!" She couldn't believe her eyes. She knew the house had been previously burglarized and the police had obviously tossed the place looking for evidence, but geez, it was like Hiroshima had blown up inside!

Light sockets were removed, holes smashed into the walls, vents pulled out, pieces of rug cut out, lamps hurled to the ground so shattered it appeared as if it had blizzard glass inside.

She carefully trod in her white sneakers through the living room, glass cracking with each step, and into the kitchen where the same scene hit her.

Cupboards hung open, some doors actually yanked clean off, chunks of the linoleum had been cut out and some of the floor boards sawed through, all the contents of the cupboards and fridge dumped covering the tiny kitchen like the town landfill.

The floral curtains had been yanked off and thrown on the floor. Chairs had been thrown against the primrose wall, which really seemed more of an act of rage than an actual search.

"Wow." She wandered around in a daze. "There is no way I'm going to find anything."

There's no way the searchers before her had missed anything, not even a contact lens could have gone unseen.

Unconsciously, she stroked her long braid as she checked each room, everyone was the same like a tornado had roared through. On her hands and knees she rummaged around, moving broken things, looking behind ruined furniture.

She looked and pushed and lifted until she was beat.

Defeated, she made her way back to the kitchen. Looking around she felt sad. The beautiful, romantic flowery wallpaper, curtains, cushions were ruined.

"How could someone be so heartless?" She shook her head morosely and stood there scrutinizing the room.

"What am I to do now?" she murmured to herself. "I need to find something that will exonerate Miss Milan. There's just no way if it was here someone else hadn't already found-" she picked up a chair someone had thrown at a wall, righted it and sat down.

"Wait, what was-" She heard a tinkling, sounded like it came from the chair when she righted it.

Getting off the chair, she turned it back upside down. All of the black plastic casings that covered the bottoms of the chair legs, except for one, had been knocked off.

She pulled off the remaining casing and shook the chair. She could hear something rattling inside the apparently hollow leg. She shook harder, a USB drive slid right out into her hand.

Holding it up between two fingers, Pepi grinned from ear to ear and spoke out loud, "In her terrible situation it mustn't have dawned on Miss Milan to mention the drive. It had to be important or she wouldn't have hidden it. Oh yeah. Wait 'til I show Cheyne. I can't believe I found-"

She stopped, not sure if she heard something. She waited. Goosebumps ran up her arms and neck, she definitely heard something and she knew there was no cat in the residence.

The sound was coming from the living room, maybe front door creaking open.

She slipped the USB into her pocket then froze. Listening, she wasn't sure if she could hear someone also outside the kitchen door blocking an escape. Her heart started slamming, she willed herself not to scream.

She concentrated on listening, and quelling her panic and jittering hands. Moving painstakingly slowly, she crept, picking her way silently across the kitchen to a hallway that led to the two bedrooms in the back of the house.

Arriving in the late afternoon she hadn't turned on any lights, now quite a bit later she was creeping down a darkening hall. She could hardly hear from the fear whooshing in her ears and the clamoring of her nerves.

Pepi was sure her fast shallow breaths could be heard a mile away. It was hard to move slowly, her legs wanted to run but there was stuff thrown all over the hall too, she could step on something noisy or trip and sprain an ankle.

The front door squeaked again so slightly it was barely discernible, but Pepi's heart raced swelling into her throat. She could hardly breathe. *How many were there? Were they bad guys or police? She doubted it was the police. They wouldn't have been so quiet.*

She shut the door to her imagination of what could happen to her if they were the bad guys- perspiration ran down her temples. They hadn't hesitated in killing two other women.

Barely able to see down the dark hall, it was quite a long hall for such a tiny house. She pressed her back against the wall with, one arm leading in front, brushing along the wall. Stepping gingerly, she thought for sure she was going to faint from terror.

When she reached the first bedroom, she could clearly hear someone traipsing through the living room cursing, kicking flotsam aside and tromping on broken glass.

There wasn't any reason for the police to be there, so it must be bad guys looking for who knows what.

She slipped into the bedroom, not daring to close the door in case it squeaked too. Still moving painstakingly slowly and cautiously she crossed the room on rubber legs to the window.

Praying it wasn't painted shut, she held her breath and pushed the lock slowly so it wouldn't click loud.

With shaking hands she gently pushed the window up. *Thank God*- it slid up fairly easily and quietly.

Sliding one leg over the sill, she pushed through, landing clumsily on the ground. She was athletic but she thought, *Cheyne with her gymnastics probably would have done a somersault backflip through the window and land on one toe!*

The fanciful thought lit a tiny smile as she ran away from the house, her sneakers quiet on the grass.

Keeping close to the neighbors' homes, she stayed in the lengthening shadows, the sun had almost set now. She'd catch a bus and come back tomorrow for her bicycle.

"Whew!" Pepi wiped her brow, heart still banging mad like the clanging parade cymbals.

She patted her pocket feeling the drive inside, with a self-satisfied smile she hurried down the street.

Chapter Eighteen

Early the next morning, Cheyne leaned her bike against the garage.

Up on the porch Pepi was waiting for her, she stood on the threshold with the door open. "Come on, I got something really, really cool to show you." Triumph rang clearly in Pepi's voice.

The morning sun just beginning to brighten the horizon drew lazy yellow streaks across the trees, caressing some of the leaves and bringing out their brightest greens. Squirrels dashed along power wires, a spectacular day was unfolding.

"Cool, because I got some information too." Carrying her notebook, Cheyne followed Pepi inside. Both in t-shirts and jeans they moved briskly through the house to the study in the back, to their 'murder room.'

Pepi closed the door and sat down at the table in the center of the room. They sat close together facing the wall plastered with the photos, graphs, timelines and other info they had collected.

"You go first," Pepi said. Crossing her arms over her chest she could barely contain her excitement over her discovery.

Still standing, Cheyne opened her notebook and skimmed the page she'd written yesterday. "Well, yesterday, as we planned, I went to Chalessa Chung's party to chat up Lareina's friends, you know, dig up any information I could get. So, only one person gave me anything at all relevant, most just wanted to spew about how nasty Lareina was, sorry, shouldn't speak ill of her. Anyway, one of her friends, Frieda Mills-"

"The toothpick with the fuzzy hair?" Pepi asked. "She's in my Latin class. Spends more time on her nails than on the lesson. Anyway…"

"Yeah, that's her. She was out of town the day of the murder so she's not a suspect, but she said the last time she saw Lareina was the day before the parade and they had a big fight. Apparently Lareina was cheating on Adonai Alamanni with some stranger." Cheyne moved a few steps to the center table and set down her open notebook.

Pepi's eyes widened. "*Really*? I thought they were the perfect Prom Royalty."

Cheyne nodded, tapping the book with her hand. "Oh yes. According to Frieda, Lareina hooked up with some foreign looking guy with a funny name. He's like a supervisor or something of a warehouse or shop. He's a lot older than her. And get this," Cheyne lowered her voice and leaned closer to Pepi. "Supposedly, he's dangerous and Lareina found that hot."

Her mouth puckered into an O, Pepi asked, "Dangerous? Like how?"

Cheyne shook her head, the blonde tresses swished across her back. "She didn't say. All Frieda was interested in was jumping poor Adonai's bones. She figured if Lareina was tossing Adonai aside she'd be there to pick him up before he hit the ground!" She sat back down at the table.

Shaking her head, Pepi's lips pulled in. "That's sick, they're best friends for Pete's sake. Even if you break up, your ex is off limits, that's girl code."

"Yeah. But apparently Adonai got around a lot himself. There were rumors about him and Finella Finestone. Don't you remember, it was all over the salon that day we had the photo shoot that Lareina about clawed Finella's eyes out over the guy."

"Yeah, young love, so wonderful," Pepi muttered sarcastically. "So what else? What is the dangerous guy's name?" she asked.

Setting her hand on her notebook, Cheyne shrugged one shoulder. "That was all she had. She doesn't know where the guy works or his name, she said it was something like Kibbet, sort of like the frog Kermit."

She glanced down at her notes. "Oh, did I mention she said something about a warehouse or shop with a warehouse or something."

Pepi looked disappointed. "Yeah, but it's so vague after it had started out so promising. This dangerous foreign guy could be a great lead with some more specific information."

Cheyne stared down at her notebook to see if she missed anything, but that was all there was. She smiled at her friend. "Yeah, well, it's a beginning, we may come across a Kibbet that works in a warehouse, you never know. So, what'd you get that's making you swagger?"

Pepi laughed. She pulled the USB out of her pocket. "Does it show that much? I am pretty pleased with myself." She briefly described her escapade at Miss Milan's house.

"Oh my gosh, Pep," Cheyne's sky eyes widened. Lips a hard line, she shook her head. "That was too dangerous, you shouldn't have gone there alone. I told you we'd go there together and search. You could have been hurt or- or even killed! Next time we need-"

"Yeah, but we hadn't expected anyone else to be there, and it turned out okay and I might never have found this." She set the drive on the table.

Both girls' eyes fastened on the drive like it was studded with diamonds. "You wouldn't believe it, Chey, how really bad Miss Milan's place has been torn up. It's outrageous, a sin really. I feel so bad for her."

"How'd you find that tiny thing then if the place was destroyed? I don't recall Miss Milan mentioning anything about it."

Pepi grinned. "I'll tell you while we're viewing it. It was sheer luck." She looked less than modest about her great discovery.

Cheyne said, "Well, what are we waiting for, let's plug it in!" She pulled her legs up on her chair, crossing them Indian style on the seat.

Pepi went and got her laptop, turned it on and plugged in the drive. It only took a few minutes to open.

When it was running it displayed photos. The teens studied them. Pepi said, "It looks like they're pictures I think of her time in the Peace Corps."

They clicked through the entire drive to the end. They sat motionless for a second, trying to make sense of the pictures, wondering if they could be relevant to their case, and if so, how or why.

Cheyne said, "It's pictures mostly of people, I guess her students and the other teachers, a nurse and a few maybe parents or visitors. There's also some pictures of the miserable little huts they worked out of, and some landscapes of the scrubby turf and surrounding wilderness. It's going to be difficult to even know if this is important, she didn't write any notes."

Pepi clicked the mouse. "Let's watch it again."

They reviewed it completely end to end 6 times.

Pepi sat back in her chair, one arm resting on the table, her feet propped up on a chair rung in front of her. "I have a feeling that it's the men she was focusing on."

Cheyne nodded, unwrapped her legs and let them dangle. "Me too. There was something, oh, odd about some of the pictures, like she didn't want them knowing she was taking them."

"Yeah," Pepi agreed. "The children were smiling at the camera, and the others that looked like teachers, doctors or nurses were smiling too and dressed appropriate for their roles. Even the soldier, he even grinned for the camera. But a couple of the men were dressed in like native clothes, not peasant stuff but not American or khakis and t-shirts like the teachers."

Pepi's eyes trained on the pictures like she was willing them to talk to her. "We're going to have to give this to Detective James."

Nodding, Cheyne made a moue with her mouth. "Yeah." She leaned forward on her elbows, cupping her chin in her palm, she moved her face closer to the screen. "But let's first print out the pictures of the people and then make copies."

"Absolutely," Pepi smiled, "we still think the same." She got up and retrieved a couple of her own drives and copied the material on them. Then she moved the laptop to the printer, hooked it up and made 2 copies of the photos.

When she got done they tacked up the pictures on the wall and put the other copies in a folder.

Cheyne stared at the drives Pepi had pulled out and laid on the table.

"We need to find good hiding places for ours and take Miss Milan's right away to the detective. After what you described of Miss Milan's house, well," she shuddered. "I'd hate to think what would happen if anyone had an idea we had these."

"Absolutely," Pepi repeated. Shoving her hands in her jean's pockets, she hunched her shoulders and looked at the closed door. "I don't want to tell Grams about this, but do you think our families could be in any danger?"

Cheyne sat and Pepi stood. They contemplated this new, closer to home fear. Pepi shifted from one foot to the other.

Standing up, Cheyne said, "I think if we give this right away, like now, to Detective James there wouldn't be any point in anyone coming after us or searching for the drive. What do you think?"

Pepi handed a drive to Cheyne and stuffed one in her pocket, then put the third in a desk drawer.

She shut down the computer and headed for the door. "I say let's hide this dupe on the way to the police station, cops are always losing things."

Chapter Nineteen

Detective James chewed the girls out for an hour and wouldn't let them leave until they promised him they would stop sleuthing. He paced back and forth behind his desk raking his hands through his hair.

"Enough!" He flattened both hands on the desk, mouth like a bulldog's.

"Pepi Nok, you were very foolhardy to have gone into Miss Milan's house. What did you think the yellow tape plastered across the doors meant? Come on in, make yourself at home?" He didn't wait for her to answer, just paced back and forth again bellowing.

"You could have encountered treacherous thugs who could have-" he raked a hand through his thick wavy hair. "Well, never mind, this is it, no more snooping. I am forced to tell your parents about this." The girls were stunned, he broke eye contact- they looked so scared. "I'm sorry, but I must. Now," he rattled on some more, both girls had tuned him out.

They were busy picturing their family tearing a strip off them and maybe even grounding them. Getting grounded would slam a lid on their investigating.

Ignoring their hangdog faces, he saw them out of his office, down the hall and held the front door open for them. They looked so forlorn he said, "Listen, don't think I don't appreciate what you've done and discovered. You may have really helped the two cases. You were brave, especially you, Miss Pepi, but-" he spoke quickly as the girls brightened.

"But no more. I mean it. Ok," he sighed heavily wiping the back of his hand across his forehead. "You girls go on home now." He ushered them out.

Standing in the open doorway he watched them morosely unlock their bike chains and pull on their helmets. He called out as they rode off, "And go straight home!"

They cycled down the drive and out to the center road and onto the sidewalk. Staying to the outer edge of the walk they dodged a pedestrian here and there as they rolled past the city structures they'd seen for years.

Although designed like a European city with a center square and smaller streets down and around it, it was obviously rustic, pure homespun, as American as the proverbial apple pie.

During warm seasons umbrellas sprout like crayon colored mushrooms on outside patios shading round tables and wrought iron chairs.

Sundays the avenue looks like a Renoir Paris street painting with people strolling dressed to the nines and buildings spilling a potpourri of lights. On drizzly days the misty vapor smears the street like runny watercolors, blending dripping and blurry.

Towards the end of town almost to the burbs, the girls stopped at a mom and pop diner and gobbled burgers and fries.

When they were stuffed full, they left the city riding on a bike path that ran beside a four-lane highway to a wealthy neighborhood.

The high end of the aristocratic tract, half hidden in such a dense chaparral of evergreens and oaks, the black estates with pointed roofs, spires and turrets, and guarded by black iron fences conjured up a dark gothique beauty.

Further in, last century Victorian mansions loomed greyly mystique behind huge twisted and knotted ancient trees, their gnarled branches canopying the genteel neighborhood appearing as if draped in gossamer Spanish moss.

Their tires roosh- rooshing along the dewy blacktop, it took them a little over thirty minutes to get to Megan Milan's sister's house.

Cheyne had called ahead to ask if it was okay to come and talk to her. Advancing deeper into the area the houses turned into a harmony of romance and classical culture.

The girls parked their bikes on the kickstands in the driveway. As they removed their helmets they took in the beautiful, old Victorian house with a glass-enclosed portico.

It was softly commanding, the large house with latticed parquetry, ivy crawling rose brick, and frilly white curtains flirting in the lead-paned windows. To one side there was another entrance, a mudroom for entering in colder and messier weather, and a detached two-car garage stood behind and to the right of the house.

They stepped in dappled light from the driveway to a cobblestone walk to the porch. Through the large windows they could see an inside door open and a figure step out to the porch.

By the time the girls got up the steps Margo Milan already had the porch screen door open for them to enter.

Margo tried to smile a welcome but failed, her face noticeably strained. The sweater and flowered dress hung on her body grown thin from worry and sorrow. Avoiding the media had added further pressure, blessedly the press had finally backed off. She invited the girls in.

After what happened to her sister Megan, Margo had moved back home with her parents.

The ladies stood on gleaming hardwood floors in the spacious entryway. Electric candles in antique light fixtures on blush walls lit the round vestibule in a soft vintage glow.

To Cheyne and Pepi it was like stepping into another world, an elegant, refined world from ages past.

Margo closed the door and said, "Come with me, we'll go to the morning room. We'll be comfortable there and my parents won't, um," her sad voice dropped to almost a whisper, "overhear our conversation."

It was hush quiet inside. Margo trod wearily down the hall. A tapestry runner carpeted the middle of the polished hardwood floor. The girls followed her, past a few rooms with closed doors then turned into one.

"Come on in, please sit down." She said politely, but her words faltered.

Margo had placed a pitcher of iced tea with three glasses and a bucket of extra ice on the lacquered coffee table along with a plate of cucumber sandwiches with the crusts trimmed, and plates and napkins.

"Would you care for some tea?" Margo asked, her voice void of any feeling or emphasis, like she was just a talking mannequin. The girls said yes, so Margo filled each glass with ice then poured in the tea, stuck in a straw, added fresh mint leaves and a lemon and handed them to the girls.

She gestured absently to the sugar bowl. "Please help yourself." Taking a melancholy sip of hers, Margo perched on the end of a gingham pink and blue cushioned chair. "Please help yourself to the sandwiches." She waved a limp hand at the platter.

Cheyne demurred, casting a leery eye at the sandwiches, she just sipped her tea politely.

Pepi reached for a sandwich.

Still standing they looked around. The focal point of the room was an ancient yet beautiful fireplace trimmed in the same rose brick as the outside of the house.

A huge mantle overhung the fireplace. Two candelabras adorned each end of the massive mantel with an ivory sculpture reminiscent of a Michelangelo piece in the center.

Over the mantel and sculpture hung an obviously very old painting of an ethereal young woman from perhaps the late 17th, early 18th century gilded in an intricately designed gold frame.

The fireplace was unlit as it was too warm, although the way Margo wrapped her sweater tightly around her thin frame looked like she was never going to lose the chills again.

Several landscape paintings of the Victorian era hung around the room interlaced with portraits of ancestors long moved on to the big Landscape in the sky.

Two cushiony chairs in gingham pink and blue sat facing a matching couch, Margo was sitting in one of the chairs. On either side of the couch were two lacquered end tables and in front a coffee table. The room was like a sophisticated quilt, elegantly comfortable.

Margo had moved out of her apartment since her sister's death and back home with her parents. Although she had no desire to converse with anyone, she couldn't stand to be alone, and her parent's hearts were broken too.

The small family closed in, they still could hardly grasp that they'd lost one of them and now they held tightly onto each other fearful that another one of them could-

"So, uh," Cheyne started. "We uh, asked to see you because..." holding her glass she sat down on the sofa. Pepi joined her.

Margo gazed through dull sparkless eyes from one to the other. "Yes?"

Cheyne cleared her throat, stirring her tea with the straw. Her voice a soft feminine whisper with a hint of tears threatening, "Well, we, I, we were very close to your sister..." she stuttered off awkwardly.

Pepi smoothly helped out, pert yet sympathetic. "Yes, we thought so highly of your sister, Miss Megan, and we were devastated when all this happened."

Margo nodded, her lips pulled in. Her eyes appeared momentarily bereft of tears she'd been weeping for so long now.

Pepi continued, "Yes, we were so distraught, you might know that we went to see her at the jail?" Holding her tea glass with both hands, elbows resting on her knees, she sat on the edge of the couch.

Pepi liked to streamline her situations, keep things easy, not exerting her energy on trivial things. Sometimes it drove her crazy shopping with Cheyne because Cheyne liked to try on everything and took forever for her to put something on, then remove it, put it back on the hanger, button all the buttons.

She even annoyingly brushed her tousled hair in between outfits.

Pepi pulled things off the rack and bought them without trying them on, she had no patience for these things, she knew her own size for Pete's sake, she knew what would fit by looking at it. She set the glass on the table.

Sadly, Margo nodded again. "Yes. We were able to have a few private phone conversations. She told me how she so appreciated you girls coming to see her and trying to build up her spirits, and how you managed to sneak yourselves in-" a tiny wan smile at that, then she sighed.

She drew a hand across her forehead, rubbed the tops of her cheekbones with a few fingers, fatigue building, she dropped her hand in her lap. "But you said you wanted to come by to ask questions about my sister. I don't see why, I mean you're welcome and all but I don't see how I…"

The corners tightened around her eyes once lively and filled with gay mischief were now racked with pain, turned into tortured vessels containing only grief. She stared unblinking at the fireplace.

Cheyne squirmed to the edge of the sofa and set her glass on a coaster on the table. She retrieved another coaster and picked up Pepi's glass and set it on the coaster ignoring Pepi's huff.

Cheyne's blue eyes exhibited compassion, but they were direct. More controlled now, she said to Margo, "Well, this is it, we know you may think we're a bit daft, but, we think your sister was framed and murdered, and somehow it's tied in with the murder of Lareina Wittgenstein. We're sure she was innocent," she took a breath.

"And we aim to prove it!" Pepi announced.

Margo's tired brows shot up. "Huh?" Her pained eyes floated from one girl to the other. She shifted forward. "I don't understand, how, I mean the police are…"

All three women now perched on the edges of their seats like anxious birds on branches.

Pepi explained, "You see, Miss Margo, of course the police are doing all they can, but they're a little resistant to the idea that Miss Megan was framed."

"Yes," Cheyne chirped in. "But we have absolutely no doubt she was innocent."

Pepi said, "We think we can find stuff out more, more, what's that word, Chey?"

"Surreptitiously."

"Yes. Sneakily." Pepi knit her fingers together set them on her knees and hunched forward, honey face aglow, braid sloping over one shoulder.

"We think because we're basically kids, teens, that people will talk over us and around us and say things to us that they don't think about what they're saying."

"And we can ferret out more information than people may be less willing to tell the police." Cheyne added.

Margo rose and slowly poured them all some more tea. The ice chinked as the glasses filled. She settled back down and studied the two teens sitting across from her.

They looked so zealously impassioned, backs straight, knees together, hands folded resting primly on their knees as if wanting to be polite yet barely able to contain their verve and impatience.

Her hair in one long braid, blue band at the end, Pepi wore her regular jean shorts, the blue plaid shirt tied at the waist contrasted with the gingham couch. She kept her white sneakered feet together on the floor.

A Persian rug covered most of the hardwood floor.

Cheyne wore jeans so faded they were almost white, pink short sleeved sweater, white, ankle length cowboy boots, her hair pulled back tight in a high ponytail. Riding bicycles was hard on long hair.

144

"Well," Margo's face deflated a little more. She slid back stiffly, like her body ached, crossed her ankles tucking them to the side. She tiredly picked lint off the drab dress covered in mini flowers.

Misery apparent in every movement, she smoothed the dour skirt, simple and long now compared to the sexier minis she had been wearing, draping it down over her knees as if it could protect her from feeling.

"I don't see how I can help, but ask away. I can't have my sister back but the sick, *animals*, that did this should be brought to justice-" her voice cracked, she dabbed at the corner of an eye with a napkin.

Picking up her ice tea, Margo cradled the glass in both hands, ice cubes jostling against each other. Shivering slightly, she said listlessly, "I don't know why I made cold tea instead of hot tea."

Her gaze drifted to the carpet. "I guess it's spring and all…" She pulled herself back with effort. "So, how can I help?"

Both girls had brought their notebooks, they had set them on the table. Now they opened them and took out pens.

Pepi started, gently. "Okay, so, if you could tell us if you noticed anything unusual or maybe didn't seem suspicious then but now something doesn't strike you as quite right?

"What Miss Megan was doing, where she was going, who she was seeing in the past few weeks? She told us briefly but there might be something else you heard or noticed that she didn't mention."

Margo stared cross-eyed at her drink. She swiped at an escaped tear. "Uhh," it was obviously quite painful for her to recall the past few weeks that were the end of her beloved sister's life. She turned her head to the window.

Her baby sister, Megan, would never again see her favorite tree right outside the window, gaudy with shimmery pink and white blossoms like bows on a child's summer sandals, standing now a desolate watchman against a pearlescent summer sky, a pitiful disparity to the dark ugly feelings Margo was experiencing now.

Sniffing, she willed herself to sit straighter. "I don't know, girls, you are so young..." sigh. "But as you say, people may underestimate you and it can't hurt to have as many people as possible investigating Megan's case. Especially since it appears law enforcement still holds a ridiculous belief that Megan was a terrorist and committed suicide when caught."

She tried to ease the bitterness from her voice, but failed. "Absolutely ludicrous if one knew my gentle, compassionate baby sister..." she blustered weakly but then trailed off.

The girls wriggled uncomfortably, gulped their tea.

Pepi said, "Miss Margo, we-"

Margo held up a hand. "No, no," she didn't smile but there was a frail warmth in her voice. "I'm sorry to digress. Megan told me how you girls so serious and grown up had braved getting in serious trouble and put yourselves in peril to come and see her and how clever you were to get in. If you can do that you may be capable of more intelligence than the police."

Her voice a sad sneer, she pulled in her lips, not as thin as her sister's, and unlike her sister's nut brown eyes and hair, Margo's eyes were a cyan green, light green, and her hair a russet chestnut.

Now grief had stripped the curls of their normal healthy sheen, she'd pulled them back into a severe bun, limp tendrils floated around her face.

The eyes paled to a washed out bare hint of her normal vibrant green, now looked more like dead leaves. "I will tell you what I can remember of her- her last few weeks before her arrest and- and..." She took a long shuddering breath.

She told them the same innocuous things about her sister's last weeks that Megan had. Going to work, church, writing her book was basically all she did.

Margo's brows drew down, she held her drink in one hand aimlessly rocking the empty glass back and forth following the last melting cubes slide from side to side.

Then, tapping a finger against her chin, her eyes moved back and forth like she was reviewing a scene. "You know," her brows now like inverted parenthesis, "there was something odd, that does kind of tie into the whole pub-bombing thing."

Their pens poised. "Yes?" Pepi prompted.

Thoughtfully, trying to remember precisely what Megan had said, Margo set her drink on the table beside her chair. She looked heavenward trying to remember. "Yes, it began at this wedding I forced her to go to." Shaking her head ruefully, "If only I hadn't insisted-"

Cheyne leaned forward, her forearms on her knees. "Miss Margo, you can't go there, you aren't at fault."

The woeful, dried leaf eyes misted, Margo nodded. "I know, still..." She tightly clinched her hands in her lap as if keeping them plaited she could hold herself together.

Staring at the floor first, then wistfully out the window at Megan's tree, she said, "Anyway, we went to this wedding. She was really dolled up, very glamorous. I loaned her sky high pumps and a bit of a risqué sequined dress." She looked guilty for a second, then sadly at the teens.

"That girl was always so shy and timid, except when it came to you students, she'd fight hail and fury for you kids." She smiled remembering.

"Anyway, I was a dancing fool so I left her alone a lot, bad sister me. Apparently at some point some students who had graduated a few years ago came in and she was embarrassed to be seen in the dress, thought it would be all over social media."

Cheyne nodded grumpily. "Nothing is sacred or a secret anymore."

"And people can be so judgmental these days," Pepi said. She clicked the end of her pen open-closed-open-closed-click-click-click- Cheyne glowered at her. Pepi set the pen on her notebook, laid her hands in her lap and tapped her fingers on her lap.

She could feel Cheyne's eyes on her, she stopped tapping, then, quietly plucked and fiddled with the blue band at the end of her braid.

"Yes, so true, the way of the world takes your- self, you practically don't own yourself anymore," Margo agreed.

"So, Megan left the wedding and ran down the hall to hide somewhere, but she found herself in the hotel's bar. She was too embarrassed to leave so she sat at the bar. And, she was too embarrassed to not have an alcoholic drink. So she did, had a lot. She wasn't used to drinking." Margo's smile hovered with affection of memories of her sister.

"After a while she started getting bolder. A group of, I think she said three men were at the bar. One of them, David, Don- no Devin, yes it was Devin, blond, cute, caught her eye. She said he had some kind of accent, but she couldn't place it."

Megan had already told them this, but the girls remained intent on Margo's tale listening for any new detail that could help.

Margo might even say the same exact thing, however in a different way than her sister had and put a whole new meaning to it.

Margo picked up a napkin and blankly pulled at it. "To make a long story short, she brashly made a date to meet him at that sleazy saloon, Dhreu House. The one that blew up- I didn't want her to go, I said I'd go with her. I should have insisted…" the catch was back in her throat.

She hesitated. The warm room was causing the girls to perspire slightly but Margo only wrapped the sweater around herself more tightly. She twisted the napkin, pulling pieces off it.

"Well, the no good lowlife stood her up." The sorrow turned to confused anger.

"She said the police had a video tape of her going into the bar with a package and leaving without it. But she said it was shoes she'd had repaired and didn't want to leave them on the front seat for thieves to break in and steal."

Margo snorted, tossed the tattered napkin on the table. "Ha, she was worried about nickel and dime thieves when a killer-" she broke off, eyes downcast, her entire body sunk like a melting snowman. She clutched at her dress with fraught fingers, shoulders caved in.

She looked up at Cheyne and Pepi, their rapt attention on her every word. "But, uh, that's it. That's all I remember. Megan lived a very quiet life."

Everyone sat quietly each in her own thoughts, Pepi jotted down some notes. Margo hadn't added anything Megan had already told them.

"Well," Cheyne murmured, getting ready to stand up.

"Oh, there was that peculiar moment at the bar," Margo perked a little.

Cheyne and Pepi leaned forward with renewed interest.

Margo said, "It's probably nothing, but she said she had almost left the bar right away because those old graduates had come in and were conversing with the three men at the bar.

"At first she was going to run off again before they could see her, then it appeared they were only retrieving drinks. They left after just a moment apparently not even noticing much less recognizing her.

"But, she recalled having a funny feeling about the interaction of the three young men with the three older men, but couldn't explain it. She said it was just a- 'flash of oddness' about the brief incident. Plus she was getting pretty intoxicated by then. Do you think that has anything to do- nah," she shook her head.

"What could college boys have to do with the death of my sister?"

Pepi tapped her pen on her notebook. "Did she happen to say if she knew these boys, what any of their names were, or the three men, maybe Devin's last name or even possibly his workplace?"

Margo's lips pressed contemplating, then she shook her head. "She intimated the graduates were much older than boys, more like young men. But no, that was all she said, she just had an odd feeling. Sorry I can't be of more help. I wish-"

Cheyne said solidly, "You never know how much help you've been, something trivial now could fit in the puzzle somewhere else and bring everything together. Every little bit helps."

Louise Furley

Softly saying, "Miss Margo," Pepi stood up and went over to the bereaving sister. "I'm going to show you some photos, okay?"

She wiped her damp hands from the glass on her shorts then pulled out the pictures they'd made off of Megan's USB and handed them to Margo. "Can you see if you recognize any of them?"

Margo took the photos and sifted carefully through each one. Her lips pulled in tight then puffed out. She shook her head and handed them back. "No. I'm pretty sure I've never seen any of them before. Why? Who are they? What do they have to do with Megan's, um, death?"

Pepi took the pictures back and stuffed them back in a folder. "We're not sure of anything yet, Miss Margo, just checking everything and see what hits."

Cheyne got to her feet. She said, "Well, if that's all, we'll be leaving you to your, uh, uh, day."

"Yes," Pepi added, jumping in at Cheyne's awkwardness. "But of course if you think of anything, any time, day or night, please- please don't hesitate to call us, or the police of course." She tore a piece of paper out of her notebook, scribbled down both their numbers and handed it to Margo.

Margo walked them out of the room and down the hall. "Are you sure you girls are safe? I mean, asking questions, and you have those photographs, are you putting yourselves, or, even me and my family at risk?"

Cheyne hugged her notebook to her chest. "We, you, are safe. Everything that we do or find out we immediately give to the police."

"Yeah," Pepi said, shrugging into her leather jacket for the bike ride home. "We stay in close contact with Detective Douglas James and give him everything we come up with. There would be no reason for anyone to come after us or you." They waited at the door as Margo opened it.

The girls thanked the grieving young woman for her time and promised to keep her updated with any relevant news.

Cheyne set her notebook in the basket attached to the front of her bike. "I can't wait until we get a car, this bicycle thing is getting old."

Pepi climbed on her own bike and laughed. "Yeah, we finally get our driver's licenses and we have no car to drive. That's why we need to get jobs. Did you hear anything from the Fresh Food place?"

Cheyne pushed on a pedal, glided standing straight up, then sat down and pedaled, propelling her out to the street. "No, I think we need to hit some more places. Let's go home and add what we got to the Murder Board."

"Murder Wall," Pepi corrected her and laughed since she didn't get to correct her friend all that often. She followed Cheyne's flying blonde ponytail down the road.

Chapter Twenty

Even though Detective James ordered them to stop snooping, they called him detailing what Margo Milan had told them about Megan's last days.

The police had already spoken with her, but the girls may have gotten something the police didn't.

On speakerphone, the girls could hear him scribbling notes. He didn't yell at them for still investigating, he probably thought Margo Milan would be a harmless interrogation.

"Well, Detective James," Cheyne spoke, "what do you have for us?"

Silence at the other end. They could hear him sigh.

"All right." Paper rustled like he was pushing pages in a notebook. "The uh, not that this will help anything, but the poison that killed your, uh, Miss Milan, was," he hesitated as if looking for the specific note. "Here, it was called Meadow Saffron."

The girls looked at each other then at the cell phone on the table. "Say again, yellow saffron?" Pepi asked.

"No, no, *Meadow* Saffron."

They could practically hear him reading as he said, "It's uh, says, 'All parts of the plant are deadly poisonous. The toxic effects appear slowly and gradually within 3 to 6 hours. These are nausea, excessive vomiting and bloody diarrhea, abdominal pain, shortage of breath and eventually, death.' It's a," he read, "'a pink-violet crocus. A flower I guess."

Pepi repeated, "A flower?"

"Uh huh. An autumn crocus, grows in the meadows of Europe and the Middle East."

"So how did someone get it, I mean it's not grown here, and give it to Miss Milan without her knowing?" Cheyne asked, confused about the whole thing.

A killer flower from Europe for Pete's sake? "What, does it do, stalk down the street on its- stalk- strangling, stabbing- what? It can't hold a gun with its leaves,"

"Really, Chey," Pepi said, eyes rolling, "I don't think that's what he's saying. So how, Detective, could they get it into the jail?"

"Well, it could have been smuggled in as tea or something. Anything can be grown these days in green houses," James replied.

"That's the craziest thing I've ever heard." Cheyne announced. "What next, killer petunias?"

They made small talk, the detective admonished them again to not get involved and they rang off.

The girls conversed, trying to make sense of all they'd learned so far and discussed the strange flower.

Pepi wrote on a paper about the meadow saffron then pinned it to the Murder Wall. Pepi's older brother Thomas put Cheyne's bike in his trunk and gave her a ride home.

The next day, Saturday, Cheyne had gymnastics practice and Pepi had ROTC, the last one until after spring break. They had agreed to meet after lunch and go over to the hotel bar where Miss Milan had gone for the wedding, and ask questions.

Early on Saturday, staff would be prepping, there shouldn't be any patrons in there drinking yet so the girls figured they could get some information, show their photos around without getting in trouble for being under-aged.

Exiting the locker room, still towel drying her hair with one hand, the other toting her gym bag, Cheyne rounded the corner with her head down- wham!

She collided with another body and was slammed backwards- unable to catch her balance, she landed hard on the floor, towel went flying, gym bag skittered across the floor.

Stunned, Cheyne sat for a second to let her spinning head wind down.

"Oh my gosh, I am so sorry, here," a voice from above said. "Let me help you."

Peering up through wads of wavy wet hair, Cheyne saw a young man hovering over her with his hand extended, an inch of brow furrowed in concern.

Without thinking, Cheyne held out her hand, the young man took it and gracefully hauled her to her feet.

When he let go of her, she swayed so he grabbed her around the waist to steady her.

Pushing away from him, Cheyne shoved her clump of tangled tresses back off her forehead.

The young man leaned over and scooped up her towel and gym bag. Four very concerned turquoise eyes quickly scanned her for injuries.

"I am so sorry, miss, um, uh, here-" he handed her the gym bag and towel. "I didn't see you, I guess I was going too fast, kind of a habit of mine I guess, but I don't usually wipe out beautiful girls along the way.

"Of course today I was in a bit of a hurry because I need to get to work, and I got out of last practice late, and I am of course now rambling like an idiot. Are you okay?" He shoved back a wild flop of hair almost identical to Cheyne's own bright flaxen mane.

But his was sun kissed; underneath it was darker. He grasped her wrists turning her arms in and out. Then he held a wrist while cupping her chin, and he turned her head back and forth examining her.

Her vision resorted back to normal Cheyne realized there was only one pair of turquoise eyes trying to see if she had any broken limbs or bruises.

She snapped her wrist from his hold and jerked her head to make him let go of her chin. "I am perfectly all right for heaven's sake. I just took a tumble. Quit pawing at me."

Her words came out harsher than she had intended, but with all of the events these past weeks she was on edge. She tried not to feel guilty at his hurt expression.

"Well, I did say I was sorry. If you don't need medical care I'll be on my way. Do you need me to take you to the school infirmary?" he asked stiffly.

"No," Cheyne shook her wet head. "I am fine, really. Listen, I'm sor-"

"Well then, that's good. Again, I am sorry for knocking you down. See you around I'm sure." He nodded, the flop of blonde hair bopped up and down and with nary another word he stalked off down the hall.

Shoulders of a brawny football player blocked half the light in the hallway as his long legs ate up the tile and out the door he went.

"Oh," now she felt bad for her rudeness. "Oh well, it was his fault really, going way too fast for the corridor, and my eyes were covered by the towel."

She threw the towel into her bag and tossed the bag over her shoulder before she could accept half the blame for the accident.

"Hmmph. Didn't even have the manners to introduce himself. What a clod." She sniffed, nose in the air, she started down the hall, a little slowly at first, she didn't want to run into the bulldozer again in case he returned.

Then she sped up remembering her plans with Pepi. She stalwartly pushed away the vision of strong shoulders, wavy blond hair with contrasting black lashes over stunningly unusual turquoise eyes.

The girls met at the far end of the schoolyard closest to the exiting drive to unlock their bikes. They greeted each other

155

cheerfully, happy to be out of school and excited about their investigation.

Pepi had changed out of her ROTC uniform into dress slacks and a buttoned down long sleeved blouse, suit jacket and heels.

She'd pulled her hair back into a low ponytail that divided itself into three long fat spools that bounced down her back. Fastening the strap of her helmet under her chin, she looked up.

"I'm glad those nasty clouds are moving on. I could hardly sleep last night with the crashing thunder like bombs exploding, and bolts of blinding lightning lit up my whole room. And it was raining so hard, the drops sounded like rapid-fire beating on the roof- about drove me mad!"

The cheeriness abruptly drained from her face, her expression transformed from day to night. Memories she had worked all night to keep at bay suddenly drilled at her like locusts.

She struggled to fight the swarm of black biting memories. Grimacing, she strained to keep her eyes open, forcing her gaze on the thick dark clouds that were pulsating ponderously away by the wind allowing a fragment of the brilliant blue sky to appear.

The humidity and blackened clouds still heavy with rain, oppressed, bending the athletic but emotionally brittle girl, pressing mentally down on her until she bent at the knees, her back rounded, she covered her eyes with her hands.

In seconds a stranger appeared to take Pepi over. The clear, honest, radiant face tightened into a wrought ball.

Clawing at her helmet, she yanked it off, threw it in the bike's basket. Dark words tumbled out of her mouth, "The rain, the gloom, it crept over me like a black plague, I couldn't breathe, I had to- to go in my closet, and, and close the door."

Her hands curled into tight fists, teeth clenched, but couldn't stop her jaw from trembling. "It's taking me over, Chey, it's winning, I can't fight it any-"

"Pepi, Pepi," Cheyne quickly unlocked her bike, in her haste she dropped her key.

"I- I can't help it, can't stop it!" Pepi's guttural voice faltered, her breath choked in gasping gashes. Clutching the bike handles, her arms grew rigid, her head dropped.

"I, it, it-" in grated breaths she cried in a hoarse whisper, "the thunder, it brings the unbearable memories, the utter fear. The loneliness, it..." Pepi's eyes shut tight.

Cheyne scrabbled to grab up her keys.

Pepi gasped, her hands clutched her throat as if she couldn't catch her breath. Wounded words kept spilling out, "It sometimes brings on," gulped a breath, "you know, the darkness comes on me...it takes over, I can't..."

She put her hands over her stomach to quell the nausea the memories brought. There were no tears though, no matter how tormented she was, she never cried. It had never done her any good before anyway.

Cheyne hurried over and threw her arms around her friend.

Pepi stood with her arms hanging at her sides, allowing her friend to hold her. They stayed like that for a while.

Still holding her gently, Cheyne murmured, "Hey Pep, it's spring, it rains. There'd be no tulips or daffodils, no sweet smell of roses without the rain. I like to think it washes the world clean, pristine and shining, all new, all fresh. A new day, like moving forward, away from the past. Don't ya think?"

She babbled giving Pepi time to regroup.

When Pepi appeared to have relaxed a shade, Cheyne dropped her arms, giving Pepi the personal space she always craved.

Jagged breaths decreasing, Pepi regained control of her emotions. Now embarrassed, she put her helmet back on and fussed with the strap.

She straightened her notebook in the basket, taking more time to calm. The black moment, for now, had passed. She climbed on her lavender and silver bike, her voice small, she replied, "I guess."

Back to her own bike, Cheyne said, "Pep," she waited until her friend looked over. "You're never alone. You always have me, you know that. Right?"

Pepi's head barely bobbed in a nod.

Her voice solemn, Cheyne said, "And, you know that if something ever happened- like, you know, like before, I would search the ends of the earth until I found you. I would never stop looking. You know that. Right?"

Pepi nodded weakly.

Cheyne chuckled. "Besides, you'd never ever be able to run Grams off with a stick now, would ya?"

Pepi nodded again, a tiny smile tugged at the corners of her pillow lips. "Yeah, you could say that again."

"Yeah, your Grams was dogged before and she'd do it again."

"I know."

Also in business clothes, black slacks and a black blazer over a red blouse, Cheyne pulled her helmet over her head. She'd managed to wrangle her wet hair also into a low ponytail while she had waited for Pepi to arrive at the bike rack.

"At least it poured at night and not now. A storm would highly dampen today's venture." Cheyne grinned at Pepi.

A corner of Pepi's mouth pulled in to a tight smile. She struggled to shake off the compressing weight of despair, push away the heavy black cloud that threatened to engulf her.

She knew there'd come a day when she would no longer be able to thrust away the pain, fight off the flood of grave memories that now only crept in by bits and pieces.

She knew they were coming full force and could- will- one day, crush her down and bury her. For now she needed to move, distract herself from her unspeakable past. "Yeah. Let's go."

They took off down the sidewalk following the main road, a four-lane highway. Cars passed, many honked, some knew the girls and were saying hi, some were just being obnoxious.

The duo tried to talk but the traffic was too loud.

"Let's-" The deafening roar of a passing motorcycle drowned out Cheyne's words, she gave up.

After a few miles, they turned away from the city to a two lane paved road, then less than a mile later veered off to a shortcut through the woods.

Riding along the dirt trail with both sides a woven mesh of limbs blooming so fast green starbursts of leaves popped and stretched as they sped past.

Intent on their destination, each deep in her own thoughts they breathed in the loaming smell of damp soil and the new spring grass with a lingering whiff of sweet honeysuckle in the air.

Sunlight stippled through the bristling branches, sweeping lemon stripes across the girls and the trail as they rode.

Twenty minutes later they evolved out of the wicker den and back onto Main Street.

Using GPS on their cells, they found the hotel where Megan Milan had attended the wedding. Locking their bikes, they left their helmets hooked to the chains and ventured inside.

They had decided the other day that carrying backpacks they looked like children, so they each had borrowed slim briefcases to hold their notebooks and photos.

When they got to the hotel, Cheyne combed her hair into a bun, pulled a pair of glasses out of her purse and slipped them on.

Pepi did a double take. "Seriously, Chey? Where'd you get those glasses, you look like a bug." In fact the bun and glasses did nothing to alter the baby blues or heart shaped face.

Cheyne sniffed and lifted her head to peer down at her friend. "I do better when I look the part. I borrowed them from Gran. Cool, huh?"

Pepi bit back a retort. "Uh, yeah, real librarian buggy cool. Come on Detective- Reporter- what are we today by the way?"

Cheyne cocked her head to one side looking at Pepi. "I don't know. Let's let them decide."

Carrying their briefcases, they trod the durably carpeted hall slowly at first, feeling as if they were interlopers.

"Really, Cheyne, we don't need to feel guilty we're trespassing or something, we could be guests just as much as the next guy." Pepi perked up her steps, feeling a little more assured in her business-like attire.

Grinning, Cheyne straightened her shoulders, raised her head like she was the president and they strode with confidence down the hall acting like they belonged there.

It didn't take long to find the lounge.

Hesitating briefly in the doorway, they pushed through and marched up to the bar.

The only other patrons were four men playing cards in a corner, and a single woman reading a book in a booth, they never looked up.

Not dim like in the evenings, the now well-lit room lost much of its intrigue and mystery. The darkness had hidden the dusty beams and stained carpet. Without the wavering candle glow, under the brighter lights crow's feet deepened, shadowed faces paled, everyone aged 10 years.

Except Pepi and Cheyne who bellied right up to the empty varnished bar.

Chapter Twenty-One

Hovering for a minute, unsure if they should call out or ring a bell for service, what appeared to be the bartender sauntered out hauling a case of bourbon. He dropped the box on the bar, the glass bottles jangled.

He then noticed the girls. Frowning, he stepped over to them.

They waited with their practiced, professional model smiles.

"Uh," the bartender looked them up and down, shook his head. "I'm sorry, girls, even if you have fake ID's there's no way I'm serving you. You need to-"

Cheyne smiled, held out a hand, her other hand held the briefcase, gold watch glinting on her slender wrist. "Oh no sir, we're not here to drink, we have some questions we would like to ask you."

Brows drew down between cherry brown eyes in a gaunt face. Before the suntanned, thirtyish man could respond, Cheyne set her briefcase on the bar, hit the snaps, plat-plat, opened the lid and pulled out the manila envelope that held the copies of the pictures they'd made from Megan's USB.

He sifted through his dirty blond soul patch, scratching it with two fingers watching her. Thinning dark blonde hair combed straight back hung stringy-wavy to his collar.

One hand, long fingers spanned like a knobby fan rested on the bar top. Although gangly, the bartender looked like he could use a workout at the gym. He held up a palm, "Wait, I don't-"

"Oh, I'm sorry," Pepi cut in quickly. With offhanded authority she held up her ID badge, waving it while she spoke, at the same time Cheyne with bored affectation flashed her wallet ID.

"It's all right, I am Pepi Nok, and this is Cheyne Somerset." Pepi introduced them giving their names an important ring. Her silvery eyes narrowed at him, she looked him up and down as if she found him lacking, something.

Pulling her petite athletic body up as tall as she could muster, she stretched her neck and lifted her chin. "We have a few questions, sir, I'm sure you want to cooperate?"

Sounded like a question, however not requiring affirmation.

The bartender tried to see the ID hanging around her neck, but Pepi tucked it under her jacket. His eyes darted to Cheyne's, she had already snapped her wallet closed and dropped it in her purse.

"Wait- I-" The bartender sputtered.

"So," Cheyne pulled out the pictures and laid them down on the bar one at a time. "Now, Mr. um, yes, what is your name, sir?" She smiled her smile of 'pretending to be polite but not really reporter smile.'

Her lips closed, pulled back and slightly up, eyes bored behind lenses, waiting impatiently.

"Well, I uh, I'm Nestor, Nestor Ramonez. But I don't see-"

"Yes, Mr. Ramirez," Cheyne pointed at the first photo, almost missing it as everything was slightly blurry from the borrowed glasses. "Please tell me if you recognize any of these men."

"That's Ramonez."

Cheyne tapped a pale pink nail on the first picture. "Please Mr. Ramonez, can we puhleeze have your cooperation?"

He looked at her, but she rolled her eyes slightly like he was short a brain and tapped the picture again. "Mr. Ramonez, really."

"Okay, okay, don't get excited, geesh." His head dropped to the pictures. Shrugging, he scanned the first picture, then the next, the next, the next, then his nostrils flared, pupils widened. He pointed at the fifth picture.

"They're pretty fuzzy, but I'm sure that's uh, oh what's his name, Kimet, um, Khirbet or something like that," the little cherry eyes turned up to the right while he thought.

"Comes in all the time, with, let's see, there's Ahmet and," his eyes rolled over the pictures, settled on the last one.

Tapping the photo with his finger, he said, "This guy here, looks kind of like Devin, hangs with Khirbet and another guy. Hunky, the girls are always throwing themselves at him. You know, blond, blue, but with skin sand dark like from the Middle East- he has like an exotically foreign manner.

"Has a heavy accent, turns the girls on. He never gives them the time of day." He leaned closer to the picture.

"Ya know, looking closer at the picture, that's not Devin, just blond like he is." He stared at the pictures, wiping the end of his nose with the side of a finger.

The scraggly hair dangled in his face, he pushed it back behind his ears and crossed his arms. "Don't recognize anybody else. That it?"

Pepi asked him, "What are their conversations like? Any particular topic?"

He looked the young teen up and down. "You mean the three guys? Dunno, business, mostly sounds like business."

"Business?" Cheyne asked. "What kind of business?"

He shrugged one reedy shoulder, stuck his hand in his pants pocket and jingled a few coins. Though tall and wiry, Nestor had a little round beer gut.

He turned his attention to Cheyne. "Dunno, their voices drop whenever I'm near. They are cold fish, like I get a creepy chilled feeling from them. You know, like an oily croc eyeing a waddling duck on the bank kind of thing."

"How do you know it's business then?" Cheyne asked.

Shrugging again, he replied, "I dunno, they say stuff like, 'you get the order, tell them we mean business, they'll know the cost when we're through', stuff like that."

He gestured to the back with his head. "Ginger, Ginger Wren, the barmaid, she knows everyone, the regulars anyway, especially the good looking men. Lemme get her, she's better with names."

Knocking at his forties, the dissipated bartender had been around the block for a long time, but he clung desperately to his youth, hence the long un-styled hair.

Not a *really* bad guy as he always told himself, he never killed anyone. He did do some minor stealing and dealing, picking up every girl he could to party hearty.

Unfortunately, his type was under 25, sadly though, now with his skull peeking through the stringy hair and the beer gut, no one under forty will give him the time of day.

He took a last look at the picture and headed back through a door to the galley area behind the bar.

Cheyne laid her forearms on the bar, dropped her head and let out a whoosh of air.

Copying her, Pepi wiped her forehead. "Wow, can you believe it?" She nudged Cheyne with her elbow. "Can't he see we're just a couple of young teenagers?"

"Shhh," Cheyne whispered. Standing up straight, shoulders back, she straightened the glasses and slapped the bored look back on her face. "It's all in the attitude."

Her friend nodded, nose slightly up in the air, eyes hooded. Pepi sniffed, studied her neatly trimmed, short nails, a coat of clear polish made them slightly shiny. She looked up at Nestor returning with apparently the barmaid.

Ginger Wren had arrow straight, pitch-black hair. Hardly an eyebrow, lip, or ear was not pierced with something. What wasn't pierced was hidden behind thick makeup, red, red lips and a harsh streak of cat's-eye eyeliner.

If her hair had been pulled up in a beehive she'd look a little like the late Amy Winehouse. Tattooed arms poking from a black, thin-strapped blouse with lace ruffling around the bodice, she was skinny to the point of drug emaciated.

Spider legs in skintight black tights and pointed high heels, she walked like she'd been sitting on a fence post for years.

Gum snapping, Ginger set a tattooed hand on a sharp hip, false lashes spiny around Goth lined eyes swept at them. "So girls, wassup?"

Pepi stepped forward. Authority ringing, she said in a moderated voice, "I'm Ms. Nok and this is Ms. Somerset. We want to thank you for your cooperation in this matter." She nodded to Cheyne who was prepared, she again flashed her ID and snapped it closed before they could get a good look and dropped it in her purse.

Pepi pushed her jacket back and wrapped one thumb over her belt acting like she had a badge clipped to her belt like the police on TV do. People saw what they were led to see even if it wasn't really there.

She wrote the woman's name in her notebook then quickly, leaving the other pictures on the counter she held up the photo Nestor had recognized, Pepi asked, "Ms. Wren, Mr. Ramonez said you know this man?"

Ginger squinted at the picture. "Uh huh, wait a sec, hon." She went to a corner of the bar and came back with a pair of reading glasses. Slipping them on, she peered at the photo.

She nodded, spikes of black hair flapped on her shirt like brittle black icicles. "Sure that's that guy, Khirbet, don't know his last name. Those guys he hangs with seem a little paranoid about letting out personal info, they're generally careful with names but they slip out sometimes.

"He hangs with, lemme see," she leaned over the other pictures, pushed them around with an inch long curved nail. She hesitated over the picture of the blond man but pushed past it.

She looked up at the girls over her glasses and shook her head. "Sorry, hon, I can't recall what I heard his last name was, and I don't see the guys he comes here with in any of the pictures. Is that a help?"

Pepi pursed her lips. Cheyne smiled. "Yes," she said. "That helps us a lot. Can you tell us anything about them? Where they work? Live perhaps? What do they drive? Maybe what country they're from?"

Ginger gazed back down at the photos. "Hmmm." She looked back and forth, shuffled them around, placed the picture of Khirbet on top. Pulling off the glasses, she folded them into one hand and then gestured with them.

"I'm sorry, ladies. They're pretty private guys. Really, they're barely polite, more like they're, um, dismissive. Act like other humans are just an annoyance like so much droning flies. They even run off the prettiest girls.

"I don't think they're gay, I think they are just very serious about their business or something, maybe they're illegal and don't want to get picked up. That guy Khirbet drives a black SUV, I've never noticed the plates.

"Like I said, I can't say I know any of their last names, only overheard them call each other by name a few times and they always pay with cash. Then again, a lot of the patrons do, don't want a paper trail, don't want their wives or bosses knowing where they're hanging out. Who knows? These guys give me the willies, they're-"

Nestor cleared his throat, cut in, "I've heard scraps of talk about, a, uh, I think it's a warehouse." His white sleeves rolled up, he crossed his arms above his tiny potbelly, legs akimbo he leaned back slightly on his heels.

"Down on the east side, the district near the edge of town, where those old farmsteads are. You know, a few miles before the Iceplant Inlet? I remember one saying that when he closes up later he would pick up some aspirin from the shop out front before he leaves."

He thought for a moment then shook his head. "I don't recall him saying the name of the place."

"Okay. I need you to look at another picture."

The bartender and barmaid watched Pepi pick out a photograph of Megan Milan from the folder. She set it on the bar in front of Ginger. "Have you seen her before?"

Ginger slid her glasses back on and leaned over the picture. She bit her lower lip in concentration. "Um, she looks familiar, I'm not sure…"

Shaking her head she pushed the photo in front of the bartender. "What do you think, Nestor?"

The bartender set his crossed forearms on the bar, leaned closer to the picture. His forehead wrinkled, he rubbed the sparse soul patch with a knobby finger. His face brightened a bit, he smiled slightly at the girls.

"Yeah, I think I remember her. She was here, uh," his eyes turned up, trying to remember. He moved his attention from Pepi to Cheyne. "I'm pretty sure she was here a couple of weeks, a month or so ago."

He gazed back down at the picture, nodding more assuredly. "Yeah, yeah, I remember, she was this shy, really prim and proper teacher type but dressed way out of her comfort zone in a sleazy, sequiny dress. Almost broke her neck in the high heels on the way in."

He glanced at the door. "Came in from the restaurant. There was a wedding going on in the back party room." His lower lip pushed out as he perused the photo.

"You could tell she was uncomfortable, she kept tugging the skirt down and the cleavage up, and she kept accidentally smearing her makeup like she wasn't used to wearing it or kept forgetting she was wearing it."

He chuckled. "After several drinks, she grew bold, I don't think she was used to drinking either. Do you remember her, Ginger?"

Black spikes prickled with a head shake. "No, I really can't place her."

Nestor set a palm on the bar, his arm rigid, he picked up the picture with his other hand. Holding the photo in front of his face he nodded. "Yeah, she got pretty trashed, started hitting on

Devine, I mean Devin. She maneuvered herself right into their little group. I didn't see what happened next, I went to take care of Cissy Lane,"

"Really, Nestor, I don't see what you see in that tramp, except for," Ginger motioned in front of her meager chest.

"Anyway," Nestor continued, annoyed. "When I got back to that end of the bar the lady was gone."

Cheyne tried to hide the contempt she was feeling. "Did she leave alone?"

He shook his head, shrugged one shoulder. "Dunno, didn't see her leave. But I think she left alone. She'd had her purse and car keys in her hand before I went over to Cissy, and she was still in the midst of the three smarmy guys. When I returned, she was gone and I think they were all still there."

Pepi hid her disdain behind a placid mask, yet she couldn't help saying, "Did you think maybe about calling her a taxi? I mean you said she was trashed and all, and about to drive. Maybe make sure she didn't leave with total strangers in her condition? Or drive for that matter." She and Cheyne exchanged a censorious glance.

His face stiffened, Nestor stood straight up. The sarcastic censor had come across clear as a bell. "I'm hardly responsible for a grown woman. She said she was a teacher, she should know better, stop drinking before you're out of control."

Pepi tried to restrain her mouth and angry expression. She asked, "Can you think back, remember for sure if the three men remained after she left?"

Nestor eyes slowly drew down Pepi's body, and back up.

She could feel her face burn.

He knew it. His gaze travelled to the bar. He looked like he was trying to picture that night. He crossed his arms, turned from Pepi to Cheyne.

"Yeah, I actually do remember now. Right after the teacher left they all ordered sandwiches and another round of beer." He looked back over at the bar then back to Cheyne.

"Yeah, that's right. The teacher left alone. I remember when I was talking to Cissy I could see the teacher stumbling past the window. I thought, 'boy that girl is headed for trouble.'"

She couldn't help herself, Pepi slapped a hand on the table and exclaimed, "So why on earth didn't you go after her, see that she got in a taxi or have her call someone to come and get her? Why didn't you?"

Ginger smirked at the bartender. These girls didn't know who they were talking to. Nestor cared only about Nestor and his next conquest. If the teacher had been a hottie he would have made sure she got home okay, with him.

Nestor faced the angry teen. Her ire didn't bother him. "Like I said, sister, she's an adult, she should learn to handle her liquor."

"She won't have a chance to now," Pepi responded quietly.

Cheyne scooped up the pictures, shoved them into the envelope a little harsher than she meant to. She shot the bartender a disapproving look. "Hmmph. Sometimes a person can be grown up in looks and education but be ingenuous in life experience."

Reviewing her notes, Pepi muttered, "When you know better it's your moral obligation to look out for the innocent." She asked Nestor before he could respond, "Do you recall a few young men, maybe college age that came in at the same time that this lady was here?"

Forgetting the rebuke, he thought for a second. He was used to women reaming him. He had thick skin to go with his thick head.

"I think so, there were some guys that had slipped out of the boring wedding and came in for some drinks. I didn't see the lady or them connect. At first I thought they were just getting drinks, then I think they knew the three men."

"What made you think that?" Cheyne asked.

He set his knuckles on the bar and leaned forward, rocking back and forth on his toes. One eye squinted, "I uh, what they, uh. I can't say exactly. It's just the feeling I got. The young guys ordered drinks, they just seemed familiar with the men. They were only there a few moments so the conversation was short.

"They all laughed kind of, but not the joshing kind. It seemed to be not real merriment, like they were acting, putting on a little show."

"A show for who?" Pepi asked. "Who was there?"

His brows rose, Nestor said, "That's the funny part, no one was really paying any attention to them except for the drunk babe. It was like for show in case anyone had noticed them all talking. Hard to explain. Besides, there was a bar in the ballroom. What was the point to come in here and get drinks if they weren't going to stay?"

"Did you know any of the young men?" Cheyne asked.

"No, not really. They've been in before, come around every few months or so." Nestor said.

"So it sounds like they're locals. About how old would you say they were?" Cheyne asked.

He thought about it, his expression showing he couldn't understand why they were so interested, and what difference could it make anyway. "Like I said before, college age, maybe 22 to 26 or so."

He ran a finger under his nose. "Hmmm, you know, they looked like they could be like ex-military or something."

"Oh?" Pepi asked. "What makes you say that?" She clasped her hands and laid them on top of her notebook, set one foot on a barstool.

They all looked up as a couple came into the bar and sat at a booth.

Nestor grasped the edge of the bar and sighed heavily. "Geez ladies, I got work to do-"

Cheyne tipped her face up to him. Twining a spool of hair that had escaped from the bun around a finger, she slipped off the glasses and fluttered her lush eyelashes.

"Of course, Mr. Nestor, we can see how important you are here, and that you have to get ready for the dinner crowd, but can't you spare just a wee bit more time? It's really ever so important…" Pink glossed lips curved in a charming smile.

A flush rose up Nestor's neck. "Uh, yeah, sure, I-"

170

"Oh for crying out loud, Nat, you fall for anything female. Think jailbait, you dumb oaf." Exasperated, Ginger turned on her heel, spikes flapping on her back she strode off to the new customers, stick legs cleaving across the floor.

"So," Cheyne drew his attention back to her. "You were saying they seemed military?" She held the envelope of photos resting her arm on the counter.

His eyes ran up and down Cheyne's figure, lingering on her chest then moved to her glossy lips. He wormed closer to her. "It wasn't nothin' really. Just a clipped way of talking, ramrod posture you know- way they stood, and it looked like buzz cuts starting to grow out."

Sliding a hand over hers, he dipped his head in close, voice low, husky he suggested, "Say, what about you and me going around the back for a few minutes, have a drink, get to know each other a little-"

Pepi tossed her notebook into her briefcase snapped it closed and slid it noisily off the bar. "Well!" she said loudly. "Would you look at the time, we must be moving on, many more people to interview before the day is over."

She headed for the door then turned back to Cheyne. "You need to come on now, Ms. Somerset, you know we have a deadline."

Cheyne extricated her hand out from under the bartender's, dropped the glasses in her pocket and grabbed up her own briefcase. "Maybe some other time, Mr. Ramonez," she gave him a pretty smile. "Thanks so much for your time and information." She hurried to catch up with Pepi.

The bartender called out as they exited through the door, "That's Nestor, babe. Call me Nes-"

They waited until they were outside before dissolving into giggles.

Pepi mimicked her friend, "Ever so important, some other time? Where do you get that stuff from, romance novels?"

Cheyne threw her briefcase into her bike's basket and climbed on. "We never know if we're going to need him again.

We need to keep our options open, keep him on a leash. I never claimed to be the great speaker, that's you, I just have a good vocabulary. Next time *you* play the femme fatale."

Buckling her helmet, she scowled. "Believe me, he knew I wanted to rail at him for letting Miss Milan leave drunk, and forget about him inviting a minor for a drink,"

"Yeah, and whatever else." Pepi spat, "Pig."

"Colossal," Cheyne agreed.

They took off for home.

Chapter Twenty-Two

The next morning started out dreary and soppy.

Fortunately, by ten the sun dug long golden fingers through the clouds, pulling them apart like they were airy Krispy Kreme donuts, a light breeze helped dissipate the last of the frumpy clouds.

The girls met to go to the mall to apply for positions at the Soda Pop Shoppe.

After they applied at the Shoppe they went over to the Crisp & Crunch Café.

Mr. Nordstrum, the owner, a short, rotund man with a face like a meaty clenched fist, interviewed them.

Clear glass lamps attached to the walls cast lights that reflected little amber circles atop his pink balding pate. Tufts of curly white hair fringed in a semi-circle around the lower part of his head.

Wearing a short sleeved, light blue shirt and black slacks, a pencil tucked behind one ear, he spoke to the girls but never stopped surveying the restaurant. Servers in pale blue dresses with white aprons skillfully bustled around the small dining room. A few patrons ate at the long lunch counter.

Mr. Nordstrum reviewed their applications then asked them a few questions. Shaking his head, his lips turned down in a frown. "I don't know, you girls have no experience." If he was wearing red he'd resemble old Saint Nick.

Pepi spoke up, "Yes, we're young, but we are very fast learners, Mr. Nordstrum." Thinking quickly, she said, "And reliable. We are free to work on the weekends and since you don't serve that late, we can work a couple of days during the week especially once summer is here."

Her hands clasped behind her back, Cheyne added, "We love people and are pretty cheerful. We'll really enjoy waiting on people."

The owner looked from one beaming girl to the other. A reluctant smile pushed up the plump cheeks. "Okay, we'll give you a try. I won't need you to start for a few weeks when season moves into full swing. In the meantime, let Marla out front photocopy your ID's and SS cards. She will call you with your schedules in a couple of weeks."

The girls thanked him then left the small restaurant and ventured with giddy triumphant skips into the mall.

"*Wow*," Cheyne drawled excitedly. "I can't believe it, our very first job!" She clapped her hands.

"I am so excited, Chey, I can hardly stand it!" Pepi grinned.

"Sounds like cause for celebration." A familiar voice behind them caused Pepi to swirl around, her grin spreading.

"Karey!" she announced joyfully.

The pair hugged.

Cheyne was astounded, she had never seen Pepi hug someone willingly.

The couple separated, however the young man kept a hand possessively around her tiny waist. For once Pepi was glad she had dressed in a frilly summer dress and dainty sandals instead of her regular jean shorts and blouse. "Chey, you remember Karey?"

"Sure." Cheyne greeted the handsome guy with a warm smile. "I remember you from the funeral. And I've heard a lot about you lately." She grinned, nudging Pepi.

Embarrassed, Pepi shushed her friend. "Hush Chey, Karey doesn't care about our girlie chit-chat."

"Actually," the young man drew Pepi closer to him, his chocolate eyes softened into her glowing grey orbs. He squeezed her gently then they parted. "I'm happy to hear I'm important enough to be mentioned."

Holding hands, his bear paw completely enveloping her small one, they gazed shyly but obviously enamored into each other's eyes.

Cheyne stood awkwardly trying not to gawk at the pair.

Pepi laughed. "We're embarrassing Cheyne." Not to mention herself, PDA's were so not her style. She moved an inch away from Karey. "We have to go, my grandmother is expecting me home by five."

Karey looked disappointed. "Really? I was hoping I could talk you into coming to my house for dinner. Ma always makes enough to feed an army. You're invited too of course," he said quickly to Cheyne.

Before Cheyne could respond, Pepi said, "I'd really like to, but my grandmother said we had to come straight home after we applied for the job. Hey," she grinned wide, "we both just got hired over at the Crisp & Crunch? We're so excited!"

A foot taller than the petit Pepi, Karey kissed the top of her head. He picked up a long, fat curl soft as mink letting it wind around his hand. "I'm proud of you, Pepi. I'd hire you if I owned a business!"

They drew close again, she smiled up at him, he smiled down at her, his strong nose almost pressed against her small, snubby turned up nose.

"Uh, Pep, I hate to intrude, but, it's a quarter to five," Cheyne mentioned.

The couple reluctantly pulled apart. Holding her hand, Karey brushed it lightly against his cheek. "We're still on for this Saturday with my church group at the skating rink, right?" he asked, his voice hopeful.

"Oh yeah, I can't wait, Karey. My brother Thomas will bring me."

"Okay then, well," reluctant to let her go, Karey clung to her hand.

"Yeah, okay. See ya then." They held hands and eyes for another moment then Pepi pulled away. "Come on, Cheyne girl, let's go."

Karey watched them walk out the door. He waved as Pepi turned around one more time, the light dress swirling around her toned legs.

"Geez, Pep, where's your glass slipper?" Cheyne made fun when they got outside.

They climbed on their bikes. Pepi's face flushed vibrantly. She stuck her nose in the air with an, 'I don't care attitude' pretending her cheeks weren't tingling warm in embarrassment.

Then a slight smile lifted a corner of her lip. "You got that right, he totally treats me like a princess. He sent me a bouquet of spring tulips and has called me every night since the funeral." Now a wee bit of bragging lightened her tone and twinkled her eyes.

Cheyne rolled her eyes. "Like you haven't mentioned this six times a day. What you didn't mention was how cozy you two were."

Looking genuinely happy for a change, Pepi said, "I told you I've been to his house for dinner and he's been to mine. Last night we sat in his car out in front of my house and talked for, like hours it seemed." She rolled her eyes.

"Then all of sudden, here came Gram, in a freakin' bathrobe and slippers marching down the driveway with a look of- well, we didn't want to find out. I hopped out of the car and he drove off before Gram got to us. She yammered at me all the way inside and to my room. But, honestly," she glowed with happiness, "I wasn't listening. Nothing could ruin my night. Even with the holey robe and hair sticking out all over her head!"

They rode off giggling.

Early the next day, they called before stopping by to see Talana Castilla, the deceased Lareina Wittgenstein's half-sister. They could hear the melodic doorbell ringing inside.

The windows in the double doors had etched borders in a diamond design that slightly distorted the young girl as she promptly came to the door. The fourteen year old pulled open one of the doors and motioned for the girls to come in.

"Hi, ladies, come on in. It's so nice to see you. Follow me to the den, I'm eager to hear the progress you've made." Two pretty barrettes swept her hair back over her temples allowing the sleek veneer to cascade in waves down her back.

The lime green silk blouse she wore was a perfect foil for the fox-red hair. Young as she was, the girl dressed sophisticatedly chic like a 1920's elegant champagne flute. Her murdered sister was the sexpot; Talana is the lady.

Even the house was sophisticated, and obviously moneyed. They stood in a spacious ivory and silver mosaic floored foyer, the fragrance of lilacs almost overwhelming but pleasantly so.

Talana led them to a large yet simpler, more modern room filled with overstuffed beige furniture, cypress wood tables and urn shaped lamps.

The room was cozy plush with slightly messy bookcases, a writing table with a phone and laptop and a gaslight stone fireplace. Vividly colorful yet tasteful paintings of South America splashed with bold reds, blues and yellows added drama to the cushy den.

Although the burgeoning sun pushed through several gold draped windows, the room retained an early morning creamy sereneness.

The young hostess offered, "Make your selves comfortable. I've made some tea, would you like some?"

The girls said yes to the tea and sat at a small round table in front of a floor length window where the tea set was.

After retrieving two more teacups, Talana poured everyone tea like an experienced hostess then sat down. Her smile friendly and open she said, "So, tell me your news."

Cheyne looked around in awe. "Wow, we've been in some pretty upscale homes lately, huh, Pep? Nice to see how the other half, the half I'd like to join someday, lives."

Pepi grinned. "Yeah, and I'm getting really used to tea. It's better for you than soda I guess. I'm starting to feel like a real lady." She lifted the teacup exaggerating holding her pinky out.

The girls laughed. She added. "You do have a beautiful home, Talana."

The girls took turns filling Talana in with the latest information they'd garnered.

Talana set her elbow on the table and placed her chin in her hand. "This whole thing is getting freakier and freakier. So you don't have any idea who these men are?"

Pepi shook her head while setting her teacup down with a tiny clink. "We brought the pictures to show you too, maybe you've seen one of them with your sister or around town." She pulled out the photos and let Talana peruse them.

The redhead took her time. Matching brows drew down, she chewed on the inside of her mouth as she moved from one picture to the next.

Her head tipped curiously, she looked closer then pointed at one of the pictures. "You know, maybe this guy. Lareina was pretty shady about her love-life lately. She was seeing Adonni less and less, and wouldn't talk about where she was going or who she was seeing. But," her eyes dropped to the picture they'd copied off Megan Milan's drive.

"You can hardly make his features out, but there's something about this guy, see here at the back of the photo?" Talana pointed to a man standing far from the group. It appeared he didn't know his picture was being taken.

"I can't say I've actually met him, or could tell you anything about him, but one day Lareina was dolled up to the max, big hair, perfumed to the sky, she flurried out the door and down the drive where she hopped into a car, black I think, dark, SUV." Bending over, she squinted at the picture.

"The guy driving, yeah, it could have been this guy. Dark hair and skin, foreign looking with a hawkish nose and like a cowboyish mustache. The way he held his body, rigid, arrogant-kind of superior like, made me think of a soldier or captain or something." She looked at the girls. "Do you think he has anything to do with all of this?"

Cheyne shrugged. "At this point, we really know nothing. The bar staff where Miss Milan went also thought they recognized him, but he's far away in the picture and when we enlarge it, it grows grainy. It's like a game of pick-up-sticks, we keep picking up a stick to build a house but it just makes another room."

Pepi gave her a screwy look. "What? What does that even mean?" She and Talana laughed at Cheyne's miffed expression.

Cheyne turned her nose up. "You know what I mean, puzzle pieces but no picture."

"Anyway," Pepi shot her friend a loopy grin, then turned to Talana. "We were wondering if your sister kept a diary?"

Talana nodded emphatically. "Oh sure. I never read a word of it of course. Lareina was way too sneaky to let her diary get around and I didn't see it in any of her things. We've packed up some of her clothes, shoes, purses and some other things to take to Goodwill; the diary wasn't around.

"Still, I know she had one because I'd seen her sometimes at night when I popped into her room to a have a word or something. She'd have her favorite pen, pink flowing feather attached to it in one hand and she'd slam the book closed whenever I came in. She wasn't the chummiest of sisters I'm afraid." Her lips curved down, lids lowered over her spring-green eyes, she reached for her tea.

The girls chatted to each other about school for a second to give Talana a moment to gather herself. She just held the teacup not drinking any, the steam misted her pretty patrician features, softening and turning her cheeks dewy. Tears lingered in her eyes.

Cheyne said kindly, "Talana, do you think it would be all right if we, uh, you know, looked for the diary?"

Talana blotted the corners of her eyes with a napkin. She nodded, pulling out a tremulous smile. "Sure. Of course."

The girls waited, smiling compassionately at the younger girl.

The three girls continued to smile and nod at each other, then realizing they were talking about the present moment, slightly pink cheeked, Talana said, "Oh, did you want to look now?"

"That would be great," Pepi said with a smile and stood up.

Slightly flustered, Talana ushered them out of the room and down a hall, walking on a carpet, like cashmere so deep and thirsty, their shoes sunk with every step leaving pockets of footsteps behind them.

Pepi thought fleetingly of kicking off her shoes and running barefoot down the hall.

The house was extravagantly decorated. Magnificent mirrors and clinquant-framed paintings glittered along the hall and lined the wall as the girls trod up the wide marble staircase, the gleaming railing swelled down and around.

Talana led them down another hall passing several rooms before stopping halfway to the end. She opened a door and stepped aside. "You guys go ahead in, I need a minute to, uh, you know."

Cheyne wrapped an arm around the younger girl and gave her a hug. "It's cool, we understand. You don't think anyone would mind if we searched the room?"

Somehow she felt like she was intruding, stepping across the dead girl's grave or something, even wearing a long sleeved T-shirt and jeans, she shivered.

Still not a big hugger, other than apparently Karey Kissoon, Pepi pulled her lips in, trying to wordlessly express her sympathy.

"It's okay. Go ahead. I'll just be a second," Talana said. She couldn't mask the heavy burden in her graceful face. The loss of her sister, venomous girl or not, still hurt, still left a hole in her heart that will never be replaced.

Her full lips trembled with the strain of trying to keep the sorrow buried inside. Yet, ever polite, the young girl pasted a smile on and stood to the side of the door.

The girls stepped past Talana and went into the room.

"Wow," Pepi gushed, looking around in awe.

The room was vast, like a mini castle in its own right. Taking up a quarter of the immense space was a king-sized canopied bed against the far wall with a burgundy and white antique loveseat curved in front of it.

A coterie of yellow printed cushioned chairs with a matching settee nestled charmingly by a tower window. The dresser and bedside tables all dark and heavy were trimmed in gold with matching handles.

A teardrop shaped space off to the side held a glass topped desk and more chairs.

The walk-in closet could have housed four families it was so enormous. It was so big it had a chaise lounge so one could rest while deciding what to wear.

"Yeah, this is what's called 'ornate'." Cheyne rotated in one spot to take in the room. "For a young, modern, hip chica, Lareina had some old fashioned taste."

Pepi agreed. "It reminds me of an antique Hollywood mansion with its burgundy and gold, look at that burgundy canopy trimmed in gold tassels over the bed."

She took in the rest of the room. "I mean it's so- like old world glamorous with the crushed velvet burgundy floor length drapes and bedspread and everything. *Spec-freakin-tacular*."

Her forehead furrowed as she kept looking around, she stifled a shiver. She couldn't imagine living in this movie set of a bedroom, so heavy, and, old.

Cheyne walked around a little, taking in the elaborately decorated room. "It's a little cloying for my taste, but, to each his own." Near the bed she said, "Check out these lamps."

She gently touched one of the huge, heavy bottomed lamps next to the bed. "I bet they weigh a ton." She ran a hand down the painted vase of the grandiose porcelain lamp and over the thick marble base feeling its coolness.

Fingering one of the purple glass diamonds that dangled around the lamp's globe, she watched it dance colored prisms against the wall. The infamous pink-feathered pen lay on the nightstand beside the lamp.

Pepi moved to a bureau in a far corner. "I feel like a spy or something." She grasped two gold handles and gingerly pulled out a drawer. It didn't slide open easily, so heavy she really had to pull hard.

"It's okay, really," Talana said, entering the room. "She's dead so she can't care and we, Mom, Dad and Talco want to know what happened. We want justice and the police aren't doing much."

She walked over and stood in front of a medieval rounded dresser with big drawers and sculptured lion legs that curved into claw feet. "It'll go faster if I help."

Cheyne sent her an encouraging smile. "Okay then, let's go." She started rifling through one of the bedside tables. Used to her little brothers rummaging constantly at will through her own bedroom, she had zero privacy, Cheyne wasn't that uneasy going through someone else's drawers.

Pepi on the other hand, moved more slowly, cautiously, it went against her grain to snoop into people's private belonging.

Fruitless hours later, they exhaustedly thumped step by step back down the long staircase.

Talana led them back to the den. She left and returned shortly with a fresh pot of tea and clean teacups and a plate of scones with jam.

They all plopped ungracefully onto the chairs at the table by the window. They sipped and ate silently, each deep in their own tired thoughts.

Talana smiled wanly at Pepi. "Girl, you looked so pretty when you guys arrived, you with your silver blouse, matches those unusual silver-grey eyes. Now you're pretty dusty. Mom has kind of kept the maids away, I guess in her mind she keeps the door closed and in some way she can pretend that Lareina is still inside."

A bit of a smirk, she said, "And we can all pretend Lareina was a nice, sweet angel since she isn't around to contradict it."

Cheyne shrugged one shoulder, licked jam off her fingers. "Who knows, maybe now she truly is a sweet little angel."

"Uh yeah, sure, Chey, dream on, you and your saccharine fantasies. Little red devil is more like-" Pepi shot an apologetic look at Talana.

"I'm so sorry, I keep forgetting you are, were, sisters. You're so opposite, but then so are a lot of sisters. Anyway," she glanced down at her blouse. Indeed there was a fine layer of dust across the front. She brushed at it, didn't help much.

Without chagrin, she smiled at Talana. "Into the wash it goes."

Cheyne asked, "Where else might she have stashed the diary? What about another room in the house? The attic? Basement? Kitchen?" She glanced up at the high rounded ceiling and around at the bookshelves lining two walls. "In here?"

Talana shook her head. "I doubt it. We can look, but I don't think she would chance someone, a maid or one of us coming across it."

Cheyne got up and went over to the stone fireplace. It was a gas fireplace with fake logs inside. She bent over and pushed at some of the stones to see if any were loose enough to have a book hidden behind one. All were solid as a rock.

Crouching, she peered inside, looked around, patted the walls. Nothing. Picking up a napkin she wiped her hands.

Next, Pepi and Talana watched as the blonde beauty headed to one of the bookcases. Cheyne walked back and forth eyeballing the rows of books to see if the diary could be hidden in plain sight or maybe behind a bigger book.

She pulled some books out to check behind them. She opened large books in case the diary could be hidden inside a cut out larger book, pushed some back and forth that were lying stacked un-neatly rather than standing up.

Talana and Pepi chatted about school and music and people while watching Cheyne give up on the bookcases and pull out drawers in the end tables and lastly the writing desk.

Finally admitting her search was futile, she returned to where the others were sitting and plopped down aggravated on her chair.

Crossing her arms over her chest, Cheyne crossed one leg over the other and leaned back in her chair, letting her head flop over the back of the chair.

In a second, she sat back up and set a palm on the table. "Didn't Lareina have a job?"

Nodding, Talana topped off their tea then spooned sugar in hers, added cream, stirred, set the spoon with a tiny clink on the china saucer. "Yeah, I don't know why, she certainly didn't need to work, and, she tended to look down at people that did work.

"I think one reason is she liked to round up more attention and was not getting it from her friends and acquaintances she's known most of her life. People were avoiding her more and more.

"Plus, Daddy told her she needed to go to college to keep getting the big allowance, and I think this was a way of getting out of it, at least for a while. She was a hostess at that upscale restaurant, Bodvoci's, on the weekends. Adonni used to pick her up after work and take her out, but he hasn't done that in months."

Pepi asked, "What are you thinking, Chey?"

Her legs still crossed, Cheyne set her elbows on the table. "Maybe she had like a locker or back room or something, front desk where she could have kept the diary."

Her dark red brows drew down briefly. Talana said noncommittally, "Not likely, but maybe. I can check it out tomorrow."

Cheyne pushed back her chair. "Well, I guess we should boogie." She glanced at her watch. Her eyes popped. "Yikes, time for dinner, we'd better hurry."

Talana walked them out.

The girls ate dinner at Pepi's house. After pork chops, applesauce and parsley potatoes they trod halfheartedly up to the murder room.

Pepi added notes to the wall. She noted the diary with a question mark next to it and wrote that they thoroughly checked Lareina's room and would check her workplace next.

Chewing the end of the marker, "What else?" she asked standing in front of the wall looking it over.

Cheyne pulled a sweater over her head. The days were warmer, but the evenings still chilled. Tugging her hair out from the sweater, she joined Pepi in front of the wall.

She pulled the sleeves over her hands and held the ends curled in her fists. "Did you put down all the info Nestor and Ginger Wren told us about each of the men, their names and descriptions?"

"Yes, I put, no I didn't." Pepi wrote on a note. "I didn't include the descriptions. There." She stuck the note to the wall.

Cheyne said, "Oh, and add that Talana kind of confirmed the black or dark SUV and that Khirbet guy from the picture."

"Right." Pepi added the information. "Tomorrow we should show the pictures to Lareina's friends, including party princess Chalessa Chung and especially that frizzle stick Frieda since you said she saw him."

"Pepi! So rude!" Mirth in her admonish, Cheyne shook her head. "Frizzle stick, really. Anyway, I don't think she got a great look at him, just a quick blur same as Talana did, but it could still help, and we still need to find Adonai Alamanni and question him, see if he has an alibi."

"Yeah," Pepi agreed with her. "He's disappeared, like off the map. I'll try to call his family tomorrow as none of his friends I've talked to have seen him."

"Good. Hey, make sure you add to the wall, that Khirbet what-ever-his-name is does keep coming up. Maybe Detective James can run his name and hit on something. I also think we should talk to Finella Finestone and Collie and Holly Eden. They could be suspects, Lareina was pretty spiteful to them."

"Sure, Pepi said with derision, "them and half the town of Corbiestep."

"And beyond too, probably," Cheyne added. She flopped down in a chair. "I'm beat, that's enough for today."

Pepi finished making last notations and set the marker and notepad down.

They stared at the murder wall for a few minutes hoping something would jump out at them.

After ten minutes or so, they gave up.

Cheyne stood up, stretched, yawned. "I gotta go."

Pepi yawned deep and long, closed her eyes tight for a second then blinked. She said, "I'll get Thomas to drive you home."

On the way out, Cheyne said, "Hey, Thomas graduated a couple of years ago. Can you ask him if he still has his yearbook?"

Pepi left Cheyne to gather her backpack and purse then returned. "Thomas will be out in a sec. He says he thinks he still has his yearbook. Needs to dig it up. What're you thinking about?"

Cheyne yawned again. "I don't know. A farfetched thought that maybe we could show the yearbook pics to that barmaid. I'd like to try Nestor too, but he was really peeved at us by time we left."

"Yeah, and vice versa, the pig. However," Pepi said shrewdly, "maybe we could kind of blackmail him. Like say if he doesn't help us we'll tell the police he let Miss Milan drive drunk, and how he offered you, a minor, a drink. It's a stretch but…"

Cheyne smiled through her yawn. "You girl, are devious, you have a detective's mind. I am so proud of you!"

Chapter Twenty-Three

The next day the girls met early at Pepi's house.

As she arrived, Cheyne sniffed the kitchen. "What, bacon and eggs? All I had was some boring blueberry oatmeal. Gee," she said with a doleful hint, "that sure smells good…"

Elma Mae chuckled over at the stove. An open jar of her own canned salsa waited on the counter. The two eggs she flipped sizzled and spat in the bacon grease. "You growing girls, child, always hungry."

"Hey Chey, let's go!" Running into the room, Pepi grabbed Cheyne's arm to take her off to the study.

"You hold on up now," May told her. "Here hon," she handed a plate brimming with bacon, eggs topped with homemade salsa and a biscuit oozing butter to Cheyne. Steam followed the plate from the range to the girl.

"Oh, Gram Elma, thanks so much," Cheyne crowed as Pepi pulled her around the corner.

"Ya'll bring back that dish you hear, don't be leaving it in the study!" Elma Mae called after them.

Pepi had added to the murder wall that Talana had searched Lareina's job, to no avail. There was as expected, no sign of the diary.

"Talana called?" Cheyne asked seeing the addition. She perched on the thick arm of the dark blue divan balancing the plate on her lap.

"Yep. It was a long shot but had to be done. She got her mother to drive her right after we left yesterday. The manager, Mrs. Minchon, told her there were no dressing rooms, just a couple of lockers that were supposed to be emptied every night because they were shared.

"She said Lareina always showed up already dressed in her hostess outfit then shamelessly vamped around, flirting with customers more than she worked. Apparently, she used the job as more of an entertainment than employment. Mrs. Minchon let Talana look around but it was useless," Pepi told her.

Both girls were dressed casually in jeans and summer blouses. Pepi's blouse was light blue, a hairband held back her thick, curly mane, and on her feet were her usual sparkling white sneakers.

Cheyne's long blonde tresses were loose over her shoulders flowing down over a white blouse with a frilly lapel, she wore her favorite cowboy boots.

"So, I thought we'd head out first to the bar-" Pepi started but Cheyne cut her off.

She stood up, a hand to her head, her eyes narrowed she looked like she was trying to remember something. "Wait, I was thinking last night that, there's something..."

"What?"

The sky blue eyes cleared. "I think we need to go back to Talana's and re-search Lareina's room."

Pepi frowned. "But why? I think we did a pretty thorough search. Even the police had given the room the once over for clues to her murder, and they found nothing as well."

Cheyne paced a small circle, her head down. "Yeah, yeah," idly she gathered up her thick yellow hair, piled it on her head, held it for a second then let it tumble back down. "I just think there's more there than meets the eye. It's so grand, kind of baroque in rich detail, heavy, thick-ish, a perfect room to hide things, you know?"

Pepi concentrated on her friend's words. She pictured the large room decorated in bold, dramatic curving forms. Nodding slowly as she tried to visualize each lavish article that was in the room. "I guess I see what you mean, but, I still can't think of anything we didn't check."

"I know, let's go again anyway. Remember the USB drive you *almost* didn't discover?" Cheyne reminded her friend of her important find at the last minute.

They called before they left and Talana was waiting at the door when they arrived. She welcomed them with a sad yet warm smile. "Come on in."

While Talana closed the door, the girls stood in the wide and round white and silver foyer. Under their feet the mosaic tile was so highly polished their shadows bounced off it.

Cheyne caught their reflections in the massive mirror hanging over the entryway table.

She thought to herself, *we're like three jewels, Pepi a cognac quartz, Talana a green emerald, and me, hmmm, what am I? Aquamarine, an aquamarine crystal? No,* she laughed, *aquamarine diamond, yeah, that's me! Na, more like a soft blue pearl* she laughed out loud at her fanciful silliness.

The other two looked at her in question at her private hilarity.

"What?" Pepi asked.

Cheyne grinned and shook her head. They'd think she was nuts if she told them her fancy thoughts. She looked around at the cultured setting.

Silver lamps and a silver bowl decorated the lace-wood sideboard. She breathed deeply of the strong yet pleasing, mildly sweet fragrance of lilacs.

On a marble table in the center of the room sat a bouquet of colorful flower shot with shades of a purple constellation. A few lavender florets lay like splotches of acrylic paint on the marble table. Loosened by the breeze from the open door, one furled and twirled delicately to the floor.

A canoe-shaped window frame arched outlining the big double doors, letting in little squares of light that replicated like dominoes on the glossy floor.

Pepi leaned an arm on one of the two wing-backed chairs that bookended the massive mirror and sideboard. She admired the stained-glass chandelier twinkling over the fresh lilacs. "That's so pretty, sparkly, Talana. Must be wretched to clean."

"Pepi," Cheyne shook her head, sighing dolefully, "Leave it to you to take the magic out of the cut glass beauty."

Talana chuckled. "So, do you want to go straight to Lareina's room?" She asked.

"Yeah. I have a hunch. We're really sorry to bother you like this, Talana," Cheyne said. Her head cocked to the side, sympathy wreathed her features from her heartfelt smile to the benevolent blue eyes.

"Come on, let's go. Follow me," Talana said.

The trio crossed the wide gleaming foyer to the stairs three pairs of shoes clacking, echoing behind them.

Talana jogged up the long winding staircase, down the hall and to her sister's room, Pepi and Cheyne at her heels.

Talana opened the door then turned to face the older girls. She held onto the doorknob, leaned back against the open door.

"Listen," she said, "it's never, ever a bother. I just can't believe how fabulous you guys are for going to all this trouble for my sister, and I want to do all I can too, to help. So, what first?"

The three girls moved slowly into the vainglorious chamber. They stood scanning the room, touching on every single grandiose item.

Silver backed hand mirror, comb and brush engraved with Lareina's initials still lay on top of the dresser. Pots and pots of make-up and utensils covered the vanity.

The maids normally straightened up after Lareina had dressed for the day, picking up the carelessly tossed garments she tried on but decided not to wear, placing shoes back on their shelves, and putting lids back on and neatening the makeup.

They put away the blow dryer and all the hair products the lazy careless girl had used that day to get ready, dropping them wherever she finished with them.

Pepi watched Cheyne standing undecided so she moved to the walk-in closet to check it again.

Talana wasn't sure what to do so she followed Pepi.

Cheyne stood in the same spot, her eyes like a clock's hands going from bed to dresser to table to settee to desk and back around again and again.

When she was falling asleep last night something had drifted hazily into her dreams. Now, something pulled her eyes to one of the lamps on the bedside table.

She moved towards it feeling a little foolish, but yet... she could hear Pepi and Talana's chatting murmurs in the walk-in closet across the room, sliding hangers squeaking, boxes moved and stacked, drawers opened and closed.

Standing beside the table, Cheyne gently touched the luxuriously painted lamp, drawing her fingers up the side and along the cold bronze arms that held the frosted glass dome.

Drops of cut glass with a purple tint dangled around the dome atop a painted vase, she touched a few watching them dance the diamond dance.

She trailed her hand back down to the base. It was made of thick marble. She wrapped both hands around the base and tried to lift up the lamp. "Wow, that is heavy," she muttered.

The lamp didn't appear to be soldered to the base, it wiggled slightly, a barely perceptive movement, Cheyne almost didn't detect it.

Holding the base with one hand, she grasped the vase part with the other and twisted. It moved.

"Oh my goodness-" quelling the excited tremors in her hands, she rotated it again and again until the vase came off the base. She set the painted vase and frosted globe with its jangling purple glass bangles on the bed and peered inside the marble base. *Oh yeah-*

"Guys! Come here!"

She didn't have to call twice.

Pepi and Talana could hear the thrill in Cheyne's voice. They dropped what they were doing and hurried out.

Cheyne held the big fat, red diary up in one hand. The girls ran over, squealing.

"How the heck did you-" Pepi saw the lamp on the bed. "Wow, aren't you the clever one!" She slapped her friend on the back.

"I just kept picturing Lareina in this room," Cheyne explained. "Like we discussed, she wouldn't put this book someplace someone could come across it. And when you write in a diary it's usually at the end of the day, sometimes people write while in bed, recording their last thoughts before they go to sleep.

"And Talana said she had seen Lareina writing in it while in bed so it had to be nearby where she could hide it easily and drift off into dreamland. I remembered these huge lamps, they kept floating in the back of my brain."

"Well, you done good, me friend," Pepi teased.

"Let's freakin' read it!" Talana yelped in uncharacteristic, unrefined glee.

Chapter Twenty-Four

Pepi carefully moved the lamp globe, vase and base off the bed to a chair.

The three girls kicked off their shoes, plumped up pillows against the headboard and settled back together for story time.

They took turns reading out loud, skipping some, paraphrasing much, starting at this past year.

Pepi read first. She glossed over the very personal parts and the boring stuff. Lareina wrote so much about the splendor of herself and how beautiful and superior she was to everyone else Pepi skipped most of the self-adoration parts too.

After a while, it was Talana's turn. Only a few pages in she shrieked, appalled.

"Holy cow! Holding the book, Talana dropped her hands in her lap. "I had no idea the life my sister was leading! This is sordid; our parents would just die! We can't let them read this."

"Not to worry," Pepi assured her, taking the book again, "as soon as we're done we're taking it to the police." She skimmed some pages.

"Listen to this, she writes a lot of poetry in the margins, rhyming romance. In the beginning she wrote about Adonai and then she moves onto a different guy. You'll recognize this, listen, 'I am lovin' and livin' for my hunk of Devin heaven.'"

"Are you serious? That's that blond guy that Miss Milan had the date with!" Cheyne practically shouted.

"Oh yeah, the plot is thickening as we speak. I'm even more sure here's a connection between Miss Milan and Lareina," Pepi said, her eyes flew back and forth like a keyboard over the pages.

"She doesn't say how or when they met, or even if they ever went out, only that she gets peeved because he ignores her and blows her off. She only writes a small bit about his hunky body, she says his accent makes her swoon."

Pepi slid a low side glance at Cheyne. Those weren't exactly the words Lareina had written, but Pepi was embarrassed herself over what Lareina wrote, she didn't want to embarrass Talana any more than she already was.

"Anyway, I'll pick up where Lareina wrote how she was growing bored of Adonai." Pepi paraphrased, "She was growing bored of everything, the pageant, her job, her friends, everyone and everything, but she was excited to be seen at parade.

"After all, she is the most beautiful woman in the town, probably the whole state and everyone should have the opportunity to get a glimpse of her. Still, she was even getting bored with the pageant crap. Her word, not mine.

"So one day on the way to Iceplant Inlet for a boat ride with yet another unnamed date, she stopped in a store to check out some celebrity magazines. It was like a drug store but without a pharmacy, like a bodega sort of, I think. Attached to the back of the store was a warehouse. You hear that, Chey? Warehouse."

Pepi leaned over Talana to high-five Cheyne. "Anyway, no one was in the front store. The staff must have been back in the warehouse. Lareina looked around and decided to purloin some makeup. Purloin?"

"Purloin?" Talana asked.

"Steal." Cheyne told her.

Pepi muttered, "Why didn't she just say ste-"

Cheyne said, "Never mind, Pepi, sometimes people call things odd names to kinda distance themselves from admitting they committed a crime or did something wrong. Go on. What happened next?"

Talana took the book from Pepi and read about how Lareina had dropped makeup in her purse as fast as she could. The fear of getting caught and the thrill of committing the act pumped adrenalin fueled tingles up her spine.

If there'd been a camera, it would have recorded her model's face in villainous delight. Then, she heard the rumble of voices coming from the back, and the hairs on the back of her neck stood up.

Realizing it didn't sound like they were coming up front, she snuck around, hid behind the wall and eavesdropped.

Several male voices talked over each other, about a plan, a scheme. Stunned, she couldn't believe her ears.

Someone was planning on murdering half a town of people! Her town! Corbiestep! She had grabbed her purse stuffed with stolen merchandise and fled.

Talana sighed heavily, set the book in her lap. She lowered her head, the vibrant hair swayed back and forth as she slowly shook her head.

Resting her head back against the pillow, she pulled a crumpled tissue out of her pocket and dabbed at her eyes. "I knew Lareina wasn't the best shining star in the land, but I had no idea she had a soul of coal. Here," she handed the book to Pepi, "I can't, you read."

Cheyne patted Talana's shoulder. "Honey, you don't have to hear all this, we can-"

"No, no, go ahead. I have to hear it all, I just don't want the words coming out of my mouth and etching onto my heart. Go ahead."

So Pepi read again, continuing to paraphrase Lareina's words. She flipped a page back and forth looking to where Talana had left off.

"So, uh, where did you stop..." she ran a finger down a page.

"Oh, here. So the next day, Lareina returned to the store and hung around until the person she thought was the supervisor, the blond guy, was there alone.

She made it clear she was interested in him. She worked him until he asked her out. Unfortunately, he only saw her a few times, then he made dates but put her off. She grew annoyed with her tiresome blond hunk."

"There's Devin," Cheyne proclaimed, very sure.

"Sounds like." Pepi continued, "A week or so passes and Lareina is back at the store when she finds out Devin wasn't the supervisor after all, this other, older, hawkish looking man was.

"Lareina wrote that she found him sexy in an older, swarthy, dangerous kind of way. She let him know she was attracted right away, and hinted she knew a secret about him and others at the warehouse. She made several exclamation points-"

Pepi cleared her throat and went on, "She wrote she uh, felt electrified when with him. He took her back to his place where they made wild passion-"

"Uh, Pep," Cheyne warned, directing her flashing gaze at the younger Talana who lay sideways curled against the pillow, an arm under her head.

Pepi cleared her throat again. "Um, yeah, so anyway after he fell asleep, she slipped out of the bedroom and read his computer entries. Not expecting to be bringing someone to his apartment that day, he had left it on in the other room.

"Well, actually, the laptop was closed and in a hutched desk, but it's not Lareina's fault when she nosed around and opened the hutch, then opened the laptop and it came right on when she pushed enter."

"Sure, nothing was ever her fault," Talana put in wryly.

Pepi shot her a surprised look. Cheyne's eyebrows rose.

Talana never spoke ill of her mean older sister. The sarcasm was so not like the sweet as a kitten young teen.

"Uh, let me see where was I…" Pepi searched until she found her place. "Lareina noted the information she read about killing off a bunch of residents in her town matched what she'd overheard at the warehouse. Wow-"

Pepi stopped, her mouth dropped open. "Wait 'til you hear this part- Lareina had written in bold letters, '**OMG It's the same information about how they planned to wipe out this town that I had read on someone *else's* computer!**'"

Pepi read the next page before saying out loud, "She hadn't told anyone about this other intrusion of privacy of the other person's computer whom she doesn't name, nor of the knowledge of this planned devastation because she was curious to see the outcome. Remember, she was bored, bored, bored with life."

"What the- was she dreaming?" Brows furrowing, Cheyne shook her head trying to lean over Talana to peek at the book. "I can't believe she would have learned information that the entire town was in danger and she wouldn't tell anyone because she wanted to see what the outcome would be?"

Wiping at a falling tear, Talana mumbled morosely, "I knew my sister wasn't a nice person, but her diary makes her sound like a- a sociopath. I can't believe what I'm hearing."

Pepi took a deep breath and read on, paraphrasing, "She continued her affair for a couple of weeks. Then, she decided she could get something out of the information she'd come across. So she told her lover, K, here she wrote his initial, but I don't think she ever entered his full name in her notes. She told him what she'd heard and read, and that she thought it was worth some money to keep quiet about it."

"Oh my gosh, my sister was a freaking blackmailer!" Talana blurted, flabbergasted at what she was hearing. "How foolish! She could have been hurt-"

Cheyne and Pepi looked at her.

"Oh," her mutter filled with dismay. Crossing her ankles, she folded her hands together then set them primly in her lap. "Go on."

Her head bowed to the book, Pepi read, "K told her he felt she could be trusted to keep his secret and that he would make it worth her while. Lareina was ecstatic! Her new life was exhilarating – perilous and daring- hot and romantic- and financially promising."

More tears escaped down Talana's cheeks, Cheyne's lips pulled in tight.

Pepi, said, "She decided she was quite good at this espionage stuff. She was a cunning seductress! She could leech cataclysmic secrets from men, hold countries ransom, have the whole world at her feet!" Pepi rolled her eyes with a huff of incredulity.

"She would become rich, and powerful, maybe she'd become a full-fledged spy! Of course she would sell her pillow talk, extracted information to whoever the highest bidder would be!"

Shocked, wide-eyed, Cheyne exclaimed, "Wow, that girl was insane. What an incredible ego and imagination." She turned to the teen beside her. "No offense, Talana."

"None taken. You speak the truth," the young girl responded sadly.

"Anyway," Cheyne shifted her attention back to Pepi, "the K guy might be our Khirbet."

"No doubt," Pepi concluded. Then she sucked in a deep breath and wet her drying lips with her tongue. She flipped through several pages skimming them quickly.

"The last pages of the book were just more about her beloved rogue and her fantastic ruse. On the last page she wrote that she planned to hook up with her paramour after the parade.

"She described her dress and her hair, she wanted it swept up in a high bun then part of it to come down and swirl in one big curl over one shoulder. Kinda like yours was, Chey." She cut a glance at her friend.

"Further on, she maligns a few of the other participants in the pageant, including us," her lip curled at Cheyne who shrugged.

"The last few lines, she wrote how angry she was that no one had offered to drive her to the event. Already running late, she would need to call a taxi in a minute. '*Then I hear the knob turn in the front door, who could that be?*'- *it* ends there."

Pepi closed the book, the silence was like an uneasy balloon filling the room.

After a disquieting few minutes, Cheyne said, "Gee. I am just, just, I just don't know what to think." She grabbed fistfuls of hair and rubbed them against her head then let the hair drop in a messy halo around her shoulders.

Her palms turned up, she said ruefully, "I mean, I hate to say people do bad things, but then again we're kinda hypocrites."

Pepi's face twinged in bewilderment. "Huh? What'd we do?"

The three girls lay back against the pillows sinking in the downy marshmallows.

Cheyne waved a hand in the air. "Well, we planned on basically blackmailing Nestor into giving us information when we know he doesn't want anything to do with us."

A snort came from Pepi's side of the fluffy king-sized bed.

"Come on, Chey, we're using our powers for good instead of evil. We're not hurting anyone, we're just trying to clear Miss Milan's name and find her and Lareina's killer. It's not actually blackmail. Besides, Nestor's a foul piece of work." She set the diary on the table next to the bed.

Cheyne leaned forward looking around Talana at Pepi.

Talana laid back with her eyes closed, tears shimmered in the corners, the thick hair like a red hoodie pooled around her head.

"I see, Pep," Cheyne said with a shade of sarcasm, "so basically it's the ends justify the means, or you're saying it's okay to do something wrong if your intent is for good. You're usually the one who's the big uncompromising stickler for the honest-"

Pepi sat up looking around Talana at her friend like they were in a 3-seater on a plane and Talana was in the middle seat.

"That's not fair, Chey, we agreed to do this. We're not breaking the law or hurting someone. We're not profiting from our so called blackmail, or using it for harm. Besides, we could have turned his gnarly butt in, in the first place for letting Miss Milan leave and drive intoxicated. Hitting on juveniles. If anything, it would hurt his job if we told." She crossed her arms and flopped huffily back against the pillows.

"Pep, I'm not saying we're really doing anything wrong, I was just pointing out-"

"Uh huh," Pepi cut her off. "You're trying to play the honorable card. That makes me feel like-"

"Oh, you're being silly. Move over Talana." Cheyne crawled over the younger girl to sit beside her friend. She wrapped an arm around Pepi and squeezed, ignoring Pepi's struggle to move away from her.

"Jeepers, don't get so serious, girl, I was just busting your chops. Gee you're sensitive, a couple of little pokes at your integrity and you just fall apart." She squeezed the girl harder knowing she hated to be hugged.

In retaliation, Pepi grabbed her pillow from behind her head and put it over Cheyne's face pretending to smother her.

Cheyne kicked and swatted and giggled until she got out from under then grabbed up her own pillow and started bashing Pepi with it, who of course slammed her back.

Not to be left out, Talana joked, "Thank goodness we're not in the kitchen with food-" then she joined the melee with her own pillow, bashing one then the other.

Soon, they were all jumping and shrieking and laughing, hair and feathers flying, bedsprings squeaking- having the biggest pillow fight the billowing canopy overhead had ever seen, it threatened to tumble down on them.

Chapter Twenty-Five

At the crack of dawn, Cheyne gobbled down a frozen waffle and an OJ, zipped through her chores then rushed out the door. She'd learned Finella Finestone had a part time job at an exclusive shop in the city.

She locked her bike a few shops down from the store, Ubersphere. Strolling along the sidewalk, she window shopped until she was standing in front of Ubersphere.

Cheyne stood, pretending to be transfixed on a dress in the window. She hung around until she was sure they'd noticed her from inside, then she went through the door.

It was a typical upscale boutique on the rifled through a few clothes on a rack against the wall, then wandered back to the dress in the window.

"Cheyne Somerset, hey girl, how're you doing?"

Cheyne swung around pretending surprise. "Oh, hi Finella. You shopping today?" She took in the sophisticated girl standing in front of her.

The gamine, humiliated girl that Lareina Wittgenstein had so ruthlessly slapped and pushed to the ground that day in the salon had suddenly turned into a cultivated, self-assured young woman.

"Wow," Cheyne gushed sincerely. "Finella, you look fabulous!"

Finella ducked her head a bit coyly and smiled. "Thank you. I've been working here for 10 months now, since last summer, and I've learned so much." She was a few years older than Cheyne, closer to Lareina's age.

She was a tall, willowy brunette with blunt cut bangs over brown eyes. Her gleaming hair flowed neatly like it had been ironed straight down her back. She was wearing a precisely tailored outfit from the store that fit perfectly. Very vogue.

"Oh? You work here? How wonderful," Cheyne said smoothly, as if she didn't know. "Do you get a discount?"

Finella nodded, red lips curved up in a pleased smile. "Of course. I started in sales and now I'm training to be a buyer. I'm beyond ecstatic. I've always been interested in fashion. Hanging around with top stylists really helps change oneself." The two made small talk for a few minutes.

"So, I noticed you were interested in the dress in the window?" Finella moved Cheyne towards the front window display.

"Yeah, it's so pretty, I don't have anything in that orangey red color. So, were you so devastated when you heard about Lareina?" Cheyne casually asked.

Finella looked at the tag on the dress in the window. "Not your size. I think we have one in the back in your smaller size."

One slender shoulder bumped up as she answered Cheyne's question. "Sure, I was so freaked when I came back from London. I was so lucky to be chosen to go on a buying trip for the shop to Europe." Her eyes drifted to the side as she recalled the dreadful day.

"I happily missed the parade. We left two days before you know, and I had to get a tutor for the short time I missed school. It was such a shock when I returned to hear about Lareina, shocked, just shocked." The brown eyes reflected the shock, but there were no sympathy tears.

Since the girl was out of the country the time of the murder, Cheyne made a mental note and crossed Finella off their suspect list. "What about that amazing blouse over there?" She spent an hour trying on clothes.

Meanwhile, Pepi looked up Collie and Holly Eden. She tracked them down at a teen music camp.

Freckles multiplying from the sun, like two nut covered orange sorbets they were happy to see Pepi. They didn't think to question what she was dong there. They babbled over each other telling Pepi about the camp.

The site was a soothing Mediterranean design of blues and greens. Refreshing ponds fanned by waving broad-leafed green plants were encircled by rambling winding trails to meditate and reflect.

The twins were at an outside patio eating mixed quinoa salad and yogurt with fruit, the sporadic breeze teasing their springy carrot-colored hair.

The sisters came from a wealthy family. They had been very sad and stunned to hear about Lareina's demise. As fundamental Baptists, they had forgiven Lareina every time she was belittling or vindictive to them.

They proudly showed Pepi a pamphlet describing the time they had been at the camp singing, along with a photo of Holly playing the guitar and Collie hammering the drums. Their names were even on the schedule of events, they had been coming there for years on the weekends.

They had been at the retreat, then returned to town with their folks the morning of the parade. Their mother had never left the twins' side, she was even a chaperone on their float. They left right after to return to the camp.

Pepi could see they were a dead end as viable suspects in Lareina's murder, the camp was a strong alibi. She accepted an ice cream and hung around to hear them sing, they actually weren't too bad. After an hour or so she left to call Cheyne.

Thomas provided his yearbook the next day. Built like a vertical railing, Thomas was in his fourth year of college on a basketball scholarship.

"Gram says you guys are investigating a murder, who do you think you are, Sherlock Holmes?" He handed the book to his sister.

"More like Nancy Drew." Pepi took the book. "Thanks, appreciate it."

"I'm kinda partial to Agatha Christie's Miss Marple, or Angela Lansbury in Murder She Wrote," Cheyne piped in.

"Who?" Pepi and Thomas said in unison.

"Never mind. You don't watch the old channels, PBS, Hallmark and stuff." Cheyne exaggerated her exasperation with rolled eyes and a sigh. "I forget your family is more physical than cerebral."

"Okay, Miss Intellectual- who's the gym-rat gymnast in this duo?" Pepi retorted with an elbow jab and sidelong smirk.

"Just 'cause you like to be all feminine and prissy on the outside," Pepi teased, "but an insane acrobat on the inside, and I'm a sporty the tomboy on the inside trying to be more girly on the outside, or at least a little more polished."

"Come on, Peps, you know I was only joking!"

"Uh huh. Besides, that crack about my family's intelligence, you know Gram never lets anyone forget she has her Master's in Biometrics."

"Joking," Cheyne repeated. Grinning, she flipped Pepi's hair. "It is *so* easy to get your goat."

"Whatever. Girls." Thomas rolled his eyes, leaving the room, the teeny curls on top of his short-cut afro almost brushing the door frame he was so tall.

Pepi wore a blue shirt that made her grey eyes tint silver blue. Her athletic legs were encased in black jeans and she wore black booties. She tied her hair back in two long plaits with two blue barrettes high on the sides of her head to keep it neat.

Cheyne was flowery in a summer dress, the cowboy boots made her look country. Her loose hair flowed gaily around her shoulders.

"All right, let's go to the hotel," Pepi said. "I called Nestor and told him we're coming. I didn't give him an opportunity to say no. And," she put the yearbook in a backpack. "You'll be pleased to know that I didn't blackmail him. I don't think I needed to, I think he knew he'd stepped over the line a few times and it could come back to bite him."

"Good. I feel cleaner about going there now," Cheyne remarked, following her friend out the door.

"I keep telling you, stinky, that you need a bath!" Pepi joked. She ducked when Cheyne feigned throwing a punch at her, yelping, "You know what I mean, you banana head!"

They decided to make a quick stop on the way to the hotel.

Cheyne called Chalessa Chung and asked if they could stop by and see her for a second.

Conveniently, Chalessa told her she was with Frieda Mills getting mani-pedi's. So the duo hopped on their bikes and rode over to the salon. Thankfully it was only a ten minute ride away.

"No thanks," Cheyne said to the receptionist when she went to get up to service the girls. "We'll only be here for a minute."

They spotted Chalessa and Frieda immediately.

The pair were sitting side by side with their feet in tubs of hot swirling water. No one was working on them yet, so the girls went over and Cheyne sat in the empty seat next to Chalessa and Pepi sat next to Frieda.

Cheyne showed her pictures from the USB to Chalessa asking if she recognized anyone in the photos. Chalessa shook her head at every one. Disappointed, Cheyne passed them to Frieda who, between yawns and chugs of cola did the same thing.

"What's this about?" Chalessa asked.

"Oh, um, we're doing a story for the Newsnotes. You can read the article next month when it comes out," Cheyne answered.

Before Chalessa could ask any more questions, Cheyne and Pepi jumped up, bid adieu quickly and hurried out the door.

They were back out on the street in less time it took them to them to get there. Pepi said, "Quick thinking, Chey, about the school paper. Heaven knows we don't want anyone to be onto what we're really up to. But still, it didn't get us anywhere."

"Oh well, we had to try." Cheyne sighed, putting on her helmet. "An investigation is a step-by-step process. We'll get there."

Pepi snorted, "Yeah, it can't be too easy you know or the police would have figured it out by now."

They laughed, hopped on their bikes and headed down the rustic, tree crowded street.

In the latter half of spring in Northern California, the days were moving from sharp nippiness with sometimes still blustery winds to more languid summer warmth.

Just the tops of the tallest firs swayed in the slight wind, everything else was still.

If they had stopped for a moment and listened they would have heard the sounds of nature; small animals rustling in the growing grass, flap of wings soaring in the garden-fresh air, even the woodpecker deep in the forest pecking insects rat-a-tat-tat out of the timber.

The congestion of trees thinned when they reached the city. As the wide country road turned onto a four-lane boulevard, and as the cars increased in number and speed, the girls moved to the sidewalk.

Forty minutes later, they reached the hotel, locked the bikes, left the warm sunny outdoors and entered the cool, fluorescent-lit establishment.

They quickly bypassed the typical hotel lobby arranged with groupings of easy chairs in sturdy green and orange fuzzy fabric and glass covered tables atop sound absorbing green carpet.

Desks with computers pocketed in corners, and stands filled with pamphlets advertising the wonderful adventures and sights to see in Corbiestep lined a wall.

Although the desk attendants in their navy blue and gold uniforms were busy checking in several families the girls didn't want to be seen going into the lounge.

They got blocked at the far side of the lobby.

A bride-to-be and her family were pushing and pulling one of those luggage trollies jam-packed with a tower of haphazardly stacked suitcases and at least a dozen garment bags containing wedding attire swinging from the horizontal bar.

The girls waited out of the way while the bridezilla ordered and directed and cursed, cried and screamed at her entourage as they bumped the cart from one wall to another.

They watched the fretful bride and frazzled family finally crowd into two elevators, they could still hear the bride whining and complaining as the doors closed.

Cheyne said drolly, "My ears are scratching from the inside, makes me want to elope."

"I'll avoid the entire debacle and skip the whole marriage thing," Pepi said.

Cheyne gently touched her friend's arm and lowered her voice. "I know how traumatic and wretched your childhood was until you were rescued you from that place. And the dark, dark days you still suffer through when you can't- never mind," she patted Pepi's arm.

"But girl, you'll change your mind when the right guy is asking you to share the rest of his life with you and raise your kidlets. A guy not like your father that um, anyway, maybe even you and Karey…"

Pepi shook her head, cinnamon plaits bounced down her back. "Nope. I told you, I have plans, the Air Force-"

Cheyne gave her friend a tender shove. "Oh yeah sure, you forget I've seen the way you two besotted lovebirds look at each other. He can hardly keep his hands off-"

"*Oh kay*, let's go, quit yammerin'-" Pepi yanked the backpack over one shoulder and moved purposefully down the hall ignoring her chuckling friend behind her.

"Hey," Cheyne called out.

"What?" Pepi tossed over her shoulder.

"I am proud of your word 'debacle.' Where'd you pick that up?"

"Movie. It was called, "Who killed the bride?" Pepi replied.

"Really?" Cheyne asked, intrigued.

"Nah, just funnin' ya. Who's the easy one now? Ha!" Pepi stopped. "Here's the bar."

She straightened her shoulders and lips, let her eyelids drift down a bit staunching her nerve, then raised them. Eyes focused straight ahead, Pepi raised her chin. Fearlessly, she pushed the door open.

Chapter Twenty-Six

Nestor was standing behind the bar filling the maraschino cherries. He looked up when the door opened and sighed loudly in exasperation.

"You girls," Nestor complained. "I never should have let you in, in the first place. You're gonna be nothing but trouble." But while complaining, he let them sit at a table and pulled out a chair to join them.

Pepi looked at the bartender through slit eyes. Her voice harsh, she accused, "You've made your own trouble, Mr. Ramonez."

A bit softer, Cheyne said, "We're just trying to do the right thing, Nestor." She set a smooth pale hand on his tanned forearm. The pastel nails were covered by his arm hair like pink ladybugs in tall tawny grass.

His gaze went to her small hand, then up to her big blue eyes before shifting to the glossy pink bowed lips slightly curved up. His jaw loosened, a snide smile tugged at a corner of his mouth.

"Yeah, me too. I'd like to do the right thing too..." The smile turned lewd. Just as he went to cover her hand with his, she pulled hers away to reach for the backpack Pepi dropped on the chair between them. Both girls reached for the backpack at the same time.

Pepi grabbed it first and opened it.

"Well Mr. Ramonez, that's great!" Pepi crowed, merrily pulling out the yearbook and setting it on the table. She pushed it in front of Cheyne then took out the notebook and a pen. "Then you can do the right thing and help us."

The bartender jumped slightly, jerked his head at Pepi then at Cheyne, then he held his head still and his eyes darted back and forth. He just wasn't sure what to do or say. His sweating palms on his knees, he resisted the urge to grip them. No way was he gonna let a couple of teenyboppers discombobulate him!

"Here," Cheyne opened the book and looked up seriously at him. "We'd like you to look through this book and see if you recognize any of the young men in it, see if any of them could be one of the young men that spoke with the foreigners at the bar the night Miss Milan was there."

"Anything for you, Blondie. And you can call me Nestor." The bravado back, he set a hairy knobby hand on her thigh and gave it a squeeze with smarmy smile.

Surprised, Cheyne's creamy complexion turned pink.

Pepi went to stand up, objecting, "Mr. Ramonez-"

The bartender grudgingly removed his hand. He smoothed back his ratty blond hair, patting it right on the top where it was the thinnest.

Rattled, Cheyne resisted the urge to brush off her leg where he'd touched her and go wash her hands. It was all she could do not to shove her chair away from his. Regrettably, they needed his cooperation, they had to tread lightly.

Discreetly pulling her skirt down as far as it would go, Cheyne tried to motion to Pepi with her eyes to take it easy, she could see the ire and fire sparking in her friend's opalescent eyes.

"All right, all right, calm down little brown sugar." Nestor gestured with his hands for Pepi to sit back down.

All that did was ignite the fire in the teen. She stood up moving closer to him, fingers tightening into fists. The plaits swung forward lining her chest like fat braided suspenders.

The look on her face made the tall bartender wilt from the angry petite girl. "Okay, okay, sorry about the brown sugar comment. Let's just get down to business, all right?"

Pepi fumed, about to explode.

Cheyne brushed her fingers through her long hair, the action caught Pepi's attention as it was designed to.

Though Cheyne's expression appeared blank as vanilla ice cream, no one else could see the unspoken words between the girls.

Exhaling long and loud, Pepi returned to her seat. She yanked the chair, scraping the legs across the floor then in contrast to her angry aggressive body language, she settled herself back down with delicate ladylike comportment.

"There then," Cheyne pronounced cheerfully, turning a page in the yearbook. "Mr. Ramonez, Nestor," his name sounding sensual from her glossy lips, one shoulder drew up coquettishly. "If you could please…"

Nestor eyed Pepi nervously. The girls were playing something like good cop- bad cop, the enchantress and the enforcer; it was throwing him off-balance.

He dropped his head to the book, uncertainty showing in his unsteady hands, he turned the page.

The table was tensely quiet as Nestor flipped each page, scanned it carefully then on to the next. The long scraggly hair covered his narrow face.

Cheyne itched to push it out of the way but no way was she touching the greasy strings. She kept her own hands clasped tightly in her lap.

He was well past halfway when he pointed at a photo. "This was one of the college boys, I think. I mean he might be a year or two older now."

Both girls leaned in to get a view of the picture of Black teen standing with the rest of his basketball team. They both shook their heads. "He doesn't look familiar to me," Pepi said, her bottom lip pushed out.

"Me neither," Cheyne stated.

Pepi drew a circle around the boy with a pencil and made a notation in her notebook, his name was Gary Gunther.

Another ten pages and ten minutes later Nestor pointed out a second young man.

Pablo Gomez had been one grade below Gunther. This boy was shorter, Mexican by his looks, name, and the Mexican flag on his t-shirt. His hair was buzzed short, his shoulders deliberately caved inwards.

He scowled out from the photo like he wasn't happy about his picture being taken. He was standing next to an American flag on a stand. The end of the flag was wrapped around his hand and clenched tightly in his fist.

"Huh. That's peculiar. I hate to say it, but he looks like a white supremacist even though he's obviously Hispanic. See the tattoos- the 88- that's a gang sign for Hitler. Wait, I recognize Gomez' pants, they're ROTC." Pepi frowned at the picture, studying every detail. "I don't know this guy either."

"Me neither." Cheyne was disappointed. She was so sure, she had such a feeling that she would know the men. Nothing she could explain, just a goosey feeling.

Pepi circled the picture, stuck the tip of her tongue out the side of her mouth as she noted the name and page number and all incidental information regarding him on the page.

Holding the pencil, she rested her hand on the open notebook. "Doesn't matter that we don't know them, the police will check it all out." She straightened her arm, tapped the table in front of Nestor. "Keep going. You said there were three."

"*Yes Ma'am.*" Nestor sighed heavily and started scanning the next page of pictures.

Pepi waited, pencil poised over notebook, she watched Nestor as he searched through the pages. Pepi watched his eyes go up and down and back and forth, she wanted to make sure he didn't miss a picture.

He must be getting weary, that might make him lazy and skip pictures. Her hand rested on her thigh, her heel jiggled up and down impatiently.

Cheyne sat quietly, cool as a winter breeze. Hands clasped in her lap, her gaze drifted around the bar.

Other than an elderly threesome of two men and a woman way in the corner gabbing over martinis, they were the only other inhabitants.

She watched people stroll past the window in the closed door. Young, old, some talking, some with their heads engrossed in file folders, maps, or sights to see pamphlets, children skipped by.

Stifling a yawn, she asked for something to drink. "Nestor, do you think we could have some water or a soda or-"

"There. There's the third guy. I'm pretty sure, like 80- no 90% sure. I think. Yeah, that's him." He nodded emphatically, stabbing a knobby finger at a picture.

The girls leaned in, the three heads lowered together to the book, then Nestor leaned back.

The girls slowly raised their heads. Eyes as wide as saucers, they blinked at each other.

"No way," Pepi said.

They lowered their heads again, not believing what they saw. Cheyne's face turned ashen.

Pepi sucked her lips in, shaking her head. "No way."

Gulping, Cheyne nodded. "Yeah. That's his name. It's him. Oh my gosh." She couldn't believe it.

"What? Who?" Nestor butted in. "You know this guy?"

The girls gaped at each other, they ignored Nestor.

With slow, deliberate motion, Pepi circled the photo with her pencil. Uncertainty huge in her eyes she said to Cheyne. "You write his name in the notebook. I don't think I can." She handed the pencil to Cheyne, then dropped her hands in her lap like they'd lost all feeling.

"It can't be a coincidence," Cheyne murmured. She wrote slowly. Pepi stared at the picture shaking her head in disbelief. Her knee stopped jiggling.

Nestor sat between them, watching. A line of perplexity drew between his brown. The girls were obviously distressed, but he held his tongue. Peering sideways at Pepi, he wiped a hand across his upper lip then scratched the soul patch. Just a damned teenager and she scared the crap out of him.

He sidled a look over to Cheyne. Her disconcerted face wrinkled in confusion stared at her friend, then they both looked back down at the picture.

Nestor slid his veiled gaze from the top of Cheyne's blonde head, over her china clear skin like Snow freakin' White, and down over her young curves. He licked his lips, swallowed, the knotted Adam's apple bobbed.

He could feel a steely glare burning through the side of his head. He knew without looking it was that little firecracker Pepi glaring at him. He tweaked his nose guiltily, wiped at it then pinched it with his finger and thumb and swallowed hard again.

Sucking in his lower lip, he said, "So, uh, you gonna clue me in? You wouldn't know nuthin' if it weren't for me you know."

They ignored him.

"Hey," he said, "lookit this, most of the stuff the students write around the pictures, you know, like, 'Good Luck, Buddy', or 'Gonna miss you, see you-' junk like that. Ha," he chortled rubbing the sparse blond patch under his lower lip.

"This is stupid, listen," his eyes shifted side to side to see if he got the girls' attention. Cheyne was writing and Pepi was watching her write.

"*Anyways*…it's goofy, makes no sense. It says, 'Don't catch the flu, Bro- ha ha, see ya at the Fact.' It's signed, Pablo." Nestor's empty laugh sounded doltish in his ears, the girls ignored him like he had dissipated into a noxious gas and wafted out of the room.

"The Fact could be some kind of bar, or maybe a frat house, ya know?" He was invisible to the girls. Bristling, he stopped talking and resumed his lustful perusal of Cheyne.

He tipped his head sideways, letting the scraggly hair hide his face so Pepi couldn't see where he was looking.

Unaware of the bartender's lascivious study of her, Cheyne was writing in their notebook. She included the information Nestor had just added, then set the pencil down and looked at her friend for affirmation.

Pepi nodded with a short jerk, the plaits hopped.

Cheyne regarded Nestor coolly. "His name is Talco Castilla. He's the murdered girl's brother."

His brows shot up. "You mean that beauty pageant girl that was killed on the parade float? I thought this was about the schoolteacher-"

Pepi slammed the yearbook shut, Nestor yanked his hand out of the way just in time. She snatched up the book, shoved it in the backpack.

Cheyne handed her the pencil and notebook and Pepi tossed them in after the yearbook. The girls stood up, Pepi pulled the backpack over one shoulder.

Nestor sat bewildered as they stalked out the door. "You're welcome-" he called at the swinging door.

Chapter Twenty-Seven

Dazed, shaken, and abjectly confused, the girls rode back to Pepi's house.

They passed through the empty house and went straight to the study.

Dropping her backpack on the floor, Pepi flopped on the couch, kicked off her booties and slouched down on her back in the cushions, her legs stretched out in front of her.

Cheyne paced in front of her.

"Stop it, Chey, you're making me dizzy, it's like watching a tennis match," Pepi groused.

"I can't help it. I can't believe it. This news is sending shock waves through my body. I can't sit still. I don't know what to think, my brain is spinning. We shouldn't have told Nestor who it was." Cheyne rubbed her arms as if she had the chills.

"Doesn't matter. He was looking at the yearbook and reading quips that people had added. Lareina had written a note to my brother, she had signed it Lareina Castilla Wittgenstein.

"It would have hit him at some point, today, tomorrow, some day. He's a jerk, but he's street smart and things don't get past him for long." Pepi yawned watching Cheyne pace past her.

Cheyne removed a folder from the backpack then strode over to the murder wall and pinned up pictures they'd gotten today.

They'd stopped in the lobby on the way out and used the hotel's computer to google the Aura High School students of the years Talco Castilla attended and printed a picture of him and the other two boys Nestor recognized.

She pinned Talco's picture right next to Lareina's, then she stood back with her hands on her hips and contemplated the resemblance.

They could be twins with their valerian hair, olive skin, same arrogant tilt to their heads, smug faces. Almost identical except Talco had the same emerald green eyes as his half-sister Talana while Lareina's were brown.

The conceit had always screamed from Lareina's mien, but Cheyne had really never noticed it in Talco before, until now with the pictures side by side. But still, brother involved in the- the harm, the *murder* of his sister?

"I just don't get it," she railed out loud. "It doesn't make any sense."

Pepi picked up a pillow, put it on her lap and set her palms on top of it. She leaned her head back against the sofa cushion and closed her eyes. She could hear Cheyne pacing again, her cowboy boots shuffling across the rug from one end of the small room to the other and back.

Pepi sighed loudly, still holding the pillow on her lap. "We need to see or call Talana." Subdued, she rolled sideways then sat up. She got up from the couch and went to her backpack, took out the yearbook and notebook and set them on the table.

Cheyne continue pacing, but her steps slowed. "Yeah, I don't think we should tell her though, what we know. It's hard enough for us to comprehend what connection Talco has with his sister's murder much less his baby sister thinking about it. We just need to ask her some more questions and figure it out."

They took the time to write up their notes.

"I'm recording everything we know to date, all the people we've talked to. Plus, I'm making an outline of what we should do next," Pepi said while writing.

"Okay. Put that we're going to see Talana. Then I think it's time to look for-"

"Oh yeah, it's time," As always Pepi read her friend's mind. "We need to go find that warehouse."

They finished the notes then went out to the kitchen.

A late lunch of turkey and Swiss sandwiches, chips, and sodas to wash them down, a quick change of clothes, t-shirt and jean shorts for Pepi, and summer dress for Cheyne and they were back out the door.

A scattering of fallen leftover winter leaves flew behind them like old shoes tied to a 'just married' limo as they rode down the lane to the main road.

Most of the houses on Pepi's street were more like bungalows. Fortunately, her gram had a good-sized family home.

Each unique house on the street was nicely maintained with neatly mown lawns and carefully tended flower gardens. Gnomes and birdbaths, faux deer and ceramic frogs abounded around the yards making the street appear as a whimsical forest.

Cute, but not Pepi's cup of tea. 'You can keep the whimsy,' she had said when Cheyne announced how adorable her street was.

Pepi told her she preferred more geometrical, squares and rectangles, plain neat yards, none of this Disney, childish fake animals prancing around the yard stuff.

Talana's street was even more tree-shrouded, yet much more upscale. Larger houses, some the size of a corner street, Bentleys and BMW's rather than Hondas and pick-ups were tucked away in two or more car garages.

Talana was surprised to see them, nevertheless she welcomed them warmly. She led them back to the room they were in before. It was filled with huge, stuffed beige furniture, soft ivory carpet, grand gold drapes at the windows and crammed bookshelves, the space was creamy cozy yet roomy.

Depositing the girls in the room, Talana left then returned moments later with a pitcher of lemonade and three glasses. In each glass there was a spoon, ice cubes and a fresh lemon circle attached to the top.

She set the tray on a table, poured them each a glass of sweet and tart lemony liquid, then joined the two girls at the small round table in front of the floor length window.

The gold drapes were pulled back to let in the light. Even so, the room retained a soft low glow. The cypress tables shone blurry reflections, the highly polished glass tops glared.

Sipping her cold drink, the auburn crowned teen sat back and asked what brought the girls there. "I can tell something's up. You both look really edgy, and neither of you is looking me straight in the eye. What's going on?"

After neatly tucking her skirt under her, Cheyne squirmed uneasily, probably wrinkling the freshly ironed dress. She rolled her glass thoughtfully between her palms, the ice cubes chinking. She and Pepi exchanged gloomy glances.

Pepi pressed her fingers into her temples, then set her arms in a triangle on the table with her lemonade in the middle, saying nothing.

"Talana, you know we're on your side, right?" Cheyne said slowly, dragging the words out. She crossed one leg over the other, her cowboy booted foot flopping up and down.

The young teen nodded cautiously. "Uh huh." Although she was always dressed casually, somehow she came across elegant, more beauty pageant queen than her sister who had dressed more like a Latina hip-hop performer.

Today, Talana wore an amethyst silk blouse tucked neatly into a dark violet short skirt, her deep scarlet hair in a French braid. Earrings the color of her blouse twinkled in her ears, purple ballet slippers adorned her feet.

She waited expectantly, holding her breath. Green eyes dynamic and calm at the same time.

The girls shared another look.

Cheyne expelled her held breath. Pulling her hair nervously around to one side, she absently stroked it. "Honey, we need to ask about your brother, Talco."

Talana looked more curious than terribly shocked. "Sure. My half-brother. What do you need to know?"

"Well, uh, tell us about him, what kind of kid was he, what were his interests in high school, stuff like that," Pepi said.

Her back rigid, Talana tried to relax against the chair, but her body was on alert for whatever the girls hadn't yet told her. Her intelligent eyes bobbled from one to the other.

"Well, as I came around a good 10 years after he was born I didn't spend a lot of time with him. Thank goodness. There was, I think you know, a lot of anger and resentment from him and Lareina about my birth."

She looked sad yet resigned that her siblings pretty much hated her because they had different fathers, and both parents fawned over Talana while barely giving Talco and Lareina a moment of their time.

"Our mother ran off with another man, had me, then she and her original husband came and got me and brought me home and raised me as their own. My real father stayed out of the picture. There must have been some deal made.

"I've never met him and they refuse to tell me his name. Anyway, Lareina and Talco got dumped like yesterday's mail on relatives for a while. That would screw up any kid." Talana was mature for her age and her IQ was high up the charts. Another reason for her less intelligent siblings to begrudge her.

Cheyne and Pepi sat wordlessly drinking their lemonade, letting Talana describe her childhood.

"It was I think, a confusing time for our parents, all of them," Talana continued. "They were young and hot-blooded and made nonsensical choices. I was the result of a love affair or scandal, jealousy or renewed love, whatever the enticement was, and my half-siblings were tossed aside. It made no sense, but then," she held her palms up, "people often don't make sense when they're in love. Or lust."

Glancing down at a water spot on her t-shirt from the sweating glass she held, "Oh," Pepi muttered, "so much fun times to look forward to."

Cheyne glowered at her then turned to Talana. "You are so mature, Talana, it's nice-" she glanced at Pepi pointedly then back to the younger teen, "for a change. Go ahead, ignore the side show."

Talana chuckled at the pair, then her eyes dropped to her hands clasped in her violet lap. She smiled wistfully. "I envy you your," she sought the word, "sisterliness. I have a few friends, none really close. People were, you know, wanted to keep their distance from my, from Lareina."

Cheyne touched Talana's hand, inclined her head and said thoughtfully, "None of us had perfect childhoods, honey. But you know, we would love for you to join our BFF sisterhood. What do you say?"

Agreeing with her friend, Pepi nodded earnestly. "Yeah, we can be like foster sisters. Strength in numbers."

Talana's eyes welled. "You guys are really so kind. You're not like most pretty girls like my sister, conceited and shallow. One of the kids in school wrote on Lareina's social media page, 'vain and slain.' That's so-"

Cheyne patted her hand again. "It's okay, they're just words, people are cruel." She sat back. "So, sister," she smiled when Talana smiled at that, "let's get back to our purpose. You were telling us about your wonderful brother."

Talana smirked. "Yeah, wonderful." Her sigh angst-filled she told them, "So anyway, my siblings were pretty angry and were not, let's say, very nice, towards me."

Seeing Cheyne and Pepi looked concerned, she quickly said, "Nothing severe, really. Just verbal abuse, tripping me, doing pranks and stuff. They never hurt me, too badly. Really." She smiled weakly at the pair.

"Anyway, Lareina and Talco burned with resentment and jealousy. Not that I blamed them, I was very obviously given more attention."

She looked self-conscious, embarrassed that her parents would let their feelings and attention be so skewed. And it didn't make any sense, why care for the love-child accident of another man more than your own flesh and blood?

It had never made any sense to her, she knew even as a young child she wasn't entitled to better treatment.

"We all lived on careful alert all the time. Lareina and Talco were like little ticking time bombs, the littlest thing would set them off. Their tempers were legendary."

Pepi and Cheyne nodded knowingly. They'd been the brunt of Lareina's anger on many occasions for just being pretty.

Talana's lip nicked up in chagrin at their meaningful looks. "Yes, so, anyway, I walked on eggshells so fearful that I would say or do something to set one or the other of them off. Mama and Daddy were constantly under attack. Lareina could be bought off with gifts, but Talco seethed every second with rage."

Cheyne offered, "I think maybe your mom held you over your stepfather's head like a, taunt I guess. Saying, 'You behave and treat me right or I'll leave again and bring back another one.' And your stepfather really loved her so he went overboard treating you so well so your mother would not stray again."

"But what about her other two children? That's so stupid." Pepi appeared about to spit. Annoyed, she leaned way over to hug her knees then noticed a shoelace on her sneakers was undone and leaned over further to tie it.

When she sat back up quickly the blood rushed to her head and made her cheeks glow.

"Yeah, it was dumb, but they were young," Talana quickly said. "Anyway, the three of us privileged kids attended private schools, but all at different schools and at different times. Talco spent his last year of high school at a public school.

"Unfortunately, actually, it was probably fortunate that what I know about Talco I got mostly from other people, like neighbors and relatives, and Lareina because he was so much older than me. He wasn't there enough to make my life too miserable."

Her expression saddened, eyelids drooped, the pretty lips curved down slightly at the edges. At 14 she didn't wear makeup, she didn't need to, her face was all dramatic coloring and striking features without enhancement.

If she was going somewhere special, she'd slick on a little nude gloss. She stared down at the purple ballet slippers.

"Anyway, apparently Talco was the kind of kid that liked to, um, I guess he liked to hurt animals. The small defenseless cats and dogs, frogs, birds, whatever. And they said he was always conniving how to get a lot of money with the smallest of effort. Lareina still lived at home but Talco was in the military for a few deployments.

"He came and went, usually without notice. He had been quite clear that he was his own man and no one was to tell him what to do. At least until he joined the military." Talana's brows dipped somberly.

The three teens shifted positions, getting more comfortable.

"Even then it seems he had a motive to get rich quick with as little effort as possible. Lareina said he joined the army because he thought he would be sent to third world countries and he could loot them at will, that no one would catch him or even care. He hung with a couple of guys from school.

"I think one of them went into the army with him, the other I'm not sure what he did. Like my sister," she hesitated, willing the tears to stay away, "it was- difficult- but in a different way- to love Talco. He could be quite, um," tensely she pushed back her hair then pulled at her silk blouse.

Her expression strengthened, she went on. "He could be secretive and cold, callous even, and remote- and malicious." The pretty lips puckered sourly, then feeling guilty she shook her head.

The braid flopped forward, she moved it back off her shoulder, pushing it around her back and crossed her arms.

223

"I guess I was lucky he more or less left me alone. But like I said, he was so much older and gone mostly while I was- am-growing up."

Cheyne touched Talana's hand again, holding it for a second. "It must have been so hard for you. You were kind of alone in a house full of family. It sounds like your parents only gave you attention for the effect it had on each other yet in reality they didn't really, uh," she trailed off, her cheeks flushing pink.

"Right," Talana's smile turned bitter. "They didn't really care about me, I was only a pawn in their game. Whatever that was."

Pepi mumbled under her breath, "I can understand how you felt."

Talana's mermaid eyes spilled over. Impatiently, she wiped at them. "I was okay, really. I had my own friends, and books, and did a lot in the church, plus now cheerleading takes up a lot of my time. Please don't feel sorry for me. Feel sorry for Lareina and her short life. She'll never be a mother or an aunt, or-" she choked back a sob.

Cheyne got up and wrapped a consoling arm around her while Talana pressed a napkin to her flowing eyes.

Pepi waited a moment then asked, "Can you remember those two friends of Talco's? Their names?"

"Yeah, uh," Talana blew her nose. "Yeah, Pablo and um, what was... Gary, yeah, Gary. But I really don't know their last names."

Cheyne and Pepi shared a look. Cheyne said calmly, "That's okay."

"But why are you so interested in Talco?" Talana rolled the soggy napkin into a ball then clutched it tightly in one hand.

Cheyne returned to her chair and took some big swigs of her lemonade. She peered at Pepi over the rim of the glass. Pepi stared back evenly, *it's up to you*, her big grey eyes said.

Wiggling her glass, listening to the ice cubes chink again then Cheyne set her glass down.

She cleared her throat, spoke gently, "Well, I don't remember how much we told you, but, we talked to the bartender where Miss

Milan met those guys. He said he'd seen some college-aged men speaking to them, acting like they didn't know them but he could tell they did."

Talana blinked at Cheyne but kept quiet.

"That in itself was suspicious, like they were trying to hide something. Even Miss Milan had mentioned the incident to her sister because it had struck her as so peculiar. It also sounded like they were locals."

Glancing at Pepi, Cheyne went on, "Since we only have three public high schools in this small town, we took a fifty-fifty chance and borrowed Pepi's brother, Thomas' yearbook and took it back to the bar," she hesitated, they had decided earlier they weren't going to tell Talana what they'd learned.

"Go ahead, I guess we shouldn't keep secrets from her, it's not fair," Pepi said, thankful she wasn't the one doing the talking, spilling the shattering beans about the girl's brother.

Cheyne pulled her legs up and crossed them tailor style on her chair. "Well, uh," she rubbed an eye. "The uh, bartender pointed out your brother and two other guys as the men who seemed to know the older men at the bar."

She said rapidly, "We think they all had something to do with Miss Milan's death," she hesitated, then her words slowed. "And, uh, possibly also your sister's." Her mouth an embarrassed line, she blinked meekly at Talana.

Talana sat stock still. She looked down at the table, her eyes widened. She snatched up another napkin wiping the tears that rolled out. "I, uh, I, I can't *not* believe you."

She raised her eyes up to Pepi then Cheyne. "It's so, he could be capable of, I mean, it's shocking enough about Miss Milan, but Lareina? His own blood sister?" She shook her head in bewildered disbelief. "I just can't-"

Cheyne pulled her chair closer to Talana. "I know, Tal, we can't fathom it either. We need to do more investigating." She massaged Talana's shoulder with one hand to comfort her, the silk blouse smooth and cool to her fingertips, but she could feel Talana's body heating up from her anguish.

Gulping back tears that nevertheless ran a race down her cheeks, Talana cried, "He was always a nasty child, never got over the way the folks abandoned him, but I never expected this." She rolled her head back, covered her face with her hands, her young shoulders heaving with quiet sobs.

Keeping an arm around Talana's shoulders, "We, uh," Cheyne said, halting, giving the younger teen time to regroup and take in this over-the-top unbelievable new info.

She started again, "We're not a hundred percent positive about this, Talana, the only thing we're kind of sure of is that we don't think he was involved with Miss Milan when they were overseas."

"He wasn't in any of the pictures we found on her USB drive," Pepi said.

Cheyne continued, "She would have recognized him right off the bat at the wedding or the bar, drunk or not. And she would have talked to him if she'd seen him while in Africa, and I'm pretty sure she would have mentioned that to us."

Leaning back in her chair, Cheyne moved, tucking her feet up on a chair rung while Pepi squirmed in her chair to get her feet on the floor, her thighs sticking a little on the chair.

Adjusting her shorts, she said, "Yeah, but he may have met the other men over there. Everyone mentions their accents and secretiveness. Miss Milan may have known or crossed paths before with one of the other men at the bar, but at the time didn't realize it."

"But *they* might have," Cheyne added quietly, ominously. Sucking on her straw, she watched the emotions grip the younger teen. She watched as the pain of her brother's betrayal of her family strike her beautiful face.

Excruciating loss traveled through the agonized eyes and trembling lips; loss of her sister, the loss of her own innocence, finally the realization that life has changed, things will never be the same again. And it's only the beginning of the end.

Talana smoothed the sides of her hair that escaped the braid and wiped her eyes. Teardrops soaked into the amethyst blouse.

Getting control of herself, she struggled to steady her voice and gain control of her weeping. She asked, "What's next? The police, are you-"

"Yes," Cheyne said. "We're going to call Detective James later with the information. In the meantime, if you see Talco, Talana, *please* do not confront him or question him at all. Avoid him. You could put yourself in danger. Promise me you'll do what I ask?"

Talana covered the lower part of her face with her hands, only the green dripping pools were visible, she nodded. Then nodded again stiffly, dropping her hands.

"I promise. I understand what's at stake. Besides," she said wryly, "it's doubtful I'll be seeing him for a while anyway. Before the, uh, funeral, he only came by every few months to see the folks for money. I don't see that changing."

She fidgeted with the end of her braid, then pulled the band off and raked her fingers through her hair, like she was pushing away horrible thoughts.

"You know," Pepi interjected, getting up, she came around to the other side of the table closer to the others. "I've been pondering that comment in the yearbook, the one that Nestor noted about the guy Pablo, what he'd written about 'See ya at the Fact, don't get the flu.'"

"And?" Cheyne asked.

"I googled it last night to see if it was a fraternity or bar or club, but I couldn't find anything. I think it might have been some kind of coded message. Coincidentally, we have a flu vaccine factory in Corbiestep. Get it? Flu- factory- remember the guy wrote, 'See you at the Fact- don't get the flu ha ha?'"

Cheyne perked like a light bulb went off in her head. "That makes sense. There's never coincidence when there's murder involved." She was thoughtful for a minute then her face brightened.

"You know frizzly Frieda? Her cousin, Jumper Hudson, works at the factory. He picked her up from school one time in this like white hazmet suit."

"You're kidding," Talana said, astonished.

"Yeah. Wasn't even Halloween, she was furious. Besides being mortified to the max that he was such a dork, he shouldn't have had the suit at all, apparently they're supposed to leave their suits at the factory for safety issues."

Pepi scooped up her purse. "Let's go find him!" She came back around to Talana who had gained her composure. "Are you okay if we go? We won't leave if-"

"No, no." Talana shook her head fervently then got up. She gathered the glasses and set them on the tray. "Anything that will help solve this mystery and bring justice to my sister, the sooner the better. Whatever I can do to help, just tell me."

She walked them to the door.

A rush of balmy summer air flowed in when Talana opened the door.

Cheyne quickly grabbed the bottom of her dress to hold it down. Talana giggled. "I don't know how you ride a bike in a dress."

Cheyne laughed. "It's a talent, takes practice, and lately we've been getting a lot!" They stepped outside.

"Oh," Cheyne said. "I know what you can do to help."

"Anything," The young teen said, erasing her sorrow. Pulling her shoulders back, she raised her head high and waited with her hand on the doorknob.

The playful breeze tickled her fiery hair teasing it into gentle jumps and flips, and frisking the purple skirt making her look her young age.

"Lareina's boyfriend, Adonai Alamanni. He must have been pretty angry if he knew about her cheating. Lareina wasn't one to not throw her exploits in someone's face, to annoy or to make him jealous. She rarely concerned herself with other people's feelings. Sorry Tal," Cheyne said quickly when she remembered she was degrading Talana's sister.

Talana pulled her lips in, her eyes dropped. She murmured, her tone not accusing, "I understand, I know."

228

"Anyway," Cheyne's sympathetic voice softened further. "Do you think you could find out where he is? Maybe even where he was when Lareina was, uh, killed? We haven't gotten around to doing that yet. We're kind of afraid he'd be suspicious of us, why we'd be talking to him."

"Yeah, we hardly knew him, he was a couple of grades older. But," Pepi admonished, her arms crossed, "only if you can do it without talking *to* him, Talana."

Her voice as firm as she could make it, "We insist you do not talk directly to him, it would not be safe. Promise us-"

Talana nodded adamantly. "Sure, sure, no problem. His mom and sister would probably tell me. I'll explain that I just wanted to see how he was doing, how is he handling things, you know, mourner to mourner."

"Okay, great. I mean, well you know what I mean. Call us if you learn anything. Meantime, take care, and call us no matter what, if you find out anything or you just need a friend to talk to." Pepi gingerly patted the younger girl's shoulder.

She looked at her hand, surprised. It didn't feel- itchy. Maybe Cheyne and Karey, and even this gracious, young teen with an old soul are rubbing off on her. This physical comforting thing wasn't as grody as it had always felt. Maybe.

"Remember," Cheyne waggled a finger in Talana's face, "don't talk to Adonai in person, or go see anyone. At this point we don't know who all is involved. Ok?" She smiled at Talana's nod.

Cheyne hugged her. "All right, later, girl."

The sun had strolled up the sky and was now slinking slowly down behind the horizon.

The fortified shadows beefed up, elongating, chasing the girls as they flew off down the street on their bikes to their respective homes.

Chapter Twenty-Eight

*C*he next morning, Cheyne called Pepi to see what time they wanted to get started, they'd left the night before without making specific plans.

Pepi didn't answer her cell. Cheyne assumed the battery had died so she dialed her house phone.

Pepi's grandmother, Elma Mae answered the phone. "Hello?"

"Hi Grams, it's Cheyne."

There was a length of unusual silence. Normally, Elma Mae was a chatty-Cathy and a morning person, she was one of those sing-song chipper people in the morning.

It drove Pepi nuts to hear at the crack of dawn Grams cheerfully singing sappy songs as she wandered around the entire house cooking breakfast, getting ready for work, making sandwiches.

She would go into each kid's room and give each one a smooch on the forehead and sing 'it's uppy-get time! Rise and shine everybody!'

Pepi would squirrel down to the bottom of the bed groaning and cover her head with her blanket and pillow. It never stopped Grams. She would just peel back the covers, pull up a corner of the pillow and sing cheerfully into Pepi's face. At least Grams had a good voice. She was often asked to sing solo in the church choir on special occasions.

"Grams?" Cheyne said. "Is everything okay?" More unusual silence. The lack of sound was starting to grow deafening.

Then Elma Mae said, "Um..."

Cheyne's stomach fluttered. With a growing urgency, she asked again, "Is everything all right? What's going on? Is everyone okay?"

"Oh honey, I'm sorry, I didn't mean to worry you. Yes, um, basically everyone is...okay, um." Grams words and voice didn't match, she sounded obviously a little distraught.

"Grams wha-" Cheyne started, stopped, then said, "Is it Pepi? Is she having, you know..."

Again a silent patch ensued. She could hear Elma Mae sigh heavily.

"Yes," Elma Mae murmured quietly, disheartened.

Cheyne switched her phone to her other ear and jogged off to find her mother. She said into the phone, "I'm coming over, I'll be there in fifteen minutes."

She didn't wait to see if it was okay with Elma Mae, she hung up and found her mother in the living room. "Mom, I'm going over to Pepi's."

Seeing the distress on her daughter's face, Laura asked, "Is everything all right?"

Cheyne didn't answer her, she hurried over to the closet by the front door.

"I'll call you later ma and tell you what's going on. You know what it is... I might be there all night." She grabbed her purse and helmet and fled out the door.

A knowing look replaced the confused look on Laura Somerset's motherly, lovely face. She set the book she was reading down in her lap, lowered her head and said a quiet prayer.

Cheyne reached Pepi's tan house in less than the twenty minutes.

The wrap-around porch was filled with toys and chairs and pitchers of flowers, flowers also flourished in baskets under the windows.

The house stood inviting, but Cheyne felt a pall of dread lowering as she approached. She rode up the driveway and ignored cement walkway leading to the porch she headed straight to the side kitchen door.

Parking her bike, out of the corner of her eye, she could see neat rows of planted vegetables in the backyard behind the garage. Some were already poking tiny green tops out of the churned dirt.

Little sticks with strings on them lined like pickets waiting staked along the fence to hold up tomato vines and other veggies that needed to climb.

Elma Mae was already opening the door before Cheyne reached it. Cheyne scooted in.

Shutting the door, Elma Mae said, "Listen Cheyne dear, it's not, I mean, I don't know if you should go in. You know she acts all strong and tough, but really she can be as fragile as a seahorse."

She twisted her fingers then wiped them on her slacks. "When she has these, uh, fugues, she won't let anyone near her, not even me. I just don't-"

Cheyne gave Elma Mae a hug. She set her purse and helmet on the table. "I have to go to her, Grams."

Elma Mae stood back and looked at the teen.

Pretty as a picture as always, but there was a determined set to her jaw. Elma Mae sighed. She knew Cheyne, and she knew that look, and she knew how stubborn the young girl was.

"I know. Go on, dear. I hope it's not like last time." She stepped aside. Cheyne shot her a hopeful smile and headed towards the stairs.

Elma Mae pulled out a chair and sat down heavily. She set her elbows on the table and her chin on her hands. She sat for a few moments, her face lined in sadness, her heart heavy. Then she shook herself out of her revelry and got up and did what always made her feel better, cook something.

She opened the fridge and studied the contents to see what kind of delectable treat she could whip up for the girls.

Cheyne moved quickly up the carpeted stairs and down the hall to Pepi's small room. She knocked but knew there'd be no answer, so she opened the door and went right in.

It was very dark and cool in the room. The lights were off and the shade was pulled down over the window and the curtains were closed over the shade. The room was desolately buttoned up. No light, no cheer.

She approached the closet, the door was closed as she knew it would be. She knocked lightly. There was no answer as she knew there wouldn't be. Cheyne had been here during times like this before. So she did what she always does and opened the closet door.

"Pepi," she spoke firmly, lovingly. She waited a moment for her eyes to adjust to the light. It was dark in the room but it was pitch black in the closet.

"Go away." The disembodied voice came from back in the closet, it sounded like it wanted to sound mean, stern, but it came out weak and wobbly.

Cheyne stepped inside the closet and closed the door. Pushing clothes to the side, she knelt on the floor trying to see exactly where her friend was.

She heard a small movement in the corner.

She crawled to the movement on her hands and knees and huddled up- without actually touching- next to Pepi.

Her friend was rolled in a tight ball. She was leaning exactly in the corner with her back against the wall and her knees drawn up with her arms wrapped around her legs holding them close to her chest as she could.

Cheyne leaned her back against the wall too and pulled up her knees. She rested her hands on her stomach and let the quiet envelope them. She could hear Pepi trying not to sniff. Pepi hated to show any kind of weakness.

After a few quiet minutes passed, "So," Cheyne drawled, "what's new?"

Pepi sputtered out a choke at her friend's whimsy. "Really, Chey? I'm rolled up and stashed on the floor in a dark closet and that's what you say?"

Cheyne smiled in the dark and squirmed over closer to her friend, but still didn't touch her.

"Go away," Pepi muttered.

Very carefully choosing her words, Cheyne spoke gently. "You know me well enough Pep, you know I'm not leaving, so save your breath."

Pepi muttered again, "Whatever."

Knowing it would anger her, Cheyne anyway reached around her friend and wrapped her arm around her.

Pepi stiffened and tried to pull away, but Cheyne held her gently. Pepi struggled for a second, Cheyne wouldn't let go.

After a few moments of rigidness, Pepi gave in. Going limp, she laid her head on Cheyne's shoulder.

The girls sat for a long time like that, not moving or speaking, just being.

After a while, Cheyne took her arm off from around her friend and moved around turning to her. Pulling her legs, she crossed them and she sat facing Pepi. She could now just faintly make out the fat ringlets around Pepi's shoulders and face.

She couldn't see her well enough to make out her expression, but she knew Pepi was in grave despair. Cheyne sat directly in front of Pepi and took a big, steadying breath then exhaled long.

"It's going to be different this time Pepi. This time I'm not going to sit in silence in this closet with you for hours like I have before. Not that I mind, because you know I don't. But, this time," she hesitated to make sure she had Pepi's attention.

"This time is going to be different. This time we're going to attack what is attacking you inside, what's killing your soul. This time," she took a breath, said firmly, but with light affection, and with not a drop of sympathy, that would have turned Pepi into stone.

At any hint of sympathy, Pepi would cease any interaction with Cheyne, she might even leave in a fury.

So, carefully Cheyne said, "You're going to talk. You refuse to see a shrink. You're letting your past eat you up, it's killing you. Each time you go through this it's longer and worse. Enough."

She wriggled closer to Pepi. She could see Pepi had her head on her knees, she couldn't tell if Pepi was looking at her or the floor.

"Seriously, enough. I refuse to sit by and watch you die a little more every day. The only way you can face those demons and get beyond them is to talk about them. I know you have never spoken about that time… not even to Grams."

Cheyne wiggled her legs, crossing them more tightly. Bending slightly, she laid her arms on her legs and folded her hands. "So…"

"So?" Pepi snorted. "You can't make me."

Cheyne pulled her lips in, nodding. "I know. But, you know what I said is true. You have to talk about it and you know you can trust me. You know I won't judge you, or think badly about you, or hate you or whatever, you know that."

Pepi sniffed. "But you'll feel sorry for me."

Cheyne shook her head in the dark. "I won't if you don't want me to. I promise. I promise whatever you want, I'll do. Just," she took a deep breath, "trust me."

Pepi was silent so long Cheyne thought her words had been to no avail. They sat motionless in the coffin closet. Cheyne would have thought Pepi died but she could hear her breathing.

She waited. And waited. And waited until her legs were pins and needles from being crossed for so long. Just as she was about to unwind her legs, she heard Pepi take a deep intake of breath, and hold it.

Cheyne held her own breath with her friend until she heard her exhale. She waited some more, a little lightheaded now.

"Um," Pepi started, then stopped.

Cheyne said quietly, almost a whisper, "You're safe now, Pep. They can't ever hurt you again."

A little whiny Pepi said, "I don't want anyone to think I'm a weak sissy."

Cheyne covered her laugh and said seriously, "Pepi, no one thinks of you as weak. You're the strongest person I know. And that's no lie."

"Hmmph. You're right, I am."

"So? Spill your deplorable past. I know the gist of it. Get it all out and it'll drain away, evaporate, gone." She snapped her fingers.

"Yeah." The strength in Pepi's voice waned. "I know, I know it's ridiculous to let my past keep a stranglehold on me like this. I know."

Cheyne could hear her move in the dark, could hear some of the longer hanging clothes move too. She could see Pepi's silhouette now wearily lean back against the wall, her legs pushed out in front of her, one ankle crossed over the other.

Pepi's voice disjointed, she said, "It's just, there's these, how do I describe it?" She thought for a second.

"In my mind, there's like these people, but they're not people, they look like people but they become these perverted, venomous, snarling monsters that float in and out and around me. At first they moan and groan. Then they grow louder, get closer, get inside my head and then they scream." She lapsed into silence.

"Pep, let me be a bridge for you. A bridge from this horror inside you, back to safety and peace, and love."

Cheyne held her hands together clutching as tightly as she could to resist the urge to reach out and touch Pepi, to comfort her. She knew it would have the opposite effect. She sat still again, and waited.

Pepi cleared her throat. "I uh, I can't fight them, Chey. I've tried, but…"

Cheyne asked gently, "Do you know them? Do you recognize them?"

Pepi snorted. "Oh yeah. There's, you know, my mom," her voice thick with bitter anger and hurt, "and my dad, and... them..."

"Them?"

Pepi was quiet again so long Cheyne was about to speak then Pepi, her voice clear of emotion, detached, said. "Yes."

She took a giant breath, several more big breaths, then exhaled letting out some of the strain.

"Okay, you know part of it. You know my mother, was, is, mentally ill. Bi-polar. Not uncommon these days, seems everybody has some form of it. It seems like the movie stars all have it, like it's an accessory." She snorted. "It's like next to ADD Bi-polar is the current popular disability to have."

"Yeah," Cheyne said to keep Pepi talking.

It worked. "You know when I was around three years old, we were all living with Gram because daddy had been swept up in a net with a bunch of people he knew and sent to prison." She sighed miserably.

"And you know that he's still there. Anyway, when she was on her medication, Mom was, well, tolerable. Looney, but tolerable, and present- in mind, most days anyways. She decided though, one day that the meds made her feel lazy and fuzzy and slow, so she flushed them down the toilet. It didn't take long for her to come unraveled."

Cheyne changed her position to lean against the wall and replicated Pepi with her legs stuck out, ankles crossed.

"Yeah," she said. "I heard, stories. Mom and Grandma Marylou would talk about her and worry about her. They didn't know I was listening. Even if I could hear them, they thought I was too young to comprehend what they were saying."

"Uh huh." Pepi mumbled. "So, she, Mom, soon became totally unmanageable, incoherent, downright crazy. Gram got her into the hospital countless times, but after 72 hours of 'observation' they would always let her go.

"Gram was trying again to get her involuntarily committed, at least to get her stabilized, Mom got wind of it. The littlest kids were just babies so I guess that's why she left them, and Thomas was away at school. Unfortunately, I was there and vulnerable and she grabbed me up, and ran." She grew still again. Remembering.

Cheyne waited patiently.

Heaving another big sigh, Pepi said, "I think she took me just to show Gram she could. So, like a lot of people that need medication but won't take it, they self-medicate with drugs. And that's what she did.

"Right away she hooked up with a guy who said he'd take care of her. Mom was so beautiful then she'd take your breath away. Rich dark hair that flowed long down her back, silvery eyes that you could see from across a crowded room they were so brilliant. And when she was normal, she was sweet as peach pie in the summer. When she walked into a room, people stopped talking and stared."

"I know how it is," Cheyne interposed, "you look just like her." Immediately she regretted her words. She clamped her mouth shut vowing to not speak again. Pepi had already mentioned a few times she feared she could be like her mother as she grew older, and not just in looks.

Thank goodness Pepi ignored Cheyne's comment. "So, this guy, Vincent," she continued sourly. "He got her hooked on crack, then other stuff. He kept her strung out all the time, she was so confused and hardly ever coherent, barely present. There were days she didn't get up at all..." Pepi trailed off then grew quiet again.

Cheyne waited, biting her lip. She couldn't help herself, she asked, "What about you? What was going on with you during that time?" She braced herself waiting for Pepi's reaction to her question; shout angrily, run, clam up for good-

Pepi grunted. She pulled her knees back up and wrapped her arms tightly around them. "Me? We went from Gram's wonderful, comfortable, loving home, where food and hugs were plentiful to horror-" a swift intake of breath sounded like she'd been hit suddenly in the stomach.

This time, carefully, slowly, Cheyne set her hand gently on Pepi's arm. Cheyne could feel Pepi's arm stiffen and imperceptivity start to move away, but she didn't. Her head dropped. Her words went to the floor.

"Sounds like a sordid movie, Chey, but we went from Gram's home to a crack house." Pepi heard Cheyne's gasp but went on.

"And just like in the movies or TV, this house was just like them. A broken down, cruddy, I almost said shack, but it was too big for a shack. It actually had a lot of rooms. I think it used to be a hotel about two hundred years ago."

"So, uh, were there other people there with you since it was so big?"

Pepi nodded and grunted again. "Oh yeah, there were other, for now we'll call them *people*.

Chapter Twenty-nine

On the dark, Pepi's labored breathing chugged around the small closed space. She stopped talking again.

Cheyne prompted her. "So, there was your mother and you, and uh, Vincent. Who else was there?"

It took a minute, but Pepi went on. "Well, there were always slimy disgusting people coming and going all hours of the day and night. Luckily, I had found a tiny cubbyhole under the stairs so whenever I heard the front door open I scurried into the hole until I felt it was safe to come out.

"The entrance was hard to see, so no one knew where I was hiding. I mean, you know," she sounded sarcastic, yet the pain was clear and intense, "if anyone cared to know where I was. So," she sighed, "besides the *people* coming and going-"

Cheyne cut in, "Why were there so many people coming and going, was it still a hotel?"

Pepi laughed unpleasantly, short and hard. "No, Chey, it was now a house, not a hotel. It was like I said, a crack house. People were buying and selling and doing drugs, all day, all night, constantly.

"It was like being in a lamp where there's moths just constantly flying, flying, flying, in and out, batting against the walls. At one point, someone had started to remodel the hotel into a house so they took down walls and stuff, but then they must have run out of money or something because they stopped. Just left it like it was. Open beams, dug up floors, some rooms had no doors, electric wires sticking out all over.

"Anyway, people were always lying all around the big center room. I'd call it a family room except it was anything but that. They did drugs and passed out then woke up and did some more and passed out and woke up- left to get more money to come back to do more drugs, on and on." Wrinkling her nose, Pepi said, "Half of them slept in their own vomit."

"Gross. Must have stunk."

Pepi let out a huff. "Yeah. That's an understatement." She paused again before continuing.

"There were mattresses all over the main room crammed with filthy strung out people. Some just crashed on the bare floor, they couldn't feel anything anyway. There were people laid out all over the other rooms in the house too. There was no space that wasn't empty." She licked her lips. "I wish I'd brought some water in with me."

"You want me to-"

"No," Pepi said abruptly. "Anyway, the place was a flea-bitten dive. I don't know what was filthier, the people or the building. It had never, ever been cleaned. No mopping, something spilled it stayed there until it dried.

"Cobwebs and slime covered the ceilings and windows so you couldn't see out anyway, the sheets and stuff were never cleaned. Sometimes when Mom was able to get up, Vincent would take us to the Laundromat. But it wasn't very often." A shiver rolled across her slender shoulders at the memory of sleeping in filth.

"I scrubbed myself with a boar brush someone had left behind every day as hard as I could in the skanky bathroom. We seldom had electricity, but someone managed to keep the water on."

Pepi pushed her legs out then pulled them back up.

Cheyne leaned forward to stretch her back, then settled right back against the wall. She said very matter-of-factly, "Sounds pretty rough, Pep." She waited for the spout of sarcasm to slap at her.

There was none. Pepi spoke faintly, "Yeah, it was rough." She waited a beat, "It got rougher."

Cheyne could hear her friend start sniffing again so she sat silently.

Letting some time pass, Cheyne said, "So, Pep, you've got to tell it, tell it all. Get it out. I'm not leaving until the ghosts are out."

Pepi laughed, not totally mirthless. "Yeah, sure, I know you, girl, you get hungry. As soon as Gram starts cooking and the smell floats up the stairs, into my room and slips under the door- you'll be gone before I can say 'ghost'!" Her laugh was short, however she sounded more relaxed.

"Uh huh, so you better get going. What happened next?"

Pepi leaned her head back and rested it against the wall. "I was dirty and hungry, and believe it or not, with a house full of people, so lonely I thought I'd die. My mother was always passed out in a room upstairs and I stayed away from-" she gulped, "from Vincent."

His name sounded ugly on her lips. Her voice tiny and shaky, and scared, she told Cheyne, "He would try to, I mean even in a room full of people, drug addicts, he would try to get me. I used to sleep in the same room, actually the same bed with him and Mom, but then," she trailed off.

Cheyne waited silently.

"He, uh, he would, well you know, he molested me, Cheyne. Even as a three year old child while we slept, he would cover my mouth with his big clammy hand and climb his big gross body over mine-" Her voice broke in a rough sob.

Cheyne threw her arms around her friend. Pepi let her. She laid her head on Cheyne's shoulder.

Cheyne wrapped an arm around her and stroked Pepi's head as she wept. They stayed like that for some time.

Then Cheyne said, "You need to go on. I know there's more."

A few minutes went by. Pepi rubbed her nose, moved to sit back against the wall. "God you're a bully."

Cheyne smiled in the dark. She murmured softly, "Yeah."

"Okay. I guess I was lucky, because he was always so high or drunk when he, uh, tried to rape me, because he would pass out before he could get to it.

"It didn't happen but a few times before I got a smelly pillow and a blanket as thin as paper and found my cubbyhole and slept in there from then on. Because, unfortunately, he wasn't the only sick swine to come after me.

"I had to be quick and invisible to avoid pinches and cigarette burns and, anyway, I had to sneak out in the night when no one could see me to scavenge some food and bathe in one of the bathroom sinks.

"I was too little to figure out the shower at that time, and there was no hot water, ever, and no one to ask for help. Pretty much everyone was out or OD'd by the nighttime, and that's when I could creep around without getting caught. Being small can have its advantages. I became the twilight ghost." She sounded less scared and angry, even a little whimsical.

Cheyne didn't hide her perturbance. "What about your mother, didn't she, didn't you tell her? Why didn't she-"

"Cheyne," Pepi said drolly. "My mother was a hard core addict. There were weeks I didn't see her. When I did tell her-" her voice cracked, "things got worse."

"Worse? I don't get-"

Pepi turned angrily to her friend. "Yes," she spat, "worse. It was hell before, it turned to torture." She fell back, her head leaned back against the wall as she caught her breath.

Then she sat up and faced Cheyne with her legs crossed.

Cheyne turned to her, crossed her legs, pushed a pair of pants off her head and waited.

"I was scared, Chey. I didn't know what to do. So one day when she was kind of lucid, but she was also itchy and lurching, her eyes were like red glass balls, I told her about Vincent. I was nervous but sure she'd handle things. After all, I was now four, yeah, spent my birthday in that hellhole."

"And?" Cheyne prompted.

"She, slapped me. Not once, but so many times I couldn't count. Her hand went back and forth, she slapped me until I fell to the floor. She was shrieking, I was crying. I couldn't even cover my face at first I was so stunned.

"She pounded me to the floor where, surprisingly as skin and bones as she was, she was able to kick me, violently. I curled into the tightest ball I could, my vision blurred, my head, I think I started to black out. Her tirade was not over. She leaned over and hit me with her fists, screaming like the devil had her in his grip.

"Slipping and twisting in my blood splattering on the torn up linoleum, she almost fell herself. I finally rolled away under the bed where she couldn't reach me. She didn't have the strength to move the bed, she didn't have the coordination to get on her knees and get me so she just stood and wailed, for an hour. Seemed like an hour."

Pepi's voice grew hoarse, years of pent up tears caught in her throat. The words started piling up, they couldn't get out. Her head dropped, shoulders slumped over until her arms rested on her legs. It looked like she was going to dissolve into the floor.

Cheyne reached out a hand, thought better of it and clasped both hands together and tucked them into her lap.

"Pep," her own tears rolled unstoppable down her face. She could taste the salt on her lips, her nose stuffed up. "You don't need to, why don't we take a little brea-"

"No," Pepi barely squawked out.

Cheyne could hear the cinnamon ringlets rustle against Pepi's shirt from her shaking her head side to side.

"I have to, I need to tell it all now." she inhaled hard then puffed out slow. "If I don't get it out now, I'll never be able to do this again, go through this again."

Her head shifted up to Cheyne. "Unless, you know, unless you can't um, don't want to uh, do you want me to stop?"

For the first time, Cheyne could hear uncertainty in her friend. She'd heard fear and anger and sorrow, but this was the first she'd heard Pepi sound uncertain.

Cheyne moved to kneel in front of Pepi. She pushed a jacket dangling from a hangar out of her face. "Girl, I am with you a thousand percent. I told you we weren't leaving this closet until you get it all out, all said."

She sat back on her heels. "The past is like poison to you, you need to get all that noxious venom out. It's making you sick. Clean out the poison and you can heal, heal your soul. Put it in the past and move forward. You deserve- happiness, just like all of God's children."

She sat back on the floor, facing Pepi and crossed her legs again. Setting her arms on her legs she clasped her hands together and bent in slightly in towards Pepi.

"What happened next?" She thought she heard Pepi snuffle, then through the murk she saw her raise her arm, move her hand to her face. To swipe at her tears.

"Okay." A tad shaky, Pepi's voice was clearer, the blockage in her throat had moved out of the way, for now.

A shuddery breath, weak at first, then stronger, she said, "Well, so, I stayed in a knot against the wall under the bed until eventually Mom laid down on the bed and passed out."

Pepi put her hands over her face trying to block out the pain and memory of her mother who had turned into a monster, attacking, beating her black and blue and bloody. Her mother sleeping peacefully while Pepi lay in her own pooling blood.

"I uh, I mean she wasn't even, I mean she didn't look like my mom anymore. When she was beating me and screaming, her face had contorted into like an inhuman creature, unrecognizable, her eyes wild, enraged and unseeing, face red and distorted."

Pepi stopped again for a minute. She struggled to talk about it without having to visualize it, to fully revisit the torture.

"When I heard her snoring, I crawled out and sat and stared at her. Now she looked like a baby sleeping, except her body was wasted away. Her face was pinched, her forehead was permanently wrinkled, and pain-lines engraved around her eyes and mouth. My heart turned to stone, Chey, that day, that moment looking at her. Stone."

A few minutes went by.

Pepi pretended she couldn't hear Cheyne crying softly. "So, uh, needless to say, I never told her again about Vincent touching me, or really anything again. I had stayed hidden in my hole, and by time I saw her again, a few weeks later, she was strung out again and didn't even remember.

"When she looked at me, her eyeballs were shaky and unfocused. She was only interested in Vincent and what he could bring her."

"Pepi, it's so unthinkably horrible I-"

Pepi snatched her hand out and grabbed Cheyne's arm, dug her nails into it. "Oh no, Chey, that wasn't the worst." The savage words tumbled convulsively, she shook Cheyne's arm hard.

"No, that wasn't the worst. Let me tell you the worst. I managed to survive over a year in that place, ducking groping hands, getting hit by strangers for no reason, just because I was there.

"Stealing food, I stayed relatively healthy although God knows how, and relatively clean. The hardest thing though at the time was, I was so lonely. Alone in a sea of people. But I couldn't talk to them, they were junkies high as kites all the time, and I learned not to get within arm's reach. I was so desperately alone." Her voice fell from anger to a deep, spirit scraping ache.

"Pepi-"

Pepi shook her head vigorously. "No, that still wasn't the worse. Let me tell you how bad it got." She heard Cheyne's anxious breathing but kept on.

"One day I was finally tall and strong enough to reach the door knob and turn it. No one was awake, I turned the knob, no surprise the creaking door didn't wake those druggies, and I slipped out." Her lids lowered and a small smile lifted her lips.

"I couldn't believe it! Fresh air! Sunshine! I actually had to close my eyes at first I was so unused to the brilliance. I could smell the flowers." She inhaled deeply as if she could still smell the scents.

"I could smell the perfumed detergent from someone's laundry in the wash somewhere. I heard cars and birds and dogs barking. It was-" she closed her eyes and tilted her head towards the ceiling as if reliving the first moment of euphoric release.

"Freedom. Pure joy, heaven, it was glorious!" Her head dropped suddenly, her hands fell in her lap.

"Pep-"

Pepi pulled her eyes open trying to see her friend in the blackness.

"Then," her voice turned flat, detached again. "A lady walking her dog down the street passed by the horror house. The dog broke loose and ran to me. I was so excited, he jumped on me, tail wagging tongue hanging, I petted and hugged him, wow it was great to hug-" she coughed.

"Anyway, I'm hugging the dog and the lady runs up saying she's so sorry the dog got away, but don't worry, he doesn't bite- She was nice and sweet, had the kindest voice."

Pepi sucked in a tremulous breath. Her eyes closed, a gentle smile graced her sad face. She wrapped her arms around herself to remember the feeling of that moment, hold onto that brief moment.

"Then, then the door swung open and Vincent came out. He grabbed my arm and snarled at the lady, "Get away," he yelled, "stay the hell away!" He threatened her.

"She snatched up her dog so fast and ran away down the street and never looked back."

Back against the wall, Pepi pulled her knees back up and clamped her arms around them as tightly as she could like a vice, like she was literally trying to hold herself together.

It was if she let go her body could just fall apart, in pieces. One by one, her head could drop off, then her arms, then her legs then…. she stopped talking.

The girls sat quietly in the dark.

Cheyne let her catch her breath, then softly asked, "What happened, Pepi?"

Pepi let out her held breath, exhaling long and slow. "Well," The teen continued with her nauseating story. "Vincent wrenched me into the house and slammed the door. I tell you, I was petrified. I didn't know what was going to happen.

"As it turns out, I never could have imagined, in my wildest nightmares, I couldn't have dreamed up such, such-" all of a sudden it she sounded like she couldn't catch her breath, she sucked in short ragged gasps.

Cheyne quickly moved to her and threw her arms around her friend, holding her until Pepi calmed.

Pepi moved away. "I'm okay. I'm okay."

"Really Pep, maybe we need to-"

"I have to finish." She haggardly sucked air in, let it out, her stomach was pulled in tight as a drum like there was no air in her at all.

Pepi struggled to keep her voice strong, unemotional, nevertheless it shook. "Vincent dragged me by the arm, he stalked fast across the room, so fast I couldn't keep up with my little legs so he was literally dragging me by the arm up the stairs banging my hip and legs against the wood stairs, up to my mother.

"He stomped over to her and slapped her a few times to wake her up. Now I see where she got it from. Mom sat up bleary-eyed, drooling, confused and ugly. 'What?' Mom asked him. 'Did you bring me some goodies?'

"Expecting some drugs, her eyes took on a putrid glow until Vincent shook his head and pushed me in front of him, to her. She leaned back, 'what do I want with her?' she said."

Pepi hesitated, they could hear a bit of movement outside the closet door. They assumed it was Gram checking on them.

Pepi went on. "Vincent told her what I had done. He told her I could bring the police down on their heads, he said that woman that saw me might have gone straight to the cops. That should have given them a clue right then the shape I was in. It had to be pretty bad if they thought a stranger would take one look at malnourished me and head straight to the authorities." She laughed harshly.

"But, my condition wasn't their concern. My behavior possibly bringing on the police was. I needed to be taught a lesson." Pepi hesitated.

"I gotta say this fast Chey or it won't get out." Her words suddenly rushed like a faucet turned on high, "So, so Vincent held me while my mother broke every one of my fingers, *every one of my fingers one by one* so next time I wanted to turn the door knob I'd think twice."

The words gushed and it was like all of her air and will went with them, she dropped down on the floor and curled into a fetus position.

"Oh my God, Pepi, oh my God, oh my God!" Cheyne couldn't think with the horrible words striking her brain. "How could they, how could your mother do that to you? I don't understand," she slapped her hands over her ears and shook her head and rocked from side to side.

The girls grew silent again. Pepi in her heinous darkness, Cheyne in her grotesque bewilderment not even trying to hide her weeping.

Pepi made a faint keening noise like she was struggling so hard not to cry that it hurt.

They stayed like that for a long time. Pepi curled on the floor, Cheyne ragged against the wall, hiccupping, until the tears finally slowed.

After a while, Pepi stirred. She moved to sit up. Bracing against the wall she patted Cheyne's arm to comfort her.

Cheyne almost laughed at the role change. Pepi was reliving her agonizing tortuous past and she was comforting Cheyne who could hardly stand what she had heard.

"You are always surprising to me, Pep. You're the victim and you're sorry for my pain."

Pepi heard the warm smile in her voice. It actually made her feel better.

"I hate to ask, Pep, but we need it all cleared, anything else? Anything else in your hellish childhood that you haven't said?" Cheyne worked at keeping her voice even, stay steady for more anguish.

How could this petite girl have withstood all that horror? No wonder she was always guarded, wary, stoic. Kept people at arm's length, kept her heart behind a sturdy iron wall, had mind-grating nightmares.

"No," Pepi's voice was small. "That was finally the worst of it."

"But what happened Pep? How'd you get out? I mean you're here. Your poor fingers, how did you-"

"My fingers," Pepi repeated. Cheyne could see the silhouette of Pepi's hands raise up, the fingers spread open in front of her face as she perused them.

"Actually, it was my broken fingers that saved me. Luck was finally on my side. It was all downhill from there. One of the junkies happened to be a defrocked or whatever you call it, doctor.

"He'd lost his hospital job and med license from stealing and selling drugs and prescriptions. He was a regular at the house. My mother was in a fairly even state at one point, between being stoned blitzed and before the DT's started. She asked Doc, he went by Doc, to look at my fingers.

"My hands were wrapped up in gauze. After they'd done the deed, Vincent had stormed out and didn't come back for days and Mom had passed out. One of the stoners had wrapped up my hands but told me not to tell anyone." She stared at her hands still held up in front of her.

"Thankfully, Doc came in that night, because I couldn't drink or eat, even the bathroom was, uh," she let Cheyne get the drift.

"Doc splinted and bandaged me and fed me full of painkillers and put me to bed. He did his other drug business then left. Then the miraculous thing happened." Her head shook from side-to-side in amazement.

"I guess even Doc surprised himself that he still had a drop of humanity left in him. He made an anonymous call to the police then steered clear of the place. The cops swooped in, arrested everybody, including Vincent and my mother and took me to the hospital."

"Thank goodness for fallen angels," Cheyne said.

"Yeah. What I hadn't known was all this time Gram had been paying a detective to search for me. When my mother left with me, Gram called the police, but they said they couldn't do anything because my mother had the right to take me anywhere she wanted.

"But Gram knew I was in jeopardy. At first she searched for me, but, when she realized there was no way she was going to find me on her own, she hired a detective."

"Huh. Must have been a lousy detective because he didn't find you."

"Yeah. Well, I wasn't in any pre-school. Mom wasn't working, had no credit cards, old address on her expired driver's license. We were living in a crack house, there was no trail, no way to track us. Grams cashed in her insurance policy to pay for the detective for over a year."

"Pep, your grandmother cared. She cared about you."

Pepi didn't respond at first. Cheyne was about to speak again when Pepi said, "Yes. You're right. I would do anything for Gram, she never stopped searching for me. And, I'm home now." She sighed. It was a relieved, contented sigh.

"Have you seen your mother, since, uh, it was a long time ago, what's happened to her? Do you know?"

Her face and voice hard, Pepi said angrily, "I don't really care. Gram said due to her mental illness and drug abuse after she got out of jail she was institutionalized. I hear Gram talking to her sisters sometimes about my mother.

"She's apparently doing better these days. They might even let her out someday. I don't care about her, not one bit." She rolled down to the floor and curled back into the fetus position.

"Hmm." Cheyne thought to herself, *next on the list may be getting Pepi and her mother together, to get them to tell each other*

Louise Furley

how they felt then, how they feel now, and for Pepi to forgive. As long as she held hate in her heart she wouldn't heal.

Although, Cheyne was so furious with Pepi's mother for putting her through that hell she wanted to see the woman punished. The mother should be the protector, not the perpetrator of her child's pain and abuse.

Cheyne lay down beside her friend.

They stayed like that for an hour or so. Then Cheyne sat up yawning. "Hmm," her stomach was growling and she had a feeling...

Pushing clothes out of the way, she crawled to the door and quietly opened it. *Oh yeah, thanks Gram!*

Elma Mae had set a tray outside the closet in a warmer containing a casserole, buttered cornbread, cookies, sodas, plates, forks, napkins.

Cheyne pulled the tray inside leaving the door open to let in some light. She pulled the lid off the casserole. The aroma of cheese and chicken and still slightly warm cornbread fanned out, filling the closet.

She tried to quietly spoon some casserole out.

"OMG, Chey, leave it to you and your bottomless stomach. Gimmie a plate."

Chapter Thirty

Cheyne stayed the night then went home early the next morning.

The following day, she hopped on her bike and headed back to Pepi's house.

Pepi greeted her at the door, her same old perky, sarcastic, bouncy self.

They called Frieda Mills to find where her cousin was working and the exact location of the flu plant.

The girls figured they would get there around lunchtime as Frieda said Jumper usually ate his lunch across the street at a diner. It took them almost an hour to get there.

The lab and factory plant, a conglomerate of brick and cement and composite buildings was spread over several acres on the outskirts of the city, still within the city limits but at an area less travelled.

The parking lot surrounding the production facility was jam packed with cars, and a fleet of trucks lined one side. The mix of structures looked more like connected barracks or long bomb shelters as there were very few windows, only in the front offices area.

Louise Furley

Granze Global Pharmaceuticals on a sign on a cement wall indicated the entrance was between two cement columns. A metal fence with dagger pole points encircled the building. Everyone had to pass through a security gate to enter the property.

A few patrons wandered the small string of restaurants and shops jumbled on both sides of the four-lane street.

Directly across the street from the factory complex was Pumperdunk's Diner.

Jumper Hudson's straw yellow hair and long head were visible behind the diner's streaky picture window. He was alone. Instead of sitting at the counter, he took up a four-top table and was eating an enormous triple-decker Dagwood Sandwich.

Holding it with both hands, the young man opened his mouth as wide as he could and crammed in as much of the sandwich as possible.

When he bit down on the front, a smorgasbord of cold cuts, tomatoes, pickles, peppers, onions, and cheese catapulted out all sides of the sandwich, creamy goo oozed through his fingers and ran down his arms.

A wet white, mayo-ring circled his mouth. Stuffing the sandwich guts back inside the bread with his fingers, he didn't see the girls enter the sandwich shop chatting gaily.

They pretended surprise when they saw him.

Cheyne slipped up behind him and practically shouted in revelation, "Oh, hey, Jumper. Jumper Hudson, is that you?" She swung her head around as if trying to get a good look at him. "What a surprise running into you like this!"

Still holding the bursting sandwich, he stopped mid-chew when he saw her delighted grin.

At the same time, Pepi strolled around the other side seemingly happy and also surprised to see him there. "Well, Cheyne, look who's here, long time no see, Jump," Pepi crowed, giving him a quick brief wave. The girls hovered in front of his table with ear-to-ear grins.

254

Jumper's cheeks stuffed like a squirrel, lips parted slightly unable to hold in the huge bite he'd taken. He tried to close his mouth to chew, but he'd shoved in so much he couldn't.

His mouth covered in mayo and mustard, more of the cream mixture oozed out the corners of lips. After a few seconds he was able to chomp and swallow but still his mouth was full.

He tried to speak, but only sprayed, his words unintelligible. The girls took that as an offer to sit.

He forced the un-chewed food down his throat. Not used to pretty girls noticing him much less sitting with him, Jumper gulped and swallowed hastily. "Uh, what uh, what uh," he slobbered moronically.

"So," Pepi drawled, then jabbered quickly, "what a pleasant surprise running into you here. What's new, Jumper? What's goin' on? What're you doin' here? How's the job?"

"Yeah," Cheyne joined in. "What is it you're doing now? I think Frieda said you worked at a factory. Do you like put nuts in bolts or something?"

The waitress approached with her order book out, but both girls declined anything to eat. Watching Jumper eat had killed their appetite.

Not expecting them to ask questions, he had already picked up the rest of his sandwich and gobbled several huge bites at once.

He glanced around to see if all the other tables were full and that's why they had sat at his, but the restaurant was half empty. He chewed vigorously, gulping loudly like a bass snagging flies.

"Uh," he stuttered, swigged some cola to wash the bread and meat down.

Drinking too much too fast, he burped then choked then drank some more which set off a fit of choking and coughing. He doused the table and his shirt with spurting soda and chunks of half chewed food.

He held up a hand when Cheyne moved to get up to pat him on the back or worse give him the Heimlich.

Finally, hacking and gasping for air, his tongue wagging, Jumper took a napkin and rubbed it all over his face. He shook his head, straight as a whisk broom blond hair swept his forehead and dangled over pond bottom brown eyes, tufts of hair stuck out at the sides.

"No I, I mean, yes I work at a factory, but not as a bolt fitter or something. I have a degree." He sniffed proudly.

"Oh my, really?" Her elbows on the table, Pepi set her chin in her hands and leaned across the table, her head cocked coyly at him.

They'd tossed a coin outside, she lost, it was her turn to play the flirt. "I just love an educated man." She hated herself for simpering like this, but they needed information.

They'd discussed it on the way. Coming right out and asking him questions might have made him leery and clam up, and they didn't want any more people to know they were asking questions about the men they were searching for.

Jumper was mesmerized by her unearthly silvery-grey eyes. The black as velvet eyelashes curled at the ends seemed to be motioning him to come closer. He did, leaned in so far his cola stained shirt mopped up some of the goo on his plate.

He gawped at her. Not used to beautiful girls paying him any attention, he didn't know how to respond, or even if he should. The corners of his mouth still had dots of mayo in them. A wet piece of napkin clung to his chin.

Squashing her feelings of revulsion, Pepi forced herself to lean closer to the young man who was wearing a lot of his lunch.

The closer she got, the more she could see pock marks from old acne covering most of his face, and fresh pimples popping across his forehead.

Her stomach churning, she trained her eyes on a less disgusting freckle below one eye and maneuvered her reluctant little pillow lips into an enticing crescent smile.

"I've always thought you were so, uh, charming. Do tell us about your job, Jumper, we are so interested, aren't we, Cheyne?"

Seeing Pepi struggling to not gag, Cheyne wondered, *what happened with all that toughen up ROTC training?*

Figuring Pepi wasn't going to last long, she pulled her own chair closer and regarded the young man with feigned interest. She leaned in a little, not too close, not within spitting distance.

"Totally. We want to hear absolutely everything. We think you're, er, um, hot." Her voice fell flat at the end. She took a deep breath, smiled broadly and said, "We want to know everything about you, Jumper. Tell us all about your job, start at the beginning."

His narrow face flushed. He sat back importantly. If he had suspenders he would have been holding them with his thumbs.

"Well uh, since you're interested, actually it wasn't my plan to work in a factory after I graduated from four years at the university with a degree in molecular biology.

"My dream was that I could get hired by one of the big companies like Sanofi-Aventis, you know, they're a leading global pharmaceutical company in New York. Unfortunately," he stuck a finger inside his collar that was buttoned up to his chin, ran it back and forth.

Nervously, he took a small bite of his Dagwood, chewing crudely, he wiped the gunk off his mouth with a napkin. He actually resembled the real comic guy, Dagwood, with the funny nose, little round eyes and hair sticking up in tufts, except he had more of a narrow, rectangle head.

He jerked his head to sweep the broom-bristle bangs out of his eyes.

Talking out of the side of his mouth, the bit of napkin on his chin clung on even as his jaw wobbled, he said, "I wasn't actually top of my class, and besides, they wanted people with Master's or PhD's. But, because of my mega brain, and, well, vast lab experience, I had preferred doing lab work to classes because I work the best alone. I'm a little um, shy, uh, anyway."

His voice throttled, he tugged more at his collar, looked everywhere but directly at the girls.

They murmured encouraging words to keep him talking, which he did. In fact now he spouted nonstop.

"So I got hired in the vaccine manufacturing plant in the formulation center. All of a vaccine's components are merged and mixed into a steel vat then packaged into the individual shots that people get vaccinated for the flu."

Clearing his throat, he set the last hunk of sandwich next to an inch of pickle spear on the plate. His head down, he peered at the girls through the long fine bangs to see if they were still listening to him, usually girls shut off after his first five words if not before.

Most wouldn't get within an arm's length of him. But Pepi and Cheyne kept their glazed eyeballs glued to the narrow young man with holes pocking his pasty skin.

His job wasn't the most glamorous in the world, he couldn't imagine these gorgeous creatures had any interest in something as banal as flu shots or factory labs, or him.

The waitress toddled back and forth, dawdling near their table, there wasn't but a few other customers in the grill. She stared at the three wondering what on earth those two breathtaking beauties were doing with that gruesome Jumper.

Everyone knew him. He ate at the café a few times a week and left a good 5, sometimes 7 percent tip. The cook's bell dinged, she shuffled off to pick up an order.

Jumper continued in a nasally monotone. Pepi tried to smile at him while thinking *this guy has the voice and face of roadkill...*

"It's kind of a pain," he griped. "Because we have to spend the entire day covered from head to toe in a white sterile gown and booties, plastic gloves and goggles. No jewelry is allowed. Everything is constantly washed down in bleach and alcohol."

He glanced down at his oddly bone white hands from years of washing with harsh liquids. "This is not for our safety, but it's for the safety of the vaccine. Humans are basically filthy people who sneeze and lose hairs fouling up the most pristine things."

He sniffed, wiped his nose with the back of his hand. "First I was a runner. That's someone who watches through a window in a door to make sure nothing is going wrong in the vats. Then I moved up to blender. I add the ingredients and blend the vaccine."

Sitting up a bit more importantly, he said, "Did you know that the flu virus changes from year to year? So the vaccines have to be updated every year. We don't have much time to formulate, produce, test and distribute the vaccine.

"So if there're any problems they have to be caught quickly or a shortage could occur and heavily impact the supply, it could result in a pandemic. It's happened before. It's part of my job to retest the vaccine at certain stages."

Bragging now, he said, "I'm a pretty vital cog in this wheel. Technically I could save lives!" He patted his chest with some pomposity. The little piece of napkin broke loose and sailed down landing on his sandwich.

The girls nodded like puppets with forced smiles and vacuous eyes.

He glanced from one to the other, his boastful attitude quickly seeping away, his gaze dropped to the table.

The silence grew. He cleared his throat. Everyone strained for something to say.

"So, uh, like, wow," Pepi forced out.

Uncomfortably, Jumper cleared his throat again because he didn't know what else to say. "So, uh," he stammered. "Did you know that manufacturers will produce approximately 62 million doses of flu vaccine this year?"

The girls stared blankly at him.

He strove to find some other fascinating facts, but could think of nothing.

At his third throat clearing, Cheyne gave her head a tiny imperceptive shake, and blinked to bring him back into focus. She smiled broadly.

"Well, then, um, Jumper. Isn't that, uh, fascinating? Wasn't that fascinating, Pep?" She grinned at her friend who was also blinking to stay engaged in the boring, stinky Jumper.

Cheyne gestured unobservantly with her head for Pepi to talk to him.

Pepi shot Cheyne a veiled scowl.

Cheyne grinned bigger. Pepi scowled harder.

259

Rolling her eyes, Cheyne crossed her arms on the table and lowered her body closer to the table, bringing her face closer to Jumper's. She tried to keep her gaze directly on the murky irises, there was too much gross weird stuff going on the rest of his face.

"So, um, you are so cute you know? Pepi and I would just love to get to know you better. Right Pep?"

Pepi just looked at her with a baleful, barely there miserable smile.

"Anyway," Cheyne bit off a sigh, "don't you work right across the street?" Her head in a flirtatious tilt, she twirled a piece of hair around a finger, holding her breath. He smelled like onions and disinfectant.

Jumper's lips pulled to the side. He said a little sarcastically, "Yeah, duh, Granze Global Pharmaceuticals. It's like the only factory of its kind for like 500 miles plus." He scratched his head and pushed the bangs back, they flopped right back down now swabbed with a splotch of mustard.

"Oh. Hmm." Then Cheyne pretended something just came to her. She snapped her fingers. "Hey, I think I know some people that work there too."

"Really? Who?"

"Oh, let's see, I know um, Talco Castilla, and a couple of guys named Khirbet and Devin, Pablo, do you know any of them?"

He thought for a minute, the dull brown eyes circled around behind the drab lids. The fine blond hair slipped over his eyes making them look like they were looking through teeny tiny yellow prison bars.

He shook his head. "Nah, I don't work with any of them. Might be in another division, it's a big place."

"Oh." The girls deflated, slumped. Cheyne perked up. "Oh, wait, what about an Ahmet, or- or a Gary, Gary- I forget his last name?" She hoped Pepi remembered, they hadn't brought their notebooks so he wouldn't be suspicious.

But Pepi shook her head. "I got nothing." She fought with herself not to edge away from him.

"Well," Jumper said, "don't know no Aamit but there's a Gary Duggan, and a Gary Badia, there's a Gary O'Flannigan who works the production line that the flu vaccine travels on to get to the individual packaging."

The girls shook their heads. "No, No, it's none of them. Oh well," Cheyne tried hard to not let her frustration show.

Not understanding why they were so flummoxed over this Gary person, Jumper just stared at them. After all, he was the one they wanted. His shoulders raised and a shiver rolled through his gangly body, relishing the thought that one of these hot babes wanted him.

Wondering which one he was going to bag, he crossed one leg over the other and swung his foot. He wore long saggy shorts, buttoned up shirt, white socks and flip-flops. The thong went flap-flap-flap every time he moved his foot.

"So, we ne-"

"Oh wait-" Jumper cut Pepi off. "There is a Gary Gunther. He transports the vaccine from the factory to a warehouse. He's tall like a basketball player, muscular, real dark skinned. Maybe he's the one you're thinking of. It's a long shot but-" He glanced at his watch, his brows jumped.

He stood up clumsily. "I have to go, I'm late." He picked up his check, threw some money on it, looked at the last piece of sandwich on the plate. "I'm sorry I gotta run, hey maybe you girls and I can get together late-"

"Oh sure," Cheyne mooned, smiling at him, batting her lashes. "That would be lovely, we'll give you a call. Oh, hon, before you go, where about is this warehouse? Do you know the name of it?"

He was so pleased as punch they wanted to see him again, he didn't question their interest in the warehouse. "It's you know, over on the back roads deep in the country, a couple of miles before the Iceplant Inlet. It's called Galypotts." He indicated east with his head.

"It's that big grey and white cement building with the shop in front. Can't miss it, you can smell those old farms long before you get halfway there what with the pigs and chicken coops." His nose hitched, the back of his hand wiped at it catching a swab of the mustard in his hair on the way up.

"Anyway," he said quickly. "Give me your numbers-"

"Oh, *we'll* call *you*, honey," Pepi said with an awkward wink. She'd never actually winked before. It was ew, she thought to herself.

"Uh, well that's really nice." He was pleased. "Here let me give you my number." He rattled it off.

Cheyne waited for Pepi to write it down, Pepi waited for her to. Cheyne finally flattened a frown and wrote his number down.

Teeth that could use some whitening showed, his smile stretching the long pocked face. He held up his baggy pants with one hand and saluted them with the other.

"Ok, then, I'll see ya soon." He swiped up the last bite of sandwich and pickle, tossed them in his mouth, then flip-flopped out the door not seeing they were as elated over the information he gave them as the fact that he left.

"OMG. I just about went into a coma," Cheyne groaned, crossing her eyes. "That was grueling. I thought he'd never shut up!"

"Yeah, me too. I wanted to take his grubby fork and stick it in my ear. Let's go." Pepi saw the bill lying on the table. She looked closer at it. "That gross cheapskate, he only left her $1 tip on a $17 check."

She swung her purse off the back of her chair, pulled a couple of dollars out and set them on top of the bill.

"You go, Santa Claus," Cheyne chided her cheerfully. They hurried out the door.

Chapter Thirty-One

On their way to find the warehouse they called Talana.

Talana's graceful, girlish voice came through on speakerphone. "Hi guys. I confirmed that Adonai Alamanni could not have killed my sister or Miss Milan.

"I spoke with Adonni's mother, his sister Adele, and one of his best friends, Jeff Jones. They all said that Adonni was able to graduate early and before the parade even happened he hopped a plane to Berlin to go work at the BMW Fabrikar Plant and has not been back since." She took a breath.

"He took his new girlfriend, Sandylee Graystone with him, and he calls home every Sunday, collect."

Pepi said into the phone, "That can easily be verified by the police. Well, I guess we can cross one more person off our suspect list. I wonder if the police know that yet. Or care."

"I have to run an errand for my mother then I'll call your Detective James and tell him for you, okay?" Talana said.

"Yeah, that'd be great, thanks, Tal," Pepi replied.

Talana asked, "What did you find out from that spindly guy with the pocked face at the factory, Frieda's cousin, what's his name again?"

Pepi filled her in with what they learned from Jumper and told her where they were going now.

"Oh." A wave of trepidation invaded Talana's voice. "Are you sure you should do that? Maybe you should call the police now and tell them what you've learned, what your suspicions are."

"No," Cheyne said. "Because that's all they are, suspicions. They would laugh us out of town. When we find out something definitive we'll fill them in. We'll call you after we find and check out the warehouse." Pepi rang off over Talana's protests.

As they climbed on their bikes and were pulling on their helmets, Pepi said breezily, "I just wanted to say, um, thank you for, you know, the other night and all. You're a good friend, Cheyne. A true angel. I'm lucky you're my friend. Thank you."

"Back at ya, Pep. You'd do the same for me."

"Uh huh. *Bridge?*" Referring to Cheyne's supportive words when they had been huddled in the closet. "You can be my bridge? What are you now, a motivational poet?"

"Oh shut up, let's go!"

The girls rode their bikes down the main street in a single line, Pepi on her lavender bike and Cheyne on her pink.

Cars whizzed past on the busy street. Drivers irritated at bicyclists sharing their road became aggressive and unruly, honking unnecessarily and shouting obscenities out the window, so they moved to the sidewalk.

After 45 minutes they were pretty much out of the business section of town and entering a rural, more wooded area interspersed with fields and farms.

They headed towards Iceplant Inlet about another ten plus miles south.

Passing neat green rows of tender lettuce crops ripening quickly in the cool sunny weather, the pair now cycled side-by-side along a tarred path that flowed in and out through whiskery fields and the two-lane road. Cinnamon ringlets flapping against a bright red blouse, loose blonde tresses bouncing off a pale yellow dress.

The further from town they travelled, the traffic dwindled. They started passing more expansive grasslands and bigger crop fields. Oak and Maple trees blossomed emerald buds, pastures bloomed with buttercups looking like it had rained lemon drops.

Daisies poked their frilly heads from slender blades of rippling grass. Cascarilla Way was a winding stretch of ancient dairy road, dotted with rustic barns and acres of hayfields spreading long and as wide as the eye could see.

They rode for a long time without a single vehicle passing by them.

The road was originally established eons ago by farmers herding their cattle from one pasture to another, and then those that weren't used for milking ultimately once a year were mustered to town for auction.

Cows knee deep in grass and weeds stopped chewing to watch the teens ride by. An unseen rooster crowed, and the occasional whinny, snort or moo broke the stillness.

The acrid smell of newly cut hay wafted with heaps of stinky manure, flies buzzed over fresh piles. High and off in the distance vultures circled over something dead or dying.

Weathered farm houses, some red, some grey, some modern with verandahs, some it was a wonder they still stood, hulking like old toadstools deteriorating far off the road.

Clothespinned wash flapped in the gentle breeze. In a few backyards littered busted cars, rusting parts and old forgotten equipment were being taken over by nature, eventually swallowed up by the overgrowth. Rows of bright green pea sprouts zipped past like spokes on a spinning wheel.

Pepi took a deep breath, exhaled slowly. "Ahh, smell that, the outdoors, so fresh and country, the rich soil-"

"Achoo!" Cheyne's nose crinkled. "Ugh. Bugs, weeds, farm animals. Ick. No thanks."

Her response made Pepi laugh. "City girl, you liked it well enough when we were at camp a few years ago and went camping and horseback riding."

"Sure. Counting shooting stars, campfire sing-alongs and s'mores, and the guy that led us on horseback down the trails was *so cute*! But that was then, now you can bring me jewels and shoes and running water, baby, you can keep the smelly fields."

"Gawd you're such a *girl*!" Pepi scoffed. "Even though you sport those cowboy boots, you can take the girl out of the city but you can't take the-"

Pointing, "Look- I think that's it," Cheyne said abruptly in a loud whisper.

Pepi followed her pointed finger to a half toppled sign that read Galypotts with an arrow pointing east.

Beyond the sign, past a heavily timbered area that crept back off the road, an outcrop of buildings was only barely visible due to the curve of the road.

They slowed way down but kept pedaling.

"Why would they put a store way out here in the middle of nowhere? It's not even a convenient way to get to Iceplant Inlet it's quicker to take the interstate. I'll bet it's a front for some unlawful business," Pepi mused.

"Shh, we don't want anyone to hear us coming," Cheyne whispered.

"Okay, geeze, we're pretty far away-"

Cheyne suddenly turned off the tarred path and into a throng of trees heavy with new baby leaves.

"Hey!" Pepi squawked then turned sharply almost falling over and followed her into the woods. Her arms and legs scraped by twigs as she hurried after the fleeting blonde.

They made their own trail a few yards into the forest, tires cracking fallen branches and crunching dried leaves, turning every which way to avoid hitting a tree or colliding with a big rock.

Cheyne slowed then stopped next to a huge moss covered stump. Pepi pulled up next to her. They hopped off their bikes and removed their helmets.

"What are you-" Pepi started to talk but Cheyne had bent over, tipped her head upside down and was raking her hands through her hair. She stood up, throwing her head back and ran her fingers through the fluffed locks neatening them.

"I hate helmet hair!" Cheyne complained under her breath. "Look, listen," she pulled Pepi behind a wide tree. They peeked from behind the tree.

A few hundred yards away through a grove of trees and shrubs they could see a cement and grey building.

Everything was still, like a ghost town. There were no sounds of industry, not a car passed, the place could be deserted it was so quiet, a feeling of emptiness hung in the air. Only the wind rustling gently, occasionally through the thicket made a sound.

"There're no cars in the parking lot," Cheyne whispered. "We'd stand out like sore thumbs if we waltzed straight down the driveway and into the store, we don't want them to see us coming. The plan is to sneak in, look around covertly, and see if we can see any of those guys in our photos and then get the hoof out and call the police."

Pepi nodded. She leaned her bike against the tree and hung her helmet on it. "Recon."

"Exactly," Cheyne said. "Look, this whole line of trees goes from here and then stops around a dozen yards or so from the building. We maybe could stay hidden in them as long as possible to approach unseen. There're windows, maybe we could peek inside a window."

Brushing her hands on her jeans, Pepi had half a mind to mention grasshoppers, salamanders, rodents and such lurking in the timberland they planned to keep skulking through, but thought better of it.

"How about I lead?" she suggested instead, tying her hair back into a long ponytail.

Cheyne was happy to let her go first. She took a lip balm out of her purse, ran it over her lips, tossed it back in her purse and dropped her purse in the bike basket and said, "Okay. Let's go."

They proceeded to make their way stealthily towards the building staying in the cloak of dense trees, stepping softly as possible, ducking branches and pushing aside prickly vines.

Sometimes they scurried across a leaner patch ducking down as they ran. Sunlight filtered through branches tracing mellow yellow ribbons over grass and bright spots on tree trunks.

The teens sprinted faster fearing the open sun's strobe light pointed at them like a lighthouse beacon, especially on Pepi with her red shirt.

Finally they were a few dozen yards from the building, still in a thinning grove of trees but mixed with shrubbery and knee-tall grass and weeds. They stopped to catch their breath and make their plan.

Bent over, her hands on her knees and panting, Pepi said, "I think when we're done I need to call Thomas to come and get us. It's a long, long way back home."

Cheyne nodded, too out of breath to speak.

Pepi moaned, "I should have taken my cell out of my purse so we can call him while walking back to our bikes. Oh well."

Hunkering down, they hid behind the thickest foliage. Peering through the greenery to observe their target.

A vine sticking her in the ankle, trying not to snap noisy twigs, Pepi pushed aside bristly leafage and whispered, "It looks like more than two buildings. There's like the little shop out front, it's the right place there's Galypotts painted across the slanted roof."

The girls studied the building.

"There's a warehouse attached to the back and it looks like there's a greenhouse tucked behind in the meadow. Plus I can see a couple of other smaller shed like buildings," Pepi commented quietly.

She caught Cheyne's grimace. "What's the matter?"

Cheyne rubbed her nose hard. "Smells fuggy here. My boots are getting muddy and I'm pretty sure something tried to crawl up my leg. Let's hurry and get out of this jungle."

Pepi snickered at her friend. "What a sissy." She discreetly pulled a spider off the back of Cheyne's hair, tossing it away off to the side. She stood on tiptoe in her sneakers to see over the tangle of broad leaves in front of her.

"This shelter of trees thins quite a bit but I think like you said we can stay in it until maybe a dozen yards or so of open space to the building."

Cheyne said, "We're going to have to move fast. We stand out like a bullfighter's cape, you in your red shirt and blue jeans, at least my pale yellow dress isn't as bright as a neon light." She flapped both hands at her calling, "Toro- Toro."

"Are you done now?" Pepi shook her head. "You ready?"

"Let's do it."

The girls darted from skinny tree to skinnier tree, then at the last one they sprinted over yards of open space to the building.

Throwing themselves at the wall, they quickly pressed their bodies against the warm cement. Holding their breaths from the tension and from running the last few yards had them panting again.

Pepi turned to face the building. There were windows all around the building about nose high to the girls.

The top half of the building was wood painted grey, the bottom half cement painted white. Very cautiously so as not to be seen, Pepi slid near a window and tried to peek in from the side.

After checking out a few windows, she said quietly, "Darn. They're covered. Can't see a thing."

Cheyne motioned to her. Pepi scuttled over to her.

Cheyne put a finger to her lips and pointed to the window she was standing under. If she stood up straight, someone looking out the window would have been able to see the top of her head so she was bent over slightly so she couldn't be seen.

Pepi mirrored her. The window was open a hair.

Cheyne straightened very slowly, gripped the edge of the window and pulled her head up inch by slow inch until she was on tiptoes and could see through the tiny open crack.

After a minute she slid back down. Eyes huge in her pale face, she appeared frightened but excited.

Pepi waited expectantly, her expression asked '*what did you see?*'

Cheyne cupped her hand to Pepi's ear and whispered. "There're people inside. I saw," her voice shook. "I saw that guy, the hawk nose one in Miss Milan's picture."

Chapter Thirty-Two

$\mathcal{P}$epi's mouth dropped wide open. "No kidding, are you su-" Cheyne clapped her hand over Pepi's mouth and held her finger to her own lips to be quiet.

She whispered, "Yeah, I'm sure. And that's not all, Talco's there too. And I think that Pablo guy from the yearbook is there, the Mexican man with the buzz cut and Hitler symbol tattoos, but it's kinda dim inside so I'm not sure it's him."

Pepi looked apoplectic. She pressed her hands together and held them over her mouth and nose, her bulging eyes flicked from Cheyne to the window, out to the forest of trees and back to Cheyne.

They weren't in any cover, the spindly grass was only about 8 inches high surrounding the warehouse. Anyone driving by could clearly see the two teenagers loitering outside the building, they were like red and yellow thumbprints against the white cement.

But, Pepi just had to see too. Reaching over her head, she pressed her palms against the wall and crept up until her fingertips gripped the ridge of the window. Slowly, on tiptoes she pulled her head up until her eyeballs were even with the open window.

About 10 seconds passed before she slid back down. She motioned for Cheyne to follow her a few steps away from the window.

Then her lips close to Cheyne's ear she whispered, "There's a blond guy in there too, must be the heartbreaker, Devin."

Cheyne whispered back, "Let's see if we can hear them talking."

Pepi just nodded, she didn't trust herself to speak.

Their eyes as wide as satellite dishes and hands clamped over their mouths, they plastered their backs flat against the wall.

The raw cement pricked and scraped their backs as they inched back over and slowly moved up the wall until their heads were just below the window.

There they stood perfectly still, slightly hunched over, holding their breaths, and eavesdropped.

Murmuring drifted through the crack.

The girls endeavored to steady their wildly pounding hearts and quiet their breathing. To their ears, their hearts and frantic breathing sounded like drums beating so loud they feared the men inside could hear.

They pressed their hands and backs against the wall to hold steady, struggling to quell their exhilaration of finally finding the people they were seeking and the panic of getting caught. They were dying to hear what was going on but frighteningly aware they were in a very precarious position.

If they were caught, they could get in trouble, or more likely worse could happen. These men, the girls believed, were cold blooded killers.

When they finally settled themselves down, they realized they could make out much of what the men were saying. Mostly it was trivial chit-chat about cars and money. But then the talk turned nefarious.

One accented voice said, "Did they have a hard time getting the first batch of the saffron crap into the vaccine?"

Cheyne slapped a hand over her own mouth to keep from gasping.

Another voice answered, "Nah, Gary cooked it like it was a tea, then when that idiot blender went on break, twenty freakin' times a day, must have a pea sized bladder, lucky for us, Gary was able to keep slipping in and pouring it into the mix that was being blended. No problem."

Cheyne's knees buckled, she started to move to the side of the window so she could stand up.

Suddenly, Pepi threw out her arm grabbed Cheyne's arm and yanked her down in a low crouch to the ground.

At Cheyne's surprised look, Pepi pointed to the front of the building.

An old beat up Chevy truck with a closed cab was crunching rapidly up the stone drive. Apparently in such a hurry, the girls hadn't seen or heard him speeding towards them on the highway and veer off into the driveway.

The driver sped up as close as he could to the front of the store then came to a tire screeching halt.

The door threw open and, Gary Gunther unfurled his basketball player's body, leaping out onto the gravel and rushed through the front door.

The girls tried to melt into the grass, praying he was too distracted to see them.

They could see his silhouette pass by the shaded windows until it appeared he had gone through the front store to the back warehouse.

Instead of wisely making a run for cover, in unison, the girls crept back up the wall and stood slightly stooped over to listen. They could hear Gary Gunther when he got to the warehouse. He was clearly upset. His deep voice belted stridently as soon as he crossed the doorway.

"Dudes, somethin's goin' on. Somebody is on to us. We're in trouble- about to be exposed-"

"Gary, man, get a grip," An authoritative, calmer, heavy accented voice cut him off.

Pepi mouthed to Cheyne, *"That might be the Khirbet guy."*

Cheyne nodded.

Gary's distraught vocal chords strained, his deep voice squeaking high. "Listen, I'm tellin' you, we're screwed, we're-"

"Slow down you jerk, take a deep breath, what the hell are you spouting about?"

Both girls recognized Talco Castilla's slight Spanish accent. Except now he sounded different than when they'd ever heard him speak before, he sounded coarse and callous with barely restrained anger.

"Ok, all right." The girls could actually hear Gary Gunther's shallow, quick breathing, he was that perturbed and close to the window.

A second passed, then over the other men's grumbling he said, "You know that freak geek, Jumper Hudson at the lab?"

"The blender? The scarecrow with the stretched out face?"

"Yeah, that's him. The blender. He just called me. He said these two girls were there an hour ago and they were asking about us. All of us," Gary ended abruptly.

"What?" Khirbet asked, his voice gravelly harsh even with the short word. "What are you talking about? What girls?" His accent might have given Lareina thrill shivers but it gave Pepi and Cheyne shivers of terror, he sounded so darkly sinister.

Even pressed against the warm cement they felt an unnatural coldness ease out the crack and down the wall, covering them like a nightmarish cloak, sucking away the air.

It felt weirdly dark and chill, as if a black cloud had passed over the sun blocking its warmth and light. Hair stood up on their arms, their throats tightened. But they stayed.

Gary still sounded worried, but steadier. Impatiently, he forced himself to speak slowly, grinding out his words in halting steps, like he was explaining to a four-year-old.

"Hudson said his cousin Frieda called him and said some girls from school she knows wanted to talk to him. But apparently these two high school girls had already showed up at the diner across the street from the lab and sat down at his table. What later struck him funny- funny peculiar not ha ha, was when the girls came into the diner they had acted like they had just come across him by accident."

"Yeah, so what, who cares about a couple of teenagers. Empty-headed things only interested in shoes and gossip." Impatient annoyance tinged Talco's words.

Gary didn't care for Talco's dismissive sarcasm. He snapped back at him, "What makes it crucially significant to us is that," he repeated his prior sentence, again slowly like talking to a child, "Hudson said when these two girls came into the diner they acted like, and actually said they had just come across him by accident and sat themselves right down."

"The jerk thought they were really into him. Two gorgeous honeys that are beauty pageant contestants, right. Have you ever seen this guy, he's practically hideous. He should have been suspicious right then, dammed scarecrow."

"Gary, get to the point," Khirbet barked.

Gary huffed, "Yeah. So, after the girls left, Hudson's cousin, Frieda called him to tell him these girls were looking for him and she had told him where he worked and ate lunch."

His patience expiring, Talco snarled, "So *who cares*?"

"All right, dude, don't get your boxers in a twist. Apparently these girls lied about just happening to run into him. Why would they do that? Then, they grilled him about his job, the lab," he paused, "and us."

Silence.

"Us? What do you mean us?" A different voice, accented, but smoother, softer, maybe Devin had joined the conversation.

The girls turned to each other, fright screamed wordlessly across their faces, they'd been found out! Their knees turned to melting butter.

They pressed their bodies hard against the wall to hold them up on their trembling legs. Cheyne's hair stuck up and around the wall from static electricity.

"Yeah," Gary was talking again. "The freak said they asked about us *by name*. You, Talco," it sounded like he was pointing at Talco, "and all of us, Pablo, Devin, Ahmet, and me, and even you,

Khirbet. Sounded like they didn't seem to know much about you or the correct pronunciation of your first name, and didn't say your last name at all, Ahmet or Devin either. I think they're fishing. But, they know something, how much, who knows? Khirb, someone let the lid off the caper. The teacher..."

The men's murmuring grew unintelligible, they must have moved away from the window. Then the girls could hear them clearly again.

Talco was saying, "I can't see how two little girls could figure out that we're poisoning the flu vaccine and planning on killing half the town."

Cheyne almost slapped her own face again to stifle her horrified gasp.

Gary spoke up, "I thought you taking out that schoolteacher," then it sounded like he turned to a different person, "and you doing your sister squashed any focus on our plot, or us."

"*Shut – up* you bleating sheep!" Talco's growl low in his throat carried to the open window.

The fierce threat in his voice sent fresh tremors through the eavesdropping girls

As scared as they were, the teens couldn't help sneaking another quick peek.

They saw a small man with a round, olive-toned face and a little slash of black mustache. He wore heels on his boots that made him look taller. His hair was a buzz cut on top with a braided pony tail on the bottom. The tail fell almost to his waist.

Scratching the top of his head, he pointed at hawk-nose and accused, "Yeah, I agree with Gary. This is all your fault, Khirbet." His arms and neck were covered in tattoos.

"Hey Pablo, I didn't say it was Khirbet's-"

But the Mexican churlishly shook his finger at hawk-nose, his heavily accented voice hostile. "You should have ensured that your daughters were dead before you left that house. This all started from you thinking that schoolteacher could have recognized you from overseas." He snorted.

"A chance spotting, she might not have even recognized you, but you said she had to go anyway, that she could have drawn attention to us and to our scheme. Plus, she'd seen all of us 6 together at the bar and down the road might have put something together."

"Aw, let it go, Pablo," one of the men said.

But Pablo was steamed, he shouted, "Now all our plans of wealth and power after we see if the first deaths at Corbiestep are traced to the meadow saffron poisoning of the vaccine! You said," his beet red face purple, kept shaking his finger at hawk-nose.

"That you believed with the delay element we added to make the poison not take effect until days later no one would catch on that they had been poisoned by their vaccines.

"People would think they had a stomach virus and blame a restaurant for food poisoning or something. If we deposit other poisons like rat poison into a few water supplies, the authorities will not be able to tie the deaths together, not trace them to the vaccine." He drew in a quick breath before surging on.

"Then we can go bigger, bigger cities until we can take control of the cities- threaten- extort-" the man blustered furiously- "But no, you, *you* had to screw it all up and bring your disgusting, sordid child-killer past into our plot-"

BANG!

At the sudden gunshot the girls dropped to the ground.

Incited voices jumbled over each other. "What the hell did you do that for?" Talco's belligerent voice could be heard above the fray.

"He needed to shut up," Khirbet's sociopathic voice replied calmly, coldly.

"What's going on in here?" A new, middle-eastern accented voice entered the room.

The girls glanced at each other. Must be the other guy who had been with Devin and Khirbet at the bar, Ahmet.

"Hey, what happened to Pablo?"

Talco answered him, "Who cares. Stick him in the freezer out back. Let's get this saffron crap loaded and get the hell out of here. Someone might have heard the shot and called the cops."

Ahmet said, "No worries. We are way out in the middle of nowhere. Farmers out here are always shooting varmints and hunters frequent these woods. The shot wouldn't have attracted any attention. Come on, you grab his legs, I got the top."

Sounds of scuffling and grunting could be heard, mumbles from the other men discussing what to load first.

Khirbet said to Gary, "Go get your truck and drive it around back."

Cheyne nudged Pepi and motioned with her head.

There was a rusted freezer sticking out from the back of the building. The sound of a door made the girls scramble to their feet desperately looking in all directions trying to decide where to run.

Pepi started for the trees but Cheyne grabbed her arm and pulled her towards the front of the building. "This way- we don't have time to get into the woods."

In a rushing panic, they ran along the side of the building and up to the driveway.

A store buffeted the warehouse. They stopped in front of the store and urgently scanned the area. Except for weedy grass the structures were surrounded by wide open space.

Gary's pickup was parked a foot from the door. There was nowhere to run that they wouldn't be seen.

Chapter Thirty-Three

"Come on," Pepi whispered, tugging Cheyne's hand.

They ran to the door. Pepi pulled the handle praying it was unlocked. It swung open.

They both looked up as they stepped over the threshold hoping there wouldn't be that ever present bell many shops hung over doors to alert staff someone entered the semi-darkened shop.

There was no tinkling alarm.

Holding their breaths, they stood in the middle of the doorway searching for someone who could help them, but the store was empty.

Shades were pulled over the windows, and only slivers of light coming in was from around the shades and emergency lights in corners illuminated parts of the shop. But it was light enough they could easily make out merchandise on shelves, racks and the front counter.

A door scraped open, male rumblings came through, then the door slammed shut. Then they heard footsteps coming their way.

Urgently, the girls hastened to find a place to hide. They dashed across the floor. Pepi flung herself behind a magazine rack.

Cheyne raced to a soda machine and squeezed her body between it and a low counter. Crouching down, she tugged her dress over her knees, her hair spilled over her face. Her brain was running like a freight train.

Pushing the hair out of her eyes, she tried to find Pepi through the gloom. *Oh no* Pepi's red shirt stood out like ketchup on snow behind the meager shield of a magazine rack.

Cheyne willed Pepi to freeze, maybe the thug wouldn't spot her if she didn't move.

Gary's heavy boots thumped soundly on the wood floor. He trod purposefully through the store, then he slowed minutely.

Cheyne held her breath, he was only a few feet from Pepi. She released the breath as he continued on out the door. He carefully closed the door behind him.

The girls stood as statues until they heard the truck rev up, back up, then drive around the side to the back of the building.

Cautiously, Cheyne stood up.

Pepi stretched her neck around the magazine rack. Cheyne waved the all clear.

The girls moved quickly but quietly to the front door. Pepi grabbed the handle to open the door but the handle didn't move. She tried again, it didn't budge. She shook it then jiggled it then hit it.

"Are you kidding me?" she wailed in despair.

"He locked the door?" Cheyne asked redundantly. Her eyes welled up with instant fright.

Pepi threw her arm around her friend to comfort her. "It's okay. As soon as they leave we'll just throw something through the window."

Without warning the door jerked open- Gary was standing there. "Hi girls." He grinned.

"What's going on?"

The girls swirled around at a second voice behind them.

Ahmet. Black hair slicked back, black slacks, shirt with several buttons undone and the collar spread well open to expose a handful of black spirally hair and a gold chain. Along with the tasseled loafers, he looked like he stepped right out of a Mafia family photo.

Stunned, the girls stood immobilized. There was no point in trying to talk their way out, act like they were just customers, they could tell by the way Gary was smirking at them he knew who they were.

"Doing a little Dick Tracy are ya?" Gary joked.

Suddenly, Cheyne screamed "Go!" and burst into a run and at the same time Pepi took off like greased lightning in the opposite direction.

Too bad Gary was an athlete with extraordinarily long arms and legs, and Ahmet was a military man. It took them five seconds to catch the girls.

Gary bounded after Cheyne, she screamed as he grabbed her around the waist and lifted her feet off the ground. "Come on, sugar, you need to come talk to my friends, you have some explaining to do."

Screaming louder, she kicked against his jeaned legs, clawed at the t-shirt. He laughed, she wasn't even hurting him a little.

Meanwhile, Ahmet raced after Pepi.

Although Pepi was a natural runner, the bigger man easily caught her. He held her hands with one of his and circled her waist with the other.

She struggled, jerking her torso back and forth, she tried to step on his toes but her sneakers didn't make an impression on his steel-toed boots. He dragged her screaming to the back of the shop.

Held up in the air, Cheyne kept kicking out, trying to connect with some part of Gary. He dropped her to her feet on the floor, spun her around so her back was to him. He gripped her upper arms and pulled her to join the others.

She kicked and tried to punch him to the point he twirled her around to face him and shook her hard. "Now listen little girl, I don't want to hurt you, you're just a kid, but if you don't knock it off I'm going to backhand you good."

He shook her again so hard her head rattled. "Besides, there's nowhere for you to go. There's six of us men, you babes haven't got a chance against us stronger guys." He laughed at her angry expression.

She continued to struggle. He frowned, squeezed her arm until it burned and raised his hand in warning as if to strike her.

The warehouse door opened. "Did you get them?" Talco was in the doorway. He wasn't wearing a uniform, but his crisp stance, starched and creased clothes made him look like he was.

"Come on, are you letting a couple of children hold you up? Let's go. We take them out then get the truck loaded and get the hell out of here. Quit foolin' around. Bring them back." With a click of his heels, Talco turned and disappeared back in the warehouse.

"You heard him, let's go." Gary held Cheyne in a steel grip forcing her to go through the door.

Right behind, Ahmet still held Pepi's hands with one of his huge paws and wrapped the other around her neck and dragged her into the warehouse.

"You got them. Good. Let us have a look at our little snoopers." Khirbet's ominous voice got to them before his body did.

The girls were finally standing in front of the man that murdered his young wife, raped his daughters, tried to burn them alive and was involved in killing Miss Milan and probably Lareina too.

His plain black shirt and trousers were non-threatening, but his hawk-nosed face, full mustache covering his mouth and thick black eyebrows over eyes that levered open and closed like a reptile made up for it.

Gary and Ahmet pushed the teens in front of them and held their arms behind their backs.

The girls stood desperately trying to hide how petrified they were, their eyes riveted on the puddle of blood smeared on the floor from the slaughtered Pablo.

"Hey, I know these girls." Talco moved to stand in front of them.

Relief rippled through the teens, he knew them and their families, he wouldn't let these men hurt them.

Then their stomachs curdled when he said unpleasantly, "You should have minded your own business." A corner of his mouth twitched, he looked them both up and down like a coyote viewing a couple of helpless lambs. He crossed his arms over his chest and stood legs akimbo.

"Your sister-" Cheyne cried,

"My sister. My stupid greedy sister," Talco spat. "She hacked my computer and found out I'd met these guys overseas and that we devised a plan to poison the flu vaccine and wipe out half of Corbiestep. Everything was confirmed when she read Khirbet's private computer.

"We figured if no one connected the deaths with the flu shots, we planned to move to bigger cities eventually taking over, maybe holding the government hostage, ransom lives, hadn't gotten that far in our plans yet. But my damned sister comes across Devin there," he motioned with his head to the blond man standing off to the side.

"She thought she could get him interested in her." His sardonic chuckle held no humor. He said, "Devin only has interest in money and power, not women, right Dev?"

The blond remained impassive. Black booted feet stayed strongly planted. He stood there with his arms crossed over in his leather motorcycle jacket not speaking.

A black knit hat covered most of his blond hair, a cigarette dangled from a corner of his sensual lips waiting to be lit. Eyes so blank and uncaring they looked like glass with nothing behind them.

"Then, the dumb girl sets her sights on our friend Khirbet here." Talco nodded to the ex-officer. "She thought he was," Talco rolled his eyes, "she said, 'treacherously hot', her silly words not mine. What a twit," he sneered with disgust.

"Then, instead of just hooking up with him, she decides to blackmail him. Fool, tried to blackmail the wrong guy, a child playing an adult's game." He spat on the floor in rancor, his olive skin darkened more.

Gary chimed in, "Wouldn't give me the time of day, the little witch. What is the attraction to these foreigners anyway, what do they have that we red blooded Americans don't?"

Ahmet snorted. He elbowed Devin in jest, then looked way up at the tall Black Gary. "We know when to shut up, maybe that's it. You American boys talk too much."

Talco continued, desiring to let everyone know what a heartless brute he was. "So, it fell to me to silence her. I knew she'd be alone getting ready for the parade, she'd bitched about it for a week. I showed up to drive her to the parade. She didn't even say thank you, acted like it was everyone's duty to wait on the queen." Shaking his head, he laughed.

"She suspected nothing. We went up to the dressing room. We were late, everyone else was already gone. The problem was she started acting up, said I had to leave now she no longer needed me.

"I planned to wait until she was dressed and ready then do her, throw her out the window, make it look like an accident, like she'd leaned out the window to wave at her fans and, oops- fell out.

"But she wouldn't get dressed with me there, so I admit my anger got the best of me. I came up behind her and broke her wretched little neck. Snapped like a twig." He expressed absolutely zero regret. Sounded like he had stepped on a bug.

Uninterested in Talco's family fable, Devin strode off to the back of the warehouse and lit his cigarette.

Talco's sneer was so evil and emotionless, he no longer resembled anything of the handsome young ROTC officer he'd been.

He went on with his unremorseful confession. "So then of course I had to dress her, put on her makeup, do her hair. I didn't want anyone to realize she'd come from home and start thinking about who could have brought her. What a hassle that was."

"And you did a lousy job," Pepi taunted. "You did her makeup like she was a clown, that's what made us suspect right from the start she'd been murdered, some fool had obviously dressed her." She shared a glance with Cheyne.

"The dress and petticoats were all crooked and messed up. You put her hair into pigtails that she hadn't worn since she was a toddler, but that's how you remembered her. You never really looked at her as a person, a sister, a human being. You're a disgusting sorry excuse for a human being, you're an animal-"

Furious, his face bombastic scarlet, Talco slapped Pepi across the face. Veins popping on his neck, teeth gritted he turned and stalked away.

Cheyne gasped out loud, then cried out, "Talco!" He didn't look back at her.

She screamed, "You're a dog! A vicious no conscience dog! You have no moral fiber at all, you're a coward to strike a woman! A coward!" Shrieking at him, tears tightening her throat the words burst out in a husky sob.

Talco strode off to where the boxes were being loading on the truck like he could care less what happened to them. After all, he had killed his own flesh and blood, what would he care about a couple of acquaintances?

Pepi felt her cheek burning, she didn't care. He was an animal with no shame.

The hawk-nosed Khirbet moved directly in front of the girls. Like empty holes, his depraved eyes regarded them with not a shred of compassion. "Tell me how much you know. Tell me who else knows about us."

The black mustache melted into his five o'clock shadow. Dark skin with a deeply lined face for his age of mid-thirties. The scariest part of him was his cruel, heavily accented voice. He sounded like one of those butchers from a war movie, and he looked as merciless as one.

The girls stood mute. Tears rolled down Cheyne's cheeks, she refused to wipe them away.

Pepi stood stoic, but Cheyne could see perspiration dampening her temples, she was just as terrified as Cheyne was.

"That is the way it is, huh?" Khirbet smiled like a demon at them. "We will see."

Suddenly he yanked a huge knife from the back of his belt, grabbed Pepi from Ahmet's hold, wrapped a muscular arm around her chest and pressed the blade against her neck, forcing her head to tilt back.

"No!" Cheyne screamed. Pepi was too frightened to make a sound.

"Now then, you are a smart girl," Khirbet directed his words to Cheyne. "You can see what is going to happen. You have three seconds to talk or I kill her with one slice and then you are next, finger by finger, foot, hand, you get my drift."

His smile was as cold as a croc's. "Now, tell me who else knows about us."

Cheyne couldn't control her shaking legs, she clutched her stomach afraid she was going to throw up. Gary grabbed her arms and viciously jerked them behind her back.

Pepi's head was held so taught she could only see the ceiling. Tears ran down her face into her ears, but she cried out, "Don't tell them anything, Chey, they're going to kill us anyway-" letting go of her body, Khirbet grabbed a fistful of her hair, jerked her head back and pressed the knife tighter to her neck, a pinprick of blood trickled out.

"Shut up, girl!" he snarled. He looked at Cheyne and said, "One, two..."

"Please don't hurt her, please! We don't know anything, we won't tell anyone anything, please!" Cheyne cried.

"Three," Khirbet said emotionless, his face a stone he raised his hand-

"Stop! I'll tell you anything you want to know! Please! Stop, don't hurt her!" Cheyne screamed at the top of her lungs.

Khirbet loosened his grip on Pepi, he let go of her hair and wrapped his arm around her waist, her arms trapped under his. He moved the knife a spare inch from her throat.

286

"Go on," Khirbet ordered.

Cheyne took a big stuttering breath and told them everything they knew. She didn't lie about anything, she didn't know if he could tell if she was lying or not.

She admitted they hadn't told the police their suspicions yet, she woefully regretted now that they hadn't. Who cared if Detective James laughed at their ideas.

The only thing was, when he asked if anyone else knew anything, she never mentioned Talana or their families knowing anything. Visions of the murder room danced in her head.

Scared out of her wits, her brain went delusional picturing her and Pepi's or their family's pictures up there.

Satisfied the girls hadn't told anyone about them or their operation, other than the bartender and barmaid, but they could easily take care of them. Khirbet threw Pepi at Ahmet who held her in his steel grip.

Khirbet checked them for cell phones, however they had left their purses on the bikes hidden in the woods.

Khirbet said, "Take them out front in the store, make sure the door is locked, pull the bars on the windows and padlock them. Kill them and burn it. We will relocate, we do not know if they were followed."

Dismissing them like they were nothing, he turned and went to join Talco to pack boxes.

Devin pushed up the big door at the back of the warehouse, the metal door and chains clanging and banging. He then went out to move the truck closer to the bay to load the boxes. Several cars were parked out back.

Without a word, Gary picked up Cheyne and carried her through the warehouse back to the store. Ahmet dragged the struggling Pepi, then he followed Gary's lead and picked her up too, her kicking feet couldn't make contact on his body.

He laughed at her futile struggles. Once they got back inside the store section they set the girls down.

"They're not going anywhere, they got nowhere to go," Gary said. "Let's bar up those windows."

The girls stood helplessly watching the men pull bars across the windows and padlock them then pocket the keys. The front door was locked and Devin had locked the entry door to the warehouse as soon as they had passed through.

After the windows were sealed, Gary said, "Okay, I'll tie them up, you start the fire."

Ahmet moved over to a rack towards the front that held all kinds of newspapers and pulled out a lighter. He picked up a newspaper and held the lighter under it. It flamed immediately. He took the paper and tossed it on top of the other newspapers and stood back laughing.

Gary reached for Cheyne first.

Chapter Thirty-Four

His extraordinarily long arms reached out for Cheyne, but she was ready.

She ducked under those freakish arms and kneed him as hard as she could in his bullwinkles- He cried out and instantly bent in half gagging –

Pepi slammed him in the side of the head with a full metal toolbox. He dropped like a bag of dirt.

Hearing the commotion, Ahmet swiftly ran over with a gun in his hand. He yelled out, "Gary?" He stopped near the cash counter. His face split into a deliciously nasty grin.

Cheyne was standing in the middle of the aisle poised as if he'd caught her about to run.

"I got ya little princess, don't move. Where's the other one?" Without taking his eyes off Cheyne, he called out, "Gary? Dude? Where the hell are-"

Whack! Pepi popped up from the side of the counter and slammed him in the back of the head with a sledgehammer. He didn't make a sound as he slunk to the floor.

Cheyne came over and peered down at the collapsed man.

"Geeze, Pep, where'd you get that thing? You might have killed him." She tried to roll him over to get the gun, but he

289

weighed a ton. He grunted. She stepped back quickly in case he reached out for her.

"Forget the gun, Chey, we wouldn't know how to use it and they would know the minute we waved it at one of them." Pepi smiled at the huge hammer in her hands. She leaned it against the counter in easy reach in case any of the other men came looking for them.

"The hammer was a lot easier to wield than that tool box. I don't feel bad, he tried to kill us." She stared down at her handiwork. "He won't be getting up for a while and should have a nice headache when he does!"

"Okay, I don't care about them," Cheyne said, tension building in her voice. "We need to get out of here, fast!"

The front of the room was filling up with smoke. Flames ate up the newspapers and were now licking at the magazine rack.

The girls ran frantically around the shop looking for a way out, but every window was barred and they knew the front door was bolted even if they could get through the rapidly growing flames to get to it.

Pepi cried in horror, "What are we going to do? We're trapped, there's no way out!"

The girls stood hugging each other still desperately scanning the room for an exit.

Cheyne lamented, "My mom's gonna *kill* me when she finds out we disobeyed them and kept investigating."

Pepi gave her a wry look. "That's the least of our worries."

Cheyne looked over at Ahmet, blood spattered on his head and on the floor. "We need to get the key to the warehouse door to-" Ahmet moaned, stirred slightly.

"No," Pepi shook her head. "We can't trust going near him. Besides, going out the back of the warehouse, even if we could- the others are there."

Anxiously she ran her hands over her head again and again as she searched the room for an escape. The room was getting hot and so smoky it was hard to see Gary lying over by the warehouse door but they could hear him moaning.

Cheyne wrapped her arms around Pepi as if they could gain strength from each other. Through tearing, stinging eyes they kept searching for an escape.

"Look," Pepi declared, "even the plaster on the walls is burning. There must just be a thin layer of cement on the outside of the walls. It looked like it was built on solid cement blocks, but it isn't, cheap jerks. This stupid building is going to collapse like a card house."

"Um, yeah. So we'll sue the developer," Cheyne said sarcastically. Then she exclaimed fearfully, "I can't believe this is happening."

"We should have called Detective James even though we weren't 100% sure," Pepi bemoaned. Clutching each other, they shuffled as one from the marauding flames towards the back of the store.

"Yeah, well, too late now."

"Cheyne, there's no way out," Pepi cried in desperation.

Cheyne was looking up.

Pepi followed her gaze. "What are you look-"

They transfixed on the same thing. Twenty feet up in the wall between the two buildings was a vent.

"Do you see what I see?" Cheyne murmured in wonder.

Pepi let go of her friend, nodding excitedly. "Oh yeah. Come on we need to hurry."

"How are we going to get up there?" Cheyne followed her.

Pepi hollered, "Look for a ladder!"

They scrambled about searching for a ladder but to no avail.

"Wait, there." Pepi pointed to a stack of pallets against a far wall. She shouted over the roar of the burgeoning fire, "Help me pile 'em!"

The girls carried and dragged and stacked the pallets under the vent. They stood back surveying their work.

Pepi shook her head glumly. "Not high enough." She stared despondently at the unevenly stacked wood. She could hear Cheyne crying in frustration.

"We're not giving up," Cheyne announced adamantly. "We're not," she repeated for emphasis. "We need to find something to pile on top of them that won't fall over."

The room was so smoky visibility was rapidly decreasing, the situation was growing bleaker by the second. Their eyes watering, the girls started coughing.

"Cover your," cough- cough, "cover your mouth," Pepi choked out. They snatched towels off a counter and held them over their mouths.

Cheyne hit her friend on the shoulder then ran over behind the cash counter and came out with a stool that she thrust into Pepi's hands. Quickly, Cheyne climbed up the pallet.

Pepi handed the stool up to her then climbed up on the pallets with her.

The girls had the towels tied around their faces like they were bandits. It would have been funny if their situation was not so dire.

Cheyne looked up at the vent. "I think I can reach it. I should try, I'm taller than you."

Pepi snorted, "What, a quarter of an inch?"

"Whatever. I'm going first. You need to hold the stool."

Pepi grasped the rim of the stool, her eyes on the vent. "Wait!" She scurried down from the pallets ran to a wall and came back with a screwdriver. She handed it to Cheyne.

The vent was screwed into the wall. Cheyne held the screwdriver and climbed on top of the stool. She hesitated, took a deep breath. "I hope it doesn't lead to an attic." Her lips pressed tight, she said, "Smoke and hot air rises."

Pepi yelled, "It probably leads to the warehouse."

Cheyne looked down at her. "Oh great, back to the killers?" Her voice came muffled through the towel.

Pepi replied satirically, "I'd rather get shot than fried. Go."

Cheyne stood on the stool and actually had to bend her knees slightly to unscrew the vent. The stool made her about a half a foot taller than she needed to reach the vent.

"Hurry!" Pepi shouted. She glanced over her shoulder, half the room was ablaze and the flames were moving like a wildfire towards them. The heat was already making her skin feel like she was a piece of sizzling bacon.

The bottom of the stacked pallets they were standing on convulsed with deadly orange and yellow torches. The rest of the room was becoming an inferno. Most of the merchandise was already consumed, the walls were peeling and crackling. The lights snapped, popped then shot sparks across the room.

Sweat poured down Pepi's face and arms. She looked up fearfully, how was Cheyne going to climb into a vent that was over her head?

They were doomed.

Cheyne managed to unscrew the screws letting them drop. She stuck her fingers through the grate and pulled. It didn't move an inch.

"It won't budge!" she cried, edging towards hysterical.

"Keep trying!" Pepi yelled. The flames were devouring the pallets only a few inches from where she stood. Her sneakers were actually melting. "Hurry!"

Cheyne pulled and twisted but nothing. Then she pushed. The vent pushed up. Relieved, Cheyne pushed the vent all the way up and to the side. She tossed the screwdriver inside the hole.

Her fingers tightly gripped the sides of the vent opening, and in one movement she did a modified kip-up –

She got her head and shoulders inside the vent, then she was able to kick up. Her arms rigid, she pushed then bent them and pushed and kicked herself up inside the vent.

Pepi watched as her friend's cowboy boots disappeared into the vent hole. With no time to waste she climbed up on the stool.

Cheyne leaned out of the hole, dusty blond hair tumbled out. She reached down. "Grab my wrists!" she instructed.

"Cheyne, there's no way, I'm not a gymnast like you. I can't do it. You go, get out- call the fire department! I'll, I'll-" her voice broke in despair.

Cheyne leaned out further. "Okay, shut up. Grab my hands, we can do it." The pallet was in flames, the fire was eating up the stool, it was disintegrating, the stool's legs were crumbling- it rocked under Pepi's feet-

Coughing, Pepi wiped her slippery sweaty hands against her jeans and raised them. The girls gripped wrists.

"Okay," Cheyne said, puffing, coughing, "on the count of three, you jump and swing, try to grab the wall with your feet and I'll pull."

Tears streaming down her face mingling with sweat, Pepi didn't dare look down, the stool was shrinking as the flames flared up it.

"One- two- three- jump!" Cheyne screamed.

Pepi jumped and Cheyne pulled and swung her up and towards the wall. Pepi kicked up and slammed her feet against the wall.

"Grab the vent!" Cheyne called, terror and fear tightened her throat already clogged and half closed from the smoke and heat. She let go of one of Pepi's hands to free it.

Pepi threw her arm up and just caught the edge of the hole. Cheyne released her other hand, Pepi grabbed at the hole, her fingers slipped, she jerked and got it at the same time Cheyne reached down and grabbed her upper arms.

"Okay, now," her voice calm, hoarse from the scorching heat and heavy smoke, her tears falling on Pepi's face, Cheyne said, "I'm going to pull you up, try to walk up the wall, kick up the wall and pull yourself into the hole. Now go!"

They struggled together, it took moments of sheer blood coursing terror as the flames jumped, hacking at them.

Pepi kicked and both pulled, grunting and coughing. Pepi was finally able get her torso in the hole. Working together they pulled her inside the attic.

Pepi threw herself on her back gasping for breath.

Cheyne knelt beside her, panting. She allowed them a few seconds to catch their breath then she stood up. She held a hand to Pepi pulling her to her feet. "We've got to go."

Breathing heavy and hacking up a lung, Pepi looked around their surroundings, but it was dusty and smoky and dark, and hot.

"Go where?" She asked. The closed in space was already thick with black smoke and broiling hot.

Cheyne hurriedly surveyed the small attic. "Look for a window, some opening, there has to be something." Her voice more muffled now, the towel was covered in soot and wet from her tears, it kept sliding down.

In a frantic frenzy, the girls searched the tiny space.

"Here," Pepi said excitedly. "There's an exhaust pipe." They studied the pipe.

"We might be able to get the pipe out, I don't know if we can fit through that little hole. And then what, climb out on a burning roof?" Cheyne cried in despair, "Should we jump to our deaths?"

Pepi shook her head. "I thought I was the pessimist, girl. Just keep going, that's all just keep going. One foot in front of the other-" she broke off in a fit of coughing.

Wiping at her eyes, Pepi's voice hoarse, she rasped, "I had looked for any kind of rope when we were downstairs, but I couldn't find anything like that, or even clothes to tie together. The ones that were there were already burning up. We just need to do the best we can."

Cheyne coughed out a guttural, "Okay," and squinting through the thick smoke, scanned the attic.

The ceiling slanted so they were able to easily reach the pipe in the ceiling. They pushed, twisted, pulled. It moved, yet only barely.

Cheyne ran back to the vent hole and felt on the scorching wood floor in the dark for the screwdriver. She found it and hurried back.

She bashed at the sides of the pipe with the screwdriver until it worked free. They pushed it one last time and they could hear it rolling and clanking down the side of the roof.

They didn't hear it hit the ground, which worried them. It made them aware of how high up they were and how loud the fire roared.

Pepi said, "That ought to attract their attention if they're still here."

Louise Furley

"Let's just hope they're not standing there waiting to take pot shots at us as we come out," Cheyne replied through a coughing fit.

This time Pepi went first. It was a tight fit. She held her arms straight up and pushed the top half of her body through the pipe hole. Then she put her hands on the roof and squeezed and twisted.

Like getting a cork out of a wine bottle, she managed to extract herself from the hole.

Then Cheyne did the same contorted winding and turning and twisting. She stifled the picture of getting stuck in the hole and the building burning around her, the flames moving closer and closer-

She shook her head to dispel the claustrophobic harrowing image and gave a mighty push, and with continued grinding back and forth, she squeezed out leaving some skin and strips of dress behind.

Chapter Thirty-Five

They stood on the roof gasping and panting.

The wind tossed Cheyne's sooty hair and ragged dress. "With the blazing inferno below and the burning sun above, I feel like the witch on the Wizard of Oz, I'm melting, I'm melting..."

Pepi laughed then coughed.

"What?" Cheyne asked.

Pepi pointed at her sneakers. The bottoms and fronts were melted.

"Hmm, funny. That'll be us next girl, if we don't get off this roof." Cheyne said.

They were towards the back of the store, they could see the men on the ground still on the premises, jogging with boxes from the warehouse to the waiting truck.

The girls could see periodically one-by-one each man look back, the store was already engulfed. The fire was breaching the warehouse, flames stroked higher, closer, faster, the men picked up their speed.

Pepi and Cheyne could just barely hear Khirbet barking orders to move faster- faster, over the thunder of the fire and the crashing of falling beams and shelves, and explosions from chemicals and other accelerants inside both burning buildings.

Flames lashed out from the exhaust hole the girls had climbed out of. Burning embers hopped onto the roof skittering in all directions looking for a place to attach and burn.

The girls jumped and scrabbled sideways to the far side, trying to keep their balance on the slightly sloped roof.

They slithered to the edge. Holding onto each other, they gingerly leaned over and looked down, way down.

"It's too far to jump," Pepi faltered, "even if we cling to the edge and- and let go-" a catch broke off her words. She looked around wildly for something to make into a ladder, or a rope, to no avail. There was nothing on the roof but them.

"I'm so sorry to have gotten you into this," Cheyne cried, she was also fiercely searching for any means of escape.

Pepi stood motionless. She stared at the searing fire, red and yellow flames reflected, flared in her eyes. She looked at Cheyne, then her eyes lifted to the sky. She watched the thick smoke plume then spiral up and away filling the sky and blocking the sun.

A peculiar look crossed her ashy face. Then her expression cleared and she seemed almost radiant, rapturously glowing, even through the grimy sweat and dirt.

"Pep, are you all-"

Pepi swung frightened but determined eyes to her friend. A wavy smile emerged, weak at first, then grew firm. For once she reached out and lightly held Cheyne's arms. "Listen, Chey. We may die here today,"

"Pepi! Don't say that! We'll-"

Pepi shook Cheyne's arms. "Hush. We might. But, if we don't, I want to tell you that- that standing here on top of a building on fire about to perish- I finally realize that I have been hanging onto my detested past like a, like a suffocating shroud that I couldn't shake off."

She blinked back the tears. "It was like it was asphyxiating me, slowly. Feeling as if I was at the bottom of a well and rocks and dirt were burying me alive, I couldn't draw a breath. I couldn't claw my way out."

"Aw Pep," Cheyne tried to shake off her friend's hands so she could hold her. But Pepi held tightly onto her.

"Listen. What I want to say is, standing on this burning roof I finally feel- free. The burden of the past is kind of burning away with the fire. This danger has brought things into perspective. Life is precious. Friends," she smiled peacefully at Cheyne, "are precious. I feel now I can move on. I *want* to live. Get it? For once, Chey, I really, truly want to live!"

She let loose of Cheyne's arms and threw her hands joyously up in the air like she was tossing confetti to the wind, she threw her head back and laughed.

Cheyne hesitated trying to decide if her friend was delusional from fear and the smoke they inhaled. But Pepi looked- no other word for it- free. Free and jubilant. And triumphant.

In the thick, broiling grey air, Cheyne threw her arms around Pepi and hugged her hard. Her tears rained onto Pepi's back.

Pepi hugged her back, comfortably, happily. After a second she gently pushed away and looked at her friend and snuffed.

"For the love of-" she rolled her eyes at the weeping Cheyne. "Look at you, you crying baby goofball. Go cry on the fire and put it out!"

Cheyne grinned, her tears making paths through the soot. "They're happy tears, girl." She glanced around, a third of the roof was gone and the fire was eating at the rest. "We need to do something fast or they'll be tears of sorrow."

She frowned. "What are you doing?"

Pepi was unbuttoning her blouse and staring at Cheyne's dress.

Cheyne looked down. "Are you kidding? You're insane-" However, she understood and reached down and grabbed the hem of her dress to make a rope-

"Wait-"

On the last button, Pepi paused. She looked up.

"Listen-" Cheyne stopped motion and craned her ear. She dropped her dress.

Sirens. They could hear sirens coming.

"Yee-ha! We're saved!" Cheyne yelped, so elated she almost lost her footing.

Pepi grabbed her arm to steady her. "Hold on they're not here yet." Buttoning her shirt, she looked back at the roof starting to burn behind them.

They crept as close to the edge as they could get, waited, hoped, prayed.

A fire truck, then a second, burst from the road behind the line of trees and tore up the drive.

Pepi and Cheyne jumped up and down waving their arms hooting and screaming. "Here! Help us! Up here!"

A dozen fire fighters jumped off the trucks, unhitched ladders, hoses, one ran to locate the fireplug. Another hopped on top of the moving ladder with a cherry picker basket attached while another maneuvered it.

Ever so painstakingly slowly, the ladder rose and stretched swinging towards the girls.

Dense clouds of heavy black smoke billowed and coiled, a live thing storming all around the building, Pepi and Cheyne were almost invisible in the midst.

Flames burst, rupturing through the roof, red hot sparks blasted in the air. The fire convulsed and licked, thundering around the girls.

The cherry picker finally reached them through thick flumes of black smoke and came to a shuddering halt.

The fireman inside the basket reached out his arms. Encircling Pepi, he picked her up and deposited her inside the basket. She moved to the back of the basket and clung to the sides while the fireman went for Cheyne.

As he reached for her through the vault of smoke, the basket toddled suddenly, hit Cheyne's foot, she tripped then went sliding down the roof tiles!

Pepi screamed.

Cheyne frantically tried to catch a hold of tiles with her hands and stop her sliding fall with her feet, but momentum and gravity pulled her and she slid right over the edge-

Throwing out her hands, she caught the gutter with one hand, leaving her body swinging in the open air. She struggled to reach up and grab the metal furrow with the other. Flames spat and forked at her feet.

Gasping for breath, she caught the gutter. Legs flailing, she kicked, scissoring her legs trying to catch the side of the building to brace herself, but her boots slid on the boiling hot peeling building.

Fire licked at her from under and hissed from the side. Too stricken with terrified hysteria to even scream, Cheyne could feel her grip weakening her fingers slipping-

She felt something on her hands. Bending her head back, she could see a fireman's hat peering over the edge. Two gloves reached down and grabbed her wrists.

He leaned over further and gripped her arms, then grunting, he pulled her up.

So scared, Cheyne didn't feel her arms and torso, and then legs scraping over the metal and tiles as he hauled her up and over until her body slammed onto the roof.

She sat stunned. He didn't let her gather her wits, just swept her up in his arms, ran the few steps to the cherry picker and practically threw her inside.

Pepi grabbed her and the two girls clung to each other sobbing. The fireman signaled the driver to lower them.

Pieces of the store burst in all directions, the front half collapsed, crimson sparks shot up like fireworks. Brilliant orange flames erupted, breaking out of the roof and whipped up towards the sky.

It seemed to take forever, but it was only a moment before the carrier reached the ground. Other firemen rushed over to help pull the girls out. Police cars now wailed up the gravel drive.

Pepi yelled out hoarsely still in the basket as the police leaped out of their patrol cars, "Around back- they're around back!" Gesturing madly, she saw Detective James hop back in his unit and tear around the building to the back of the warehouse.

As a fireman set Pepi on the ground, she caught sight of her grandmother climbing out of a police car. They ran to each other.

Elma Mae hugged Pepi so tightly, Pepi thought her head would pop off.

Getting out of the other side of the police car was Karey, even more handsome now that she thought she'd never live to see him again!

He raced over and joined them, hugging and cursing Pepi while he stroked the filthy cinnamon ringlets, the rubber band had busted, setting the scorched hair free.

Holding her back from him to check out that she was uninjured, Karey saw the cut on her neck from Khirbet's knife. He leaned in and tenderly kissed the wound while murmuring, "Geesh, baby, what did you get yourself into?"

Not waiting for her to answer, he moved his head and said against her lips, "I am so happy to see you alive! So happy," and he kissed her.

The fireman that saved Cheyne hopped out of the basket then reached back inside for her.

Her dirty face streaked with tears of relief, she looked up as he wrapped his jacketed arms around her, and their eyes met.

Her sky blue eyes widened in sudden recognition of his unusual turquoise peepers. "You!" she exclaimed and leaned back.

It was that rude young man she'd literally run into at school the other week.

He smiled, his face almost as dirty as hers did nothing to hide his masculine good looks. He tipped his hat, soot covered tufts of blond hair poked out. "Interning fireman, Rome McAdams at your service."

She couldn't help grinning, he looked so absurdly adorable. He swung her up in his arms and valiantly carried her across the lawn away from the burning building which was completely engulfed in flames and coming apart at the seams.

Cheyne breathed deeply and greedily of the delicious fresh air, then had a brief coughing fit then breathed deeply again, slowly this time.

Cradled securely in extremely strong arms, Cheyne snuggled against the broad chest like she'd been born there and asked him with a raspy voice, "How in the heck did you find us? This place is so far from the city, even the surrounding farmhouses are far away and half are vacant."

Smiling down at his precious cargo, he told her, "Talana Castilla was concerned you two rogues would get yourselves into danger so she called Detective James. He had a bad feeling, so he sent a deputy out here to check things out.

"The deputy was still a few miles away, but he saw the smoke and called it in. You know," he shifted her slightly. "Even with a smudge of soot on that cute nose, you are still one striking young woman!"

"What? Darn-" Cheyne rubbed her nose with her soiled hands which made the situation worse making him laughed. It was a pleasurable throaty sound that gave Cheyne a jolt of electric shivers.

"What did you say your name was? Rome? It's kind of different?"

He looked embarrassed. "Yeah well, my mother the romantic named me Romeo. I needed to get through school so I shortened it, ya know-"

He still held her in his arms as a car containing her mother, father, and grandmother raced up.

Rome gazed at her nestled in his arms. "I freaked out when I saw that blond mane up there billowing in the wind, red flames raging behind you like a firestorm." He shook his head with a shudder.

"I was so scared, then when I saw you go over the edge- my heart leapt into my throat."

He smiled sheepishly as he admitted, "I couldn't get you out of my mind after our- meeting, ah crash- that day in the hall. I tried to push away visions of the rude little girl that haunted my dreams, but I couldn't. I tried to find you."

He nodded at her brows arched in disbelief. "Yeah, I did. Then, I saw you. A breathtaking siren bravely standing on a burning roof- I thought, after searching and asking if anyone knew you, just when I finally found my golden beauty with singed hair I'm going to lose her before I even get to know her name, or get a first kiss…"

His lips parted, her lips parted, eyes hooded, he lowered his head, their lips met-

"Cheyne!" Her mother was running across the lawn with her father and grandmother at her heels.

Rome raised his head and smiled reluctantly. "Another day, my beauty." He gently set her on her feet but kept his arm around her shoulders to help her steady her quaking legs.

Cheyne's family scooped her into a mass hug.

Chapter Thirty-Six

The girls descended the staircase admiring their reflections in the mirror by the foyer.

Pepi in her favorite lavender, full length flowing gown as light as air, held up by spaghetti straps. Her hair in loose waves for a change, one side pulled back by a silver bow.

She straightened the lavender and white corsage Karey had brought her, he had a matching boutonniere in his sophisticated grey tuxedo.

He waited beside Rome, who was wearing a black tux, blond hair slicked back.

Cheyne attired in coral sequins squeezed Pepi's hand and they giggled. "What a spring break!" Cheyne laughed.

"Yeah, let's not try to duplicate it too soon," Pepi said.

"Getting grounded for all these months was a bummer, but totally worth it. And Detective James tearing us a new one, still, then you could tell he was proud of us. He had to be nice to us after he met your sister and fell hard! I'm glad our family relented and is allowing us to go to the prom!"

They tread gracefully down the stairs and into the waiting arms of their escorts.

After pictures, they were preparing to leave for the prom when the doorbell rang.

It was Detective Douglas James. He was expected. As they were wrapping up the investigation, Douglas had met Cheyne's sister, Suchie Rose. It was love at first sight.

Home on a break from school, Suchie Rose left a few weeks later with her sorority sisters to study another semester in Istanbul.

Douglas and she had Skyped a few times a week, but tonight Douglas and her whole family would be Skyping together with Suchie Rose.

Detective James had filled everyone in on what had happened since the fire.

They had caught all the men trying to escape from the burning warehouse. They'd all crowded in the truck when they saw the police and fled around the building.

The police gave chase down the road right at their heels.

Rounding a hairpin bend, the driver lost control and the truck skidded, hit the grass, rolled like a ball, then landed upside down in a gulley.

A few piled out and made another run for it but they were quickly captured. The others wounded were easily caught.

The two the girls had left knocked out inside had woken in the midst of the fire. Not seeing the teens disappearing through the vent in the wall because of the smoke, the two injured men leaped through the fire and just made it as the building was falling down around them.

However, they'll have a long, painful recuperation in the burn unit before going off to prison when they're adjudicated guilty at trial.

They all pled not guilty to terrorism, murder, attempted murder, kidnapping, and a plethora of other charges and were pending trial.

The girls had been correct in believing that Khirbet Beteiha was the ringleader, and he was also the man from overseas that had killed his teenaged wife and tried to leave his young daughters to die an agonizing and terrifying death.

When Megan Milan had gone into the bar that day of the wedding, just by pure chance Khirbet Beteiha was one of the three men sitting there.

He had managed to leave Africa and shaved off his thick beard and wore contacts instead of glasses. A knit hat covered his shaved head. He looked completely different.

At first he couldn't place why she looked familiar to him. Then he remembered his home in Africa. When he learned his daughters hadn't died in the fire he went searching for them.

Under pretense of some other mission, he had visited the rural school looking for them there and now remembered the priggish homely teacher who had spoken with him and rushed him out.

He normally wouldn't have noticed such a plain Jane as Megan, but the way she acted so peculiar around him, she made no eye contact, she appeared unnecessarily nervous, discouraging him from speaking to the other children there and tried to hurry him through the tour of the school.

Unbeknownst to Khirbet, his infamy had preceded him so the teachers had quickly hidden the girls when they learned of his arrival at the school.

Khirbet wasn't sure if Megan had recognized him or not in the bar, or if she had overheard their plans to poison Corbiestep as she was sitting close by.

He didn't know if she had been pretending to be drunk in order to learn more, or insinuate herself into their group to spy on the men then sick the police on them. So he had Devin make a date with her.

Tragically, Megan hadn't recognized Khirbet in her drunken stupor, yet there was a possibility in a sober moment later on, his monstrous face could punch her memory like a nightmare, and she'd remember him.

Khirbet took no chances. They ransacked her house to see what information she had regarding them and they found the photos and the story she was writing.

They had planned on setting her up for the bombing anyway to destroy her credibility as they didn't know how much she knew or who she'd told.

However, shortly afterwards, they thought the police might believe her after all, so they decided she had to go.

Detective James told Cheyne and Pepi that after Khirbet is tried in America for his crimes, he will be extradited to the country he's from for killing his wife and attempted murder and assault on his little girls.

The courts will decide where he spends his incarceration. Likely it'll be where he receives the harshest sentence for the abhorrent acts he committed.

The greenhouse behind the warehouse contained the meadow saffron. The fire didn't get that far so it would be used as evidence against the killers.

Their devious plot to poison the flu vaccine with the saffron was thwarted.

The prosecutors didn't think Jumper Hudson was involved with the scheme so no charges were brought against him. But he was fired for stupidity, and taking too many breaks.

He became a minor celebrity after his interview on the Paul Castronovo Show down in South Florida. Changes in procedures were put into effect immediately at the lab.

The authorities had located the black SUV parked outside the residence of the three, Devin, Ahmet and Khirbet's, an apartment in a rundown section of the city.

Evidence of bomb substances, guns, ammunition, more evidence that can be linked to the lab and the saffron, and blood from people they hadn't discerned yet who they were, was discovered by CSI.

The rolled truck was loaded with the saffron and materials to sabotage the flu serum, along with a detailed description on a tablet on how they were going to do it, as well as a list of other confederates inside the lab, that were then sought out and arrested.

Pepi and Cheyne's names were kept out of the papers in case the police hadn't rounded up all of the thugs and they decided to retaliate.

The family along with the girls' dates and Detective James gathered around the dining room table.

Cheyne's father turned on the computer. They conversed while waiting for the computer to power up and get the Skype up and running.

Cheyne and Rome made dove-eyes at each other, Pepi and Karey did likewise. They all couldn't wait to get out and get slow dancing...

The picture came up. Everyone's attention turned to the girl at the other end.

It was Melanie, one of Suchie Rose's sorority sisters. She did not look happy. In fact, she looked highly distressed. Huge globules of tears swelled and heaved then dropped as the brunette hiccupped and bawled.

There was an uneasy silence.

Then Cheyne's father said, "Melanie, what is it? Where's Suchie Rose?"

Melanie became hysterical, between sobs she blurted out, Suchie's gone-"

Douglas James leaned closer to the monitor, frowning. "What do you mean she's gone? Melanie?" The family tensed around him.

When she just kept crying, he demanded, "Melanie, what do you mean by she's gone?" his voice grew louder yet icy calm. Only the pulsing vein at his temple betrayed his tension.

"Answer me, Melanie," he ordered, steel bracing his voice.

Melanie gulped and wept and sniveled, she dashed at her eyes with her hands. She moved in closer to the monitor, so close her despairing face filled the screen.

They could see the reflection of her computer in her eyes and tears. She wiped her eyes and said, "I mean she's gone. She's missing. She hasn't been home or called for three days." Melanie broke into a wail.

The shocked family started asking questions all at once; why'd she wait so long to tell them? Where was she last seen, could she be with other friends?

All they got was that Suchie Rose had gone to a historical site and never returned. Her friends called her cell but it must be turned off. They went to the police, but they said there was no need for alarm, it was just a young woman feeling her oats, leave her alone.

Her friends were going to call the family today, they had decided to wait for the Skype appointment.

Cheyne pushed her chair back and stood up. "We've got to go find her." She looked at Pepi who stood up and sharply nodded her agreement.

Pepi said, "Call the airport."

The End

Dear Reader, thank you for choosing <u>Shots, Plots & Diva Down</u>!

I know you could have picked any number of books to read, but you chose this story and for that I am extremely grateful.

I hope you enjoyed this novel, and if you did, **please leave a review** *where you acquired it, and look for other exciting titles in my name!*

About the Author

Louise Furley is the author of numerous published adult novels. When not researching or writing, she is dreaming of unique plots, and discovering fresh ventures she hasn't yet experienced in the world.

Ride along with her as she travels new and thrilling journeys!

311

www.ingramcontent.com/pod-product-compliance
Lightning Source LLC
Chambersburg PA
CBHW020910200626
46814CB00001BA/269

* 9 7 9 8 9 8 5 9 9 6 3 6 4 *